MW01138008

To Journey in the Year of the Tiger

(Book 1 from Tails of the Upper Kingdom)

H. Leighton Dickson

To Parker,
Every Journey Begins with the First Step!
H. Dickson
2017

ISBN-13: 978-1478127093

DEDICATION

To Brynn, Graeme and Megan
(my own little lion cubs)

ACKNOWLEDGMENTS

I would like to thank my children, Brynn, Graeme and Megan, for taking this journey with me over the last few years. I would also like to thank my husband Alan for letting me stew over a hot computer evening after evening. I would most especially like to thank that gang at Fanfiction dot net for rewarding me with reviews and letting me know that I did, in fact, have it in me.

DHARAMSHALLAH

It was hard to believe that a man could see twenty-three winters before he began to live. It is harder even to believe that his life began all at once, on one night, with the occurring of three obscure and apparently random things: the death of a bird, the flash of golden eyes and the first of One Hundred Steps. But for Kirin Wynegarde-Grey, it did happen, just this way. His life began, as all great and terrible things do, in the Year of the Tiger.

***

It was almost the close of the Second Watch and the falcon soared high above the Great Mountains. She was small and speckled with the familiar mask of peregrine grey and the wide fantail of the raptor. Bells streaked from the leathers that wrapped her thin legs, securing a tiny parchment in place. She scanned the land below, her wing dipping slightly as she spied the first of the torches lining the road into the city. She had flown all night, navigating the violent winds that blew through the mountains but now, with her destination in sight, she tucked in her wings and dove like an arrow.

Still the swiftest creature of earth or sky.

Suddenly, without chirrup or cry, the falcon died. Her head

twisted back, her wings folded neatly over her spine. She never pulled out from her dive and plummeted to the ground within seconds. A snowdrift became her tomb, silent and unadorned, save for the single small, dark pit to mark the bird's passing.

In a Hall far to the North somewhere, a priest died as well.

It was the close of the Second Watch.

***

He could see his breath when he paused at the top of the One Hundred Steps. The Imperial banner flapped above him in the darkness and lanterns burned all around, throwing golden light into the night sky. He was very high up and it was not quite dawn, so he turned back to look across the rooftops of the city at his feet.

It was the quiet hour before sunrise. A few windows already glowed from lamps within and smoke curled from every chimney. The winter had been cold and hearths were kept fed long into the night. But winter would not last forever and now, as he stood under the Imperial banner, he could see the first streaks of purple behind the mountains and he knew that they were greeting another morning in peace.

DharamShallah, the Jewel of the Upper Kingdom.

This was the Roof of the World.

Towering above it all, the palace of *Pol'Lhasa* slept like a baby, cradled in the arms of her Mother the Great Mountains. She needed no fortified walls, this Palace. The peaks themselves were her soldiers, spears of white against the morning sky. *Kathandu* herself was guardian, her snowy cliffs serving as battlements, her glaciers deadly moats. Bitter winds and treacherous paths were both nursemaid and sentry, allowing only the chosen to enter the courts that were the heart and soul and will of the Upper Kingdom.

He felt a rush of pride, which warmed him more than hearths or lanterns. He turned and made his way underneath the pillars of the Outer Court. Leopards watched him as he passed and large ebony doors swung open to allow him through. Of course they would let him through. He was a lion and he wore a sash of Imperial gold. He was Kirin Wynegarde-Grey, Captain of the Empress's personal guard. Like his father had been before him, and his father's father before that. His was a noble family, theirs a royal house.

In this early hour, the Palace was awake but quiet. Leopards lined the walls, eyes roving, swords and staffs ready. Servants moved along the corridors on slippered feet, carrying baskets of linens and food. Ministers moved to and from offices to the tune of a lone koto. It was bowed at night, not plucked, and sounded like the Palace breathing. At this hour, when most cats were sound asleep in their beds, a few worked to keep them safe and unknowing and fed. It was the way of things.

They were at the cusp of a New Year and the entire Kingdom would celebrate as the Year of the Ox withdrew into the waters and the Tiger prowled onto the Celestial stage. The Ox had been a good year, a productive one and stable. Policies had been made, alliances built, and the Wall had advanced into *Shyria* half a world away. But the Tiger meant other things for Tiger years were turbulent and full of social upheaval. Things would change during a Tiger year. Society would change and for a man charged with the security of such a Kingdom, 'change' was not a good thing.

And he was a very young man.

He strode past the Seven Candles, a prayer room for the ministers and chancellors of the Court, and he smiled. There were far more than seven candles in the vast scarlet room, with torches and incense pots and kettles. Already several ministers were engaged in early morning rituals of cleansing or forgiveness, of sanctification or supplication. Prayer wheels spun, holy beads counted, parchments written and burned with prayers rising up to the heavens on trails of smoke. It was a room filled with talismen and idols, purified water and sticks of incense. They were a religious people, a favored people, and they held fast to many holy things. Cats are, after all, a holy people.

The Minister of Fields spied him, bowed slightly. Kirin nodded but continued walking. He cut an imposing figure, twin swords at his hips, dark golden mane fanning down his back like a cloak. He was the ideal Captain for such an army, being tall, square-shouldered and regal like his father before him. The *Bushido* was strong in him too. He was *Shah'tyriah,* the warrior caste and the Way of the Warrior shaped his very being. In fact, he was in many ways like his father, possessing the same quiet authority, the same sober intelligence and the same deep, soft, rumbling voice accented in the tongue of the Old Court. Indeed, it was said that much of his authority came from his voice, for when he spoke he used few words and his men were forced to listen carefully for his orders. He had never been heard to raise his voice, never been seen to lash his tail, never been seen to unsheathe his claws. It was simply not his way.

He was a lion among lions, ideal to command such forces of men.

(And, according to the ladies of the Royal Court, he was also rather pleasing to look upon and he was often the subject of their fancies. Another thing that pleased the ladies of the Royal Court, was the fact that, like the Empress, he had not chosen a suitor, which was also and often the subject of their fancies, and his mother was constantly beset with offers. I know this for fact. His brother has told me many stories.)

His boots echoed as he trotted down a winding staircase made of polished teak and soon, he was in the Hall of Warriors.

Which was really a misnomer. It was more a hall of diplomats, of government officials overseeing the armies of the Kingdom, and it was located on one of the lower floors of the Palace. He loved this Hall though, loved the smell of the cedar and teak and the leather, loved the shine of the swords and the gleam of the armor lining the walls.

At the far end of the hallway, a panther stood outside his office, wearing the uniform of the elite and personal bodyguards of Her Excellency, the Empress. A messenger from *her*. Kirin's heart thudded in his chest but was interrupted by a voice to his right.

"Kirin-san." He turned to see Master Yeo Tang St. John, Minister of Horses, in a doorway. St. John was also a lion, and he wore robes of Imperial gold. His mane was shot with silver and pulled back into an elaborate top-knot. Kirin rarely wore top-knots. He preferred a simpler style, his mane pulled off his neck in a simple queue. It fell down to his waist, straight as a razor.

St. John bowed slightly. Kirin did the same, out of respect.

"You have the drill plans?"

"Yes," Kirin said. "In my office."

"I will need them soon. I hear you have asked for twenty more horses."

St. John spoke in the Accents of the Old Courts but his voice was reedy, not at all like a normal lion. In fact, a little more like a horse.

"No," Kirin sighed. "I have not asked for more."

"Chancellor Agarwal said that Master Turlington said that Major Laenskaya said—"

"I have not spoken with neither Chancellor Agarwal nor Master Turlington since the Moon Festival, and Major Laenskaya…" He did not smile. "Major Laenskaya does not *speak* to anyone."

St. John grunted, made a move to slip back into his office. "I will need those plans soon."

"You will have them."

The door clicked shut.

He shook his head.

Two more doors clicked open, Ministers of Fireworks and of the Armory, and he reigned in his impatience to speak with them. It was difficult when there was a panther waiting at his door.

It was the middle of the 3rd Dynasty, when the Sacred Empress was still young. In fact, she had not yet chosen a suitor and her people were growing anxious. They needed assurance, as much as they needed diversion. So, it was with all seriousness that he, the Captain of Her Guard, was occupied with the Drill Ceremony for the upcoming Festival. The Drill Ceremony required precision troupes to ride Imperial horses through a succession of patterns. There would be fireworks of course, and dancing dragons, and speeches - a spectacle designed to enthrall the entire city, held in two night's time. All to impress a potential suitor arriving from *Cal'Cathah.*

He smiled as he thought of it. Had *he* been Sacred-born, he would have no need of such horses, nor fireworks, nor speeches.Or had *she* been lioness...

But that was blasphemy and Kirin Wynegarde-Grey was no blasphemer.

And truth be told, he did not mind making arrangements for ceremonies such as this, for it reminded him of the blessed price of peace, for the succession of the Monarchy, and the perpetuation of the Pure Races.

And so he spoke with the Minister of Fireworks and the Minister of the Armory, before finally setting off toward the panther at his door.

"Sir," the man said and handed him a scroll. It was unopened, but it needn't have been. None of the Queen's Panther Guard could read. Kirn's eyes flicked downward, to the Imperial seal of coloured beeswax. Red dragon entwined around a golden cat over a black lotus. *Her* seal.

Kirin steeled his heart, took the scroll and entered his office, closing the door softly on the Hall of Warriors.

***

The panther could hear the sounds of humming.

After searching for hours along dark, bleak corridors, he had finally found the door. *Agara'tha* was notorious for its caverns. It was a labyrinthine monastery carved into the deepest rock. Its floors and walls and ceilings were granite, veins of marble and amber occasionally breaking the blackness. Torches burnt from infrequent perches, anchored into the rock with heavy iron casings. And the incense was everywhere, heavy and heady, making him wonder if he hadn't in fact been searching for days.

Yellow smoke seeped from beneath this peculiar threshold and with a deep breath, he knocked.

"Come."

The panther pushed the door open, the ebony warm under his palm. As he expected, the chamber was thick with incense, clouds of orange and scarlet billowing from a central hearth. It was an unnatural flame. He shuddered. The Alchemists were just as unnatural. He hated coming here.

A figure sat, cross-legged, with her back to him, facing the hearth. Clothed in absolute black, she was almost a part of the shadows herself, silhouetted as she was by the hearth's brilliant light. A burst of white erupted from somewhere and the incense folded dramatically around her like a shroud.

He cleared his throat.

"I am looking for Sherah al Shiva."

"You have found her."

Her voice was deep, throaty, and he imagined it was due in part to the large amounts of smoke she breathed daily. It only added to the mystique, however, and the Alchemists were fond of their mysteries.

"I have a summons, *sidala.* From the Palace."

"Leave it by the door."

"Hand to hand, *sidala.* It bears the Royal seal."

There was only the briefest of pauses, while she turned her profile to him. It was long, elegant, proud - *Aegypshan.* Small dark spots ran the length of her hairline, framing her face, gracing her neck and disappearing beneath the wild crush of mane along her back. A black streak ran from the inside of her kohl-rimmed eye, down her nose to curl on her cheek like a serpent.

Cheetah.

"Hand to hand," she repeated. "Very well. Choose."

She raised her arms, palms upturned. Suddenly, she was Kahli, with many palms and many arms, moving, undulating like many serpents flowing from the shadows of her body. He watched for a moment, spellbound before shaking his head. *Of course.* The incense. Only two hands, naturally, both completely still, awaiting the scroll that would end her divinations and bring her up from *Agara'tha* into the light of morning.

He placed the parchment in one and backed away. The wax melted without a touch, the scroll unfurled on its own. Her black lashes flicked down for the briefest of seconds as she read, then she slid her eyes to look at him. He was a senior in the Empress' Panther Guard, having faced dragons and dogs and the great leathery behemoths that roamed the foothills of the Lesser Kingdoms. But never had he seen such a look as the one sent him by Sherah al Shiva that night.

"You shall accompany me. How delightful."

She rose to her feet and her legs went on, and on, and on. When she approached, he could make out her pelt, smooth, fine, the colour of churned cream. Her hair was as black as night, rising from a peak in the centre of her forehead. Her eyes, spaced wide apart, seemed both wicked and wise, the insides golden, the lids painted with colors found only in stone. The tip of her thick, spotted tail curled about her ankles, and she wore both choli and salwar of black silk. Her midriff was bare, and silver vestments hung from her hips like curtains to a shrine.

He swallowed. She smiled.

"Some say the caverns of *Agara'tha* are tombs, *sidi,* waiting to claim lost souls in sleep. A man may get turned around in such darkness, in such shadow. But do not be afraid..."

Long strong fingers brushed his chin as she passed and she paused to lean into him, fanning his neck with her breath.

"…I believe I know the way."

He believed she did.

***

Emerald eyes gazed out the small open window, drinking in the breathtaking splendor that was the palace of the Empress. According to her studies, architecture was one of the truest tests of culture, and *Pol'Lhasa* was so very beautiful. With her steep stepped courts, blackened cedar beams and high, winged rooftops, she towered over the city like a monarch. In her many rooms, torches had begun flickering into life as the sun rose from behind *Kathandu*, the Fang of the Great Mountains. This was her view every morning. It sent her to sleep every night. She still marveled that she was here at all.

And so, with a dreamy sigh, Fallon Waterford dragged her eyes from the window and back to the cramped, cluttered room that had served as her home these past eight months. It was so very different from her real home in the foothills near *Parnum'bah Falls.* There she and her parents and sisters had had all the space they could ever need. Groves of banana, flocks of crested pheasant and glacier-fed rivers stocked with fish. Again, she smiled, for thoughts of home brought pleasant memories. *A tiger's paradise,* her father had called it, and she heartily agreed. She would be enjoying it all still, if only she hadn't been so cursedly, maddeningly, wonderfully clever.

She snatched the scroll from her workbench, the ink still dripping and fresh. She cleared her throat and began:

"THE YEAR OF THE TIGER – A LAMENT
by Empress Faisala the Wise, Second Dynasty,
Year of the Tiger

The Year of the Tiger brings war.
The Year of the Tiger brings change.
Kingdoms rise, Kingdoms fall.
Nothing is the same.

The Year of the Tiger means joy.
The Year of the Tiger means strife.
Beginnings end, Endings begin,
The heartbeat of life.

The Year of the Tiger brings change.
Nothing is as it seems.
Big adventures, Grand schemes,
Nightmares and Dreams.

The Year of the Tiger brings war.
The Year of the Tiger brings change.
People rise, People fall.
Nothing is a water buffalo."

"Water buffalo?? *Water buffalo?!*"

With a dramatic cry, she crumpled the scroll and tossed it to the floor. There were many scrolls discarded there.

A pheasant peeped at her from its bamboo cage and she rolled her eyes at it with shrug.

"But it's so *hard* to write in MandaRhin! It's so different from anything else. Bad enough to memorize it but to have to write it as well! Oh mother! Imperial is so much easier! I don't know, Sica, sometimes I think I've bitten off far more than I can chew here, and believe me, I can chew a lot..."

The pheasant tucked its head under its wing, dismissing her.

"Yes, yes, I know. Mother would be proud, but father, father would be pulling out his fur. 'You're a *girl!'* he would say. 'What *girl* needs to know how to write poetry in MandaRhin? Just find a fine young tiger and settle down like your sisters. Have kittens, be happy.'"

Her golden-orange face grew wistful, the exotic stripes of darker fur creating worry-lines along her brow. Truth be told, there may have been some ink.

"I wonder if he'll ever understand. I *am* happy now, here, in the University. The things I am learning, Sica! The ideas! The books - Oh, the books! I have never dreamed there could be so many books, all in one place! Who needs men when you have such books?"

The pheasant rebuked her.

"Okay, men would be nice too."

Grinning, she reached out to close the window, drawing the iron latch toward her with a click.

Naturally, her reflection came with it.

The face in the glass was that of a tigress, not having yet reached her 18th summer, with a slim, graceful build atypical of her Race. Her pelt was tawny-orange, her arms, legs, back and tail banded with black. Splashes of white accentuated her long throat, curved ears, and bright, wide eyes. Rings of kohl exaggerated her lashes and arched over her brows to create a perpetual expression of wonder. The stripes ran off her forehead like a river delta, her mane from her face like a waterfall. It cascaded to her shoulders only to curl upwards on itself once there, and each strand of hair was tipped in snowy white. Her mouth was small but generous, and frequently contorted into a variety of smirks and smiles, pouts and frowns, for she was both a creature of sunlight and a creature of stars.

She stared at that face in the window glass.

What had her mother always said?

"'But Fallon, dear, you have such nice markings...'" She yawned, stretched, blew a stray lock of hair from her face. "Right up there with Good Family and Plentiful Harvest."

There was a knock at her door and she froze. No one knocked on her door. Not even Anoop, the studious leopard down the hall. She bolted to the door and flung it open to find a panther standing before her, a shoulder-to-hip standard identifying him as a messenger from the Palace.

In her surprise, she closed the door in his face.

"Oh dear, oh mother, oh dear… A messenger from the Palace. Oh dear…"

She opened the door again.

"Oh! Hi. Um, I was, um... just resting, here – *there* – for a moment...I thought you might be a man. I mean, well, you *are,* um, a man…but…um, oh never mind. So? Who are you?"

"Fallon Waterford?"

"No. *I'm* Fallon Waterford. We haven't determined who *you* are yet."

There was no reaction, none whatsoever. The guard handed her a scroll and stepped back into the University's hall, hands folded stiffly behind his back.

She stared at the scroll.

"Is it written in Imperial?"

He nodded.

"Well then, it's a good thing I can read Imperial, isn't it? I mean, what if I didn't read Imperial? What would you do then?"

He stared at her.

"Because I'm having a real problem with MandaRhin, let me tell you. Even writing Hanyin. Mother, that is tough. Imperial is so much easier. You can't read, can you?"

He blinked slowly.

"Well then, never you mind. Thanks for this. Thanks a lot. Really sweet of you to deliver this in person. To *me,* Fallon Waterford. That's me. Not you. *Me.*"

She closed the door and sagged against it.

"Oh, Mother. I really am hopeless, aren't I?"

The scroll was sealed with the Empress' personal seal and she swallowed back a rush of nerves. But her curiosity got the better of her and she peeled it open, her eyes growing larger by the moment.

"Oh no, oh dear, oh no. Oh, Fallon Waterford, what have you gotten yourself into this time? The Palace? Me?"

She glanced down at her garments, at the loose man's tunic and leggings and kujuh coat of forest green, at the russet suede over-vest and bootlets and belt. Her father's clothes.

"I can't go to the Palace like this. I'll have to change my clothing, brush my hair, to brush my face, my tail!"

She peered out the door. The guard was still waiting.

"I can't go to the Palace like this! I'll have to change my clothing, brush my hair, my face, my tail!"

"Now."

"Okay."

She stepped out into the hall and closed the door behind her.

***

A pair of ocelots were talking softly as they passed through the antechamber toward the prayer room called Green Tea. It was for Imperial guests, and some of the best gossip could be found just inside Green Tea's rice paper doors.

"It is a dragon," said one. "A fire dragon, lost in its search for the sun."

"It is a dragon, to be sure," said the other. "But Kaidan's dragon. The one he rode to the moon. It has fallen in love with the moon and is going back."

"With Kaidan?"

"Nonsence," hushed the other. "Who would believe such a thing. *Without* Kaidan, of course. He has other things to do than visit any place twice. I hear he's a-courting the virgin *Shagarmathah.*"

"No!"

"Indeed!"

Kirin rolled his eyes. 'Kaidan' and his adventures. Popular myths. Stories for kittens. People confounded him sometimes. But still, their curiosity was understandable. There *was* a new star in the heavens. It was brilliant and bright and had set everyone's imaginations racing as it rose and fell with the moon. Diviners and worshippers alike were set on discovering its meaning. He paid it no mind. Stars had little to do with panthers or armies or negotiations. Although they could help with New Year's spectacles, if only he had the skill to move them.

The woman at his side growled and the ocelots hurried to leave the antechamber. With a snort, she resumed her pacing and the chamber filled with the sounds of sharp, angry clacking. Kirin gritted his teeth and tried instead to focus his gaze on the great red and gold door at the far end of the hall. It was impossible because of the clacking of the heels. In fact, he'd often wondered if she indulged those heels in order to compensate for her size, as she was a rather small woman. The heels, along with her long, marbled tail lashing from side to side and her long, marbled hair swinging in straight, coarse lines across her back, it almost worked. Add to that the facts that she wore a uniform of white doeskin, bore both long and short swords and sported blades strapped all over her thin, muscular body, she *was* rather imposing. A snow leopard among snow leopards. Swift. Fierce. Lethal. She was his right hand.

And right now, she was giving him a headache.

"Patience, Ursa," he sighed. "They are on their way."

Her ice-blue eyes flashed at him.

"The summons went out over an hour ago, before the sunrise. This is insubordination and it is completely unacceptable."

"Can civilians be insubordinate, Major?"

"Obviously. Can they even speak Imperial?"

"We shall see."

"Pah. I have no with to be discussing Imperial matters in Hanyin."

He grinned and turned his back but from the corner of his eye, he watched her. She was perhaps the most striking woman he had ever known. A study in the colors of ice and snow and cold winter skies, her pelt as silver as a full moon and just as untouchable. Beautiful, remote, and confrontational, she had clawed her way through the ranks at breakneck speed, literally carving herself a path through those who stood in her way. It was only when he had realized that she was closing in on his job that he had found it necessary to remind her of one of the First Laws of Nature.

Lions are bigger.

Good thing too, for she had almost killed him.

Unconsciously, he raised a hand to rub the old wound and was distracted by the feel of braided leather. He had not had the time to inspect his uniform, the laces, straps and buckles that outfitted him and he hoped he looked honourable. His hands searched for creases – found none. He adjusted the brigandine across his chest and shoulders, straightened the epaulets and tightened the golden sash that had loosened at his waist. Like the Major, he wore both long and short swords and his hands fell to the scabbards of their own accord. *Katanah* and *Kodai'chi,* a warrior's blood brothers. He sighed, not for the first time wishing he'd had a mirror in his office. Only perfection was acceptable when the Captain of the Guard was summoned into the presence of his Empress.

He felt Ursa's eyes upon him and he straightened, focusing back on the door at the end of the hall.

Finally, a muffled clang echoed through the antechamber. A quartet of panthers accompanied a pair of civilians and Kirin could immediately tell them apart. Their very strides gave them away, as different were they as day from night. He noticed the one, eyes wide and overwhelmed by the splendor of the Palace. The other however, seemed unmindful of the gold and ivory and kept her painted eyes fixed on him. Finally, the guards peeled away, breaking formation with precision, and he was faced with the two women known to him as the Scholar and the Alchemist. Complete strangers whose very lives now rested squarely on his shoulders.

He gave a very small bow, cupping his fist in his palm. A mere courtesy, for he needed bow to no one save the Chancellor and the Empress. Perhaps not even the Chancellor.

"Fallon Waterford. Sherah al Shiva. Thank you for coming."

The Alchemist did not return the bow, merely lowered her heavy painted lids. The Scholar, on the other hand, bowed quite formally though not quite perfectly. At his side, Ursa was scowling.

He straightened to his full height.

"I am Kirin Wynegarde-Grey, Captain of the Imperial Guard. This is my adjutant, Major Ursa Laenskaya—"

"Wow," the Scholar interrupted. "You have a great voice."

He frowned at her, the tigress, the Scholar. Fallon Waterford.

"Sidala?"

"I mean, not just that you speak Imperial so well – I'm still learning myself but your accent. It's very old, Old Courts. But you're a lion so that's natural I guess. I've just never actually *heard* a lion before or met one, now that I think about it. There aren't that many in the University but I'm sure they're smart, even if they are so very pretty…"

She snorted with laughter.

"And your name, Kirin Wynegarde-Grey? Means 'unicorn.' At least, the *Kirin* part does. It's really old, isn't it? And your sire name, wow. So, do you have any?"

"Any?" He blinked, confounded.

"Yes. Greys?" She was chewing her bottom lip, appearing deep in thought. "The suffix 'Grey' is significant, perhaps indicating a predilection for grey pelts in your line. Pretty rare among lions, really. So I was just curious... to see, um, if there were any... um, greys..."

She seemed to catch herself, for her eyes grew very round.

"...in in in your line, I mean..."

He released a deep breath.

"There are."

"Wow," she said again and she smiled.

The one called Sherah was eying him the way a hungry kitten might eye a marzipan.

Ursa was growling.

And for the first time in his life, the Captain of the Guard felt out of his depth.

"Sidali," he began, clasping his hands firmly behind his back. "The Empress has summoned you here, along with the Major and myself, on a matter of great importance. Therefore, I should not have to remind you that, as in all things pertaining to the security of the Upper Kingdom, we demand your absolute discretion. Nothing less than complete and utter dedication to the work will be accepted. Failure is not an option.

"So first I must ask you if you are willing to accept this standard, even before the task is made known to you. As the Captain of Her Excellency's Guard, I order you all to search your hearts and your souls and your wills before you answer. If you say no, then go in peace. No shame shall come to you, no dishonor on your houses. But if you say yes..."

He studied the three faces spread before him.

"If you say yes, then nothing less than your hearts and souls and wills will be demanded of you. Your lives will be hers and thus, as her Captain, mine. Your deaths, if it come to it, will also be hers and therefore, mine."

His blue eyes tried them like fire.

"So, this is the charge. Ursa Laenskaya, how do you speak?"

"Yes." Without hesitation.

"Fallon Waterford?"

"Oh yes." The tigress swallowed, nodded earnestly. "Yes sir."

"Sherah al Shiva?"

There was a languid pause. She arched a black brow.

"Of course."

Not quite an answer, he thought, *but it would have to do.*

"Very well. On your oaths, I now amend your birthrights, granting you status in the Court of Thothloryn Parillaud Markova Wu, Twelfth Empress of the Fangxieng Dynasty, Matriarch of *Pol'Lhasa,* and Most Blessed Ruler of the Upper Kingdom."

Because of her name, he bowed to them, fist to cupped palm.

As one and likewise, they bowed back.

And with that, the great red and gold door at the end of the corridor swung open, summoning them all into the Court of the Empress.

***

The Throne Room of the Empress Thothloryn Parillaud Markova Wu was breathtaking, the most splendid, most regal, most tranquil court in all of *Pol'Lhasa.* Its walls were scarlet-stained cedar, with beams of ebony and columns of ivory to support its high winged roof. Timbers ran the length of the ceiling, depicting legendary scenes with behemoths and dragons, cranes and monkeys carved into the wood. Temple chimes sounded in the breeze, brightly colored peacocks strutted freely within the walls, and banners of blue and gold hung from the very tall windows. Stained glass painted light from the early morning sky.

Torches burned in many lampstands, filling the Throne Room with incense and with a serenity that defied the rushing of feet. Stepping inside, one breathed peace.

A nod as they passed from Chancellor Angelino Devino d'Fusillia Ho. Quiet, authoritative and brilliant, he was of Sacred blood and the

Right Arm of the Empire. He was also of *Pershan* descent and his lush white pelt was barely contained within his orange and blue robes. It was accepted amongst the Courts that he knew Everything. His flat-faced expression was somber as they walked past him toward their matriarch and they dropped to their knees at her feet.

Like a carving herself, she sat perfectly still, perfectly straight, upon the ages-old seat, the symbol of Dynastic power for 12 generations. She had not yet her 22nd summer, but her golden eyes glowed with wisdom beyond summers. Her lips were painted red as cherries, high cheekbones dotted with white. With the carriage of a swan, she was the spirit of the Mountains incarnate, as beautiful as she was iron, as fragile as she was stone.

And like the Chancellor, she was Sacred with a pelt as black as night. The Sacred Ones were a small race, a people thin of bone and delicate of feature, and the many layers of red and gold that draped her body did nothing to hide the slightness of her frame.

She was glorious.

She regarded them now from that ages-old seat - the four bowed figures in gold and green, black and white. Behind and before them, the Leopard Guard waited in absolute stillness and for several long minutes, not a word was dared spoken until she herself gave leave.

"Rise."

As one, they obeyed and she surveyed them all the more closely, weighing their very souls in the depths of her eyes. Perhaps, she allowed her gaze to linger a moment longer on the face of her Captain…

Yes, it did indeed linger much longer on her Captain. It was rumored amongst the Court that he held her heart in the palm of his hand and that her spirit leapt like a lamb whenever she looked upon him, like a lamb newborn playing on steep, wonderful, dangerous slopes.

"Captain."

"Excellency."

"And your brother? The summons was for him, as well."

The Captain lowered his eyes. "Kerris... is traveling, Excellency. I do not know when to expect him home."

"He is home."

"Excellency?"

She smiled with her eyes. "Your brother is charmed in more than coat, Captain. His party has returned to *DharamShallah* this very night. I believe he is presently deep in his bed, dreaming of sea shells and monkeys."

"I was unaware, Excellency," he replied, gritting his teeth. "I shall send for him at once."

"No. As I have said, he is charmed. Let him sleep. But make certain he knows of my good will."

"He will know, Excellency."

She offered him her hand. It was as slim and delicate and completely covered as she. He took it as if to kiss her many rings, but the rustle of silk told him to wait. She rose from her throne and began to step down the three steps to the mosaic floor.

"Walk with me."

She did not withdraw her hand.

Cupping it as one might hold a baby bird or an eggshell, he fell in at her side, breathing deeply to control the lightheadedness that suddenly threatened to overcome him. This was an honor for none were allowed to touch the Imperial person. He did not need to see the look from Chancellor Ho. He could imagine it well enough. The Green Tea would be buzzing by noon.

They walked in quiet of the throne room toward a far curtained corner, glowing in tones of scarlet and jade. The three women fell in behind, none daring break the spell of the moment. For his part, the Captain could have held that hand for a lifetime.

"What do you know of the Council of Seven, Captain?"

"Your Seers, Excellency. Seven men of learning and wisdom, blessed with the Gifts of Farsight and Vision."

"It's a community of 500 or thereabouts, if I'm not mistaken…" added Fallon Waterford.

She was strolling behind them, speaking very casually and not seeming to realize her breach of etiquette. She had not been given leave to speak.

"Mostly acolytes and students, I think. Some scholars. All who devote themselves to the search for Truth, the pursuit of the Gifts, and other such monastic endeavors. Simplicity, honesty, humility, that kind of stuff. Ultimately, only seven are chosen, seven in whom the Gifts are pure and strong. They advise the Courts on their Visions, and interpretations of Visions, and so on, from the cliffs of, um..." Her mouth twisted upside-down as she thought. "From the cliffs of *Sha'Hadin*."

Ursa was growling once again.

"Indeed, child," purred the Empress, "They advise *me*."

"Oh." Fallon's face fell. "Oh mother..."

The silence was unbearable.

"I see Guru Navheen has trained you well. He was always insolent with my mother."

"Forgive me, Excellency! I - I just—"

"Enough, child. You are, of course, quite correct. The Seers are learned men, gifted and wiser than most. The Seven are my most trusted advisors and, with present company excepted, the truest protectors of the Upper Kingdom. These are their familiars."

She swept a scarlet-clad arm in the direction of two falcons, hooded and perched on a simple, wrought iron pedestal, hearing all but seeing nothing.

Immediately, Kirin's head snapped up. Ursa had caught it as well, for her eyes were sharp and shining.

"Two?" he asked, for Ursa would not. "Only two?"

"The Council of Seven is dying."

Again, that unbearable silence.

"How, Excellency?"

"That remains a mystery, Captain. Each of the past four nights has seen the death of a Council Member, always near the Close of the Second Watch.

"And the manner of death?"

"Also a mystery. The first man, Agis Marelius died in his bed. He had eighty-three summers to his credit, and the physician declared his death as natural for one so old. But when the second died, and then the third, all with similar contorted expressions and violent cries, it became clear that only 'unnatural' causes were at work. The falcons have been relaying messages to and from *Sha'Hadin* as swiftly as they fly. We expect - no, we *pray*, for the arrival of another at any time. Perhaps, this curse has not yet claimed a fifth, this very night."

Thothloryn Parillaud Markova Wu extended her hand to remove the first hood. Small, black eyes blinked several times before the falcon unfolded its speckled wings and lifted into the air, exchanging black iron for red silk.

"This is Na'rang, companion of Petrus Ishak Raphael Mercouri, the Ancient of *Sha'Hadin*, eldest of the Council and a dear, dear friend. As of last evening, he yet lives. And this,' She reached for the second hood. "This is Path."

The second falcon chirruped loudly as her shiny eyes met sunlight. She too, spread wide her wings, talon bells jingling, and rose from her perch. She did not follow Na'rang however but streaked past the Imperial forearm, landing instead on the arm of Ursa Laenskaya.

All eyes turned to the Major who stared at the bird in horror. She shook her arm, pushed at its small body, attempting to dislodge the creature but resulting in a series of angry protests from the sharp, hooked beak.

Ursa turned to gape at the Empress.

"Why?! Why did it do that?! *Why?!*"

"I do not know, Major," murmured the Empress. "It is most interesting. Perhaps it is because her Seer is new to the Council. Sireth benAramis is the youngest ever to sit on the Council of Seven, not having yet reached the Age of Perfection. Indeed, it is said that his visions are never wrong."

Kirin nodded slowly. Most Seers did not attain Council status until well past sixty summers. But to have accomplished such before the age of forty-nine was unimaginable. And therefore, suspect.

"You have not met him, Captain?"

"No, Excellency. I was delivering your last terms to the *Chi'Chen* ambassador during the time of his confirmation."

"You have heard of him, though." It wasn't a question.

"Such a man on the Council, Excellency? Who hasn't heard of it?"

"And what are your thoughts on the matter?"

She was watching him carefully, weighing the meaning behind his words. He would choose them well.

"You have allowed it, Excellency. That is Enough."

That seemed to be Enough, then, for her.

The Empress reached out a gold-clad hand. The falcon sprang from its unwilling host to its Imperial one, bleating its displeasure. She smoothed the ruffled feathers before transferring both falcons back to the pedestal and replacing the hoods.

"There is a new star in the heavens—"

"Yes!" exclaimed Fallon, clapping her hands together. The leopards flinched but still did not move. "We've all seen it! Everyone in the University is so curious as to what it means!"

Kirin sighed yet again. This child had no training. Indeed, he wondered if she possessed any sense at all.

"Our Alchemists are working on divining the answer to that, child," said the Empress. "And my dear Petrus believes that this youngest council member has seen something of it, but refuses to speak of it."

"Refuses, Excellency?" growled the Captain. "This cannot be allowed."

"Sometimes oil is more effective than a stick for opening a lock, Captain. That is why I sent for you."

He lowered his gaze, shamed by his temper. She touched his arm and he was instantly restored.

"You four, with the addition of Kerris Wynegarde-Grey, will journey to *Sha'Hadin,* to discover who or what is killing my Seers. You will use any and all means at your disposal, all of your venerable skills to see that it is stopped and stopped soon. Without the Gifts of Farsight and Vision, *Pol'Lhasa*, *DharamShallah,* and all of the Upper Kingdom will be vulnerable and once vulnerable shall surely fall."

Her deep, soul-searching eyes burned into them like the sun. All four – Ursa Laenskaya, Fallon Waterford, Sherah al Shiva and finally, Kirin Wynegarde-Grey, Captain of the Guard. Yes, most especially, her Captain.

"To you I bind our lives, our civilization, our future. Do not fail me."

And she added one final word, which when spoken from those lips, could break bone.

"Please."

***

"He is dead," said the physician.

There was a long silence in the Hall of the Seers. Of course, they had known he was dead. They had felt him pass violently at the End of the Second Watch. There seemed no stopping it. Physicians, acolytes and attendants could offer little more for sympathy than silence.

The physician nodded and left the two men to grieve alone. The central hearth was smoldering now, its embers dying as a cool wind reached its fingers inward towards their kneeling forms. Surrounding the hearth, three tiny flames flickered from three earthen bowls, the last of seven oil lamps still burning in the Hall of the Seers. Small grey fingers reached to snuff one out and darkness advanced into the room.

"Did you see it this time?" came a rich, quiet voice. The voice of a lion, accented in the tongue of the Old Courts. "Please, Petrus, tell me you saw it."

"No, Sireth," said the elder as he struggled to his feet. "Again, I did not."

"It *must* be wrong. Perhaps this time... perhaps I..."

He did not finish, but let the words hang with a sigh. He did not move to get up.

The old man regarded him gently. "Sireth benAramis is never wrong.

"I would give anything to be wrong. Just this once."

Tattered brown robes swept the floor as Petrus laid a hand on the younger man's shoulder.

"Your vision is the only key, Sireth. Do not disparage it. It may be the only thing we have."

The one called Sireth pulled at his hood, hiding his angular face further in shadows and bent lower, as if calling the warmth from the hearth.

"What now, Petrus? What if we can't stop this?"

"Then we can't."

"I don't understand. This makes no sense."

"You should sleep."

"I can't sleep anymore. There is no peace in sleeping."

Petrus Ishak Raphael Mercouri, the Ancient of *Sha'Hadin*, smiled and slipped his frail hands into his sleeves. He turned to stare out the black window.

"There never is."

***

Kirin watched her for several long moments as she sat by the great charcoal brazier in the kitchen. Ever since he could remember, she would be up with the servants, tending them as a shepherdess tends her sheep. She would not cook nor would she clean, for she was too well bred – a lioness of the Imperial Courts. But she would be there at first light of dawn, working on some tapestry or piece of porcelain that required a lady's touch. This morning, with her tea at her side, she embroidered a slip of purple silk with beads so tiny that she held them on the tips of her claws.

"Mother."

She looked up at him, eyes small and dewy and brilliantly blue, before bending back to her work.

"Sit with me."

"I haven't much time."

"I know, my son. But sit."

He could do nothing but obey, so he pulled up a magnificently embroidered stool in front of the brazier. Silently, a servant placed a cup of hot, sweet tea at his side. Her attendants sat on similar stools behind her, passing her beads and refreshing her tea as required. It had always been this way, and its familiarity warmed him more than the coals.

"He is home," she said.

"I was informed."

"He has something for you."

Kirin smiled. "I am not surprised."

"How is Lyn-ling??

Now he felt the warmth in his cheeks. *Lyn-ling.* The pet name for the Empress since a kitten in the Imperial Nursery. Only a handful of people could get away with calling her that, only nursemaids and nannies and Mother. She knew the secret places in his heart.

"She is well."

"Good."

She nodded quietly, pursing her paper-thin lips, her small, bird-like fingers weaving intricate patterns into the silk. She did not look at him, would not, and he knew she had something on her mind. While part of him cried to get moving, the other ordered him to sit. It would be dishonorable to do otherwise. Her long golden hair was streaked with silver and pulled up into a knot of many braids. She wore a kimonoh of Imperial gold, the mark of their noble heritage. Patiently, like the maid-servants, he waited on her.

"I have spoken with Tamre d'Elsbeth-Ford," she said.

His heart sank.

"Her daughter has made inquiries."

"Yes."

"Dellanana is a lovely young woman. A lioness of fine features, grace and intelligence. You would be well matched." Still, she would not look at him. "I would like you to consider her."

He said nothing.

"I am growing old, my son. I do not wish to face our Ancestors with nothing to show for my life but crafts and dreams and no heirs to your father's legacy."

She held up the slip of silk. It was a kitten's presentation gown. She smiled now, few of her teeth remaining. It puckered her face like a withered apple.

"But more than these, I wish you to be happy."

"I am happy, Mother."

"You will be more happy with a wife."

"I will consider her."

"Your brother will be happy to see you."

She bent back to her work. It was a dismissal. Quietly, he rose to his feet and bowed his most formal bow. She deserved it.

"I will bring him home safely, if not soon."

She nodded again and he left the warmth of the kitchen, feeling a familiar weight fall heavy on his shoulders.

***

Kirin padded up the winding stone staircase in utter darkness. There was no danger for each step was as familiar as a finger or a toe. Indeed, he often felt as if this place were a part of him. It had been their ancestral home for at least ten generations, longer if the city's record-keeper was to be believed. And he treasured every step, every stone, every hearth in its ancient halls, every measure of what it was and what it had always been.

The House Wynegarde-Grey.

He stopped at the uppermost door. The outside wood was surprisingly clean, not at all what he knew the *other* side to be. On the *other* side, there would be etchings and carvings and paintings, and every gap in the wooden surface stuffed with paper or fabric or twigs, transforming ordinary cedar into something extraordinary. Something other-worldly. Something that reflected the uniqueness of the individual living behind it.

With a subtle shake of his tawny head, Kirin pushed it open.

What had the Empress said? Deep in his bed. Of course, she had been right.

He stepped over the woven mats tossed carelessly across the floor and threw open the shutters, then the windows themselves, allowing great gusts of cold air and sunrise to tumble down to the blanket-covered mound in the centre of the room. The room smelled of leather, pine and old ale, and he noticed the bottles also tossed carelessly across the floor. If Kerris was drunk, this would be a problem.

The blankets began to stir. Kirin nudged them with his boot.

"Wake up, dung beetle."

"Mm. Go away."

"The dawn sends you her greetings. As does your Empress."

"Kindly give the dawn and Lyn-ling my regards," mumbled the blankets and a grey tufted tail whacked the floor. "But tell them I shall chat them both up later. I'm far too drunk for sunny conversations, thank you. Now go away."

"I'm serious, Kerris. You were summoned to the Palace last night. Your 'services' are needed, drunken or otherwise."

A groan escaped the blankets and a grey head appeared, propped up on grey elbows.

"Kirin, are you serious?"

"I just said I was."

"Why?"

"I shall tell you that when you're standing."

Blankets and animal skins were tossed aside as Kerris Wynegarde-Grey climbed out from his makeshift bed.

"Welcome home, Kerris," Kerris grumbled. "How was your trip, Kerris? Where were you off to this time, Kerris?"

"Later."

"Later, Kerris. You're needed, Kerris. Nothing quite like 4 hours of sleep, is there, Kerris? So very good for the bones..."

He stepped into a pair of doeskin trousers, slipped a loose linen tunic over the tangle of pendants around his neck and pulled on his yak-hide boots, ones with brightly-colored laces. He ran his hands through his mane of ashen grey, which fell just below the chin - far too short for a Race that prided itself on its crowning glory. It gave him the perpetual, tousled-headed look of one just rolling out of bed.

Not an entirely inappropriate image.

In other than pelt, he could have passed for his brother for in fact they were twins, identical in form and feature. The same eyes of deepest blue, the same rich, rumbling voice in the oldest of accents, the same height, the same build, the same regal blood coursing through their veins. One silver, one gold.

As different as the stars from the sand, or waves from the shore.

"Alrighty then…Pahguah...wind stones...very special sticks..."

He looked around the room, grabbing articles of dubious importance, stuffing them in his trouser pockets.

"Right." He slapped his thighs. "I'm ready. Let's go."

"Inspiring," said his brother. "A vision of readiness. Are you really drunk?"

"Absolutely," Kerris grinned. "Not really. Maybe. I just liked the bottles. Perhaps I shall make something of them someday. I brought you something."

His hand dug into one pocket, then another. He dumped the pouch. He scratched his head.

"Uhm, hang on... Now where did I put that thing? Where's my

cloak?"

"In the hearth."

Kerris spun around, frowning.

"Hmm. Not a good place for it. It's new, you know. I lost my old one. Can't seem to remember where..."

He pounced on the smoldering fire pit, snatching the cloak and shaking it out like a flag. Ashes and bits of charred wood rained to the floor as he rummaged in a deep pocket to produce a pendant, which he proudly dangled from long grey fingers. Swinging at the end of the leather was something flat, triangular and white. Kirin eyed it with suspicion.

"Is that a tooth?"

"A shark's tooth, actually. The bugger tried to have me for breakfast. Instead," he patted his stomach. "We had him. He was quite surprised."

"The ocean! You went to the ocean?! Kerris, you idiot!"

"You're welcome."

"Why would you go to the ocean, Kerris? The Empress has no agenda there."

"Agenda? Who needs an agenda to go to the ocean, Kirin? Winter in *Hindaya* is decidedly more pleasant than winter here." His eyes gleamed with the memory. "More tigers too."

Kirin shook his head.

"And am I to assume that you went to the edge of the world - in the company of *tigers*?"

"A whole pride of them, actually. They paid me too. It was great fun. I love tigers. I should have been born a tiger."

"Yes, Kerris. You should have."

Kirin took the pendant, still dangling from his brother's fingers. He slipped it over his neck, tucking it under two layers of leather.

"There. Are you happy?"

"Never been happier. Well, maybe once.

"Good. Ursa is sharpening her blades as we speak."

"Ah Ursa, my flower, my love. Has she killed anyone lately?"

Kirin grinned as they headed toward the door, his brother a welcome shadow.

"Say, have you heard the latest adventure of Kaidan? They say he's conquered *Shagar'mathah,* you know. Deflowered the virgin peak as it were, left his cloak as a wedding gift..."

The cedar door creaked closed behind them.

***

"Ursa, my petal! Kirin says you missed me! That you're practically on your death bed with love for me!"

Ursa Laenskaya glared down from the back of her horse, eyes narrowed in disdain.

"If it came between you and a death bed, I would not miss."

"I love you too, dearest and gentlest. I just conceal it better. You know how people talk."

"I suppose he is necessary, Captain," she snorted. "We will need someone to clean up after the horses."

"Witty *and* fatal, my love."

Kerris bent to the ground, picked up a handful of earth, tossed it into the wind. Bits rained back down, while other bits rose and floated in several directions. Kerris studied it for several moments, before turning to his brother, rubbing his arms and breathing deeply the chilly morning air.

"So, where's Quiz?"

"The stableboy is bringing him out now."

"It's really not fair, Kirin. Quiz only had four hours too, you know. Unlike snow leopards, horses aren't made of stone."

Kirin grinned and mounted up. His brother loved that horse of his. It was a mountain pony, as rugged and wild as the peaks it came from with a long, shaggy mane, an unwrapped tail and a nondescript coat of mottled brown. But the thing was quite the trail horse, as surefooted as a goat with a remarkable capacity for terrains and an uncanny sense for danger. He was certain Kerris owed the animal his very life many times over.

He knew the feeling and reached down to stroke the sleek neck beneath him, to rub the stiff roached mane. The horse nickered softly, enjoying the touch. alMassay, his own stallion, was Imperial bred, Imperial trained. Large, powerful, intelligent. More dependable than soldiers, more faithful than men.

And they would need all the help they could get.

Straightening up, he let his eyes scan the group assembled in the courtyard of the House Wynegarde-Grey. Eight leopards would accompany them, four ahead, four behind, carrying the Imperial Standard and riding stallions from the Imperial stables. Ursa naturally rode her own, a steel grey mare with teeth as sharp as hers. The Alchemist and the Scholar had been assigned quiet stock horses, for Imperial ones were at a premium in the Upper Kingdom and riding was not a skill known to all. Ox carts, goat traps and foot were still the common modes of travel in cities and villages and on the steep, winding roads that connected them.

They would take three geldings to carry supplies, books, weapons and Alchemy stores, while each rider would be responsible for his/her own blankets and cloak. There was no time for a change of clothing, for in theory, they would reach the monastery before one was needed. The trip should take ten hours at a steady trot, in time to make *Sha'Hadin* before the Second Watch. The third falcon had never arrived, signaling the loss of yet another Seer. Two left. Only two. Kirin ground his teeth, unable to shake the feeling that this trip would not end in ten hours, nor the answers found within the cliffs of *Sha'Hadin.* This was going to take much, much longer.

"Well well, I must have been very good in my last life. Good morning, *sidalady* tigress!"

Kirin glanced up. He shook his head. He should have known.

Kerris was leaning against the shoulder of Fallon Waterford's sleepy mount, smiling the smile that had charmed the Royal Courts since his youth. Wide-eyed, the tigress looked all around her as if seeking its true target, which for some reason, could not be her.

"Me?"

"You are a tigress, are you not?"

"Well, yes, yes I am. And wow! I was right. A grey lion!"

"I am indeed. And you are a clever and spirited girl! I love tigers. They know how to have fun. Not like snow leopards. Or any leopards. Or even most lions for that matter."

Beside him, Ursa's long tail lashed like a whip. Kirin found his fingers curling themselves into fists, quite of their own accord.

"My name is Kerris, First Geomancer of Imperial Quests,

Caravans and other such travelly things. The roads can be dangerous for lovely young ladies such as yourself. But never fear, I'll be there to protect you."

A high-pitched squeal pierced the courtyard, threatening to shatter old windows and ancient stonework.

Kerris grinned.

"But a moment, *sidala.*"

Slipping two fingers between his teeth, he whistled, a sharp, shrill whistle that caused everyone to wince at the sound.

The frantic staccato of hooves on cobbled stone grew louder, and louder still, until a ragged little pony burst out from the stable arches, wild-eyed and flecked with foam. It skidded to a halt only a hand's breadth from its master, nostrils flared, flanks heaving. It wore no bridle about its head, carried no rope or bit of cold metal between its teeth and the only 'saddle' on its back was a blanket tied around it's belly, as rough and mountain-made as the creature itself.

Kerris rubbed a crescent-moon of white hair on the little forehead.

"Hello, Quiz. Sorry to get you up so early. Duty calls, and all that. Still, we're game for it, aren't we, old friend. Sure we are..."

He glanced up at his twin on his shiny Imperial stallion.

"Well then, dear brother, where are we off to this fine morning?"

"*Sha'Hadin*," Kirin growled. "I trust you know the way."

"Yes. Yes, I do. Gloomy place, very serious. No one smiles much there. Don't really say much, either, come to think of it. Guess they don't need to, eh?" Again, that smile. "Ah well, at least it's better than, say, *Agarah'tha.* Now there's a place that gives me the chills."

"You know *Agarah'tha, sidi*?"

A black horse moved forward from the flank of guards, its ebon-clothed rider as foreboding as Death herself. Long, speckled fingers reached up, slowly pulling the hood from her face and heavy-lidded, golden eyes stared down at the lion with a look of obvious intent.

Kirin could have sworn he heard the sound of a grey chin hitting the cobbles.

"*Sidalady* cheetah." Kerris recovered smoothly. He always did. "Forgive my harsh words. I meant no disrespect to your Order. I meant only that to an adventurer such as myself, the tunnels of

Agara'tha are confounding and frustrating. Not to mention cold, hence... the chills?"

"Of course, *sidi.* A misunderstanding."

She offered him her hand, turning it palm upwards as he moved to kiss it.

"Fall In!" The Captain's voice boomed through the courtyard and everyone snapped to attention. "We must make *Sha'Hadin* by sunset. Any questions? If not, we head out."

There were no questions.

Grabbing a handful of mane, Kerris swung on to the back of his pony.

"Right, then. On to *Sha'Hadin!* Let's hope they can *see* us coming!"

And with that he spurred his heels into the mottled flanks, disappearing out the main gates like a whirlwind.

Ursa turned her pale eyes to him.

"Sometimes I very much wish to kill him."

"Let's get to the monastery first, shall we, Major?"

She seemed disappointed.

"Fall in!" she cried, echoing her Captain's order, and the Leopard Guard fell in like a drill team behind her. Sherah al Shiva glided ahead on her lean, black mount, leaving a glowering Fallon Waterford plugging helplessly in her dust.

Kirin rubbed his brow.

Three women. One Kerris.

How on earth would they all survive?

alMassay moved forward at the slightest pressure, out and under the great stone archway of the House Wynegarde-Grey and into the crisp morning air. Finally, they were on their way, from *Pol'Lhasa* to *Sha'Hadin.*

POL'LHASA TO SHA'HADIN

It is interesting to note that the air grows colder the closer one gets to the sky. From the Royal City, it was almost as if the Great Mountains aimed her daggers straight to the heart of the sun. Therefore, one would think the snow should melt away like iron thrust into a blacksmith's forge. Indeed, most mornings, the peaks glow as if melting, but come noontime, they are as white as the clouds only returning to gold with the approach of sunset. So, it would seem that it is the moon that forges the gold and the sun that forges the silver. Likewise, the higher the earth climbs, the colder the air becomes and it is the very depths of the jungle that brings the scorching heat of midday. It is a mystery.

They had left the gates of the Royal City many hours ago and the terrain had not varied much. If anything, it seemed the Great Mountains had grown fiercer, more protective, as they traveled the narrow roads that led to *Sha'Hadin.* Slopes sheered off sharply from the rocky paths, with inclines as steep and dangerous as any cliff, and vegetation was rare amongst the sandstone and granite of the valleys. Snowdrifts were common though, for at this height the shadows stayed cold even in summer and beginnings of streams would freeze nightly. Kirin knew from experience that, come sunset, even their breaths would be ice.

But he had to admit he loved it. Even when the Mountains were at their worst, he would never trade them for any lush jungle or fertile valley in the Upper Kingdom. Here, the air was sweet, the waters cold and the skies went on forever.

He urged alMassay forward to pull up beside the Scholar. She was panting slightly, looking uncomfortable in her heavy cloak. He knew the feeling. The mid-afternoon sun was hot on their backs even as the air was cool. Breathing quickly became labored and riders light-headed as they maintained a steady climb. The brisk trot of morning had been exchanged for the more realistic jog of noon and all horses seemed to take their cues from Quiz, the mountain pony with the eyes of a falcon and the feet of a goat.

"How are you doing, *sidala?*"

"Oh, well, I guess not too bad, really, all things considered. Why? Do I look bad?"

He smiled a small smile. "No. But sometimes, the riding—"

"Oh, I've ridden before."

"In the University?"

"No, at home." She swallowed, panting slightly before she continued. "We had a yak."

Kirin bit his tongue for a laugh had almost gotten the better of him.

"A yak? I hear they are... quite the ride."

"No. They're pretty terrible, really. This is much better."

"Good."

"Do you think we can stop this, Captain? I mean, with the Seers. Do you think we can find out what's killing them?"

He let his gaze wander out over the craggy valleys, so very far below them. But in his mind's eye, he saw *Pol'Lhasa,* her gardens and beams, her servants and courts.

"It is our duty."

"I hope so, too."

alMassay pushed onwards towards the eerie sound of humming. Ahead of him, the Alchemist's black mare seemed to glide along the rocky paths as if its hoofs never touched the ground. Across its wide cantle, several saddlebags lay strapped containing powders and potions, vials and compounds. One small pouch of blood-red satin floated above them all, with strands of spider-silk to keep it from disappearing up into the skies entirely. He had never seen anything quite like it. It whispered of unnatural things.

"Captain," she purred. She did not turn her head.

"*Sidala.* You ride well."

"I do many things well, Captain."

Good thing Kerris was ahead, he thought grimly. *Far, far ahead.*

"Are you able to detect poisons, *sidala?*"

"All manner of poisons, *sidi.* Natural, and otherwise. I have considerable experience with the dead and the dying."

"And the living?"

"Some."

"Well. That will have to do."

He pushed onward still, drawing up beside the Major's grey mare. She had twisted her long hair back in a knot, and the cloak she wore was as silver as her pelt. He could see she was irritated, however, and found a good measure of relief in those few things that would never change.

"Our time is not good," she growled. "We will not make *Sha'Hadin* by nightfall."

"We only need make the Second Watch, Ursa. Nightfall is not a prerequisite."

"I do not wish to be riding these trails in the dark."

"Good point. How are your charges?"

Her hand slipped down to the pommel of her saddle, to the two tiny baskets strapped on either side. A muted chirrup was heard from within the first.

"This one, Na'rang, seems content enough, but this one..."

From the other, a hooked beak jabbed at her through the weave.

"... I believe this one has a problem with baskets."

Kirin grinned. "Perhaps that one has a problem with you."

She snorted. "I shall be interested in meeting the man responsible for such an ill-tempered pet."

Again, alMassay moved forward, bypassing the four leopard guards riding ahead. They all nodded silently as he swept past, up a particularly steep incline. He leaned forward, easing the weight from his stallion's back. The powerful haunches engaged and they lunged forward, and forward again, sending tiny bits of shale down the path below.

Finally, they made breast of the rise and Kirin reined in his mount to breathe in the view. It was spectacular, an endless panorama of cliff and valley, snow and shale. Blue sky, bluer than his mother's eyes, and white – the spears and fangs and daggers of the Mother's Arms, Protectress of the Upper Kingdom. Blue and white. Clarity and purity. Harmony and balance. He nodded, understanding why the Seers chose to locate in these mountains for it seemed that one could see from one edge of the Kingdom to the other all the way to the oceans. Nothing could be hidden from up here, no secrets or plots, no army or ambush, from minds trained to see as a falcon sees, in the endless expanse of dreams and visions. Yes, he could understand it all quite well.

"Kirin!"

A flash of grey and mottled brown and the mountain pony scrambled into sight from behind a bend in the rock. In seconds, Kerris was at his side, looking for all the world as though he belonged right here on this particular road in these particular mountains. One would never have guessed he was noble-born.

"Splendid view, eh? We stopping for lunch?"

Kirin shook his head. "No stopping today, Kerris. We must make our destination."

"Right." A grey hand fished in his pocket, pulled out a roll of dried white flesh. He offered it to Kirin, grinning. "Shark. Care to try some?"

"No, thank you. It's bad enough I'm wearing his tooth."

"Kitten." As he chewed, Kerris waved an arm towards the bend. "Now, here's where you get to prove why you get your own office in the Palace. Just past that rise, the road takes two paths, one steep and narrow, the other broader, less severe. Come, I'll show you..."

Together, the horses jogged forward between the rocky bend. The mountain rising before them was massive, as impressive as *Kathandu* or *Purnannah* and its high snowy peak was hidden in cloud.

"*Sha'Hadin* is on the other side," said his brother. 'Still a bugger to get to, however. And see there? There's the low path. Takes you round for a bit of a dip, then a slow, gradual ascent from the base. It's as well used as you'll find 'round here and there's an inn about halfway up to the monastery. Great ale on tap. Don't touch the sakeh. It'll blow your boots off."

"And the high path?'

He followed Kerris' finger with narrowed eyes, to a small snowy mound by the main road. He could barely make it out.

"Starts right there. It's only wide enough for one horse, and not always then. Very steep, very nasty. Prone to avalanches and mudslides. Rock falls. Bandits. You get the picture."

"And the time?"

"Now, here's the thing. If all goes well, the high path can shave two, maybe three hours off your travels. If all goes poorly, well you'll probably be dead so time becomes rather less of a problem."

They could hear the scrambling of hooves and the blowing of winded horses as the rest of the party scrambled up behind them. He was not even tempted to ask Kerris' opinion - he knew exactly which path his brother would take. And had he been alone, or in the company of soldiers without a pair of valuable civilians, he would have done the same. His eyes studied the mountain, its defiant rise, its sheer walls and glacial plateaus. It was folly and Kirin Wynegarde-Grey was no man's fool.

He felt Ursa move in beside him.

"Major, you will take two guards and make your way by the narrow path. It should get you to *Sha'Hadin* in five hours. Let them know we are on our way and offer them any help you can. Kerris will lead you."

"We should kill him and follow the pony," she suggested. Kerris laughed.

"The rest of us will travel the low route. It's longer, but safer, and I have no wish to compromise our journey for the sake of a few hours."

"Understood, sir."

"And Major..."

"Sir?"

"Do not kill him."

She steeled her jaw, disappointed.

Jabbing her finger at the two foremost leopards, Ursa Laenskaya whirled her horse, making a point of heading out first. The guards fell in at her heels and soon, they were fading into dark and distant specks, throwing up clouds of dust in their wake.

"She wants to marry me. She wants to bear my children." Kerris looked up at his brother. "It's admirable, isn't it? Really, it is."

And within seconds, he too was little more than yet another dark and distant speck, quickly eating up the dust and closing in on the Major like wildfire.

For a brief moment, there was no sound but the wind. Kirin glanced around at the faces behind him - six inscrutable, one wide-eyed and eager, the last anything but. Eight faces, all waiting, each looking to him for the order to move out. He cleared his throat and gave it.

***

It had been an early start this morning in the Throne Room of the Empress, and Chancellor Ho stifled a yawn. *It may have started early,* he mused darkly, *but start it had.* There were scores of people in the room now, from white-robed attendants to musicians playing calming tunes on flute and koto. There were two other Chancellors waiting to see her, of Roads and of the Imperial Stable. They would have to wait now. He knew they would not be pleased.

It seemed that lately none of them were.

He approached her royal form as she stood lighting a stick of incense in a high window. She did not turn as he stepped in at her side.

"They will stop this," she said softly.

"Yes, Excellency. I am quite certain they will."

"But then again, they may not."

"True again, Excellency."

"And perhaps you will have your wish after all."

"None of this is my wish, Excellency. Petrus has been a long time friend."

Her breath was a fan as she blew across the tip of the stick. It glowed orange, raising fingers of smoke into the morning air. She laid it in the bowl and turned to regard him.

"What *do* you wish, Chancellor?"

"Naiamus Ivanoff Terrence Satinder from *Calca'thah* awaits presentation, Excellency."

"I have not forgotten, Chancellor. I will consider no man until this matter is resolved."

"But Excellency, all is prepared."

"My council is dying."

"But your people are not. They are expecting a New Year's festival, Excellency. Are we to make them bear the burden of our affairs?"

He lowered his eyes respectfully, but his heart was pounding in his throat. He could be killed for such insolence. He steeled his lush white jaw.

"And our young Captain has gone to such lengths for the mounted drills."

The Empress' black tailed lashed once and all breathing in the Throne Room ceased. She swung toward him and leaned in close, her voice no more than a whisper.

"You think I am a koi, Chancellor, swimming to the top of the pool at the dip of your finger. Very well. I will see Naiamus Ivanoff Terrence Satinder of *Calcah'thah* presented. I will be entertained by the ceremonies, the fireworks and the mounted drills. I will do as you advise. As always, my will is yours. But my soul will be elsewhere. And my heart..."

She froze, golden eyes gleaming, not knowing whether to be angry with the Chancellor for his insight, or terrified with herself for her blasphemy.

"My heart, like my soul, will be with my Seers, *both* of them, Chancellor, in the mountains of *Sha'Hadin.*"

With that, she straightened and turned back to the incense, allowing breathing to resume with that small gesture.

***

It was several hours before they came to the first signs of people. In fact, the Captain had found it odd that, despite its remoteness and isolation, there had been absolutely no indication that the road they were traveling was little more than a wild mountain path, used by goats, yaks or other feral creatures. But when the leopard in the fore swiveled in his saddle, Kirin knew something was ahead. He prodded alMassay forward.

"Wow," he heard the Scholar exclaim from behind, "Where did all this come from."

For suddenly and without warning, they were in the middle of a marketplace.

Stalls of flapping leather and booths of bound willow crowded the narrow highway on all sides, stretching for a good distance up and down both sides of the mountain, and creating narrower alleys between the shops. Goats and lambs wandered freely among the stalls, bleating and jingling with the bells of ownership. Chickens darted between the horses' legs, the fortunate few still retaining their heads. The cool mountain air was heavy with scents - steamed fish, sizzling coals, bubbling vats of fatty stew. Wafts of incense struck like fists, only to be replaced by something even stronger a few paces further.

People pressed in from all directions – cats of every race speaking in every conceivable language, congregating here in the remotest of places and selling wares from all reaches of the Kingdom. Without exception, their clothing was drab, layer upon layer of tan linen and brown wool, undyed leather straps and unpolished buckles. So very different from the pageantry of *DharamShallah* and life in the Palace Courts. Weathered faces watched them as they rode through the crowds, many with small, rough-hewn pipes clenched between their teeth, puffing and nodding and following them with wary eyes.

Kirin felt his own eyes grow sharp. It was his experience that places like these often bred malcontent and thievery. The crowds did nothing to allow the Imperial party passage and he disliked the feeling of bodies scraping along his shins. One little nick from a loose blade could maim a horse for life and he knew that unsavory reputations could be forged on much less.

"No, no thanks," the Scholar was insisting, "Really, it's lovely but, but I can't..."

He twisted in his saddle. Two horses behind, she was surrounded and because of it, the leopards behind *her* were stalled. Immediately behind him, the Alchemist seemed to be having trouble as well, as many hands reached up to tempt her with stones and silks and meats of dubious origin. Worse yet, she was leaning forward, golden eyes gleaming, almost as if she were tempting them back.

Once again, he cursed the presence of civilians, sat deep in the saddle and applied pressure to the reins.

Slowly at first, then with greater force, the great Imperial stallion began to back up, its haunches and lethal hooves clearing a path unlike any Royal banner as vendors scrambled to get out of the way. It wasn't until they were fully beside the Alchemist's mare did the Captain snag her bridle and release the pressure, allowing his stallion its head. Like a spring wound over-tight, alMassay leapt forward, pulling the mare with him as his powerful lunge dispersed both merchants and merchandise in every direction. A leopard followed suit, and soon both Scholar and Alchemist were free of the mass of bodies that had detained them. Still, it was not easy going and at some point, he lost count of the stomped feet and crushed tails of people foolhardy enough to stay in their way.

After what seemed like ages, the marketplace was gone and the road so congested became a ghost road once more.

The Captain let out a sigh of relief. Still riding beside him, the Alchemist smiled.

"You are not accustomed to crowds, *sidi?"* she purred, her eyes smiling with heavy-lidded humor.

"On the contrary, *sidala,* I am quite accustomed to crowds. I simply do not like them. They are dangerous."

"People are dangerous, sidi. In any number."

He studied her a moment longer before turning his gaze back to the mountain still rising into the clouds.

"True enough, *sidala."*

He spurred his stallion forward, putting some distance between them.

***

"Civilians! I can't believe this!"

"Ah, Ursa. You are as gentle as a spring shower."

She snorted, her hair almost breaking free of the knot as she tossed her head in disgust.

"I hate civilians. This is completely unacceptable."

Kerris studied the ox-cart directly ahead of them. It was askew on the narrow trail, feathery contents spilling down the mountainside and rear wheel rattling desperately over the edge. An elderly jaguar with bad teeth was pleading for help, chattering in a broken version of the Imperial Tongue and pointing wildly as if none of them had seen.

"We have no time for this. His ox is unhitched. He is safe. I feel no need to lose our remaining light to save a cart full of chickens. Stay if you want. We're moving out."

Like a silver-tipped arrow, the Major and her guards struck the trail once again, picking their way slowly toward the over-turned cart. The mountain pony did not budge however, its small hoofs clinging to the sandstone as if frozen. Small, hairy ears pricked and lay back, pricked and lay back, as if trying to solve an intricate puzzle. Kerris loved puzzles. Quiz hated them.

And for some reason, Quiz hated this. *This* was *the perfect place for an ambush,* Kerris agreed silently. The mountain rose up steeply on one side, and the narrow ledge that had been their trail now flattened out, in a wide, almost level plateau. Below them, the gradient was less steep, but deadly still, for to start a fall would surely see it to its stony end. Giant rocks dotted this section of trail like spikes on the back of a sleeping dragon. The mountains were full of such stories, of creatures much larger than cats and to his credit Kerris believed them. He had seen too much not to.

He scanned those giant stones with narrowed eyes.

He heard the moan of hollow wind, the drum of Imperial hoofs fading away.

He studied the elderly man, who suddenly seemed not nearly so desperate for help, nor nearly as elderly, as he too watched the trio attempting to pick their way around the cart and get to wider ground.

Make your move, old man, thought Kerris, his heart thudding in his throat. *All three of them are completely defenseless. Now is the time!*

As if reading those very thoughts, the jaguar turned back, fixing the grey lion with a glare that could freeze blood. There was a flash and something metallic slid out from a sleeve.

"Ursa!" Kerris howled as he dove from Quiz's back and onto the rocky path, the dagger slicing through the air where his head had been.

He scrambled to his feet towards the great rocks.

Somewhere high above, another blur of movement and the hiss of arrows being loosed.

The Major heard it too and threw herself forward on her mount, even as an arrow thudded into her arm. One of the guards let out a yelp, arching his back as a bolt from a crossbow pitched him from his horse. He tumbled head over tail, sliding down shale and bouncing off rocks in the fall that would never end.

Grey hoofs scrabbled on sandstone and the Major's mare pivoted on its back end, tucking up its forelegs and spinning in place. With the arrow still embedded in her upper arm, Ursa drew her long sword and charged.

From behind the huge rocks, the pair of attackers stood and fired again, their crossbows sending lethal bolts whipping across the distance. The lead arrow was deflected easily by her steel; the second sailed hissing past her cheek. With amazing power in its haunches, her mare took great leaps up the mountainside, bringing them within striking distance of the bandits. A scruffy-looking young jaguar raised his weapon and fixed the snow leopard with point-blank accuracy but her steel flashed again, locking into the crossbow's frame. She forced her mare forward so that the frame was pointing at the sky and flung wide her arm, sending both crossbow and sword clattering to the shale. And with another cry, she yanked the bolt from her own arm and tackled the much larger man with relish.

The surviving leopard charged up the sheer escarpment, bringing his own steel to bear. The second jaguar turned tail and began to scramble back along the path but the horse gained easily, knocking him to the ground. The guard was on him in an instant.

Kerris, however, had seen none of this. He had successfully made the giant rocks his cover, keeping at least one stone face between him and his attacker, but the man was persistent and Kerris soon found himself running out of rocks.

He flattened his back against the last stone, scanning the wide expanse of plateau left before him. He could run for it, he wagered, for he had always been fast but in order to avoid the daggers that would be sent flying at his back, he would have to weave and dodge and *that*, he decided, on *this* terrain would be a very bad idea.

The fur on the back of his neck began to tingle.

With a deep breath, he ducked as a dagger struck the rock where his head had been. He snagged the wrist, twisted and forced the man face-first into the stone. He twisted some more until the jaguar yelped and sagged in the grey lion's grip.

"Please *sidi,* please," moaned the man. "This was not my idea! It was my sons! They are so hard on their mother and I, so hard. Right now she sits at home, weeping. Please, *sidi,* spare her more agony, *please."*

Tears welled up in old, yellow eyes.

"Drop your dagger, *sidalord* jaguar, and I shall consider it."

The rusty blade slid down the rock to disappear into a drift of snow at the base.

"Pleeese, sidi…"

Kerris stepped back. He allowed the elder to pull himself into a shaky stand but kept one hand locked around the man's wrist.

"Thank you *sidi*, thank you for your kindness..."

The tears streamed down his face now, making glistening brown stripes along his cheeks. The old shoulders began to heave as shaky fingers reached for Kerris' tunic.

"Oh, thank you, good and kind *sidalord* grey lion. You are so merciful to a pathetic old man, so merciful..."

"Yes, right, well..."

There was spittle on the old man's lips and Kerris backed away but grimy fingers had hooked his tunic. The jaguar pulled himself closer.

"You must be a good son to your father, *sidalord* grey lion. Not like my sons. They are hard on their mother and I, so very hard..."

Kerris tried to dislodge the fingers. He glanced around for Ursa as the hands traveled up his shirt-front, tugging his collar, patting his cheek...

"But my sons, my sons are all I have. I have trained them well, no?"

Within a heartbeat, those grimy old fingers had found his throat.

Black claws began to extrude. Instinctively, Kerris grabbed the old man's throat in the same manner, his own grey claws pricking the tawny pelt.

"I wouldn't do that, *sidalord* very-ugly-old jaguar. I really wouldn't do that at all..."

He smiled his most charming smile, praying that his bluffing skills and fabled good luck would not fail him now.

"Let's just see what we have here, shall we? You are old and a jaguar, your claws are brittle and you likely cannot flex them as quickly as you did in your youth. I, on the other hand, am in my prime, aren't I? A lion and a grey-coat to boot. I'm charmed. You can't kill me, but I can quite easily kill you. You will be dead, while I may be only slightly... inconvenienced."

It worked. It always did. He could see it, plain as day, as the old man quickly rethought his plan. Could see the wheels spinning behind his eyes as he thought and thought some more.

"If I let go," the jaguar hissed. "You promise you won't kill me?"

"I promise," said Kerris.

"On your father's life?"

"Hm. How about on his death?"

The old man released a long breath when suddenly, he fell forward into Kerris' arms, the sharp tip of a blade appearing out of his tunic.

The force of the steel pushed both lion and jaguar backwards to the ground. The blade continued towards Kerris' chest like the tusk of a charging elephant and it was only when the tip was firmly implanted in linen and grey fur did it stop just short of breaking the pelt.

Behind and at the other end of it, hovering above him, Major Ursa Laenskaya stood grinning.

"Need help?"

"Doing quite fine on my own, actually, love," Kerris said, delicately picking himself off the well-sharpened point. The body slid to the stone and he rolled out from under it. "I had him thoroughly confounded."

With a push of her high boot heel, Ursa sent the corpse rolling down the cliff face. They both watched until it was little more than puffs of sandstone far, far below.

"You sure he was dead?"

She sheathed her weapon.

"He is now."

The surviving guard was awaiting them at the over-turned cart. He and Ursa each grabbed a corner and, like its unfortunate owner, it was dumped unceremoniously down the mountain, wood and wheels and feathers raining in its wake. The ox merely stood, watching it go.

"All those poor little chickens." Kerris shook his head. "Really Ursa, now I see why you wear white."

She mounted her horse in one smooth motion.

"Why?"

"The blood shows up so much better."

Her smile was as terrifying as it was beautiful. She tossed her head and headed out, the surviving leopard leading the spare horse behind. Kerris whistled for Quiz and followed.

***

Kirin growled at the sight.

"I can't believe this."

"Oh!" he heard Fallon Waterford exclaim. "Oh my, that's terrible!"

There, on the narrow path before them, lay an over-turned ox-cart.

He rubbed his forehead. He was getting a headache.

With a hand held high, he stopped the party and all horses ground to a halt. Two elderly people, ocelots as old as the mountains, stood at the side of the road, nodding and smiling gentle, toothless smiles. It was clear they were expecting the Imperial party to come to their aid. Both oxen were still hitched, one animal standing, the other lying quietly under tangled yoke and leathers. Fruit, fresh and dried, had spilled from a split in the rough wood. Flies were gathering.

The old man began to speak in the ancient tongue of the Manda'Rhin, his voice hushed and breathless like the language itself.

The Captain growled under his breath once again, for he spoke little Manda'Rhin. *This was the perfect place for an ambush,* he thought darkly. The mountain climbing steeply above them, falling away sharply below. Small twisted cedars grew at strange angles out of the slopes, and drifts of snow provided little cover. But there were no warning bells, no little voices cautioning him to be on alert. Moreover, alMassay was standing quiet and steady under his hand.

Fallon pulled her horse up beside him.

"He humbly asks us for help."

"You speak Manda'Rhin?"

"Oh yes! Just don't ask me to write early Dynastic poetry in it!" She laughed out loud. "There are all kinds of books in the University. In every tongue you can imagine. It's a wonderful place, the University."

"Tell them we have no time."

"S-sir?"

"We have no time. The sun is already far too high in the sky. We will not make *Sha'Hadin* by nightfall."

At the mention of the monastery the old couple smiled anew, their small, moist eyes bright with recognition. One of the oxen lowed miserably, thrashed its forelegs as it tried to rise but sank back to the ruts in the road. The pair were still nodding at him. Still smiling.

"I'm sorry," he began in slow Imperial. "We cannot help you."

His grinding teeth betrayed his words. The Scholar seemed to recognize this.

"Forgive my boldness, sir," she began tentatively, "But I think we should."

"At the cost of another Seer's life, *sidala?*"

She swallowed and looked down at her saddle.

"Sir, this morning, you said that the security of the Empire was at stake..."

"It is."

"I think..." She swallowed again. "I think that if we can't help each other, then, then, then the Empire is already lost. Sir."

He cursed himself once again. She was right. Expedience was not a worthy master. With a resigned sigh, he signaled the six mounted guards and with well-trained precision, they split into three groups, a pair to the cart, a pair to scout the terrain and a pair to stand in guard of the two civilians, tempting targets for any would-be highwaymen. They were as swift as they were thorough and once they had searched the vicinity, the first pair dismounted to attend the cart. Like the mobs in the marketplace, this proved no simple task and soon, Kirin was forced to dismount to lend a shoulder. Almost immediately, the cart began to heave and within minutes, the dislodged wheel was back on the road.

"Wow," whispered Fallon to the Alchemist. "He's really strong."

Sherah smiled, her golden eyes never having left the Captain. "It is the way of lions."

Kirin straightened up, releasing a deep breath and tugging down the sash at his waist. He approached the elderly couple with a formal bow.

"*Sidi, sidala.* Your cart is restored."

"Captain?"

It was one of the guards.

"Yes?"

"Sir, the rear axle is broken. It won't be going anywhere like this."

It was a small sound at first, a faint and distant clatter that grew louder and louder, like the onset of thunderclouds. All eyes turned to the sky, then the defiant cliff face towering above them, then with amazing alacrity, to the road ahead which erupted with a crash of wood and iron. Bits of shale rained down as well, along with wheels which continued bouncing their downward descent and, oddly enough, feathers.

"Wow," said Fallon. "Another ox-cart."

Behind her, the Alchemist began to hum.

The ocelots were still smiling.

Kirin sighed and turned toward his horse.

***

The sun was sinking behind an unfamiliar mountain, casting long shadows into the craggy valley. There was grass here, but it was sparse, cropped too short by a small band of goats that roamed in the rocky pasture. Twisted pines dotted the landscapes but those too were short and stunted, owing their crude shapes to hard summers and harder winters. Muddy footpaths seemed to weave in and out in all directions, a maze of trampled snow and hoof-worn creases that led nowhere, anywhere and everywhere, except where they needed to go.

"Where now, stableboy?" Ursa growled.

Kerris moved Quiz deeper into the valley. He rubbed a hand through his rumpled hair, bit his bottom lip several times, chewed on the tip of an oddly-filed claw but in the end, he simply shrugged.

"I have absolutely no idea."

"What?! I thought you knew where this place was!"

"Well then. You were wrong."

"The Captain said –"

"The *Captain* never asked if I'd been there, did he? Only if I knew the way. Well, I showed you the way, didn't I? But how to get in the proverbial front door is another matter entirely. In fact I don't think there *is* a front door. I recall something about the number seven..."

Suddenly one of the baskets erupted at her knees. It was Path, the ill-tempered, emitting a series of shrill, frantic cries and sending downy feathers all over the Major's doeskin.

Ursa swatted the basket lightly.

"Stop it."

The falcon struggled all the more furiously to get out.

"I said stop it."

She swatted harder, to no avail. Finally, she grabbed the basket with both hands but it resulted in a direct hit from the lethal beak and a ribbon of red running the length of her finger.

"She's hungry," said a voice.

"So am I," muttered Kerris, before his head snapped up in surprise. "Say! Who said that?"

Seated on a rock in the middle of the valley, a man was watching them.

"Was he there before?" asked Kerris.

"No." Ursa scowled, her eyes narrowing to shiny slits. "He was not."

"Of course I was," said the man. "You simply weren't looking."

The Major urged her horse forward. The man spoke with the voice of a lion, in the deep, rumbling tones and accents of the Old

Courts. He was maned, too, his hair long and dark and falling loosely past his shoulders. His pelt was the colour of pale sand, with a scar of fine white fur running across his left eye from brow to cheek. He sat quite still, clothed in sweeping robes of brown leather, and tapped a staff of twisted bamboo softly against the base of the rock. He seemed tall, being long of limb and lean of torso and his leonine tail was tufted with black.

But he was as far from Lion, or any Pure Race, as a cat could get.

This cat wore a beard.

Mongrel, she thought grimly. *Mountain Lion.* Like the stripe of a tiger, or rosette of a jaguar, a dark circle of coarse fur ran over his lip and around his mouth, framing it in a way no true lion's would. It ran just to his chin and across it, thankfully stopping there and not traveling up his jaw like she had seen in other mountain cats. *What was this called again?*

Oh yes, a goah-tee. Appropriate, since he apparently tended goats.

"Do you know where the main entrance to the monastery is?"

He seemed to consider this a moment.

"I don't think there is one."

Again, that rich, rumbling voice. She did not like this one bit. *Mixed Breeding. The scourge of the Upper Kingdom.* She decided to speak slowly, for he was also, apparently, quite stupid.

"We seek *Sha'Hadin.* Can you help us?"

"Yes. I can."

"Can you take us there?"

"Yes. I can."

She felt her claws begin to curl.

"Now?"

"Well, I don't think they'll let you in."

"Why not?"

"Why should they?"

"We're here on business."

"Business?" He was smiling at her now, the kind of patient, long-suffering smile of only the very wise, or the very dim. "Are you buying or selling?"

"Not that kind of business."

"We have nice goats."

She stiffened in her saddle.

"We're from *Pol'Lhasa.*"

"Aah. *Pol'Lhasa.*" It was only then that she realized his eyes were brown. *Unnatural.* Cats' eyes were light, like the sun, like the sky, like the grass. Dogs eyes were brown like the earth. This was unnatural. "Are you the Empress?"

"Simpleton!" she sputtered. "Let's go. This mongrel couldn't find his way into a sheep pen, let alone the monastery of the Seers!"

She prodded her horse forward, almost pushing the man off the rock with her passing.

"Sorry, *sidi.*" Kerris shrugged. "I'm just the stableboy."

The leopard fell in behind and the party rode out of the small valley at a forceful trot, picking one of the goat trails and following it as if they could make it take them where they wished to go.

The bearded one watched them, until they had disappeared into the long shadows of evening. He shook his head with a sigh, rose from the rock and began to walk in another direction, back along the way they had come.

***

Sunset was changing things.

The usually clear, bright blue of sky had faded, growing dark, muddy, almost the color of the mountain rock itself. Slopes, once red as clay, became the color of old wine and wine-colored clouds took the shape of slopes. Everything gleamed and glistened on snow. It all blurred the distinction between heaven and earth, making the narrow trail more treacherous than ever before and causing great strain on already-strained eyes. If he hadn't known better, Kirin might have thought that the coming of night beckoned the elements together, gathering them in some ancient ritual of unification or prayer.

He was tired.

And they seemed no closer to their destination than when they had set out this morning.

All conversation had ceased after repairing the ox-cart's broken axle. It was as if each word was an added hour, time they could ill afford now as the air around them grew cooler and the heavy cloaks of midday became welcome second-pelts. They had passed the inn Kerris had mentioned, but there was no sign announcing it as such. He'd been sorely tempted to stop for a flask of ale and directions but the place had seemed abandoned, the windows blackened, door bolted. Nothing on this journey was proving simple, he had concluded.

Immediately ahead, there was the sound of a hoof sliding on unsteady ground. The lead guard had caught his mount soon enough but the Captain called a halt to their progress. He dismounted and strode to the fore.

High in the distance he could see lights.

Torches, most likely, lining what could only be some sort of road. He prayed that they led to the monastery and not some other Inn or marketplace or ox-cart.

He felt warm breath on his neck.

"Can I help you, *sidi?"* purred the Alchemist, standing altogether too close for his comfort.

"No, but thank you, *sidala.*" He sighed and surveyed the river of lights, winding its way into a steep ravine far above them. "We are in need of torch, not candle."

She smiled and held out her palm. A burst of fire erupted within, and Kirin found himself shrinking away from its brilliance. It burned from no recognizable source but something in the palm of her hand sizzled and flared with the light of many torches.

He nodded, impressed.

"That... should suffice."

"Wow," came Fallon Waterford's voice, hushed with wonder. "Look at all this..."

On the rock face behind them were carvings.

The entire side of the mountain was chiseled from its stony base as far up as they could see. Kirin shook his head. The carvings did not start here, but likely had begun a long way back on the trail, the shadows of the setting sun rendering them unnoticed and incomprehensible. Even now, they remained as such for the symbols themselves were strange, likely remnants of an ancient tongue.

"Oh look," exclaimed Fallon, standing in her stirrups and pointing to a character high up on the cliff face. Sherah shone the 'torch' in her direction. "There's Buddah! And and Ramah! And Kristos, the Three-in-One! Wow! And this, this is the symbol for 'eyes', thousands of eyes, no - a *Thousand Eyes*, yes!"

"Can you read this?"

"Yes. No. Very little of it. Some of it though. Some words. Some symbols. Not much." She glanced at him, her usually bright eyes weary but earnest. "I think we're close. If that helps?"

He tried to smile. It ached to do so.

"Shall I lead?" purred Sherah al Shiva, holding her 'torch' out like a beacon.

"By all means, *sidala*. But I shall be right behind."

She mounted her horse and smiled again.

"Of course."

***

Night comes to the Great Mountains.

Night, anywhere, is a mysterious thing but in the Great Mountains, in the Valley of the Seers, it takes on almost religious tones. Night brings with it prayers and petitions, confessions of sins and admissions of guilt. It brings questions and answers and then questions again. It brings revelations and lamentations, and the soul-searching of prophets. And especially, this night, when a sixth life is demanded and ultimately surrendered, it is a sacred, somber, most terrible thing.

There is a new star in the heavens, and the people see it and wonder and fear.

In a small bamboo basket, on the back of a horse somewhere, a falcon dies.

In the Hall of the Seers, a candle is snuffed out. A lone man kneels weeping and darkness advances into the room.

And it is only the Middle of the Second Watch.

***

Kirin Wynegarde-Grey closed his eyes.

"Sha'Hadin"

They had followed the glow of eerie torchlight for the last hour, placing their trust in the sure-footedness of their horses for they had only Sherah's beacon and precious little moonlight to guide them. It had grown dark swiftly and with the darkness had come the cold, chilling them to the bones and creating treacherous ice slicks on the narrow mountain paths. They had been forced to slow to an agonizing crawl to give the horses their heads. Now, as torches burned before them and below them and finally all above them, he felt a terrible weight settle onto his shoulders.

The Cliff of a Thousand Eyes, it had once been called, and he could see why.

Hewn out of the sheer mountain escarpment, were holes – windows that stretched up the cliff face as high as seven levels, open to the night sky like many mouths, pouring forth light and warmth from within. Inside those mouths, figures could be seen moving, robed figures with bowed heads and outstretched hands, swaying in silent rhythm. And from somewhere deep within, a gong sounded seven times seven, the number of perfection.

Kirin shook his head.

They were too late.

And with a deep breath, he moved his horse forward, beginning the descent into the steep ravine that was the monastery of the Seers.

***

"Captain!"

Ursa Laenskaya spurred her horse up the stony ground as she pulled up by his side. She looked as haggard as he felt. Her long hair had escaped from the knot she had worn all day and her arm was dark with blood. Things had obviously not gone well on their end. But he was short on patience and he snarled at her.

"Major, why aren't you inside?"

"We were attacked, sir. We killed three, lost one."

Instinctively, he looked for Quiz, picked him out rambling towards them in the darkness. And thankfully his brother, bundled in the pony's blanket, looking ready to exchange saddle for shale at any moment.

They had failed.

They had made it but they had failed.

He could hear the rest of his party, the Scholar and the Alchemist and the Leopard Guard, their horses heaving and blowing in exhaustion. With a sigh, he slid from his horse and trudged up to one of the seven ground level openings. It was barred by a black iron gate, teeth across an open mouth. Torches burned on either side, casting shadows across the stone. He reached up to take one.

"You're late."

On the opposite side stood a figure hidden by darkness. Kirin lifted the torch from its perch and angled it toward the gate. It was a tall man in dark robes. Many men actually, obscured by robes, hoods pulled to cover their faces. They stood perfectly still, watching him, weighing him with unseen, all-seeing eyes.

"Yes," he said. "We are late."

"Where is the falcon?"

Kirin looked at Ursa, noticed the dread coldness in her face.

"Which?" she asked. "Living or dead?"

"Dead."

She reached under her cloak to produce the small, feathered body. Its head lolled; there was no flicker of wing or tail. She handed it to the Captain, who passed it between the iron into gloved hands. One of the figures disappeared with it into the depths of the monastery.

"And the living?"

Chirrups pierced the quiet as Ursa loosened the ties securing the lid of the basket. Speckled wings burst forth, then the head, hooded since the Palace and the bird sprang to the Major's arm as if home.

"Remove the hood," came the voice, soft now, almost purring. "I told you she's hungry."

For once, Ursa did as she was told without question. The falcon lit from her arm, talon bells jingling. Soon it was only a shrinking silhouette as it soared upwards, a black speck against the overpowering blackness of the cliffs.

The tall figure regarded them.

"Stableboy, see to your horses. Rodreigo will show you the way. "

Kerris slid from the mountain pony and began to gather up the reins of the Imperial horses when a young pair of hands touched his. Bright eyes smiled at him in the darkness.

"I will help, *sidi.*"

"Right. There you go then."

As he handed off the reins, Kerris noticed the Scholar, dismounting on wobbly legs. He swung around to grab her arms and steady her.

"You alright, *sidalady* tigress?'

"Oh, never been better."

"Well, you won't be saying that tomorrow. Come on, Rodreigo, these beasts are tired. We can all use a soft, sweet bed right about now."

And without so much as a backward glance, he followed the youth deep into the ravine, leading the weary horses into the night.

The gate swung open.

"Welcome," growled the tall figure, as he turned his back to them and disappeared into the shadows. "To *Sha'Hadin.*"

SHA'HADIN

The corridors of *Sha'Hadin* were a remarkable tapestry of carved stone that rivaled *Pol'Lhasa* for its detail. Almost every inch of wall space was chiseled with scenes and symbols, seeming to date from the time of the Ancestors or beyond. Fallon Waterford ran her fingers along the walls as she walked, as eager to stop and study as she was eager to see more but far too weary for either. Oil lamps burned at regular intervals, providing welcome light and bathing everything in warm gold. The low minor tones of chanting echoed through the halls, underscoring the mood with sobriety and strength.

The tall figure led them in silence. He had kept his back to them the entire time, his brown robes and tufted tail swaying behind him with each long stride. Kirin had grown accustomed to the futility of engaging him in conversation. Instead, he had focused his attention on the gloves. It seemed everyone in *Sha'Hadin* wore them in one form or another. Some wore only palm gloves with fingers exposed. Workers, he assumed. Others wore gloves of fine linen, others of silky satin, and others of coarse dark wool. Their 'host', however, wore gloves of thickest leather, tanned and dyed and stitched with elaborate detail. He carried them behind his back like an angry sensei.

Acolytes and robed attendants scurried around them, not rushing but moving with an efficient grace. One attendant, an elder man with the silver hair and great wide hands of a lynx, had fallen in beside their host and was now speaking softly in his right ear.

The tall man paused and with back still turned, he spoke.

"This is Tiberius. He is arranging for several mugs of hot tea for any who wish. Your journey has been long and even in the worst of times, our home is open to all." He paused. "You have with you both Alchemist and Scholar?"

Kirin nodded. "Both."

"They shall accompany Tiberius to the Chamber of the Dead. There they can begin whatever preparations they may need make for tomorrow night."

"Tomorrow night?"

"When benAramis dies."

Sherah al Shiva moved forward, her heavy, painted eyes boring holes between the man's shoulder blades.

"Do we have leave to open the body, *sidi?"*

For the first time, he turned his head just enough for his bearded chin to be seen from the shadows of the hood. Kirin was surprised. He'd assumed he'd been dealing with a lion. He shook his head. This was no lion.

"Why?"

"To determine the cause of death, of course."

"I *know* the cause of death."

Now, it was Fallon Waterford who stepped forward, brows drawn, hands wringing like damp dishcloths.

"Please, *sidi,* we - we mean no disrespect, but sometimes there are signs in the tissues and humors, signs which can help us confirm the truth."

"Or prove the lie," Sherah purred.

"Whatever their reasons, *sidi,"* said Kirin. "They have been sent by the Empress, in Her service and on Her order. Do you deny them their duty?"

There was a heavy pause. The man sighed, took a deep breath.

"Of course not. They have leave to open the body. *Bodies.* There are, after all, six. Now, Captain, Major, if you will kindly follow me? I shall take you to the Hall of the Seers."

Fallon opened her mouth, thought better of it, and closed it quickly in a frown. Wrapping her arms around her ribs, she watched as the trio departed down yet another remarkably carved corridor, leaving the pair of them to their work. The attendant, the lynx Tiberius, was smiling at them.

"*Sidali,* this way, if you please."

"He knew their ranks," sputtered Fallon. "We didn't introduce ourselves, not here, not outside, not before. I know, 'cause I was there. So, um, how did he know their ranks? How do you guys do that?"

Tiberius turned, leaving with women with nothing to do but follow.

***

The staircase was as treacherous as a high mountain pass. No guardrails were in place and the sides fell off into sheer blackness. Gone were the regular, welcome torches that had lined the walls of the monastery proper and a cold wind snatched at them, threatening to push them from the steps and send them plummeting seven levels to the stone below.

"We're following a goat keeper, sir," growled Ursa from behind. "I cannot believe they would let this happen. This man is lost and he will get us lost yet again. Look at him. He is almost swallowed by the darkness. I will not rush to catch him when he falls."

"Major, your voice causes an echo. Please stop."

"He sees with one eye, that is obvious when he talks. We are following an insolent, half-blind mongrel—"

"Major, that's enough."

"But Captain, your brother and I met him earlier. He sent us on the wrong path. I can assure you, he is simply the goat keeper."

Kirin sighed, pausing mid-step on the stairs to glance up at the figure receding into shadows. *The temper, the arrogance, the breeding... Could he have been wrong?*

"*Sidi,*" he called up. "Are you taking us to the seventh Seer, the one that yet lives?"

"You shall make his acquaintance in the Hall of the Seers."

"You did not answer my question."

"I suppose I did not."

"Mongrels," Ursa snorted. "We should kill them all."

A heavy door awaited them when they finally reached the top of the stairs. It was clearly on the seventh and last level of the monastery and they could now see the many windows carved high in the stone. In daylight, the staircase was likely flooded with sunshine and cool breezes and in need of no candle or torch. But in the dead of night, those windows served to suck away the faintest flickers of light that came near. It was impossible, even, to see stars.

The man with gloved hands wrapped them around an iron clasp. "The Hall of the Seers."

As he pulled the great door open, a cold gust of air struck them, billowing the torches on either side of the frame. First Kirin, then Ursa, strode across the threshold and into the room. Save for the faltering hearth, several black earthen bowls and a single wavering candle, the room was empty.

Large, cavernous, and completely empty.

"Empty! This room is empty!" Ursa whirled, tail lashing, her pale eyes narrowed. "Captain, I was right! This man is a fool and we are all the more so to have been led by him, this, this keeper of goats!"

Kirin said nothing, merely watched as the man brushed past them to kneel in front of the hearth, in front of the only flame of seven still burning. He watched as a strip of talon leather was drawn from a deep pocket, the bells put to quiet lips, then both bells and leathers laid in the hearth's smoldering ashes. They began to hiss and curl.

"I think rather, a keeper of falcons," said Kirin. "Sireth benAramis?"

Facing the fire, the man nodded.

"What? Who? Him?" Ursa was livid. "He said he was the goat keeper!"

"She hears without hearing. She sees, but is more blind than I."

Slowly, Sireth benAramis unfolded his long legs and rose from the hearth, pulling himself to his full height to face the Captain. He lowered the hood and finally, Kirin could see the infamous scar.

"Captain Wynegarde-Grey. I am honored."

The Seer inclined his head, but did not bow.

Kirin did likewise, fighting back the rush of indignation. The man was living up to his reputation already. He could understand why this Confirmation had been hotly debated.

"And I you. I apologize for missing your Confirmation."

"Ah yes. The price for peace with the *Chi'Chen.*"

"Yes."

"Thank you, then, for coming now." His good eye glittered in the firelight. "The journey is not an easy one from *Pol'Lhasa* to *Sha'Hadin.* Nor I fear, a necessary one. Nonetheless, your people will be well cared for here until you decide it is time to leave."

He turned to Ursa, with a faint trace of a smile.

"And I thank *you*, Major, for pointing out some of my more obvious shortcomings. I wonder if, with all those daggers, you wouldn't care to take a stab at the other, *less* obvious ones?"

To her credit, Ursa held her tongue. If he had been anyone else, she would have gutted him.

Kirin folded his hands behind his back.

"You fear the journey is unnecessary? Why?"

"What has been killing us for six nights now, cannot be stopped by soldier nor sword. Nor, I'm afraid, by all the books or brilliant imaginings of a Scholar. And I, for one, place no trust in the Black Arts of a Necromancer."

"There are many who might say the same of the Gifts of Farsight and Vision."

"Indeed, Captain, that is true. I, however, am not one of them."

With a dramatic swirl of his robes, he moved away from the hearth, toward a small, open window in the wall.

"There is a saying in *Sha'Hadin,*" he began, "That Time is little more than an old woman's knitting. A ball of yarn on one end and on the other, a scarf. Or a pair of slippers or socks. It doesn't really matter, for every time she knits, she makes something different. But you see, she always works with the same ball of yarn."

He reached down to the stone floor, scooping into his hand a mouse that had been scurrying for cover. Again, Kirin was surprised. He hadn't even seen it moving.

"Alchemists would seek to change the scarf, or the slippers, or the socks, for change is the very nature of Alchemy. They would attempt to change its color or its composition. Then, stitch by stitch, they would pull it apart until the thing was completely unraveled in a tangled up ball on the floor. And they would claim success for they would have indeed succeeded in determining her methods and her patterns. They would be very, very pleased. The woman, however, would not be so similarly inclined..."

The mouse was scrambling over his fingers now, across his gloved palm, and he rotated his hand to keep it moving.

"Those with the Gift of Vision much prefer to study the yarn *before* it passes through the needles."

And with a flick of his wrist, he sent the mouse sailing into the air, tumbling and twisting in its arc to the ceiling.

A speckled blur streaked through the open window, snatching the mouse in midair with a jingle of bells. The falcon swept through the room, crying in her shrill, sharp voice, circling the Major before coming to rest on the Seer's shoulder. She dropped the dead mouse into his palm.

"Pah," Ursa scowled. "Theatrics."

"Sometimes."

The Captain stepped forward, his hands still firmly clasped behind his back.

"You said earlier that you knew what was killing the Council of Seven. Tell me."

Sireth looked at him, his head cocked like the bird on his shoulder, and for the first time, it was obvious the blindness in his left eye.

"That which has caused the deaths of my dearest friends?" He sighed. "Terror, Captain. It is Terror."

***

"Terror? Oh, Sherah, are you sure?"

The Alchemist stopped her strange humming, but did not look up from her work.

"It is obvious. They died screaming in fear."

Fallon Waterford cast her eyes downwards once again, at the wrinkled old faces twisted into grisly caricatures. It broke her heart to think that such wise and noble men died in such terrible ways. She had always believed that death would come, no - *should* come with some measure of dignity to the aged. But, as she had begun the first of her investigations, that belief had been torn from her and it stung like a scorpion.

"You're probably right. Yeah, you're right. But still..."

She turned back to the table, to the long, polished lens that was suspended over a glass plate. Her tongue peeked out between her lips as she peered at the smear of blood she had drawn.

"But why? I mean, there must be a physical cause. The hearts must have seized, or humors ruptured inside their skulls – but all the same way at the same time six nights running no that doesn't make sense at all now, does it? And still..."

"Here. See?"

Sherah straightened up from the body, her black silk sleeves pushed up to her elbows, her long arms thick with blood. She turned toward the Scholar.

In her hands was a heart.

Fallon swallowed, but as always, curiosity got the better of her.

"Yes. Pale. Constricted. Like every fiber has been squeezed together by a fist. Are they all the same?"

"I shall tell you that soon, Scholar."

"And the lungs?"

"The same."

"And the fingers and toes, they're black as pitch. It's like, like..."

"Frostbite."

Fallon shook her head.

"How can this happen? Can this even happen? I mean, this is physically impossible, really." She pushed away from her table, letting her hands fall to her lap with a sigh. "There are no problems with the blood, other than the usual anemia of age. No signs of plague, no disease, no creatures–"

"Creatures?" The Alchemist eyed her. "You mean poisons."

"No. I mean creatures. Sometimes, if people get very ill, you can see creatures in their blood. Very small, so small in fact that you wouldn't even notice them if you didn't have a glass like this. Sometimes, the creatures are given by flies, or mosquitoes, or bad water. Sometimes, the creatures live in the tissues. The liver is particularly susceptible. Hmm, we'd better check the livers..."

She pouted, grabbed a book, began flipping the pages.

Sherah stared at her for a long moment, before shaking her head. Her hair was loose about her shoulders, the ends tipped in red.

"Creatures. You are very amusing, Scholar."

"Oh. Yeah. I have pretty markings too..."

Fallon sighed and closed her book, swept her eyes across her little table. Almost every inch of it was covered in books. Textbooks, workbooks and most especially notebooks — journals that had been with her since her childhood. While her sisters had been learning to sew and mend and cook, she had been out in the jungle with her journals, observing the leaves, the trees, the insects. She had catalogued everything she had ever seen and her books were filled with sketches. Once, when she had been in her eighth summer, she had found the body of dead monkey, a *Chi'Chen* scout most likely and she had dissected it in secret. Within those notebooks and journals, she revealed everything.

The Alchemist's table was similarly cluttered but with things other than books. There were jars of phosphorous and vials of ammonium. Sacks of animal remains were strewn about along with tiny boxes of jewels and odd, powdery rock. Spilling from a saddlebag were silks, crusted in blood and labeled in ink. And candles. Many, many candles. It all smelled of incense, Fallon thought, like strange, exotic incense. Almost like the Alchemist, herself, strange and exotic. And perhaps, just a little bit frightening.

Then there was that pouch...

She pushed herself from the table and crossed over to the red satin pouch. It floated like a poppyseed on the breeze. She threw a glance in Sherah's direction before poking it with a finger. It bobbed at the end of its unusual tether. With a frown, she tried again, pushing it gently downwards with her palm, only to have it float back up when her hand moved away.

"Um, Sherah, what, um, what exactly is in this?"

"Souls."

It took her a moment to close her mouth.

She tiptoed back to her table, trying not to hear the sucking, cracking sounds as the Aegypshan dug into yet another chest cavity.

"You may have him if you wish," said Sherah after a moment.

"Him who? The'dead guy' him? Well, I don't really think there's enough room in my bags for a dead guy, even if he has over one hundred summers to his credit. Pretty remarkable, isn't it? I mean, look at the white fur on his head, whiter even than the peaks of *Kathandu.* And his pelt, its so soft and wrinkly, like a comfortable pair of woolies. People look so wonderful when they're old, don't you agree, like the mountains? But really I don't think—"

"I meant the grey lion."

"Oh."

It had come so unexpectedly. All Fallon could say was "Oh."

And again. "Oh."

"I have no designs on him. I shall leave him to you."

"I don't understand..."

The Alchemist paused to look up from her investigations. Her painted eyes narrowed and a crooked, almost wicked smile slid across her face. She ran bloody fingers through her black hair, and stretched out her arms, arching her long back like a drawn bow. She yawned.

"You want him, don't you?"

"I still, I don't know what you mean." The tigress furrowed her brow. "I mean, I'm a tiger, he's a lion. We couldn't, we wouldn't..."

"Of course."

Sherah al Shiva turned back to the open ribs.

"Regardless. He is easy on the eyes."

"Oh." Fallon sighed. "Yeah. Sort of."

"With an agreeable voice."

"Oh. Yeah. I love the accents of lions. They sound so sophisticated." She sighed again. "Not like tigers. I'm probably the most sophisticated tiger in the jungle, and that's not saying much."

"I can help you."

"Okay."

There was silence for a very long time afterward, save the cracking and sucking and occasional sigh.

***

"Tastes good, doesn't it, Quiz my boy? Sweet, lovely hay with ground- up pheasant garnish. Chom chom chom."

Kerris Wynegarde-Grey rubbed the shaggy neck as the pony dove nose-first into the feed. *Almost as carnivorous as cats,* he thought, with teeth for both grinding and tearing. He ran his hand down the shoulder to the legs, straight and sturdy and strong of bone. No scrapes or soreness, no signs of swelling. One by one, he applied pressure to the fetlocks, lifting each hoof in turn to check for rocks, chips and tell-tale bruises. All fine. The creature was as sound as a yak. Almost as shaggy. He straightened up and winced.

Too bad the same couldn't be said for its rider.

"I must go now," came the voice of Rodreigo as he tidied up the brushes, wraps and liniments in a far stall. "I must get back for Lamentations."

"Lamentations?"

He could see the boy quickly lower his head and immediately Kerris cursed himself.

"Yes," Rodreigo whispered. "The Ancient of *Sha'Hadin* is no more."

"Sorry. I think I'll stay here, if it's all the same to you. I just want to keep an eye on the horses. It was a long journey."

"Yes. From the Palace." The boy grinned at him now, eyes bright with candlelight. "Are you really a stableboy?"

"Me? No, not really. Feels like it, sometimes..."

"A soldier, then? Lions make the best soldiers, it's true."

"Not *grey* lions, I'm afraid. Coat clashes with the uniform."

"So you *are* grey. I couldn't tell in the torchlight. This is a good omen. You will save the last Seer, I know you will. This is a very good omen."

Kerris shook his head.

"Good night, Rodreigo. See you in the morning."

"Good night, *sidalord* grey lion. Sleep well."

The candlelight disappeared along with his footsteps and Kerris was finally alone.

With an arm draped across his pony's back, he glanced around the monastery's dark stalls, savoring the aroma of cedar and leather. Tall beams of mahogany braced the ceiling, for like *Sha'Hadin* itself the stables were hewn out of mountain rock. Quiz pulled away with a mouthful of hay and pheasant entrails, snuffling the ground and turning tight circles on the floor. His front legs folded, and within seconds, the pony was lying down. He let out a deep rumble of breath and his brown eyes blinked slowly.

Kerris sighed. "Looks comfy, my friend."

He ambled back over to the door of the stable, took one long last look at the night sky and the strange new star. He could hear the clouds talking to each other, could feel the snow gathering in the north but the star was silent. He pulled a small stick out of his pocket. It had red tassels on the end and a word etched in its shaft.

"Snake?" he muttered to himself. "Now why in the Kingdom would it say that?"

At least there was no lightning.

He stuffed the stick into a deep pocket and stepped back inside, looking for and spying the loft up a narrow pole-ladder. Within seconds, he too was sprawled in the fragrant hay, yawning and stretching, not even having the time to say goodnight to the moon before he was fast, fast asleep.

***

The Captain was amazed at how much warmth was put out by such a faltering fire. Or perhaps, it was the tea, hot and sweet, that they cupped in clay bowls in their palms. But whatever the cause, as the three of them sat around the hearth, eyes mesmerized by the glowing embers, they were warmed indeed and grateful for it, for the story was chilling.

"The first night," said the Seer. "When Agis died, we suspected nothing. He had seemed healthy but then again, he had seen 83 summers. Then the next night, Meelosh Hunyadi died in his bed at the End of the Second Watch. Again, 75 summers. But simply because we are isolated, does not mean we are insular. That morning, Na'rang was sent out with a message notifying the Empress of the deaths. And that night, that third night, the remaining 5 of us kept vigil right here in the Hall. And that third night, Kim Li Poh died, right here in the Hall, with all of us present. I can assure you, it was not a pleasant thing."

"Can you describe it?"

"In vivid detail, Captain. For the next two nights, we kept vigil, none of us eating nor sleeping but giving ourselves over to the meditations which we believed would hold the answers. So, when Lashlin deWinter then Diamont ibn al-Fayed, died within our very circle, one each successive night, we felt it. We lived their deaths, we died with them, man by man."

Patiently, Kirin waited as the man took time to collect his thoughts.

"Last night, Petrus and I agreed to hold *AhmniShakra*—"

"*Imperial* Tongue, if you please," snarled Ursa.

"Ah, yes. I forgot. The ears of the Pure Races are small and delicate. I must remember to use little words."

Kirin bit back a smile. There was something to be said for a man who could hold his own against the Major.

"What is *AhmniShakra?*"

"It is, it is something we..." The Seer held up his hands. "May I?"

The Captain nodded.

First one, then the other, Sireth benAramis removed his gloves, revealing even more of his mixed heritage by the small cheetah spots running up the backs of his hands. The hands slipped under his hair, at the base of his skull, fingers spread wide, thumbs pressing deeply into his temple. One brown eye locked with blue.

And suddenly, Kirin was seeing double.

More specifically, he was seeing himself, a flat, two-dimensional version of himself, yet still seeing the Seer. There was another heart pounding his blood, another chest filling with air, breathing for him, with him, another voice in his head, not his own. It was a most peculiar thing.

As suddenly as it had come, it went, leaving him blinking and rather short of breath.

His headache, however, was gone.

"*AhmniShakra*," said the Seer, pulling the gloves back over his hands. "That was only the first level. There are, of course, seven."

Kirin nodded again, with a sudden appreciation for the power and the danger, inherent in the Gifts of Farsight and Vision.

"Tell me what you saw."

"We had initiated Seventh Level at the Opening of the Second Watch. We saw you were coming, also that you would be too late. And this time, the assault - for I can think of no other term - fell upon Petrus near the Middle of the Watch, not at the end as with the others. It was as swift as it was complete and it almost overwhelmed us both. Indeed, I believed we would both succomb to it."

Sireth closed his eyes.

"There was ice. Ice, everywhere, above and below and within. We were frozen, solid, unable to move, unable to breathe. There was no air, there was not even the drawing of breath for our lungs were full of ice. Our hearts would not beat, could not, for they too were frozen like stone. It was as if we were within a mountain glacier and our eyes could focus on nothing but the whiteness of snow. There was a name on our lips, a name we could not speak, but our minds cried it over and over, even as the panic seized us in its iron grip. It was then that Petrus pushed me out, for his heart was older and he was dying, as surely, as savagely as Agis, or Kim Li or Lashlin..."

He shook his head.

"It was more than a vision, much more than a dream, for we could not break loose from it. *It* seized *us*, not the other way round and it would not let loose until one of us was dead. It was an assault, Captain, from a living soul, upon a living soul and it was as cold as the grave. But colder, so much colder."

"What was the name?"

"It is gone from my memory. But it is dying."

"What is?"

"I don't know. But it's falling from the sky and it is dying."

"What is falling from the sky?"

"I don't know."

"This name, did you recognize it?"

"I don't remember it."

Ursa snorted. "Useful visions."

For the first time, Kirin saw the Seer's tail lash but he said nothing. There was something, however, something in the way the man avoided his gaze. It quickened his blood.

"Is there anything else you can recall?"

The Seer lowered his eyes.

"Nothing."

"In all your meditations, all your vigils, you saw nothing else? Nothing? None of you?"

"Captain, believe me when I say that there is nothing more I can tell you."

They had him.

Kirin glanced at Ursa, her sharp, feral stare never having left the man since they'd been seated. She seemed to be deciding which part of him to cut and eat first.

The Captain gritted his molars.

"You are young, *sidi,* to be sitting on Council."

"And you are young, my friend, to be Captain of the Imperial Guard."

"Not yet forty-nine summers?"

"Forty-five."

"Ah. Year of the Snake."

"Yes."

"And a Council Member for less than two?"

"What of it?"

"Well, you must be powerful then." Kirin rose to his feet, allowed his gaze to wander the earthen bowls, now empty. "Indeed, the Empress maintains your visions are never wrong."

He watched the man carefully while appearing not to, watched him grow wary, guarded. Kirin began to move slowly about the chamber.

"And why this time, in the Middle of the Watch, not the End? You saw us coming, also that we would be too late. We arrived before the End of the Watch when the deaths had previously occurred. It should not have been 'too late.'"

Sireth glanced at the Major, as if looking to her for clarification, or of all things, reassurance.

"I don't understand—"

"These *assaults*, as you call them, are obviously carried out by a very powerful soul. Perhaps one that has learned to project such thoughts into older, more trusting ones. I'm sure it wouldn't take much to stop an aged heart such as Mercouri's, would it?"

"How dare you?" the Seer growled and for the second time, Kirin saw his tail lash. He rose to his feet, Ursa a sleek, white shadow.

"How *dare* you suggest—"

"I suggest everything. And nothing. It is simply my job."

"Your job? Your *job?* I am no fool, Captain, nor am I naive. I know full well how I am regarded in the Courts of *Pol'Lhasa.* But the Empress Herself approved my confirmation despite the debates and I admired her greatly for it. Pray tell me then Captain, how a woman as revolutionary as she can surround herself with people who simply 'do their jobs'?"

"Cut out his tongue," snapped the Major. "Then blind him completely."

The Captain was not a man who relished his power. Indeed, he bore it in all seriousness and at this precise moment, when he should have been furious, he felt strangely calm. With a deep breath, he straightened his back, slid his palm away from the hilt of his sword. It had gone there of its own.

"As the Captain of Her Excellency's Guard and Under Her Absolute Authority, I hereby abolish the Council of Seven. As a result, Sireth benAramis is removed from the Office of Council Member and is placed in my custody. Responsibility for the running of the monastery of *Sha'Hadin* falls directly upon my shoulders now and will be so until my order or that of Her Excellency Thothloryn Parillaud Markova Wu."

Sireth benAramis gaped at him, the look of a man with a dagger thrust through his heart.

"How can you do such a thing? We have done nothing but serve and serve, then *die* in that service!"

"Major, I order you to accompany this man to his chamber. See that he sleeps and sleeps well. You are not to let him out of your sight for an instant. If he resists, you have leave to kill him. Is that understood?"

"Sir."

The Captain turned to regard the Seer, who shook his head in disbelief.

"How can I sleep? With what you have done, abolishing the Council, bringing *Sha'Hadin* under control of the Army… It is better she kill me now, for I shall in no wise sleep."

"I am also no fool, *sidi,* nor am I naive. I wish to believe you an innocent man. If you are so, then you are in danger and thus in need of rest and strength for that which faces you tonight. If you are guilty, then you will die by my hand so you may as well enjoy your dreams, for they shall be your last."

Ursa slunk in at his side, her pale eyes gleaming in the dim light. She stood on tiptoe, for the Seer was a good head taller than she and she stretched up her small chin, so her lips were only a breath away.

"Better to be tending goats..."

Sireth pushed off, his long legs taking him out of the Hall of the Seers in seconds, his robes billowing, tail lashing. And behind him, the Major, heels clacking like the rattling of many spears.

For a long moment, there was silence in the Hall of the Seers.

Kirin Wynegarde-Grey shuddered and released the breath he had been holding. He had, within a heartbeat of a heartbeat, almost killed the last Seer of *Sha'Hadin.* The brazen words had deserved it. Even now, he wasn't entirely certain why he hadn't.

With the remains of the mouse hanging from her talons, the falcon was watching him.

***

Two figures arrived at the home of the Chancellor Angelino Devine d'Fusillia Ho. They were not greeted in the conventional fashion - that being a message carried by sentry from the outer wall through the gardens to the house proper. Rather, the Chancellor himself, clothed in a scandalously lush bearskin cloak, met them at the gate and he accompanied them inside the garden wall. They remained outside under the careless, sleepy gaze of the moon and the new star, bright as a child of the sun.

It was a winter garden, a study in contrasts, expressly designed to be viewed under a blanket of snow. Hedges and shrubs formed dark accents to geometric carved stones, the path soft and white. Lanterns burned from many lamp stands and candles were hidden under bushes and mounds of rock. The high stepped courts and black winged rooftops of *Pol'Lhasa* were visible from here and its distant windows flickered with light. This garden was a place of wonder and secret. The Chancellor did much of his business here.

"Well?" he said in a quiet voice. One of the figures, clad in sweeping black and silver robes, motioned to the other in brown at his side.

"This is Yahn Nevye. Yahn Nevye meet Chancellor Ho."

The two men exchanged bows, the man named Nevye's being deeper, with the formal fist to palm salute, for he was nowhere near the Chancellor in status. This did not stop the Chancellor, however, from a bow of his own. Etiquette was one of the many things that separated cats from animals.

"You are aware of the situation?" the Chancellor asked.

"I am, Magnificence."

"And?"

"It is a tragedy, Magnificence."

"This is not our doing," said the Chancellor. "We did not cause this. I will have you know that before we proceed. What has happened is not only tragic, it is sacrilege, a crime against the Kingdom that we cannot begin to comprehend. I myself know Petrus Mercouri. He is a dear friend, and cousin to my wife's mother. If he dies tonight, if he dies..."

The Chancellor broke off and the two other men allowed him his silence. A long moment before he took a deep breath.

"If he dies tonight, then something I cannot accept will follow. I *will* not accept. It would be worse than no Council at all. I am led to believe you share my sentiments."

Nevye glanced at his companion before nodding.

"What happened two years ago was also sacrilege, Magnificence. From Untouchable to Brahman. That is unnatural. I too know and respect Petrus, but his decision has compromised the Council. It should not have been allowed." He raised his hands. They were gloved in thick leather. "I was but one voice."

"So you left *Sha'Hadin?*"

"Yes, Magnificence."

"And since then, you have been at *Agara'tha?*"

"Yes, Magnificence. The First Mage's dream is upon us."

"The First Mage has as many dreams as he has wives," said Ho. His face was smiling. His voice was not. "To which of them are you referring?"

The man in black and silver spread wide his hands. "Indeed, I *have* many dreams, Magnificence. But the first and last, best dream is to see our Kingdom strong and without compromise. To see our people strong and without compromise. To see our Empress strong and without compromise. This situation may serve all three."

"I trust you have someone already in place?"

"Of course."

"Kunoichi?"

"The best. Perhaps, the very embodiment of this dream."

The Chancellor turned to Yahn Nevye. "Is this so?"

"It is."

"Very well. As I have said, we did not cause this, but we can use it. Two of our worst tribulations will collide in very short order, if they haven't yet. I believe we are being tested, being given an opportunity to take *Bushido* to the highest level. We must not fail."

"But Magnificence," Nevye looked nervously at the Chancellor. "None of us is *Shah'tyriah*. We are not warriors. *Bushido* is not ours to serve."

"We are all warriors for something, *sidi,"* said the First Mage. His eyes were as white as the moon. "It merely depends on what we serve."

"Indeed it does, Jet," the Chancellor nodded. "But enough of this. We shall do nothing until tomorrow. One of the 'tribulations' may have already been taken care of tonight."

Jet BarraDunne, the First Mage of *Agara'tha*, smiled.

"It would be poetry, wouldn't it, if they simply took care of each other."

They all smiled at that.

***

"She sleeps."

Sherah al Shiva put a bloody finger to her lips and turned her eyes in the direction of the Scholar's table. In the Chamber of the Dead, the Captain followed her gaze.

It was almost impossible to see her for the mountains of books and foothills of paper, but she was there. Head down in her arms, hair splayed in a multicoloured mat across the wood, slim back rising and falling like a slow, steady tide, Fallon Waterford was indeed sleeping.

The Captain smiled a weary smile.

"She is fortunate. I wish I could do the same."

"I can help you, *sidi.*"

He shook his head.

"No, but thank you, *sidala.* What have you discovered?"

Slowly, the Alchemist rose from her table, stretching her long body like a serpent, forcing him to watch every arch and curve lest she bite suddenly and kill him with her poisons. She moved to the row of bodies, six chest cavities exposed, six rows of livers and hearts and lungs, severed fingers and toes in drying rings across the table. He cast his eyes up to their faces, for the organs did not interest him, but the faces, they were another matter.

One leopard, one lion, two tigers, a serval, and – he moved closer...

One was Sacred.

"Petrus Ishak Raphael Mercouri. The Ancient of *Sha'Hadin.*"

He felt a knot in his chest. The Empress had called him friend.

He felt Sherah move in behind him.

"Some say he had seen one hundred summers, perhaps more. That he himself had counseled three Empresses. Pity."

"How did they die?"

"Terror."

His head snapped up. *The exact word the Seer had used.*

"Explain."

She picked up a heart. It looked small and pale in her long, strong hands.

"They were old men. Something terrified them, stopped their hearts. Stopped their breathing. A dream, perhaps. Or a vision. We will never know."

"That is not the answer I was looking for, *sidala.*"

"That is the only one I can give."

"No poisons?"

"No poisons. No puncture wounds or pinpricks. No deep and hidden bruises that swell up after hours to block the path of blood. No apparent causes of any sort."

He hesitated before touching the ring of fingers, blackened and blistered as if scorched. Or frozen.

"And these?"

She shrugged. "Anemia of age. Poor circulation. A mere curiosity, I should think."

"benAramis claims there is friction between the Alchemists and the Seers. Is this true?"

Sherah leaned upon the table, rolling back her head and stroking her long throat.

"There is a mild conflict of philosophy perhaps, between the Orders. But there are Alchemists who are blessed with Gifts of Vision, just as there are Seers who practice the Arts of Alchemy. They are not mutually exclusive disciplines."

She turned her golden eyes upon him. They were hypnotic.

"In fact, there are certain factions within *Agara'tha* that seek the unification of the Gifts and the Arts. An Alliance, if you will. For the good of the Kingdom, of course..."

"Of course." He cleared his throat. "This 'Terror' as you have called it. Can you think of any way to prevent it from claiming its last victim tonight?"

She seemed to think for several moments, plucked at her bottom lip.

"There are medicines we use, medicines to slow the heart, thicken the blood, dull the senses. Perhaps a combination of these..."

"Very well. Use what you have learned here. I want him alive in the morning."

He turned his back to her, taking several long strides as if to leave the chamber of the dead. It was thick with incense and incense invariably gave him a headache.

He paused a moment.

"Can the Gifts of Farsight be projected?"

"Sidi?"

"Is it possible for a living soul to project a vision into the soul of another?"

"Those are two distinctly different questions, *sidi.*" She shrugged her shoulders. "Anything is possible at the seventh level, *sidi.*"

"Even death?"

"Even so."

He let his eyes wander over the still sleeping form of the Scholar. He should wake her, for he was curious as to her conclusions and she was sure to have no 'conflict of philosophy.' But he would not. He envied her the peace.

"She dreams of your brother."

"What's that?"

"Your brother." She hummed softly. "The grey coat. He has caught her fancy."

"Hmm. Yes. Yes, he does that on occasion. Although what he does once he has caught it is another matter entirely."

He did not turn to see the smile. He could imagine it well enough.

***

"Sleep."

"Sleep. Sleep. How can I sleep? Tell me that, oh wise Empress, tell me that."

"You *shall* sleep, for if you do not, then I shall kill you."

"Then I should sleep well, indeed, for fear of your claws upon my chance awakening."

"*Pah.*" Ursa rolled her eyes. "You talk like a scholar."

"And you talk like a soldier."

"Soldiers obey orders. My orders are to make you sleep or kill you. So, sleep or die."

With a growl, Sireth resumed the pacing that had him moving round and round the small chamber like a cobra wanting out of its basket. Ursa straddled the room's only chair, following him with her eyes and growing more frustrated with her inability to carry out the Captain's orders. She glanced around the spartan chamber. There was nothing here, only the chair, a low mattress stuffed with straw, a tray of paints and a bedside candle to break the monotony of stone.

But the sun was reaching her first golden fingers in through the long, narrow window and somehow, everything seemed right in this small, spartan room. Everything belonged.

It disturbed her.

He spun to face her, hands clasping together dramatically.

"Tell me this then, my dear woman. Is the Captain so eager to shed my blood because it is mixed? Is it because I have no claim to a single Race that you find yourselves so desperate to kill me? If that is the case, then why did you come to save a man who deserves nothing but death? Why make the journey?"

She rolled her eyes yet again.

"I don't have to tell you anything. I am not your judge. The Captain is. All you must do is prove your innocence."

"Ah yes," he nodded. "Yes, of course. By dying tonight. Effective proof, I should think. If I die, I am innocent. If I live, then you kill me. Either way, there's one less mongrel to pollute the bloodlines of the Kingdom."

Her smile was as icy as her eyes.

"You see, you understand all too well. Now," She reached out to pat the corner of the mattress. "Sleep."

To her surprise, he obeyed, lowering himself down to the lumpy surface with familiar grace. He sat a moment, looking at the floor between his split-toed sandals and nodding again with slow deliberation.

"Yes. Yes, I suppose you're right. I'm tired of this, Major. I'm tired of death. I'm tired of life. I'm very, very tired."

He stretched out his long legs, laced his hands across his middle and closed his eyes. It was merely a matter of seconds before he was deep in sleep.

And the Major did not take her eyes off him for an instant.

***

When the gong sounded for Sun Salute and morning prayers, attendants and acolytes obeyed without hesitation. An hour afterward, it sounded again, this time to break the long fast of night. The kitchens served up food for 500, porridge and sweet rolls, steamed fish and rice. Tea of course, hot and sweet, to feed the blood and purify the humors. It was as if the day were starting as usual and the cold drifts of morning quickly fled at the approach of the sun.

High in a hay loft a grey lion slept, dreamless for once, his stomach only beginning to rumble about in the absence of food.

High in the monastery a mongrel slept, stirring only momentarily at the sounding of the gong. The snow leopard, however, slept not at all and did not touch the tea that was brought to her.

Deep within the monastery, a young tigress slept while a cheetah worked, mixing medicines of questionable nature and humming to herself in strange, exotic keys.

And finally in a quiet room, once the chamber of Petrus Ishak Raphael Mercouri, the Ancient of *Sha'Hadin*, the Captain of the Queen's Gurard slept fitfully, restlessly as visions of his own intruded into his dreams.

BEYOND THE WALLS

Fallon Waterford stretched her slender arms over her head, yawning so broadly that her tongue actually curled inside her mouth. Then she shook her head so that her hair fluffed up from the flatness of sleep and curved about her shoulders like a river flowing round a rock. Finally, with an exaggerated flare of nostril, she breathed in the cool morning air, blinking as its sharpness bit the back of her throat like her father's sweet iced cream.

"Ah, the mountains," she announced to no one in particular. "The Great Mountains. There's nothing like mountain life, I always say."

She glanced around the rocky path, flung her arms up in desperation.

"Oh who am I kidding? I've never even been to the mountains until eight months ago. I'm a jungle girl, born and raised. These mountains are so dreadfully cold. I hate all this snow. There're no plants, there're no trees, no vines or bugs or anything like home. I suppose it could be worse. After all, they've amended my birthright, haven't they? I have status in the Court of the Empress! Won't my father and mother and sisters be pleased?'"

She smiled to herself and pushed off the rock, resuming the stroll she had been enjoying since breakfast. The fish and rice had been tasty, but she found the porridge and sweet rolls very filling and it was all sitting in her stomach like a stone. On top of it all, the odors in the Chamber of the Dead had been dreadful so she had abandoned the Alchemist to her bubbling pots and noxious potions and set out to clear her head and think.

Trails led to and from the monastery like goat paths and she had not been surprised to see the occasional patchy pelt scrambling up the rocky slopes. Her father used to keep a few goats and she remembered they always smelled of musk. When she had moved to the University, she had made it a point to wash her clothes many times over to rid herself of the stench. These goats, however, didn't seem to stink. Curious.

She had seen several robed people also out for their morning strolls. Odd sorts, these monks. She had noticed when they were doing their jobs or when they hadn't seen her, their hoods were down, faces exposed like normal folk. But at the sight of her, their hoods went up, drawn like curtains cross a window. *Curious,* she thought again. She would have to ask Tiberius about it later.

Silhouetted in front of a bank of high dark clouds, a small bird sat preening itself on a bluff. She had never seen it's kind before so she climbed up toward it, squeezing her backside through a cleft in the rocks and froze.

On the other side of the bluff, in the centre of a level plateau, Kerris Wynegarde-Grey was working a great shiny horse at the end of a long rope. It was the Captain's horse, she remembered, now barebacked and sporting only its leather bridle, reins laced high up on the neck. She could hear his voice, singing to it, urging it onward. It cantered around him in a large circle, collected and calm, its large hoofs springing from the ground like a hare.

She sank into the rock, sighing.

Easy on the eyes, Sherah had said and she found herself agreeing wholeheartedly. His hair, although not as traditional or impressive as his brother's, seemed to suit him, falling into his eyes and curling at the back of his neck but in need of a good brushing. He was athletic, this she could tell, for he moved within that circle with supple strength, keeping the horse cantering by the movements of his body alone. He held the rope in one hand, the excess looped in the other and she realized that those hands were not as soft as she might have expected from a lion born to a Noble House.

"Alchemists," she muttered to no one in particular, "Why can't you leave well enough alone. I was fine. Really, I was. Now, you had to go and ruin it all. Here I am, me, Fallon Waterford, Scholar in the Court of the Empress, ogling over a stable boy who happens to be a grey lion from a Noble House. Look at me. Look at *him*. Oh mother..."

As he turned within his circle, he spotted her and waved and in her flurry to disappear, she tumbled off the rock onto the hard earth below.

"Hello, *sidalady* tigress!" He dropped the line and rushed toward her. "Say, are you alright?"

"Fine! Fine!" she shouted. "I'm not needing a-rescuing, thank you very much!"

"You need water for diving, *sidala,*" he grinned as he pulled her to her feet. "I thought tigers had more sense than that."

"Well, we do, and I wasn't, so... so paws off!"

She snorted, pouted and dusted herself off, slapping his hand away when he tried to dust too.

"Yes, yes, paws off, I understand." He was still grinning. "How's your backside?"

Emerald eyes flashed.

"I didn't fall on my backside, in case you hadn't noticed. And, and, and if you had, then then then why are you noticing my backside, hmm? What *are* you thinking?"

For the briefest of moments, his mouth hung open, bewildered. But he recovered smoothly, the grin moving up to his eyes in a heartbeat.

"I meant from yesterday, *sidala.* That was a long ride for someone unaccustomed to the back of a horse."

"Oh. Oh, well. Oh well, that's different." She nodded, swallowed, looked away quickly. "That's a nice horse."

"Yes he is. Imperial bred. Just like my brother."

"Are you two really twins?"

"We are. I'm just immature, that's all."

Again, that smile. It seemed to capture the sunlight and wrap it up in one brilliant package, just for her.

"Come on, I'll introduce you."

She took a step to follow, but for some reason, one knee had turned to butter and buckled beneath her. He caught her as she stumbled

"You sure you're alright?"

"Oh. Yeah. My, um, foot just... fell asleep. Happens all the time. Feet. Can't live with 'em. Can't cut 'em off."

alMassay nickered as they approached, and Fallon was surprised at how large the horse was. In fact, when the great head reached out toward her, blowing softly through wide nostrils, she found her feet strangely planted.

"He's not going to eat me or anything, right?"

"My, my no. He's just checking you out. Here, scratch him right here. He likes that."

His grey hand took hers and laid it high on the withers, to the arch where proud neck met strong back. She scratched and the stallion sighed, a deep rumbling sound that rolled around his massive chest.

"See, he likes you. Want to try him? He's a good ride."

"Me? Oh, no. No, I can't. I'm a yak girl, really. Need that old spinal ridge to keep me on. Besides, there's no saddle..."

"Saddle? Who needs a saddle? Grab his neck. I'll give you a leg up."

Before she knew it, she was on and Kerris was backing away, holding the rope and grinning. The horse started to move and he resumed his position in the centre of the circle.

"But there-there's no mane!" she yelped. "It's all shaved off! And the reins are tied way, way up his neck! How do I hang on?"

"You don't stay on by hanging on, *sidala.* You stay on by balance."

"Balance?"

"Yes, balance."

"Balance…"

Biting her lip, Fallon sat back and began to think.

"Good, good. Lengthen your legs and... yes, just like that and let your weight fall into your feet... and... that's right and..."

The instructions trailed off, for the tigress had indeed lengthened her legs, letting her weight fall into her feet, rolling on to her seat bones, squaring her shoulders and dropping her hands to her sides.

"Yes, um, yes that's good. That's *quite* good, actually..."

"It makes sense, now that I stop to think about it," she said, finding herself now completely at ease on the back of the great horse. "The problem is that there are so many things I never stop to think about.

"My life story, sadly."

alMassay had picked up a trot now, and the Scholar's perfect position had not wavered as they circled around the figure in the centre.

"So, then, if you don't need a saddle to stay on, do you really need reins to steer—"

Suddenly and without warning, the horse stopped, planting its fore hoofs into the sand, its body almost buckling as its rear end caught up. But an unprepared Fallon tumbled over the crested neck, pitching forward to the ground with a thump.

"Don't move!" shouted Kerris.

She pushed her face and shoulders from the earth and realized it had been rather good advice.

"...oh mother..."

For a mere hand's breadth away, a giant cobra reared its hooded head.

***

The chamber of Petrus Itshak Raphael Mercouri was small. *Too* small, the Captain thought, considering the man's station. But then again, life in *Sha'Hadin* seemed to defy the usual conventions and he found the simplicity of things appealing. He could understand why people lived this way.

It was almost noon. The sun was high over the ravine, sending light in straight, strong shafts through the clouds and into the room. The window was oblong and open with no glass. He had thought it a curiosity, for this place must surely grow very cold in winter. Even now, this late spring morning was cool enough but the blankets were thick and warm. Again, the simplicity of necessity. The monks wore robes, not for aesthetics, not for dramatics but for the simple fact that the long, swirling layers caught the warmth the way no doeskin nor tunic nor leg wrap could. Everything seemed to have a place, everything belonged, here at *Sha'Hadin.*

Everything except them.

It disturbed him.

He sat cross-legged by the window, a mug of hot tea at his side and an open book in his lap. It was a journal, the last entry dated only yesterday. Under normal circumstances, he would never violate the privacy of a man's journal for he himself was a private man, keeping record of all his own deepest, innermost thoughts in the same fashion. But these were no ordinary circumstances and he had found the diary quite illuminating. There were trunk loads of journals from a hundred summers of living and the Captain found himself envious of time. He would have loved to sit for days, going through this particular lifetime of stories.

He dropped his eyes back to the journal, the final thoughts of a dead man.

Diamont died last night within our circle. It was the same as the others only he had no voice - the spell fell upon him too quickly. His falcon was dispatched earlier this evening, so no doubt it too is dead, buried in some deep mountain pass on the way to Pol'Lhasa. *We pray that our messages have reached the eyes of the Empress, else we too shall join Diamont within two nights and none shall be the wiser. Now, that would be loss.*

Sireth is afraid. He says nothing but I can tell this matter weighs heavily upon him. I can understand for he is young and I am not. I have lived long and well and look forward to seeing what lies beyond where we cannot see. Naturally, he does not share my sentiments. If only he would acknowledge the truth of his vision, this vision that has plagued only him for so many nights, he might derive some comfort in it for then to die might be gain for the entire Upper Kingdom.

Then again, it might be devastation.

We have agreed to hold AhmniShakra *tonight at the commencement of the Second Watch. Perhaps then, one of us can see more clearly what it is that strikes us down with the ease of a bitter wind. If not, then I pray that this ends with us, with the death of the Council only, and this spectre does not find 500 monks a tempting prey.*

Sireth is coming. I am ended.

Or am I begun?

Kirin stared at the last page for a very long time. It was an old book, every one of its soft parchment pages filled. In the bottom corner, Mercouri's small, scrawled signature finished it off. It was as if the Ancient had known this would be his final journal and this, his final entry. Perhaps he had seen it sometime and planned accordingly.

Kirin closed the book and gazed out the long window.

There were storm clouds gathering.

***

Over those strange, unfamiliar peaks, Ursa Laenskaya could see the clouds. Great masses of darkness obliterating the usual brilliant brightness of midday. The sun pierced those masses in several places, sending her light to the earth like a hail of arrows or spears raining down on an unsuspecting enemy. There was war in all things, she thought. The rain fought with the sun, the winter fought with the summer, the snow with the grass. Life was war, for even birth was bought through death. It was the way of things. She had always understood that simple fact.

The Major wrapped her arms around her chest and turned back to study the walls. Paintings were lavished layer upon layer on the granite surface. By the window, a portrait glistened with brighter color and she suspected it was the Seer's work, for it could not have been more than several months old. It was curious, however, for the same portrait was repeated over and over again, growing faded and muted as she suspected with age.

The subject was a woman, a panther with braided black hair and ebony pelt and eyes the color of the Queen's gold. The older, more muted portraits were lovely, very realistic and full of minute detail. But the newer ones, obvious by the freshness of the paint, were broader, more stylized, as if that minute detail were fading from memory.

This was also the way of things. She was grateful for it.

She heard something and turned, arms still tightly clasped around herself. Sireth benAramis was sitting up on the mattress, heavy-lidded and sleepy but smiling at her in that same patient, long-suffering way of his. She turned back to the wall.

"You are not very good."

"An honest critic. I never could do her justice."

"Who is she?"

"My wife."

"I thought there were no women at *Sha'Hadin?*"

"There aren't. She died a long time ago. Before I came here."

"How?"

"That is none of your concern, Major."

"Your wife. Your friends." Her heels snapped as she turned towards him, her long silver tail slapping from side to side. "Death at every turn. Is this a common occurrence for you?"

"Persecution of mongrels," he began archly. "I should think you would welcome such tidings. It is a soldier's job after all, to enforce the breeding practices of a free people."

"Idiot. We don't enforce anything of the kind. We don't need to."

"Ah yes. You simply throw us in prison."

"This doesn't look like a prison to me."

"Isn't it? But perhaps, we should ask your Captain. I'm quite certain he would know."

His level, one-eyed gazed bored into her.

"In fact, why don't we ask him right now?"

And the door swung open to the small chamber, slamming against the opposite wall with a thud. Kirin Wynegarde-Grey stood under the arch.

"Ah, Captain. We were just discussing you. Weren't we, Major?"

Ursa snarled at him.

The Captain strode into the room, drawing up in front of them.

"Major, please leave us."

"But –"

"Now, Major. Close the door behind you."

She steeled her jaw but could not protest. With a swift nod of her head, she left the room. Kirin waited for the sound of those heels to carry on down the corridor but they did not, telling him she was no more than a heartbeat away.

Kirin held up the journal. Sireth rose to his feet.

"That belongs to Petrus," he growled. "It was his private journal. Have you no honor?"

"It would seem that you, sir, are the one in need of a lesson in honor."

"Save it, Captain. I have no need of your sermons."

"You lied to me. You have had a vision."

"Is that 'your job' now, Captain? Telling me what I have and have not seen?"

"Petrus has recorded it." Kirin threw the book onto the mattress. "Or is he too a liar like yourself?"

The Seer's eyes flashed, and Kirin observed with a detached air how the blind one mimicked the good.

"Yes I lied to you! You could not handle the truth! You could not handle what I saw! I... *I* cannot handle what I saw. I'm not certain I believe it myself."

"Theatrics. Tell me."

"I cannot. I will not."

"Then you will die."

"Bah. Such is the way of lions."

Kirin bit his tongue, his fingers curling into fists of their own accord. This was all wrong. Like their presence in *Sha'Hadin*, they did not belong. It was not right. He was not a man to force and bully those under his protection. It was *not* his way, the Way of the Warrior. Somewhere, along this hasty journey, he had forgotten this simple fact and he cursed himself for so easy a loss.

He walked past the Seer, to the window. Gripped its stony edges and leaned out, feeling the darkening winds on his face, feeling them pluck at his hair, his lashes, his lips. He breathed them in, willing them to fill his chest with coldness, imagining ice in their place and the Terror that would surely follow.

The way, *his* way, could only be found in his heart, his soul, his very centre of being. *Bushido.*

"The Empress." Grey clouds, rolling around white peaks, dark and heavy with spring snow. "Would you tell the Empress?"

There was a pause.

"Yes," said the voice behind him. "I would. I would tell the Empress."

"Good." Kirin nodded but did not move, his claws digging into stone. "Can we make *Pol'Lhasa* by nightfall?"

"No. Even by the high path, it takes ten hours. It is already noon."

"The falcon, then."

"This cannot be delivered by falcon, Captain. I have seen this same vision every night for the past six nights and even yet I do not believe it. A simple message on parchment? It would be madness."

Again, the Captain nodded but this time, said nothing.

He could feel the mongrel watching him with wary eyes. Understandable, he reasoned. This man had almost overturned the Imperial Council with his confirmation for the simple fact of his mongrel birth. He was Untouchable and now Brahmin, whereas Kirin was *Shah'tyriah*, noble and warrior both. Dharma was a cruel mistress, but Bushido was more.

The mongrel released a long, cleansing breath.

"Petrus Mercouri," he began softly, "Was a wise and gentle man. He taught me much since I came to *Sha'Hadin*. More than a man wants to know about the blackness, the tangles, in his own soul. For it is through that soul we receive the Gifts of Farsight and Vision, and the darker the glass, the darker, more obscure the vision. It is the way of things."

Kirin said nothing. Bushido was a quiet master.

"We do not choose what we shall see, Captain, nor how we shall see it. We see only what we are given to see and as it passes through our souls, it is filtered by what it finds there. Our thoughts, our hopes, our fears and our prejudice. Most importantly our prejudice for although the vision is pure and true, our perceptions are not. You said I was powerful, Captain, and you were right. But it is not from strength of character or pureness of heart but rather from lack of prejudice, for I am a bastard by birth and a gypsy by choice. It is simply who I am."

The clouds were almost upon them now, completely blocking the sunlight that warmed the ravine. Kirin could feel the cold settle upon them. He closed his eyes.

"When I touched your soul last night, even in the First Level, I sensed a true soul. A good soul. Honesty, integrity, loyalty. A rare and blessed combination. Metal in its purest form. But it is not enough, Captain. It is not Enough. You are a lion, born and bred and proud of it. You *should* be proud of it. *I* would be if my blood ran pure. But it influences everything, how you think, how you are treated and how you treat others. It darkens the glass."

Kirin set his jaw, allowing the words to fold over him, shine light into dark, tightly-held places.

"But if you believe that you can handle this vision, Captain," the man continued. "This scrap of knowledge, this *thing* that will change everything... If you truly believe, with your heart and your soul and your will that you are Enough, then I will tell you."

The room was quiet for several long moments. The Captain finally turned around, hands clasped behind his back.

"In the morning, we shall leave for *Pol'Lhasa,"* he said. "There and in her presence alone, you will speak of your vision to the Empress. She is Enough."

The man nodded.

"You are wise for one so young. However, there is still one small problem..."

"You shall not die tonight."

"Words, Captain."

"You shall not die."

He held the Seer's gaze in the heart of Bushido. Steady, confident, and almost, for the briefest of moments, Sacred.

"Very well," Sireth sighed. "I believe you."

"If it is true that these deaths are caused by a living soul—"

"It is true."

"*If* it is true and if these attacks are intended to bring about the collapse of the Council of Seven then they have failed, for I myself have abolished it. The Council is no more and killing you should serve no purpose. If there is another motive behind all this, we shall discover it soon enough. And if it is you, *sidi,* if it is you..."

There was no need to finish the thought.

"Major!"

The door slammed open and a silver-white blur streaked into the room. Her sword was drawn, her hair loosed about her shoulders. She looked like a bolt of lightening.

"At ease, Major. I shall be having a meal sent up from the kitchens. See to it that both you and the Seer eat well for he will be meditating all afternoon and will need his strength."

"Sir."

"And while he meditates, you will sleep. There, if that is permissible?"

He swept an arm in the direction of the mattress. Sireth nodded. The Major did not.

"Captain, I don't need rest. You know I can work for days—"

"That's an order, Major. I will redouble the Leopard Guard at the door. I need you strong for tonight. Is that understood?"

"Understood," she growled. *"Sir."*

And with that, the Captain strode from the room, leaving Ursa flexing the tip of her sword in agitation.

Sireth smiled at her, that patient, long-suffering, infuriating smile. He leaned down and patted the corner of the mattress.

"Sleep."

***

"Don't move, *sidala...*"

"Oh-kay."

It wasn't that Fallon Waterford was feeling particularly agreeable as she lay, belly down on the ground, trying not to spit out the bits of gravel that had collected in her mouth from the fall. Rather, with the great, long body of the cobra swaying over her head, it seemed like a good idea to be motionless, given a serpent's generally suspicious disposition. She averted her gaze, trying to remember her studies in animal behavior and whether or not snakes had dominant or submissive reactions to eye contact. Or, actually, any reaction at all.

Softly, she cleared her throat.

"Kerris? Was that your name? Kerris?"

"Still is, *sidala.*"

"Um, Kerris, this might sound like a very strange thing to say right about now, but um... there are no cobras in the Great Mountains."

"You're absolutely right," he said, moving slowly around her. "It is a very strange thing to say. But I'll tell you something that's even stranger."

"Oh?"

"It wasn't there a moment ago." And he slipped his fingers between his teeth.

She winced as a sharp whistle whipped the air like a blast from a firecracker. The cobra's hood flared and it swung in his direction, brushing her arm with its warm scales.

"I don't think it likes noise," she whispered.

"Be quiet then."

Her world became at once small and profound. She could feel the stallion's hoofs trembling against the stony earth. She could feel the wind pick up, smell the oncoming storm, see the shadows caused by black clouds crossing the sun. Most of all, she could hear her own pulse like rushing waters in her temples.

Suddenly, the ground was trembling with a different pulse, a quick, frantic, growing one and she squeezed her eyes tightly when she realized what was about to happen. Within seconds, there was an ear-splitting squeal and small sharp hoofs were churning up the ground directly in front of her, sending up bits of shale and snakeskin into her face. Strong hands grabbed her, dragging her backwards and out of the way.

After what seemed like a lifetime, Quiz the mountain pony stood on wire-tight legs, wild-eyed and snorting, as remnants of the snake's body twitched on the hard ground. Of the head, hood and lethal fangs, however, nothing recognizable remained.

"He hates snakes," said Kerris. "Are you alright? I mean, First *is* Luck, after all."

Fallon puffed her hair out of her eyes as she sat, gasping, in his arms.

"Yep. Figures education is Fifth. That's *my* luck. Along with Nice Family and Great Personality."

"Well, you do have pretty markings."

"Oh, thanks. *Oh—*"

Before their eyes, the snake's body was drying, shriveling, and crackling, finally blowing away in the gathering wind. Then it was gone, leaving Quiz pawing the earth for its return.

"Um, Kerris your name was, did you just see that?"

"No, I don't think I did. Did you?"

"No. No, I don't think so either. Really. No."

"Well then, maybe we should, um..."

"Leave?"

"Yes. Leave."

"Okay."

That said, they sat for quite a while longer, staring at the flattened spot where nothing at all had happened.

***

"Where is the Scholar?"

Sherah al Shiva did not look up, rather continued to fold the silks and skins laid out on her table.

"She was bored and has taken a walk."

"Bored?" Kirin frowned as he watched her snuff out the many candles and pack them away in her bags. "She finds the deaths of the Queen's Seers boring?"

"Intrigue is found on many roads, Captain. Not everyone finds death so evocative."

"You speak in riddles, *sidala.* It is not helpful."

Now, she did look up, rolling her hips along the table's edge to face him and smiling her slow smile. It was as if she were pulling his insides out claw by claw.

"Forgive me, Captain. How may I help you?"

He glanced at her table. Her bags were packed, the cadavers wrapped in swaths of white linen. Their organs were separated, placed carefully in tall earthen jars, the little red pouch hovering over them like a vulture. *Necromancy.* He did not like it one bit.

"Your preparations for tonight?"

"Complete, *sidi.* However..." She indicated a clay cup off to one side, its contents bubbling over one of her many candles. "It will need to simmer for several hours to boil the ingredients down to the ideal concentrations. Too little will have no effect, leaving the Seer to the mercies of his vision. Too much, well, too much would not be good."

She picked up a small mortar and pestle, wiping out the contents with a long speckled finger and putting it to her tongue.

"Then, it must be cooled. Again, several hours."

"It must be ready by the commencement of the Second Watch. Is that understood?"

Without waiting for a response, he turned to leave, pausing only slightly when she purred "Of course."

He shook his head and left the room.

She, however, waited until he was well and truly gone before uncurling her hand, to reveal a slip of dried cobra skin, withered and crushed into whisper-thin ash. She drew her lips together and blew it from her fingers and into the cup.

***

They sat side by side at one of the great long tables in one of the great long dining halls of *Sha'Hadin.* It had begun to snow just as they had ridden into the ravine and they were soaked through to the bones. The lynx Tiberius had kindly offered them robes while their clothing dried by one of the many hearths in this lowest level of the monastery and the mugs of hot, sweet tea he had provided had them almost feeling feline again.

"500 people, can you imagine?" Fallon Waterford looked around with wide eyes. "I mean, I can barely manage to feed myself, let alone prepare meals for 500 people. And not just one meal, but lots of meals. 500 breakfasts. 500 lunches. 500 dinners..."

"What about a snack?"

"Well, yes, that too. I mean, you can't have 500 monks sneaking around the larders and pantries for some midnight peck, now can you? How in the world do they do it?"

"I meant for me. I'm starving." Kerris waved a grey hand in the air. "Hello? Hello, anyone paying attention? Two very important people from the Palace need food right about now!"

Several brown-robed monks, hoods drawn, scurried about

carrying pitchers and jugs and plates of goat cheese but no one attended his request. One, however, had the misfortune of having to go past their table so Kerris lunged for him, snagging a stick of crusty bread with a long grey claw. He grinned, broke it in half and tossed piece one to her.

"Good manners," said Fallon as she shoved a piece in her mouth. "Very monk-like."

"It's amazing what you learn in the Palace Courts."

"What else did you learn?"

"Ssssssnake charming."

He slid his hand along the table. She stabbed at it with a fork.

And they began to laugh like naughty schoolchildren, giddy and weary from their afternoon encounters until a figure loomed over them from across the table.

"Will his Lordship be needing a bath?"

Kerris rolled his eyes at his brother. "Yes, actually. Fill up one of the wine vats, nice and hot. My friend and I will be taking a little dip."

Fallon almost spat out her bread. It was obvious the Captain was not in the mood, for his hands were on his hips and his brow was low and dark.

"You took out my horse," he growled.

"I took out all the horses, Kirin. You can't ride all day like that then leave them to stand in a stall for who knows how long. They'll seize up. You know that."

"What I know is that I needed to speak with the Scholar and she was unavailable." He narrowed his blue eyes at her. "The Alchemist said *sidala* was bored."

"Bored? Bored?! I - I wasn't bored, I - I was... I was..." *Finished,* she wanted to cry, *I was finished!* She sank into the table. "Oh mother..."

"Relax, Kirin. She was probably choking from all the incense in 'the 'Chamber of the Dead'." He waggled his fingers. "You know how you get those headaches."

"Right now, Kerris, *you* are giving me a headache." He lowered himself onto the bench, hands folded across the table. "*Sidala,* I do require your services. *If* my brother can bear to be silent for more than a heartbeat."

Kerris stuffed the bread stick into his mouth.

"The Alchemist stated that the cause of death is Terror. Do you agree with that?"

"Um, well, sort of."

He glared at her.

"Sorry." She straightened up on the bench, pushing her hair off her face. "Okay. Okay.'Terror', as she put it, was definitely a factor in the deaths. A very major factor actually but the actual physical cause of death, *deaths,* however, would have to be heart seizure. All of their hearts were the same, all constricted within their chests. There was some secondary scarring, and the lungs were—"

"Did you open the bodies? Or the Alchemist?"

"It was Sherah. I think she enjoys that kind of thing."

"Lovely," muttered Kerris through a mouthful of bread.

"Did you watch her?"

Fallon blinked.

"Um, no sir. I didn't really think it was necessary. I was in the same room, however, if that makes any difference?"

The Captain said nothing, simply stared at his hands, jaws clenching and unclenching in concentration. Finally, he looked up.

"Any evidence of poisons?"

"No sir. No poisons, at least none that I can trace. No poisons, no crea—" She stopped herself. "No poisons. Sir."

"Very well. What else can you tell me, *sidala?"*

"Well..."

"Sidala..."

"Sorry, but I just can't figure out this 'cold' thing," she yelped. "I mean I know the mountains aren't like the jungle but really, sir, these people really should invest in some window glass. They were all suffering from extreme frostbite."

"Explain."

"All their fingers and toes were severely blistered from either extreme heat, or more likely, extreme cold. I mean, I know they all wear gloves here, but really..."

"This could not be caused by old age?"

"Not a chance. Sir. It was exposure, right and sure."

"Right and sure?" asked Kerris. "Is that like front and centre? Or well and good? Or safe and sorry?"

"More bread for my brother!" Kirin snapped his fingers and it was on the table within seconds. "The Seer claims that the vision that falls upon them is like that of being trapped within a mountain glacier."

"Ooh, that fits!" she exclaimed. "That fits exactly, sir. That would explain the hearts and the lungs and the fingers and toes..."

She fell into thought for a moment, her mouth open as if awaiting a spoon.

"But then that doesn't begin to explain how in the world this, this mountain glacier could kill all six of them, for six nights running. And all in the Second Watch? I mean, mountains do not have sundials, sir."

"I see your point. However, that question can wait until later. What we must concern ourselves with, first and foremost—"

"Oh, there's another one!" yelped Kerris, before quickly stuffing a crust of bread into his mouth.

"Is the survival of this last Seer. The Alchemist has combined several medicines which she assures me will greatly increase his chances."

Fallon frowned. "I would be interested in knowing what she's using."

Kerris rolled his eyes but to his credit, his mouth was closed. Kirin glowered at them.

"Sherah al Shiva has been chosen by the First Mage of *Agara'tha*, specifically for her skills in herbs, poisons and their like. The Empress has placed her trust in the First Mage and therefore, in his choice. Do either of you question the Empress' wisdom?"

The only response was silence.

"Good. Now, these 'medicines' should effectively slow the heart, thicken the blood and," he paused as he recalled the Alchemist's exact words. "Dull the senses. This should render him less susceptible to the 'Terror', as they both have called it. So, *sidala* tigress, what I need from you is some method to curb the cold or the perception of cold, before it can trigger a killing panic. Can you do this?"

She sat, chewing the inside of her cheek for several moments before beginning to talk in a very rapid voice.

"Well the main problem with that is this thing starts off internally." She tapped her head. "Then ends up manifesting itself externally." She waggled her fingers. "And with whatever 'medicines' Sherah is using, I would hesitate to suggest some other such drug like something to cause a fever, which would reduce the likelihood of a cold reaction but could quite easily send his body into convulsions. Not really a desirable response, oh no no. But if we take the opposite tack and warm the body up externally, the question now is will this be enough? Will blankets and a good warm hearth be enough to reach whatever is going on inside?"

She tapped her head again, took perhaps her second breath in all of that then plunged back into deep, cheek chewing thought.

So the three of them sat, very quietly now, all staring at the table, and wondering if anything they might do, would be Enough.

"Sidis, sidala." It was Tiberius, brown-robed and smiling, the tufts of his ears peaking out from under his thick silver hair. "We of *Sha'Hadin* cannot begin to express our most profound gratitude for all your efforts on our part. But if you would permit, our cooks have prepared a special goat stew for tonight's meal. I have had three bowls readied as you decide the future of our monastery."

He stepped aside to allow three monks passage and three wooden bowls were set before them, brimming with steaming, savory stew. It set their mouths watering instantly.

"Whatever our fate, we wish you peace and fulfillment. Please enjoy."

And with a most serene bow, Tiberius left them to their food.

Kerris dug in instantly, stopping only to toss two bits of bread to his fellow diners.

"See here, *sidala,* goat stew for 500! That's a lot of goats, don't you think?"

She wiped broth from her chin and smiled at the Captain.

"Your brother and I were debating the problems of feeding 500 hungry monks three times a day, and then some. I mean really, not to even mention the amount of meats and vegetables and fruits and milks, I mean milk. Just imagine the kitchens! Imagine all the pots and woks and kettles and fires! It would be worse than the jungle at midday! It would be so incredibly hot—"

As one, she and Kirin glanced up at each other.

"The kitchens!"

As one, they bolted from their benches, wooden spoons clattering to the table in a splatter of gravy.

Kerris watched them go.

"Either of you going to finish this? No? Well, alright then. Can't let two perfectly good bowls of stew go to waste. All those poor little goats..."

And with the tip of a grey claw, he snagged each bowl and dragged them across the table.

***

Sireth benAramis squeezed his eyes even tighter. But nothing seemed to help, to be able to distract his mind from the angry growling and tossing going on in his bed. The afternoon had been wasted, for it had been impossible to meditate even sitting by the open window with the snow blowing onto his face, cooling the fears that raged inside him. Someone else, it seemed, was raging much better.

"Major. Sleep."

"I can't sleep."

"You are a soldier. Soldiers obey orders. Your orders are to sleep. Now, please, *sleep*!"

"It is cold and this bed scratches."

Just like you, he thought grimly but immediately cursed himself for his lack of patience. He was accustomed to solitude, to long private hours in soul-searching contemplation, broken only by others who valued those pursuits as much as he. But now, to be thrust into the company of this thornbush of a woman for the last twelve hours, he found himself in need of all the resources at his disposal to keep himself from scratching back.

"Would it help if I gave you a robe?"

"No. It probably itches. That would be worse."

"What would be worse, Major, would be to fail to obey your

Captain's orders because of your stubborn pride. I will not bite you. I will not even look at you. I simply wish to meditate. In silence. Can you understand that, Major?"

She sat up, scowling. Her hair fell across her face and her pale narrow eyes peered out as through tall grass. She looked very, very dangerous.

"I understand more than you think, *Seer.*"

She spat the word like a challenge.

He sighed, refusing to take it up, and turned back to the open window, letting his hands fall loosely into his lap. He breathed in the snow.

"Mongrel."

The snow on his face, the cold mountain air...

"Coward."

The snow... the air... the snow...

"Answer me!"

He sighed again.

"You do not seek answers, Major. You seek bloodshed. But shedding my blood will neither quench your thirst, nor wash away that which eats inside of you like a python. Not all the blood in the Kingdom can help you with that."

With a frustrated snarl and a heavy thump, she tossed herself back onto the mattress.

The snow was falling heavily this late in the afternoon, blocking the sun and turning the sky a dull grey. He closed his eyes and was elsewhere.

"What is your favorite place?"

"I have none."

"There is a place," he began softly. "Deep in the South and far to the East, where the jungle grows like none you have ever seen..."

"I hate jungles. There are too many bugs." Her words, however, were slower. "I hate bugs."

"This jungle has no bugs. In fact, the trees grow so tall that their tops completely cover the sky. The only color is green, the green of ferns and limes and moss and broad leaves. The air is warm and rich and sweet like poppies and everything smells of rainwater and damp, damp earth. No one lives there. No towns, no villages, no roads through this particular jungle and the only sound you hear are the sounds of birds. Beautiful songbirds and chattering macaws and of course peacocks, with their great fan tails and funny little crowns. In the middle of this jungle there is a waterfall as high as a mountain. At night, it pours the moon's silver. It is said that from this waterfall, come the souls of white tigers and grey lions, and perhaps even snow leopards..."

There was no protest, no growl nor rattle of sword. Rather, soft deep breathing in slow, natural rhythm. She was asleep.

Sireth shook his head.

"Pleasant dreams, my wild little Empress. You need them."

***

Kerris was beginning to enjoy himself. He had been wandering for hours, still dressed in the great brown robes of a monk and he had drawn the hood low over his face. He was going nowhere in particular, simply enjoying the sensation of being on the move. He walked as the monks walked, with hands folded inside their wide sleeves, following one long corridor after another, nodding in solemn fashion to every passing monk he met.

They weren't fooled, but he didn't care. To Kerris, the game was everything.

The inscriptions and carvings on the walls were intriguing. He had seen many in similar caves during his lifetime of wandering, and invariably they all led to some sort of treasure. He prided himself on his treasure-hunting ability, for he always managed to bring back a trinket or two for the Empress or his mother or the Imperial Mother's Mother. Because of him, they had stores of treasures dating back to the times of the Ancestors. A particular favorite had been a small chest, smaller than a saddlebag, which once opened, produced music. It was strange music, to be sure, not at all like the flat wailing tones of the tomepipe, or the minor chords of the yangquin. No, this was like the tinkling of bells, and the Empress had been thrilled. She had financed his next journey. He had a pocket full of shark teeth and a single, exquisite pearl, waiting for her in return.

He was deep in the monastery now, utterly lost but not bothered for the earth here was friendly, when he caught the faint echo of incense.

"Hmm," he mumbled to himself. "I wonder..."

The scent led him deeper, down a dark curve in the corridor to a half-opened door. Outside that door, a leopard slouched on a wooden stool, sword across his lap, sleeping. Kerris grinned as he sneaked past. Kirin wouldn't hear about this breach from him, hat was certain. It would mean the guard's head and Kerris had always maintained that heads worked much better when attached to necks.

He slipped into the room.

There were no torches burning, no oil lamps, only a single flickering flame on a far table.

He looked again.

Only the flame. At the end of a wick. No candle.

"Alchemists," he snorted and removed his hood.

He was in the Chamber of the Dead.

"Hello? Hello, *sidalady* cheetah? Anyone home?"

There was a rustle from behind and slowly out of the shadows, came Sherah.

Half-silhouetted from the small flickering light, her long black hair cascading over her shoulders, moving like a panther on the prowl, she was magnificent. He puffed out his breath in awe.

"Sidala."

"Sidi. How may I help you?"

She was still moving toward him.

"I need your opinion."

"Opinion?"

"Yes. I had a little run in with a very unusual snake."

"Snake?"

She was directly in front of him now, sliding her strong hands up the folds of his robe.

"Um, yes. Cobra, actually. Appeared out of nowhere."

"Nowhere?" Up his throat, along his jaw...

"Yes. We managed to dispatch it, of course. No harm done."

"We?"

...passed his temples, into his hair. He closed his eyes.

"Yes. The Scholar and myself - *Aiya!*"

"Tangles. You need a brushing."

"Sorry, love," he said, catching her wrists and dislocating her hands from his hair. "Don't own one."

"I do."

And suddenly, there was a brush in her hand. He could have sworn it hadn't been there seconds earlier.

She grabbed his robe-front and hauled him over to one of the tables, the one with the odd, burning wick. She pushed him onto the bench and climbed up to straddle his arms, pinning him from behind. She sat on the table and began to brush.

"Strange technique. They teach you this at *Agara'tha*?" he laughed, only half joking. "So, um, as I was saying, about this cobra..."

"Yes. The cobra from nowhere."

"The very one. So, after we killed it, it disappeared. Dried right up before our very eyes and blew away on the breeze."

The bristles were hard, biting against his scalp like claws, but oddly enough, the strokes felt good. She was intoxicating and he was drinking her in.

"Your problem has a simple answer, *sidi.*"

"Has it?"

"Yes. It has. The serpent was a vision."

"A vision?"

"A vision. Consider this. We have come to the monastery of the Seers, where the Gifts of Farsight and Vision have free rein over the souls of men. There are no cobras in the Great Mountains. So, you see something that could not possibly be seen which disappears from sight as quickly as it came. The answer is simple. It was never there."

"Never? Hm. Well, I'm not –*Aiy!*"

Her hand had twisted his hair, yanking his head back and chin up. She bent low over him, bringing her face in very close to his and she hovered there for a long moment, her mouth only a kiss away.

"Never."

Their breaths were becoming one.

"Never?"

"Never." She inhaled him deeply and he felt lightheaded, emptied. "Never."

And with that, she rose from the tabletop, freeing his arms from the lock of her legs and pushed him into the middle of the room.

"There. Your hair is much better. Now go."

A very confused lion stepped out of the Chamber of the Dead just as the final little wick was snuffed out behind him. He scratched his head and glanced down at the sleeping guard.

"Have you any idea what I went in there for? Any idea at all?"

Naturally, there was no response so Kerris shrugged and set off down the corridor, back in the direction he had come.

***

"Well, this is hot."

Fallon Waterford was right. The kitchens of *Sha'Hadin* were very hot. All seven hearths were roaring with life, logs soaked in oil to keep them burning well into the night. Over every fire, pots were bubbling and kettles were steaming, creating within the high-roofed chamber a veritable rainforest of heat and humidity. Condensation dripped from blackened beams and the stone floor was slick as if with dew. Thick woolen blankets were everywhere.

With the help of Tiberius and the kitchen staff, they had transformed the main galley into a Hiranian steam bath in the space of three hours. Kirin nodded to himself as he prodded several logs with an iron poker. It was almost unbearable, this heat, but necessary for the ordeal which would be upon them all too quickly. He straightened from his crouch and twisted his long thick hair off his neck. It didn't help. He pushed his sleeves up past his elbows, unlaced the heavy brigandine that covered his chest and dropped it against a wall. Nothing helped. It was brutal.

With a smile, he saw that the Scholar had done the same, pulling her hair into twin braids and loosening every article of clothing. Still, she looked eager and he admired her resilience.

An equally soggy Tiberius was waiting beside her.

"Is everything to your satisfaction, Captain? Do we need more blankets? More lamps? I can have some sent up from stores."

"Thank you, Tiberius. This will have to do."

"Very good, *sidi.* I have sent for our brother, Sireth, as you have asked."

Again, Kirin nodded and, with hands on hips, surveyed the room.

"I wish all the staff to be elsewhere tonight. No one is allowed in these rooms until I give the order. Is that understood?"

"Very good, *sidi.*"

He moved to leave.

"Not you, Tiberius. I wish your counsel tonight."

"I would be honored."

Out of the corner of his eye, Kirin caught a flash of grey. He spun around.

"Kerris!"

"Don't mind me, Kirin," called his brother from the doorway. "Just popped in to grab another bit of that stew but since everyone's so busy, I think I'll just go out and feed the horses. Right? Right."

Quickly, Kerris disappeared from view.

"Kerris! Come here. Now."

"Why?"

"Because I said so."

Eyes rolling, feet dragging, Kerris shuffled back into the kitchen.

"What?"

"I want you to stay with us tonight."

"Why?"

Sighing, the Captain strode over to his brother, grabbing him firmly behind the neck and ushered him off beside the door. Still smiling, Tiberius turned his gaze away to one of the hearths. Fallon, on the other hand, watched with interest, ears straining to hear scraps of conversation. She had a sudden craving for her father's popped rice.

"Kerris, a very important thing will happen tonight," began Kirin. "I wish you would take this a little more seriously."

"There's very bad kharma in this room, Kirin. It makes me nervous. Besides, the horses—"

"There is more to life than horses, Kerris. You can't hide yourself away in stables forever. I need you here. I need your help. Please."

"But Kirin..."

"Perhaps you can reverse the bad kharma, Kerris. We need all the help we can get."

"If I knew how to reverse bad kharma, Kirin, I would have done it for myself years ago."

"Please?"

Reluctantly, Kerris trudged toward the Scholar by the far wall. She cocked her head at him.

"So where were you all afternoon?"

"Oh, here. There. You know."

"You smell of incense."

"Do I? And you look like you've gone swimming. And without me? I am wounded, *sidala.* To the quick."

She huffed, but did not respond.

And suddenly, sharp angry clacking filled the air and all eyes turned to yet another entrance to the kitchens, where two figures were emerging. One very tall in swirling dark robes, the other as slim and silver as the swords at her hip.

"Close the door behind you," the Captain ordered. "Close all the doors."

One by one, seven great wooden doors groaned on their hinges, coming to a close with muffled thuds as the last of the kitchen staff left the room. The Seer did not pause but strode up to face the Captain. Perched on his left shoulder, the falcon hissed in ill humor.

"Captain, the Second Watch is almost upon us. We must meet it in the Hall of the Seers."

"We shall not meet the Second Watch in the Hall, *sidi.* We shall meet it here."

"Here? In the kitchens?" Sireth let his gaze wander over the dripping beams and raging fires and pots of bubbling water. "Do you plan to cook me after I'm dead?"

"You shall regret those words at first light of morning, *sidi.*"

"I sincerely hope so."

Kirin turned to look at all those assembled. His brow darkened.

"Where is the Alchemist?"

"I am here, *sidi.*"

A shadow separated from the others in a corner of the room, and Sherah al Shiva slid in to the firelight. No door had opened, and the room was windowless. Kirin shook his head.

And from somewhere, a gong sounded the beginning of the Second Watch.

***

Sireth benAramis eyed the cup and the murky liquids held within.

"Drink *that?* Captain, are you serious?"

"I am always serious."

"Yes," said the cheetah. "It should help."

"How very comforting, Alchemist."

He passed the falcon onto Tiberius' waiting arm and with a deep breath, he snatched the cup from Sherah's hand, tossing the entire contents back in one gulp. He gagged instantly, drawing the back of his hand to his lips to suppress a fit of coughing.

"That is absolutely *vile.*"

"Yes," Sherah purred. "It is..."

"Um Sherah, what 'medicines' are in that exactly?" asked Fallon, her stripes making worried wrinkles on her wide forehead. "I mean, the Captain said, and I quote – 'Slow the heart, thicken the blood, dull the senses' – I remember, 'cause I was there. I'm wondering what can do all that. I'd really be interested in knowing the ingredients. That is, if it doesn't violate some secret Alchemist's oath or anything..."

"A variety of herbal ingredients," said the Aegypshan. "Among which, crushed apricot seeds, fermented rice, snakeskin and blood."

The cup shattered to the floor.

"Blood?" said Sireth.

"Blood?" said Kirin.

"Apricot seeds?" said Fallon.

The Captain grabbed the Seer's arm. The man had taken a step toward the woman, but he wished in his soul of souls that he could let go. Among a carnivorous people, there were certain rules. Certain taboos that must be followed in order to maintain their distance from the vast population of carnivorous animals that roamed the Upper Kingdom. And the First and most Sacred of those rules forbade the eating of people. No killing of any Race, pure or otherwise, for the purpose of consumption. No tissue, no organ, and most of all no blood, for the life was in the blood. It was Abomination.

"Whose blood?" the Seer snarled, *"Whose blood?!"*

"It is a fair question, *sidala.* Answer it."

"The blood of the Seers, lying in the Chamber of the Dead."

Sireth staggered backwards, turning toward the kitchen hearths and covering his face with his hands.

Kirin swung to face the Alchemist.

"Tell me this is necessary, *sidala."*

"It is necessary, *sidi.* The Seers have all died at the hand of the same enemy. The face of that enemy lies within them, in their souls and in their blood. Even now, they can impart strength and wisdom to one of their number."

Fallon stepped beside her, twisting one of her tunic laces into knots.

"As strange as it may sound, sir, Sherah is right. There is a theory in the University that not only life but healing can be found in the blood of the dying. I read about a physician who took a measure of blood from a very sick man, a man whose entire village was dying of the pox. He distilled that blood and gave it to a child and the child survived, with only a very mild presentation of symptoms. There are many things to be found in the blood, things we are only beginning to understand. Sir."

She seemed so earnest, thought the Captain, *standing in defense of one so damned.*

The Scholar turned.

"But Sherah, why apricot seeds?"

"To slow the heart, of course."

"But apricot seeds are the foundation of the deadliest of poisons. If your measures are just the slightest bit wrong—"

"They are not wrong."

"And the snakeskin?"

"Year of the Snake," she purred. "Alchemy embraces both philosophy and physiognomy."

"You had no right," growled benAramis, silhouetted by flame. "They were my friends. You had no right!"

He swung around, taking several long steps but before he could reach her, his right leg buckled beneath him. Only Ursa's swift response kept him from hitting the stony floor. Still, he came. The

Captain intervened, catching the other arm and together they pushed him to his knees. By the hearth, Tiberius held fast to the talon leathers as the falcon shrieked and cried, furiously shredding his arm in its attempt to aid her master.

"She had no right..." muttered the Seer, "She had no right..."

"She had no right but she bears no blame. I commissioned this medicine. The responsibility is mine. Do you understand this?" Kirin bent in close, for the Seer's head was bowed and his dark hair fell long past his face. "You can take this up with me later. Do you understand?"

"I will, Captain. Be sure of it."

His words were thick and slurred. Kirin sought out the point on the throat that throbbed with life, the point where heart met soul. It was slow, slowing even as he found it and the man's lids were closing like curtains darkening a window. Beneath his hand, tension drained from the muscles as the Alchemist's medicines began their work.

"Well, there you go," said Fallon brightly. "Apricot seeds."

The Captain looked up and around at his charges. This was wrong. They did not belong.

Tiberius approached, frowning.

"A word, *sidi,* if I may?"

Kirin rose to his feet. "Keep him down, Major."

"He's going nowhere, sir."

The monk led him toward another hearth, a slight distance away from the others. The humidity was taking its toll on the older man, for his silver hair was slick against his forehead and he was panting. Even still, the man radiated peace and Kirin found himself envious once again.

"*Sidi,* please accept my humblest apologies if what I say causes offence but I'm afraid I must warn you against touching a Seer with your bare hands.

"I meant no disrespect, Tiberius."

"No, *sidi,* it is not a matter of respect. It is very unwise. It can damage the soul."

"Do not concern yourself with the state of my soul, Tiberius."

"Not your soul, Captain. His."

And then, Tiberius bowed. It brought a subtle end to the

conversation, encouraged him to rejoin the group. Kirin did, slowly and very deeply in thought.

The next few hours dragged by, with hardly two words spoken by any one tongue. The fires raged on. The kettles boiled and spilled their contents over their brims, causing new steam to hiss upwards from the sizzling char. Limbs grew as limp as hair and people sat in puddles of arms and legs and discarded clothing. And Kirin was beginning to wonder if the Watch might close without incident. That, he concluded, would be a problem.

He cast his eyes over his people.

Side by side, sat Kerris and Fallon, knees up, backs against a far wall. They appeared to be comparing the tips of their tails.

"I seem to recall saying something about great hot vats of water, earlier," Kerris was saying, plucking several long grey strands from his tuft. "Remind me to keep my mouth shut in the future, will you? After tonight, I shall seriously reconsider my infatuation with swimming..."

"Did you talk to her?"

"Her who?"

"The Alchemist. Did you ask her about the snake?"

"What snake?"

"The cobra, the one on the bluff..." She turned wide emerald eyes on him. "The one your pony stomped to bits..."

"Quiz hates snakes. And there are no cobras in the Great Mountains. I'm sorry, *sidala*, but there was never any snake. Never." He looked away. "Never."

Openmouthed, Fallon looked away too.

The Seer still knelt on the stony floor, head bowed, arms loose at his sides, palms resting on the floor. His eyes were closed and his breathing was very slow, but regular. He looked as if he might be sleeping, so every few minutes the Major would poke him, prod him, anything to get a reaction. She actually seemed to enjoy it. Kirin shook his head. He would have to speak to her about it at a later date.

Only the Alchemist seemed unmindful of the heat or the crushing humidity. She sat, plaiting her hair into long ebon braids, humming all the while in strange, exotic keys.

Perhaps it was the bubbling of pots and the crackling of fires, filling the room with an endless stream of noise. Or perhaps it was fatigue, for he was tired and conditions were oppressive but at some point, Kirin realized that there was a sound.

He sat forward. It was a faint sound, a grating, whining, scraping noise that set one's teeth on edge. Much like the sound of claws on rock. *Yes, claws on rock,* he thought to himself. *That's exactly what it sounded like.*

Cursing, he scrambled to his feet.

Black claws unsheathed through slits in brown leather, digging into the floor with increasing force.

The seventh and last Seer was not breathing.

"Blankets!" he snapped, and immediately, all hands were available, working to drape the robed back in thick woolen sheets.

Kirin grabbed the man's shoulders, tried to shake the air into him but they were rigid, stiff, and bitterly cold. He bent lower, pulling the chin up and noticing the icy beard crunch under his fingers.

"Breathe. Breathe." He growled, "Sireth benAramis, can you hear me? I order you to breathe!"

But the eyes were glassy and far away, with the wild, fixed stare of one firmly in the grips of fear.

"I said *breathe!*"

No response. Ursa shook him in vain, trying to relieve her sense of helpless frustration. Tiberius hovered over them all, wringing his great wide hands. The falcon screeched. Still no response.

The Captain did the only thing he could think of doing. He balled his hand into a fist and sent it thudding into the Seer's abdomen, forcing the air out of his lungs and praying the loss would cause more to be drawn in as reflex.

The Seer breathed in a great shuddering gasp and he pitched forward, claws slicing against stone, leather, and lion flesh. The scrabble of heels as the Major lunged toward him, locking her arms under his and hauling him backwards off the Captain. Within moments, she had him pinned to her chest, fingers laced across the back of his neck, the muscles in her arms standing out like steel cords.

"Kirin, you're bleeding!"

He slapped his brother's hand away and scrambled back to the Seer's side.

"Wrong. Wrong. Wrong. All wrong."

Now panting, the Seer's eyes focused far beyond the confines of the kitchen and his teeth chattered uncontrollably. The ends of his hair, which had only minutes before had been dripping with condensation were now white with frost.

"It's all wrong. Max, what the hell is going on? Max, where are you?"

"You are here, in *Sha'Hadin*. Can you hear me?"

"Max?"

"No. You—"

"Max, it's too cold! Initiate core warming immediately! I can't breathe!"

"You can breathe. You are breathing now. And you are warm. Can't you feel the warmth? Feel it."

For emphasis, Kirin dragged another blanket from the pile at his side, tugging it up over the man's chest and wrapping it around the stiffened fingers. The claws still extruded through the gloves.

"See? Warm."

"I can't breathe!"

"Listen to me. You are talking. You are breathing. You are warm. Believe it."

"How?"

"I have no idea, *sidi,* but it is the truth. Can you feel the warmth?"

"No. Yes, I can. It's...it's warm now. Is it? But how? Is that you, Max?"

"No."

"Why am I awake? Is it time?"

"I'm not certain. But you are safe, you are warm and you can breathe."

"I must be dreaming this. Am I dreaming? How can I be dreaming? You can't dream in cryo."

"He sounds like a tiger."

Kirin glanced up. Fallon Waterford stood over them, her mouth twisting into knots of wonder. Briskly, she nodded at him, as if it were as plain as day.

"No accent."

She was right.

The Captain leaned forward.

"Who are you?"

"Initiate core warming. Begin infusion of liquid Oh Too. Get this procedure back on track, Max." The Seer closed his eyes. "Or this cold is going to kill me..."

"You are not going to die."

"If you say so."

"Who is Max?"

"Don't wake any of the others, do you understand? Not until we've got this mess straightened out. Have you got that? Have you?"

"Yes. Yes, I think so."

"You better hope so, or I'll pull your plug myself."

The strange, unaccented voice grew sluggish, the breathing deeper, less ragged and Sireth began to sink into the Major's strong arms.

"I think, I think I'm going to go back to sleep now. Wake me when the procedure's complete. And whoever the hell you are, get online with Max, will you? This is really, really bad."

Save for the bubbling and the hissing and the roaring of flame, and the soft chirruping of a falcon, there was silence in the kitchens of *Sha'Hadin.*

Kirin reached out his hand, seeking the point where heart met soul. The pulse was slow but strong. The seventh and last Seer was alive. They had succeeded. He rubbed his brow, only then noticing the bright ribbons of blood standing out on his forearms. And what was worse, he had another headache.

But tears were flowing into Tiberius' broad, broad smile and suddenly things were right in *Sha'Hadin.*

And the gong sounded the Close of the Second Watch.

THE MOTHER'S ARMS

It was the dawn of the third morning since the adventure had begun. The third morning since Kerris Wynegarde-Grey had been so unceremoniously roused from his bed after only four hours of sleep. It was a remarkably similar one, he had noted, cool and crisp with a skyful of clouds. But this morning, one thing was drastically different. Everywhere he looked, the Great Mountains were covered in snow.

It was not unusual for the mountains to receive snow rather than rain during one of her many spring storms. Indeed, snow was the lifeblood of all high places, dripping into rivulets, then streams, then mighty rushing rivers in its endless quest for level ground. And snow, being cold and heavy, falls faster than water through the valleys that channel its path, rushing like wild horses to throw itself off the very edges of the earth.

Kerris knew all about such things. He had seen it happen time and time again. He had followed rivers to their sources and discovered that these rivers were in fact simply snow warmed by sun. He had chased this racing snow through foothill and jungle alike, marveling as it changed colors from white to brown to deepest blue, always to end up in the same place. The oceans. And like a wild horse, he too had followed that snow off the edge into the oceans. Somehow he had never mustered the courage to pursue it farther out as far as the waters would go, beyond the edge of the world.

He smiled to himself. One day, he would. He was certain of it.

He tugged on the black mare's girth.

"Oh, there's more to life than horses, Kerris. Can't be hiding in stables all your life, now can you, Kerris? Oh and by the way Kerris be up before dawn, will you and have the horses ready. There's a good man."

Rodreigo was laughing behind him.

"Why do you always talk to yourself, *sidalord* grey lion?"

"Perhaps because I can hold up both ends of a conversation and quite happily too. Besides, by talking to yourself, you are guaranteed to rarely lose an argument and you always have someone to blame when you do."

Rodreigo laughed some more.

With a huff of breath, Kerris stepped back and ran his eyes along the row of horses standing outside the stable's stony walls. Not including the pack animals, they had thirteen horses. Little Quiz was herd boss. The pony stood at the head of the row, ears flat, teeth bared, squealing and snapping at any who dared contest his authority. Kerris laid a steadying hand on the pony's shoulder. Thirteen horses, thirteen riders. He shook his head.

"Rather convenient, isn't it, how we managed to lose one leopard but keep his horse. Otherwise, your Seer would be riding a goat."

Rodreigo howled this time, clutching his sides to keeping his lungs from bursting out his skinny ribcage. With such an appreciative audience, Kerris could not resist the temptation to mimic the image. He scrunched up his left eye and dragged his legs along the ground, smacking an imaginary goat with the tip of his tail.

"Hai-hai there, Imperial goat! Off to the Palace. Hai-hai now!"

Rodreigo hit the dirt now, gasping in vain attempt to catch his breath. Kerris straightened his back, clasped his hands to his hips.

"Breathe, Rodreigo. Breathe. I am Kirin Wynegarde-Grey, Captain of the Queen's Guard. I order you now to breathe or I'll punch your guts in."

Abruptly, the boy's laughter died.

"Good morning, Kerris."

Kerris swung around, smiling.

"Ah, good morning, Kirin. I was just explaining to my friend here how we saved the Seer last night. Wasn't I, Rodreigo?"

Rodreigo swallowed, waiting for the flash of steel that would take off his head.

"We, Kerris?" growled the Captain. "How *we* managed to save the Seer?"

"Yes, we. First is Luck, remember? And Rodreigo claims I'm a lucky omen. He knew we would save the Seer. Isn't that right, Rodreigo?"

Rodreigo nodded swiftly. He was a serval and he glanced between the bigger cats with quick, anxious looks.

"And he was right, wasn't he? You know, I wonder if Rodreigo hasn't got a bit of the Gift himself, eh Rodreigo? He certainly is a splendid judge of character."

"Forgive me, *sidis*. I must wash up for morning prayers."

And with that, he grabbed an armful of brushes and scurried into the shadows of the rock. Kerris watched him go.

"You enjoy frightening children, Kirin? I thought that was Ursa's job."

"Kerris..." The Captain turned to regard his brother, grinding his molars to restrain his tongue. "Kerris, thank you for saddling the horses. And thank you for your help last night."

Kerris shrugged and leaned across the back of his pony.

"I tossed the stones this morning, Kirin. The *Paghuah* says there is no good to be found on that trail and I don't like the look of those mountains. That snow won't stay. By midday, it'll be racing for the valleys like kittens for candy."

"We have no choice, Kerris. We must reach *Pol'Lhasa* today."

"Why?"

The Captain shook his head.

"Right. Not my place," said Kerris. "That's fine. But as your Geomancer and Guide then, I really don't advise it."

They turned as a party of leopard guards marched in perfect formation from one of the monastery's seven entrances. Sandwiched in between were the Scholar and the Alchemist, neither looking particularly refreshed from the few hours of sleep before early rise this morning.

"Ah, *sidali,"* said Kerris, "Allow me to escort you to your horses."

The tigress' emerald eyes flashed at him.

"Are you sure it's really there? I mean, I would hate to try to mount a horse that wasn't really there." She brushed past him and slipped her foot in the stirrup. "Besides, I think I've got the basics now. Now that I've stopped to think about it, and all..."

Within seconds, she was up and in position, head held just a little too high, back just a little too straight.

Kerris rolled his eyes at his brother.

"I gave her a bit of a lesson yesterday. She fell off," he whispered loudly. "I daresay she wounded a bit more than her pride..."

Fallon huffed but said nothing.

"Now, *sidalady* cheetah?"

The Alchemist needed no assistance however and she mounted with languid grace, her long, ebon-clad legs wrapping around the animal like a second skin. She drew the hood of her black cloak up and over her forehead so that her wide, golden eyes peered out at them from the shadows.

"Thank you for your help, *sidis,"* she purred.

Kirin shook his head.

Lastly, there were voices as three figures approached from the monastery. For each of the Seer's long strides, both the Major and the lynx Tiberius were forced to take two in effort to keep up. For the Major, this presented no problem. Tiberius, on the other hand, was puffing as the trio pulled to a stop in front of the horses. The old man smiled. The Seer did not.

"Captain, your message?"

Kirin handed him a scrap of parchment and watched as Sireth fixed it to one of the falcon's legs, binding it securely with the talon leathers. He placed two fingers on the hood over the hidden eyes.

"Pol'Lhasa," he breathed softly, then removed the hood.

The falcon launched from his arm, crying in her shrill, sharp voice as she rose into the morning sky. Within moments, she was gone. He turned back to the Captain.

"There is one final matter before we embark on our journey, Captain."

"And what would that be, *sidi?"*

"Sha'Hadin."

"Sha'Hadin?"

"Yes, Captain. You have abolished the Council and removed me from office. You yourself have assumed responsibility but now you leave, and I doubt that you intend on returning anytime soon. The monastery is left without leadership. I wish to know what you intend for the 500 who remain, 500 of the Empire's truest servants. Would you have them also pack their bags and depart?"

Kirin could hear Ursa growling behind, saw her hand move to the hilt of her sword. He shook his head and clasped his own firmly behind his back.

"*Sidi,* your anger, while understandable, is misplaced. I hereby confer all authority for the daily operations of the monastery onto Tiberius' capable shoulders, until the reestablishment of the Council and the return of its last surviving member. Tiberius, does this suit you?"

The lynx bowed most deeply.

Kirin turned to the Seer.

"And you?"

"For now."

"Very well. Major, please show the Seer to his horse. We must depart immediately if we are to make *Pol'Lhasa* by sunset." He turned to Tiberius, laid both hands on the man's shoulders. "The Empress will know of your service, *sidi.*"

The monk simply shook his head.

"Unnecessary, *sidi.* You have saved *Sha'Hadin.* That is more than enough.'

The Captain mounted his Imperial stallion and surveyed the group assembled in the deep ravine – the seven guards, the Scholar, Alchemist, Seer, Major and their Guide. He cast his eyes up the sharp escarpment, its high ridge just now glowing with the golden rays of dawn. Out of its stony walls, the Cave of a Thousand Eyes watched the Life of the World, preserving the future of the Upper Kingdom. He prayed they would watch forever.

He nudged alMassay forward.

"Move out."

***

By noon, they had reached the split in the trail, the small grassy knoll where high and low paths converged. Naturally, they had returned by the low path for on roads as wet and dangerous as these, they needed sure footing to ensure the best time. Water ran in widening streams across the trail and in some cases, the horses were made to leap over ragged ditches created by the runoff. The sun was high and hot, promising the return to more typical spring weather and again cloaks weighed heavily on their backs as they descended slowly from the mountains of *Sha'Hadin.*

They had passed the inn and the markets and the cleft in the road where carts tended to break, all without incident. It seemed that today, they might make their destination by sunset. The Captain smiled a small smile.

The Empress would be pleased.

He let his gaze wander down the trail, to the winding river of horses that comprised this Royal Entourage. Three leopards led the way, the Royal Standard waving above them, leading them like an arrow to the heart of the Kingdom. Next came the Scholar, riding quite well on her rather leaden horse. Kerris had situated Quiz immediately behind for the pony was definitely dominant in this mismatched little herd, and its sharp teeth snapped and nipped the sluggish backside whenever the pace grew too slow. The Alchemist next, again somehow managing to make her stock mare something remarkable. He had also noted, with some degree of concern, that the little red pouch floating above her bags seemed somehow fuller, more menacing than before.

It didn't matter. He would be rid of her by sunrise.

Behind him, Sireth benAramis, Ursa Laenskaya, the three pack horses and the final four leopards to complete the party. The Seer had been surly all morning and the Captain was forced to admit there were matters still unsettled. He knew what they were, for he himself had invited them. With a sigh, he reined in alMassay and pulled alongside the man.

"*Sidi,* is the mount not to your satisfaction?"

"The horse is fine, Captain. It is the blood of the Seers that sits poorly in my stomach."

"Now is not the time."

"Will there *be* a time, Captain? It is cowardice to delay such a challenge."

"It is prudence, *sidi.* There will be a time."

"I look forward to it, then."

Behind him, Kirin heard the Major sputter in disbelief as he nodded calmly, ignoring the thinly veiled threat. Under normal circumstances, he would have in no way allowed such a challenge to go unanswered. But the man had a legitimate grievance and was obviously lion enough to demand his due. Kirin would have to address it soon enough.

"And you maintain no memory of the events last night?"

The challenge postponed, the Seer shook his head.

"Nothing, Captain. *Truly* nothing," he added with a thin smile. "My last recollection is the Alchemist's cup of 'medicines' and then nothing until awakening under the Major's watchful eye. I believe that I'm growing accustomed to the sharpening of her claws."

Behind them, the Major sharpened her claws.

"Is it true I spoke in the tongue of a tiger last night?"

"It is true."

"A tiger." Sireth shook his head again. "How odd."

Behind them, Ursa narrowed her pale eyes and grinned. "Some long lost relative, perhaps?"

"First cousin on my mother's side."

The Captain tried to smile. "Very well. We are making good time. If you recall anything, at any time during the journey, tell me at once."

He spurred alMassay forward, taking his place in the winding river once again. He noticed Quiz trotting next to the Scholar's poky beast, and their riders seemed to be engaged in animated conversation. *Too bad she wasn't a lioness,* he thought wryly. Kerris might actually have stumbled on a good one in her.

Then again, perhaps his brother was more tiger than lion, himself.

"You're in quite the mood this morning, *sidala,*" Kerris was saying. "It really doesn't suit you. Makes your eyes all scrunchy, and does nasty things to your nostrils."

"Let me ask you something, Kerris your name was. Something just for clarification. If you don't mind."

"Ask away, *sidala.*"

"You say there was never any snake yesterday, is that right?"

"Sorry, *sidala.* There was never any snake."

"Well, did we get caught in the snow yesterday on the way back from the bluff? Did that really happen?"

Kerris grinned. "Yes, I seem to recall something like that."

"And did we exchange our clothing for monk's robes and have hot tea and stew in the dining hall?"

"Yes, *sidala.* We did."

"And did you snag a loaf of bread from a passing monk? And did I comment on your manners? And did you say that it was something you learned at the Palace? And did I ask you what else you learned? Did it go something like that, Kerris your name was?"

"My, but you have a good memory, *sidala,*" he laughed. "Yes, that's exactly how it happened."

"I know, 'cause I was there. So, what was your answer then? What else did say you learned at the Palace?"

"Snake charming," he said, smile fading. "I said snake charming."

"Exactly. Why? Why would you say that, if there had never been any snake?"

He scratched his chin and sat back, putting pressure on Quiz's spine and easing the pony into a slow jog.

"Well, you just stop to think about that one, Kerris your name was. Take just a scrap of time and use that little mind of yours for something other than walking, eating and talking for a change. Can you do that for me?"

That said, she tossed her head once again, tightened the laces on her cloak.

For his part, Kerris continued to puzzle for some time afterwards.

Behind them rode the Alchemist, humming to herself in strange, exotic keys.

The water on the road was growing worse, rushing in torrents now from the snow-heavy mountain slopes. It was taking the road away with it, stone by stone, as it poured headlong down the sharp incline and Kirin noticed alMassay struggling to keep even footing. He also noticed his brother, frequently glancing up at the sheer expanse of deadly white that glistened in the mid-afternoon sun above them. He set his jaw, shook his head but before he could make a decision, the Major's voice snarled from behind.

"Move," she hissed. "Get going."

The Seer had stopped his horse, his eyes focused yet far away. Kirin remembered the look. He held up a hand and the rear guard shouted orders to the group in the fore. The winding river of horses ground to a halt.

"I said *move!*"

"Major, that's enough."

The Imperial stallion performed a tight turn-on-haunches to draw up in front of the Seer.

"*Sidi?*"

Sireth blinked, refocused. "Captain, we must turn around—"

"*Kirin!*"

Kerris and Quiz were scrambling back up the path toward him.

"*Kirin!*"

It was then that they heard the boom, the faint and distant thunder of ice sheets giving way. High above them, a white spray arose from the mountainside, reaching into the blue sky like the birth of a cloud. It began to shake the very earth beneath them as easily as a child shakes a stalk of bamboo.

"Back!" shouted Kerris. "We must go back! Now!"

"Back!" echoed Kirin, and with great effort, alMassay dug his hoofs into the sloppy, vibrating ground, propelling himself back up the path and forcing the others to do likewise. The Captain threw a glance up and over his shoulder. The snow was almost upon them.

"Faster! Move!"

With a surge of speed brought only by panic, the horses galloped up the slippery path, racing to keep ahead of the death that was plummeting toward them. Tiny crystals of ice cut into Kirin's neck like the sting of a thousand wasps. He ducked low in the saddle and urged his horse forward.

And then he heard the screams.

First one leopard, then another, crying out for only an instant as their horses were swept from under them, and they were sucked into the charging wall of snow. Arms and legs and finally the Royal Banner carried on above the bank until they too were swallowed up in sheer, blinding white. The Alchemist's black mare was at full gallop at alMassay's flank but far behind, the Scholar's horse was losing ground. The third leopard plunged forward, the roar of the avalanche licking at his horse's heels and snow cascaded downwards all around him. He reached out to catch the Scholar, scooping her into his saddle just as her horse stumbled and went down. As it fell, it collided with the soldier's horse and it too lost footing. The snow obliterated sight of them both in an instant.

The thunder was deafening now, as Quiz the mountain pony scaled the mountainside, back up and over the near vertical slope like a monkey, sending shale and bits of snow onto the road. Both pony and rider disappeared into the sleet that preceded the crushing snow.

"Kerris!"

For the first time, alMassay disobeyed his rider, steeling his mouth as the Captain hauled on the reins. For in a flash, Quiz was back on the path, wild-eyed and frantic, with Kerris almost twisted in half, one hand clutching the pony's mane, the other hand clutching an orange one. The tigress swung out from under the blizzard and for the briefest of moments, it looked like Kerris would have her, until the mountain boomed again. Kerris lost his grip and both tigress and lion were sucked into the speeding front, Quiz scuttling off alone.

Without thinking, the Captain leapt from his stallion's back. He hit the wet, rumbling ground, flattened his arms and legs to brace himself and still, he slid. When he finally scrambled to his feet, he was just in time to see the body of the avalanche carry on past them, hurling itself off the edge of the mountain and sending a cloud of white raining down to the valleys below. Slowly, the thunder subsided, leaving unnatural silence in its wake and for a long moment, all he could hear was the sound of his own breathing, heavy and hurting in the afternoon sun.

Behind him, he heard voices – calling voices, arguing voices, voices snapping orders and voices hotly disobeying. He ignored them all.

Suddenly, someone was beside him, grabbing at his arm.

It was the Seer.

"They're alive, Captain. They're alive. Hurry."

Kirin needed nothing more and with the Major at their heels, the pair of them dove into the deep bank of snow.

***

For a long moment, all Kerris could hear was the sound of his own breathing, heavy and hurting in the afternoon sun. He could feel the cold empty howl of wind on his face and the cold empty expanse of air around his legs as he swung high above nothingness. But what he was waiting to feel - the sickening, sucking sensation of free fall or the sudden, harsh smack of ribs on rock - these he did not feel. He gradually got up the courage to open his eyes, hoping against hope that the last thing he would see would *not* be the Mother's Arms, rushing up to give him a bone-crushing hug.

What he did see was cliff face, dark and stony, closer then further away, closer then further away. He was swinging less than an arm's length away from sheer mountain rock. His hands ached and he looked up to see them twisted around a double strand of thick, braided leather. *Reins,* he realized. He was hanging on to a strange pair of reins that disappeared up and over the edge of the cliff. It seemed very likely that it was attached to a bridle and equally likely to the head of some horse, dead and buried under a shroud of cold, heavy snow. And finally, with a deep breath, he looked down, way down, to see the bottom of the mountain fall away as if forever, swaying and spinning in dizzying circles below.

And the tigress.

She had her eyes squeezed tightly closed, her arms wrapped around his legs as in a death grip, her face pressed into the back of his knees, squishing his tail with her forehead. *Perfectly sensible*, he thought dully. He had pulled her out of the snow so she had pulled him back into it.

"Hello down there," he called out, his voice cracking from the strain. "Hello, *sidalady* tigress. Can you look up a moment? Please?"

Slowly, she did look up, eyes wide.

"That's better, isn't it? See, we're fine. Really. Quite fine." He tried to smile, managed a grimace instead. "Um, do you think you can climb?"

"No. No, I don't think so. I think I'm fine right here, thanks, if it's all the same to you."

"Well it's not, actually. We're in a bit of a predicament right now and I don't think I can haul the both of us back up this cliff without a little bit of help."

"Oh. Okay."

And she clung to him the way a small child clings to its mother until the reins gave a small jerk. She yelped.

Kerris swallowed. He could imagine it all well enough. The reins were braided Imperial leather, the finest in all the Kingdom, and the body of the horse itself was a worthy anchor, crushed and pinned by the weight of snow covering it. But the snow was still melting, moving in its inexorable slide to the valley, bringing the dead animal along for the ride.

The reins jerked again.

"Use your claws! Now! Climb!"

She did. Her claws were fine and black and she began to scale him like a tree house, sinking them into cloak and tunic as easily as old bark. As she pulled herself up to his shoulders, she felt them dig into flesh.

"Sorry! Oh, sorry!"

Kerris gritted his teeth. "Keep going!"

And the reins slipped some more, bringing with them a rush of snow. It struck her and sent her toppling from her perch. Purely by instinct, she lashed out, snagging his shoulders once again and dragging her claws down his back like razors. They were swinging wildly now, spinning high above the chasm, and she felt her fingers, then her hands, then her arms grow warm and sticky.

"...oh... mother..."

"...just... climb..."

She began again, hand over hand, trying desperately to avoid the slices in his pelt. Higher, just a little bit higher, she climbed up until, with one boot balanced on his shoulder, she pushed herself upward, sending a searching hand past the reins, to the very edge of the cliff.

And suddenly her weight was gone from Kerris' shoulders, leaving the coolness of space in its place. He briefly wondered if she had fallen once again and this time been thoughtful enough not to take half his pelt with her.

Above the howl of the cold empty wind, he could hear voices and soon there was the face of his brother, reaching out over the edge, grabbing his arms in a powerful grip. Kirin was using his own claws and this time Kerris felt his arms grow warm as blood flowed down into his sleeves.

"Hello, Kirin," he said weakly.

His brother gritted his teeth, hanging on as if nothing in the Kingdom could make him let go. A silver set of claws flashed into view, as both Captain and Major hauled the grey coat up and over the cliff edge, into the welcome cold of the snow. Kerris glanced up to see the tigress in arms of the Seer. The man was speaking softly to her, stroking her thick, silky hair. He felt hands on his shoulders, his back, and he let his brother hold him as he sank to his knees.

"You owe me a very big drink," he grumbled.

And he closed his eyes under his brother's soothing hand.

***

Hands on hips, Kirin Wynegarde-Grey oversaw the excavation of snow. It was not a pleasant task, nor a particularly useful one, for snow had buried the narrow, winding road for a great distance beyond. *They had been fortunate,* he thought darkly. If they had been further along, they could not possibly have outrun the avalanche and all thirteen of them would have been buried along with it. As it was, the four surviving leopards had unearthed two of the dead guards and three of the four horses that had fed their Mother, the Great Mountains. Hopefully it would sate her appetite for a long time to come.

Ursa Laenskaya stood beside him.

"We should be able to clear a path, sir," she said. "The snow is not that heavy."

"No, Major. The snow is very heavy. We shall succeed only in exhausting our men."

Kirin glanced up at the sun, now high in its afternoon arc through the sky. He shook his head.

"We shall not see *Pol'Lhasa* tonight."

"Perhaps if we enlist the aid of the civilians?"

"Have the men call off their work. We shall see to our dead, and return to the monastery. Perhaps by tomorrow, the sun will do this work for us."

"Yes, sir."

He turned to leave, but paused to put a hand on her slim, white shoulder.

"Thank you, Major."

With a sigh, he trudged up the muddy slope that passed for a road to the circle of horses and people further up the hillside. The Alchemist had prepared a pot of tea from one of her many bags and warmed it to boiling with her many candles. She had done it all quietly and it had served to heal frayed nerves more readily than all the ointments or balms at her disposal. Bundled in a warm, wooly blanket, the Scholar sat beside the Seer, who seemed to have taken her under his wing. Kirin crouched down beside them.

"*Sidala,* how are you feeling?"

She shrugged over her mug of hot tea.

"Oh, fine actually. Maybe just a little wobbly. My claws hurt, though. And I still have bits of snow in my fur. And I think I might have sprained something. But really, other than that, I think I'm fine. Really."

She gave him a valiant smile, and he noticed her chin trembled, just a little.

"Why? Do I look bad?'

"Yes, *sidala.* You look bad."

"Oh mother."

"You look fine, my dear. Just a little soggy." Sireth patted her hand before turning to Kirin. "Captain, I'm not certain what you are planning for us, but I don't think it would be wise to return to *Sha'Hadin.* Not today. Not with the state of this young woman, not to mention your brother. It would be inviting disaster."

"The Inn, then."

"It is closer. Granted, the owners are inhospitable and the ale weak, but the food is good and the beds are warm. Great sakeh too, real bite to it. Might be just the trick for soggy, wobbly bones, eh?"

Fallon beamed at him.

Kirin's jaw worked as he thought the specifics through.

"You may be right. We will bury our dead, and leave immediately. We should make the Inn by sunset."

"In about two and a half hours, actually," Fallon said. "And given the poor conditions of the roads, and the fatigue of the horses, it might even be four. Yep, probably four. How will I get there?"

Kirin stared at her blankly.

"I mean, my horse, he's, he's, he tripped and… He was so slow, so slow..."

Her chin trembled again and she did her best to stop the tears that were gathering behind her lashes. Such remorse for that hapless creature was a waste of one's chi, thought Kirin. Nonetheless, it spoke well of her.

He nodded gravely.

"We have three pack horses. I will have one readied for you before we leave."

"Oh. Thanks."

"Might I see your hands?"

"Who? Mine? My hands?"

"Please, *sidala.*"

With a furrowed brow, the tigress offered Kirin her hands. He took them in his own, noticed that they were still trembling from shock. Gently, he squeezed the pads of her palms, watched the claws extend slightly through the tips of her fingers. *As expected,* he thought. Small, fine and delicate. Sharp, nonetheless.

"My brother was very fortunate," said Kirin, releasing her hands. "So were you. I'm glad you survived."

She did not seem to know the appropriate response, so the Captain rose to his feet, gave her a modest bow and left.

"Was that a good thing?"

Sireth smiled at her. "Yes, I believe it was."

She wrapped her arms around her knees. "Wow."

***

The sound of humming met his ears as the Captain picked his way over the rocks to the second pair. Sherah al Shiva had her back to him but he could tell from her movements that she was packing away the various salves and tools she had needed to treat Kerris' injuries. He shook his head. The woman had proved herself invaluable this last hour with her strange medicines and welcome brews. Perhaps the Seer had been right all along. Perhaps his own 'glass' was dangerously dark.

"Sidala"

"Sidi."

Still, she did not turn.

He shook his head again.

He passed her by to sit beside his brother, wrapped in the Alchemist's black cloak, his normally bright blue eyes heavy-lidded and sleepy. His dark grey hair was sticking up all over his head. He smiled as Kirin sat down.

"Hello Kirin."

"How do you feel?"

"Ah, rather good at the moment. 'Rah gave me some little powdery thing and a thimble full of rice wine. She would have me believe that my back is in shreds, and that you flailed fur from flesh on my arms but really I am not at all convinced. I feel nothing of the sort."

Kirin reached behind his brother, lifting the cloak and torn tunic away from his spine. Ten long gashes from shoulders to ribs, all bright and oozing with salve. He noticed her stitching, small and precise, and approved of the fine white threads she used in her work.

"Well done, *sidala.* These shall heal up quickly."

"Of course."

He let the fabric drop to his brother's back and took Kerris' arm, turning it over to study her bandaging. Again, neat and precise. Just enough wrap, not too tight. He nodded silently.

"Well, you'll live."

Kerris grinned sheepishly. "Yes. I suppose I shall."

"Are you up for a trip back to the Inn?"

"Will you pay for the ale?"

"I will."

"Unlimited then," said Kerris. "Lyn-ling owes me that much."

Kirin shook his head once again. Only Kerris could get away with calling the Empress by her pet name, the name she had been called since a kitten in the Imperial nursery. Only nursemaids and nannies, and Kerris.

"I believe Her Excellency pays you well, brother."

"You may be right."

Golden eyes turned toward them and the Alchemist tilted her head.

"*Sidis*. I have finished here. Perhaps I should tend to the dead? Prepare their souls for the next world?"

Images of candles and vats of dried organs flashed, unbidden into his mind and Kirin suppressed a shudder. It was necessary. Many of the Leopard Guard were of the Old Religions and to deny them final sacraments would diminish the honor of their deaths. With a sigh, he agreed, and she slunk from their company like a shadow. Kerris followed her with sleepy eyes.

"She's quite the creature, don't you think? I'll bet she's a good cook."

"Cook?" Kirin stared at his brother, shook his head. "Yes, Kerris. I'm quite sure she's a good cook."

"Ah, well. I'm quite enjoying the powdery white thing she gave me..."

"I don't care what she gave you, as long as you're alive."

Kirin reached out, tried to pat the ashen grey hair into place. It wouldn't go. He gave up.

"I don't know what I'd do without you."

Kerris, however, was not hearing him, finding himself in a warm and twisty world of snow and powdery white things and his brother's voice. At the moment, it was a very good place to be.

***

It was obviously the place to be.

It had no name, this strange cobbled building with tiled roof, scarlet wash and small, blackened windows. It had no sign above the door, no crest nor emblem to distinguish it from any other dwelling on the road to *Sha'Hadin.* To the general populace, it was known simply as 'the Inn' or, to the more poetically inclined, 'The Inn on the Roof of the World.' Perched on the crest of this great, remote mountain, it was an agora for all sorts of activity, serving both commerce and recreation with equal, alcoholic measure. Naturally, it was also the epicenter of all matters illegal, from whoring to the opium trade to bartering in stolen goods. It was constantly busy, this strange, cobbled Inn and even more so after dark, when the sun drew her starry blanket to cover her eyes and the impish moon came out to play.

The noise and laughter died quickly as the band of strangers walked through the door. In fact, the smoky room grew suddenly silent, the only sounds being the clinking of sakeh pots and the thudding of boots as all eyes turned toward the newcomers. Soon, even those sounds ceased as a young lion of regal bearing crossed the wooden floor to the bar.

"I wish to speak to the owner," said the lion.

There were three cats behind the bar and two of them fled, leaving a heavy-set tiger with small, yellow eyes.

"That'd be me," said the tiger, in a different tongue.

"Is Hinyan the tongue of these parts?"

"Maybe."

"My name is Kirin Wynegarde-Grey," he said in Hinyan. "I am Captain of the Guard of Empress Thothloryn Parillaud Markova Wu. We are here in her service."

"Yeah?"

"We need rooms. Four rooms, actually, and the use of your—"

"We're full."

Kirin took a cleansing breath.

"I say again, we are in need of four rooms for the night. And stabling for several horses."

"And I say again, we're full."

The tiger was grinning, egged on by the snickers of the crowd. He was accustomed to being a rather big koi in this small pond. Captains and guards and empresses had little to do with his day-to-day living, up here on the Roof of the World.

The Captain leaned across the bar.

"I'm afraid I must insist you accommodate us, sir. You and your guests will be well reimbursed, and you yourself will be doing a great service for your Queen."

"Well, why don't you just tell her Excellency to get on up here herself. I'd be more than happy to service her in person..."

That drew laughter from the drunken crowd. The lion was as still as a statue.

"That, *sidi,* was a very bad answer." He straightened up from the bar. "Major?"

The dagger whistled past his cheek and thudded into the heavy cedar barrels behind the bar. The innkeep's head went with it, pinned as it was by the tuft of a black-tipped ear. He screamed and twisted, trying to pry the hilt out of his hair, when a strong, tawny hand touched his chin.

"Do not struggle, *sidi,* for if you pull it out, I'm afraid I will have to ask the Major to pierce the other. Now, do I have your full attention?"

The tiger gave a swift nod. A thin line of blood began to trickle down his neck.

"Very good." Kirin laced his fingers across the bar. "As I said earlier, we have need of four rooms, stabling for our horses, and exclusive use of your, your 'lobby' just for tonight. Do you agree? Say yes."

"Yes. Yes."

"Major, you may retrieve your dagger." He nodded to the pinned innkeep. "Thank you, *sidi.* We are in your debt."

He turned away from the bar, catching Ursa's arm as she strode past him. With his other hand, he stroked a lock of his thick, smooth hair. Several strands were broken.

"That was close, Major."

"Sorry, sir." Her eyes gleamed unapologetically.

The Captain strode to the centre of the room, taking a position where all eyes could see.

"*Sidis, sidali.* Thank you for your patience, but I'm afraid I must ask you all to leave. The Inn is closed for the night."

Many furtive glances bounced off his tall Imperial form, but oddly enough, no one moved to obey. He sighed deeply. Sometimes people confounded him.

His hand fell to the hilt of his long sword, the *katanah*. It was drawn rarely, for it was rarely needed, but its presence was a reminder to all not only of his authority, but of his ability to see that his orders were carried out.

In a smooth, fluid motion, he flung the sword from its sheath, sending it sailing through the air like a shirh'khin, tip over hilt to thud into the wood of the far door. It wavered a moment, then grew still. Along its blade were bits and pieces of the various patrons – a lock of hair, a sliver of fabric, a slice of leather, all skewered into the door like a feline shish'khebab.

"*Taijutsu,*" breathed the Major. "Well done."

Kirin sighed. "I believe the door is that way."

"Bye!" sang Fallon as she held the door. "Good night, now! Thanks for calling! Come again!"

Within moments, the lobby was empty save the ten newcomers and the tiger behind the bar.

Kirin turned back to the innkeep.

"*Sidi,* we have traveled far, and endured much. What do you have on your menu for supper?"

The tiger disappeared into the kitchens to prepare supper for ten unexpected, uninvited guests. And for the first time in memory, the Inn on the Roof of the World was closed for business.

***

In Imperial once again, the Captain addressed the four guards standing before him.

"You will split your shift, tonight. One will guard this corridor, for I in no wise trust these people. A second will guard the stables, for the same reasons. The other two will sleep and relieve the first pair at the end of the Second Watch. I leave it to you to decide amongst yourselves who will take the first shift."

As one, the leopards nodded and split into pairs with perfect precision. Kirin smiled to himself. He was proud of these men, of their dedication to duty and unwavering commitment to the Empire.

He could not have trained them any better. It weighed heavily upon him that they had lost so many so soon.

He stepped back into the room.

It was one of the four that had been so ceremoniously 'selected' for them by the innkeep and his meager staff. It was small but adequate, cozy even, with dark mahogany walls and floor of the same. But it, like every other corner in this two-level building, was in desperate need of a mop and a broom, and the bed linens spoke volumes to years of satisfied customers. Just to think of it sent shudders up Kirin's spine.

None of this seemed to matter to Kerris. He was sprawled facedown on the thick mattress, shirtless and bootless and apparently tumbling headlong into dreams. The Alchemist had given him yet another of the strange 'powdery things' and its effect had been almost immediate. Kirin crossed the floor to check on the conditions of his wounds. He shook his head. It seemed as though they were closing up already and he wondered if something more than competent stitchery was involved.

He walked to the window and threw open the smoky glass pane.

The moon was rising over the Great Mountains.

It glistened off the snow, giving the night a surreal midday glow. There were countless stars in the clear sky, including the newest which sparkled like a crystal. Silver peaks towered all around them, and in his mind's eye, he could see *Pol'Lhasa,* nestled deep within the Mother's Arms. He prayed they were sleeping well.

More especially, that *she* was sleeping well.

But he also knew that she would be concerned that they had not arrived as promised. No, she would not be sleeping well at all.

And for that simple fact, neither would he.

***

"I can't sleep."

Sherah al Shiva turned to her companion.

"You are in pain?"

"Oh, no, not really. Not 'pain', really, just... sore. Stiff. You know..."

Fallon Waterford rolled her head forward, wrapping her hands behind her neck and stretching the muscles along her shoulders and back. She was sitting cross-legged on the bed and her elbows and knees stuck up all over.

"I don't often get swept up in avalanches and go flying off cliffs and have to climb up handsome young lions everyday, you know. In fact, I think the closest I've ever come to that kind of thing was the time I built a catapult... Yeah, that was close..."

"A cat-a-pult?"

"Yeah, I read about one once in a very old book. It's kind of a ground-based 'sling for rocks.' Apparently the Ancestors used to 'pult' cats. Anyway, I tried it out, and it worked really well but when I tried to pult someone, he sailed up and away and into the sky and never came back. Which was a shame, since he was my very first suitor and all. My only suitor actually. I never really figured out why, considering I have such pretty markings."

Sherah smiled. "You are very amusing."

"That's not what my father said."

"I can help you with your neck."

Fallon glanced up from her rather awkward position on the bed. "You can?"

The Alchemist pulled her long legs from underneath her and rose from the mattress. She crossed the room to where several of her bags lay, some neatly packed, others in total disarray. When she straightened up, in her hands was a small black bundle. She began to unroll a strip of leather.

Fallon watched as she folded the leather back on itself to reveal a long row of needles, shiny and sharp. Sherah held several up to the candlelight.

"My, my neck is feeling much better, really..."

"Oh no," purred the cheetah, and she crossed the floor towards her. "I don't think so..."

***

"I don't think so."

Ursa and Sireth studied the bed.

"Not to worry, Major. I am accustomed to sleeping on the floor. You may have the bed."

Pale blue eyes flashed at him. "You are old. *I* will sleep on the floor."

"Thank you for the sentiment," he replied. "But you are of a Pure Race, delicate of limb and fragile of form. I would hate to see you bruise your pelt."

She snatched a dagger from her hip and lunged.

Instinctively, he closed his eyes, wincing at the sound of steel tearing cloth. After a brief moment, he opened his eyes again to find himself in one piece.

The mattress, on the other hand, was not so fortunate.

With a nasty smirk, she slid the dagger back into its sheath.

"Did you think I was going to hurt you, Seer? That would be disobeying orders, wouldn't it?"

"I daresay."

Stiffly, she stepped up onto the hard board of the bed and, placing one boot heel on the far half of the mattress, kicked it off the bed.

"Your side."

She pivoted, and did the same, until the two halves lay on opposite sides of the frame.

"My side."

Sireth watched her step down onto 'her side', curling her white-clad legs underneath her. She began the process of removing all the swords, knives and shir'khins strapped all over her body, her upper arms, her thighs, her back, deep within her boots. Each was then viciously slammed, point down, along the wooden frame, until she had formed a fence of silver steel, further heightening the separation between them.

She rolled her sleeves up to her elbows and, with a toss of her marbled hair, flipped onto her belly and rose onto the points of her toes, legs taut. She began to push herself up and down on one hand. He found himself impressed with the well-defined musculature of her arms.

He moved to 'his side' of the bed. He turned his back to her and began to loosen his sash.

"What are you doing?"

"Hmm?"

She peered at him through a curtain of hair. "What do you think you're doing?"

"I was going to remove my robe."

"Why? *Why?!*"

"Well, it seems you took this room's only blanket along with 'your side' of the bed. I shall use my outer robe as a blanket for myself."

She stared at him, eyes sharp, breathing shallow. If he didn't know better, he would have thought her afraid.

He tugged at a brown leather sleeve, showed the linen and a flash of orange underneath.

"There are many layers."

"Good," Ursa snapped quickly. "It will get cold here in the night."

And in a swift motion, she flipped over onto her side, back to him, beyond the fence of silver daggers.

Sireth lowered himself onto the mattress, deciding that for the time being, it might be safer to leave his robes on. He watched her for a while longer, before shaking his head and reaching for the candle.

"Good night, Major."

"If you snore, I will kill you."

He blew out the flame.

***

The Inn was as dark and quiet as a panther. The guard on duty stood at complete attention, his spotted ears swiveling at every sound, but there were few this night save for the crackling of the great hearth that warmed the place. He could hear the Captain, moving about in his room, unsettled and sleepless as he wrestled with the losses of the day. He could hear the brother, letting out the occasional moan of pain as the Alchemist's strange medicines began to wear thin.

From the middle room, he could hear voices, as the Scholar

rambled long into the night. Her rapid-fire conversations were punctuated by whines and whimpers, almost as if she were being pricked by many sharp points. He could hear the Alchemist herself, humming in strange, exotic keys.

From the far room, he could hear nothing at all and wondered if the Major hadn't killed her charge sometime during the night. He would not have been surprised. She terrified him.

He yawned, stretched his arms over his head, flexing his sharp, black claws. Not long to go now, he thought and soon, he would be relieved, sent to slumber in a room down the hall. He was looking forward to it.

It was the middle of the Second Watch.

***

Ursa opened her eyes.

She did not know how long she had lain there awake, for the room was clothed in blackness. Pale moonlight shone in from the cold, night sky, but clouds had covered the stars, dimming their usual brightness.

She could hear breathing.

Rapid, shallow breathing, like the sound of a cornered enemy, seeing its death in her face. It was a sound she knew well.

There was a flash of movement out of the corner of her eye and she rolled to her feet, crouched and poised to spring. Her pupils grew wide and she could see shadows now, and moonlight glinting off the furniture. A figure was pressed into the far wall, back flattened against the oily wood. It was a tall figure, the mane long and dark, and she knew at once it was the Seer.

She rose to her feet.

"What?"

He did not look at her, did not seem even to have heard, his gaze fixed on the window, with its dirty, smoked glass. She scowled and moved around the bed towards him.

"What is it? Answer me."

"Animals..."

"What? What animals?"

"Everywhere... animals..."

"Your voice—"

The last thing she remembered was the smell of leather as the blow sent her backwards into a much deeper blackness.

***

Kirin opened his eyes.

He did not know how long he had lain there awake, for the room was clothed in blackness. Something was wrong, he knew it instinctively and rather than let it eat away at him, he rolled off the mattress and out of the bed.

He checked once on his brother, still deep in sleep but moving as if in dreams. He pulled on his boots, gathered his long hair into a queue at the back of his neck and crossed the room to the door.

The guard was waiting at the door.

"Sir," was all he said.

"Where?"

"The Major's room, sir. I—"

The explanation was interrupted by the sudden shattering of glass. Kirin bolted down the corridor, the leopard on his heels and together they threw open the door to the Major's room. A gust of cold wind greeted them. Kirin grabbed a torch from beside the doorframe and shone it into the shadows.

"Major?"

A groan from beside the bed, and he rushed toward it. Ursa Laenskaya lay in a crumpled pile on the floor, a smear of blood at her mouth. He took her elbow and helped her to her feet.

"He hit me," she murmured, spitting a mouthful of blood before her eyes flashed. "He hit me! I'll *kill* him."

Kirin stepped to the window, leaning out as far as he could, feeling broken glass crunch under his palm. Clouds obscured the moon and earlier, the midday sun had melted all the snow around the Inn. There was no sign of the Seer, save a skid of freshly churned earth where his feet had landed.

When he turned 'round, the room was full of people.

"You, you and you," he jabbed a finger at the three leopards.

"Alert the guard in the stables. Find Sireth benAramis now and return him to the Inn."

"Sir," they echoed as one, and left the room.

Kirin swung around to face the others, the Scholar and Alchemist, both of whom had obviously been alerted by the crash.

"I thank you for your concern, but we shall handle this. *Sidala*, if you could tend to my brother. I believe his pain is returning."

"Of course, *sidi.*"

She slunk from the room.

"Are you sure I can't help, sir?" asked the Scholar. "I was pretty good at tracking bukbuks back home."

Kirin reached out to remove a tiny needle sticking out of her forehead. He handed it to her.

"Thank you, *sidala,* but I'm quite certain the Queen's guard can locate one man, this quickly after he has gone missing."

"Oh, yes, yes I'm quite certain they can too, sir. I didn't mean to say, that is to say—"

"Thank you, *sidala.* That will be all."

He tried to move around her, but she stepped into his path.

"Um, I'm really sorry, sir, but, um..."

He glared at her. She swallowed, wrung her hands, took a deep breath.

"Captain, your men are probably really good at tracking down criminals and soldiers and monsters and things like that, but, none of them are tigers, sir. They can't think like a tiger. I can. "

"What is your point, *sidala?*"

"Well, sir, it *is* the middle of the Second Watch, isn't it?"

Kirin swore under his breath.

"Of course. Go. And *sidala,* be careful."

She smiled and disappeared out the door.

Kirin swore again, this time not under his breath and he began to pace.

"I can't believe it. I can't *believe* it!" With a snarl, he stamped the mahogany planks of the floor. "It completely escaped me! I didn't even think it might happen again!"

"I didn't think of it either, sir," said the Major.

"It is not your job to think of it. It's mine."

"We will find him, sir."

"No, Major. *She* will."

***

Fallon watched them split up into pairs and head off around the Inn, swords drawn and ready for anything.

What was she thinking? These were trained men, the best there were to be in the Queen's Elite. She was a skinny little tigress. What could she hope to accomplish that they couldn't? *Why couldn't she ever keep her mouth shut?*

Emerald eyes cast upwards, to a narrow cart-path that likely led to isolated farms up in the mountains. The sky was black, the path slick with ice and frozen mud, and to fall from such a slope would most certainly give her more than wobbly legs and snowy hair. But she remembered how gently the Seer had held her, how like her own father he had stroked her hair.

She squared her chin and set off up the path.

***

Kerris opened his eyes, only to be greeted by large golden ones.

"Hello, *sidalady* cheetah," he said, smiling. "My, but you have lovely eyes."

She kissed him.

"Well," he said, and his hands pulled her down onto the bed.

***

Fallon Waterford paused to pace in a small, tight circle.

"Now, if I was a tiger, which I am, this would be where I would want to hide. You can see everything from up here, right down to the Inn - Oh, look, I can see the guards right now. *Hm.* And it would be pretty hard to sneak up on you from above. Yep, this is where I'd hide. Wow, this is so beautiful..."

Her breath frosted the air in front of her face as she drew her cloak around her throat and let her eyes linger over the view laid out below her. The mountains in the moonlight, so ethereal yet so very real beneath her boots. She could almost see the clouds, springing up from the valleys like the breath of a dragon. And the star, brighter than any in the sky, bright as a tiny sun –

A gloved hand wrapped across her mouth and pulled her down onto the rocks.

***

Ursa glanced down at the Inn, dark save for a few windows glowing with candlelight. This was very wrong, she thought grimly, very strange. She hated to see her Captain upset. He was far too compassionate for his own good. She would have handled this matter much differently had she been in charge.

Icy blue eyes darted up to his silhouetted figure. She studied the noble carriage and stoic demeanor as he picked his way over snow and rock in pursuit of the tigress. Such was the way with lions. People rarely challenged their authority so when a challenge did arise, they were often slower to respond than the smaller cats. Her Captain was always more concerned with 'why' a challenge should be presented, rather than dealing with it swiftly and without remorse.

Ursa never needed to know why.

She tossed her head and followed her Captain, picking her own way over the rocks.

***

Her heart was racing in her chest, as the hand tightened across her mouth. She had been pulled down next to an outcropping of rocks and while a part of her was terrified, the other part felt warm and secure. She could smell leather. She knew where she was and who it was that had her.

"Shhh," said his voice in her ear, at the same time familiar yet strange. "Can you hear them?"

"Mmeea mmoo?"

"The animals. This place is crawling with animals."

She allowed her eyes to dart upwards for a glimpse of his face. All she could make out was the beard. The rest was obscured by loose, dark hair. His grip was tight and he was breathing quickly, much the same as the previous night when in the clutches of the Terror. He was in those clutches now even as he spoke, for also like the previous night, he was speaking in the common accent of the tiger.

"The others are dead," he said. "The cold – it had to be. Something's gone wrong. There's no power. No tech. Nothing. How could this happen?"

Fallon swallowed hard but, steeling her resolve, reached up with trembling fingers to lower his gloved palm from her mouth.

"Who are you?"

"How could this happen? How long have we been down here?"

"Please, *sidi,* can you hear me? Can you tell me who you are?"

"Max?"

"No. My name is Fallon Waterford. I'm a Scholar in the Court of the Empress. Who are you?"

"What? You don't you know? Check your files – I'm there. Super Seven, the comedian. I think they wrote that. Check for me, will you?"

"Oh. Um..." She frowned, understanding the context if not the phrase. "There's been a small problem, um, with the um, *file.*"

He laughed, a short sharp bark of a laugh.

"Is that what they're calling it? A small problem with the file? Six supervisors dead which means all the Subs in limbo, no power, no links, no communications whatsoever, except of course, for you, my friend, whoever the hell you are. And then, to top it off, there's all these, these horrible creepy little animals."

She felt his grip weaken, as if suddenly the strength were gone from his muscles. She too relaxed her body until he pushed her away, lowering his head in apparent exhaustion.

"It doesn't matter. None of it matters. I'll probably be dead by morning anyway."

For some strange reason, she felt sorry for him, for this strange tiger, trapped in the Seer's soul. She reached out a tentative hand to touch his cheek.

His head snapped up and he clasped her hand to his face, eyes growing sharp with focus.

"Kittens," he gasped. "Six kittens. Six grey striped kittens."

Then suddenly, Sireth benAramis was back, blinking and panting and pulling her hand away.

"*Sidala,* forgive me. I — Why are we outside?"

A darker shadow passed in front of the moon. Fallon glanced up to see a tall, regal silhouette, a shorter, slimmer one rising by his side.

"Oh mother," said the tigress.

"Sireth benAramis, you are under arrest."

TO MARKET

The sun was chasing the moon back beyond the mountains, sweeping the darkness away with her golden brooms and dusting the clouds with brushes dipped in honey. In the Great Mountains, it seemed that half the Kingdom was sky and that the other half was constantly reaching to claim it, trying to snare the clouds with her peaks and luring the heavens downwards into stark, empty valleys. Even still, the sky went on forever.

A slim, scarlet figure swept through the halls of *Pol'Lhasa,* as swiftly as her slippered feet would carry her. She had not slept and as the night had marched, watch by watch, into the breaking of a new day, she found claws as sharp as daggers digging into her heart.

His party had not returned to *DharamShallah.*

Leopard guards as still as stone watched her as she carried down the long, high antechamber to the Throne Room. The great gold and red door opened and she flowed inside, the many layers of skirt and sash sweeping the marble floor as surely as servants. The dawn sun sliced down with beams of light and color and many a day she often felt she could reach out and catch those beams in the palm of her hand. Today, she brushed right through them toward a far, curtained corner glowing in tones of scarlet and jade.

The falcon was still alive.

She breathed a sigh of relief as it chirruped an early-morning greeting. It was perched as before on the wrought-iron pedestal, hooded and belled, its tiny head bobbing with quick, sharp movements. She stroked its downy breast.

"Good morning, dear Path. I trust you slept well."

From a deep, embroidered sleeve, Empress Thothloryn Parillaud Markova Wu withdrew a slip of parchment. She held it fast as if not daring let it go. Finally, she brought the parchment to her lips and closed her eyes, letting it linger there a while longer with perhaps the most intimate of Royal Seals. Finally, she tied it securely to the banded leg and the bird sprang to her wrist as she moved to stand beside the window.

She threw it open and removed the hood. With a shrill cry, the falcon lit from her arm, talon bells jingling and streaked off into the blinding sun of morning.

"You carry my heart with you, Path of *Sha'Hadin,"* she whispered to the fading silhouette. "Find my Captain. Find him well. It is all that I can hope."

And she remained at the window for a very long time.

***

Kerris yawned and stretched his arms over his head, flexing his grey claws toward the ceiling. He flexed his toe claws as well, for he was bootless at the moment and he enjoyed the tingling sensation across the tops of his feet. *Toe flexing was an odd luxury,* he thought to himself, for since kittenhood, people were trained to curb that inborn tendency in favor of footwear. Unsheathed pedal claws made for a very good climb but were generally rather hard on one's shoes.

He sat for a moment on the edge of his bed taking a moment to orient himself to his surroundings. He was quite accustomed to waking up in strange places, in even stranger beds. It never seemed to bother him much, for most important things in life were constant no matter where you found yourself. Such things as the sky above, the ground below and breakfast. And at least he was waking, he reminded himself. That was more than could be said for some.

The mahogany floor was cold so he reached under the bed for his yak-hide boots. As he did, he noticed his arms swathed in wraps of fine linen. He tried to remember the reason for them but it was escaping him. Perhaps he had gotten drunk. Things like this frequently happened when the ale and rice wine flowed too freely, which they often did in the company of tigers. Frowning, he scratched the back of his neck only to find more problems there. Tentative fingers traced the ruts in his shoulders, his back and again, he had no recollection of the cause.

It disturbed him.

He rose from the mattress and padded to the door, cracking it open ever so gently and peering out into the hall. He saw no one but heard many raised voices from the great room down below, his brother's among them. It sounded rather touchy and since Kerris hated business of that sort, he decided that whatever it was that he wasn't remembering could probably wait.

He reached into a pocket, pulled out a stick. 'Six' is what it read.

Six.

He closed the door and went back to bed.

***

"You *hit* me!"

"I'm sorry.'

Kirin swung around. "You do not deny it, then?"

"How can I deny what I do not remember?"

"So you say," Ursa seethed, pushing her face up into his. "But your fists speak louder than your words, Seer."

Sireth benAramis shook his head, lowering his eyes to the floor. He stood in the middle of the Inn's Great Room, hands bound behind his back, the Major circling him like a shark.

Three of the four leopards were also present, each with blades drawn and ready. On top of a table nearby the Scholar sat, knuckles between her knees, her brows knit together in worry. The Alchemist leaned against a wall, apparently engrossed in braiding her hair with strands of silver thread.

The innkeep had broached the subject of breakfast only once before quickly disappearing into the kitchens. And the Captain of the Guard was at the heart of it all.

"Are you maintaining that this, this spell is the same as that which befell you in *Sha'Hadin?*"

"I don't know."

"If so, where was the cold? Where was the ice?"

"I don't know."

"He's lying," hissed the Major.

"Are you?"

"No."

"Why should I believe you?"

"Because you want to."

"I believe him," said the tigress.

"Then you are a fool." The Major wheeled upon her Captain. "Sir, I demand reparation. He hit me. He does not deny this. It is my right."

Kirin ground his molars. The Seer's words were true. He wanted to believe. But there it was, the 'darkness' in his own glass. If the man was innocent, then he was not the enemy. If he were not the enemy, then the enemy was still unknown, still at large and still capable of bringing destruction down on the Upper Kingdom. It was far easier to believe that this threat could be removed, quickly and cleanly, by the edge of a sword.

Finally, he nodded.

"It is your right, Major. Vindicate yourself."

Like lightning she struck, her small fist swinging in a fierce arc that connected with a **crack** on the Seer's jaw. Though considerably taller than she, the force was sufficient to send him staggering back into two of the guards. They caught him with well-trained precision.

"Wow," whispered the Scholar to the Alchemist. "That was good. I wish I could do that. I hit like a girl."

"You are a girl," said the Alchemist.

"Oh. Maybe that's why."

"An eye for an eye, a tooth for a tooth," said Kirin. "Major, the matter is settled. You no longer have grievance against this man."

"Yes, sir."

She took several steps back, grinding her fist into her palm with a grin.

"Interesting, Captain," said Sireth, working his jaw back and forth. "How swiftly justice moves when one is pure of Race."

"Race has nothing to do with this, *sidi.*"

"Oh, it hasn't? As I recall, you were sent to *Sha'Hadin* to save, oh do let me recall…*me!* What will your Empress think when you tell her that, somewhere along the way, you decided I wasn't worth saving?"

"She is *your* Empress as well, *sidi,*" said Kirin.

"I had thought so," said Sireth. "Until you abolished the Council."

"I saved your life."

"So you could take it later. Yes, yes, I've been there before."

"Watch your tongue," Ursa growled.

"Captain, I am not the enemy."

The exact words. Kirin eyed him with renewed suspicion.

"Convince me."

"Free my hands and I shall."

"I find many things about this matter disturbing, *sidi.* It was you yourself who suggested that we spend the night here, in this place, a place you seem to have some familiarity with. Moreover, you did not wish to make the journey to *Pol'Lhasa* at all and here again, we find ourselves not there. Yes, I find these things disturbing."

"You intend to blame me for the avalanche, Captain? Was I somehow the cause of that?"

Kirin felt a pang of guilt, for his brother had warned him of the dangers that very morning. But he had no intention of tipping his just hand yet. There was simply too much at stake. Instead, he merely shrugged.

"Many things are possible at the seventh level, *sidi.*"

"Perhaps he is a firestarter..."

All eyes swung in the direction of the Alchemist. She did not look up, however, seeming quite content to study the braid she had been working on all morning.

"A firestarter? Explain."

"It is as it sounds, *sidi.* One who starts fires, only…" Now she did look up. "Not by conventional means."

"Is this possible?"

Sireth snorted.

"Yes," purred the cheetah as she now began to unravel the braid, plait by plait. "It would not take much for such a Soul to focus his thoughts and melt the snow beneath the mass. It was happening anyway. It would simply be a matter of timing."

Kirin turned back to the Seer.

"Is this true? Are you a firestarter, sir?"

"I am the last Seer of *Sha'Hadin.* Would you be asking such a question of Petrus Mercouri were he standing in my place?"

"Answer the question."

Fallon glanced nervously at the faces all around her. The accusation had not been denied and the tension was unbearable, but she could think of no way to break it. She tugged at her laces, and waited.

Finally, the Seer smiled.

"If I were as you say, Captain, then I would have little faith in these bonds at my wrists, for it would take nothing at all to burn them clean through."

"Take him upstairs."

Two of the three guards stepped forward and with a shake of his head, Sireth benAramis allowed himself to be ushered past the Captain. He paused for a brief moment.

"Be careful what and whom you believe, Captain. It is not my soul you are damning but your own."

Kirin stepped aside and together the three men began the climb up the stairs that led to the upper rooms. Ursa pivoted to follow. The Captain stopped her.

"Do *not* touch him. Is that clear?"

She nodded swiftly and was gone, the clacking of heels on hard wood fading up the steps and down the long corridor.

The Captain lowered himself onto a bench, elbows on the table and began to rub his aching forehead.

With her heart in her throat, Fallon slid off the far table and approached him, nervously tugging a well-tugged lace of her vest.

"Um, sir, I just want to say..."

He glared up at her from under his brow.

"I just want to say that I - I'm sure you'll do the right thing. Sir."

"Thank you, *sidala.*"

"I mean, even if it is hard to understand. It's not always a distinction that is easy to make."

"I know."

"'Cause I know what I heard last night, sir, and I heard a tiger. A tiger, right and sure."

"I *know.*"

"Would you like a cup of tea?"

Immediately, he cursed himself. He was just about to ask her to leave him alone for a while. Confound him and his accursed 'dark glass.'

"That would be very nice. Thank you, *sidala.*"

She smiled and disappeared into the kitchen. That left him alone with the Alchemist. At least, she wasn't humming.

"You seem to know a great deal of this matter, *sidala.*"

"I know a great deal in many matters, *sidi.*" She seemed about to leave it at that but for some reason, she decided otherwise. "Unlike yourself, I was not sent out unprepared."

"What does that mean?"

"The First Mage is not valued counsel for nothing, *sidi.* He believes it is his duty to be informed of all aspects of the Kingdom, from the very number of guards in each regiment to the histories of the men sitting on the Council of Seven. How else could he faithfully advise the Empress?"

"How else indeed?" Kirin sat very still, weighing her words against the inner voice that nagged within. "Tell me what you know."

"I know nothing for fact, *sidi,* but..."

"Tell me."

She pouted, picked at her hair, rolled her eyes to the ceiling.

"Sidala?"

"Have you heard how he got his scar?"

"No."

"It is believed that he got it while killing a lion in the National Guard, *sidi.* Only the intervention of Petrus Mercouri saved his neck from the executioner's blade."

It is not my soul you are damning, the man had said, *but your own.*

The Captain sat back for a long moment, feeling a weight settle onto his shoulders. None of this was good. None of this belonged. He regarded the woman with a frown.

"What else has the First Mage seen fit to tell you?"

"Enough."

"Riddles. Again, riddles. You are not being helpful."

Suddenly, she was beside him, moving with such lithe grace that it caught him unawares. He had not, in fact, seen her move. She straddled the bench, bringing her proud Aegypshan face only inches away and the incense that wafted from her was rich and heady.

"I *can* help you, *sidi.*" Her golden eyes were intense, almost pleading. "Just say the word."

For some strange reason, his thoughts began to grow muddy as she moved closer still, almost sucking his breath out through his lips. He wanted to pull away but he couldn't, couldn't think, couldn't breathe. He wanted to...he wanted...

"Tea, sir. Hot and sweet, and – *oh.* Sorry!"

He broke away as the tigress placed the mug before him. He cupped it, feeling the heat radiate through ceramic into his palms. He took a large mouthful, wincing as that same heat scalded his tongue, bringing him swiftly, fiercely back to reality.

The Alchemist rose from the bench.

"I will take my leave of you, *sidi.* Your brother should be waking—"

"No!" he snapped. "But thank you, *sidala.* I shall check on Kerris soon enough. You are dismissed."

She smiled as she headed up the stairs to the middle room.

He waited until he heard the click of her door before he allowed himself to relax.

"She's a little strange, I guess, but I think she means well."

Kirin glanced up at the Scholar, sunshine after shadow.

"No, *sidala,* I don't think she means anything of the sort." He smiled a weary smile. "Please, sit. I wish to know your impressions of this matter."

"Oh. Well. Alright." Fallon slid her backside onto the rough wood of the tabletop, clasping her hands between her knees. "Can I have a sip of your tea?"

He offered her the mug and she gulped it in hungrily, and gulped again, leaving her with a wet puma's moustache. She wiped her mouth with her sleeve and handed the mug back.

"Thanks. Um, okay, you want to know what I think these 'spells' are?"

He stared into the dregs of his mug. There was nothing left.

"Yes."

"I haven't a clue."

"Hm."

"But, I have a story."

"I am not surprised."

"Well, my father used to raise pheasants. Golden crested pheasants. Pretty things. Nasty personalities though. Very aggressive. Very stupid. Any way, he had this prized hen, one he had hand-reared from the shell. He had bred her and was anxiously awaiting her clutch, when just before she was to lay, she escaped the pheasantry and was gone."

She bugged her eyes at him, as if he should appreciate the seriousness of the situation. He simply stared at her.

"Now, I had only six summers when all this happened, and one day soon after, when I was exploring in the forest, I came across her nest. Father had figured she would be a bad sitter, being hand-reared and all –"

"*Sidala*, does this in any way pertain to the matter at hand?"

"Oh, I think so. Maybe. Probably. Just hang on. So, turns out that Father was right. There it was, a clutch of four perfect eggs, left alone on the jungle floor. I knew that I should have gone immediately to fetch him, but they were already starting to crack, so... I didn't."

She frowned, and said nothing more for several seconds.

"And?"

"And? Oh, I watched. I sat there and watched, as one by one, these tiny prized chicks struggled to get free from their shells. I wanted to see it happen. I had always been so curious about it, but one by one, it didn't happen at all. One by one, I watched their struggles grow weaker and the shells got the better of them, and one by one, they died. Until I - I couldn't stand it anymore and for the fourth and final chick, I broke open the shell and helped it out onto my palm. It was all brown and wet and ugly, but it was alive and I had helped it be free."

She turned those earnest emerald eyes on him.

"It seems to me that we have the same situation here. One by one, something has been killing the Council of Seven, and I can only think that this... this 'something' has been trying to break out, to break free, just like those chicks, and using the Council to do it. I mean, who better than such sensitive and powerful souls? So finally, by helping Sireth survive, we have helped *it* survive and now it is free. But, like that little chick, it is not safe, its existence not secure. I think it still needs our help. That little chick died, Captain. Even with all my help, all my 'valiant efforts' on its behalf, it just curled up in my palm and died. This fellow with the voice of a tiger is afraid. He thinks he is going to die - he told me so last night. And I'm afraid that if he does die, he will take Sireth and the last of the Council along with him."

She shrugged, pouted and shook her head.

"I can't imagine any thing else. Unless of course..."

"Yes?"

"Well, unless of course, he's gone completely mad..." She shrugged again. "Either one."

Kirin sat quietly for some time, allowing the echo of her words to sink in. Finally, he sighed.

"You are wise for one so young, *sidala.* Thank you."

"Oh, that's alright. Don't mention it. Except maybe to my father. He's still angry at me for losing his hen."

"*Sidala?*"

"Oh, didn't I say? Yeah, I was the one who forgot to close the pheasantry door. We lost all the pheasants that night. Just like that. One little mistake and – Poof! No more pheasants. Yep, he was *pretty* mad..."

With that, Kirin rose from the table and began the climb to the second floor.

***

The sound was the sound of steel on steel, the slicing and scraping of razor-sharp edges as Major Ursa Laenskaya crouched in a corner of the drafty room. In her hands were two of the many daggers she had retrieved from the silver 'fence' along the bedframe and she was busy honing their blades lest they be needed anytime soon. Occasionally, she allowed her icy eyes to dart to the Seer, silent and seated on the mahogany floor. She was mapping herself a target area of heart, lungs and other vital organs. She could carve him like a springbuck, given the chance.

"Does the sharpening of my blades annoy you, Seer?"

Naturally, there was no response. She rose to her feet.

"Did I hurt you earlier? Perhaps you bit your tongue."

Again, nothing.

With a sneer, she flipped one knife to grasp it by the blade and sent it hissing down next to the Seer's knee. He did not flinch. Indeed, it was as if he had not noticed. She flipped the second in her palm and flung it hard, thudding into the hollow between his crossed legs. *A good shot*, if she had to admit it herself. Once again, there was no reaction whatsoever.

She wanted a reaction.

Her boot heels snapped like angry dogs as she strutted across the room, crouching down in front of him. She yanked the first dagger out of the hardwood and slid it into its sheath. The second she also retrieved but let it roll about in her palm as if deciding its fate. She regarded the Seer.

"I should kill you now."

Finally, Sireth opened his eyes.

"Perhaps you should, Major. It would seem that your Captain has no taste for bloodshed. As for me, I am looking forward to seeing Petrus again. We have much to discuss."

"Pah! An old man's folly. When you die, you die. There is nothing beyond that. Nothing."

"Even that would be preferable to this."

Ursa sat back on her haunches, flicking the hilt up and down in her fingers.

"Perhaps I won't kill you, then. Perhaps I will just take out your good eye."

"I would still see more clearly than you," he whispered.

She waggled the point of the knife under his chin.

"See? That's what I hate about people like you."

"People like me? Mongrel people?"

"Seers. Scholars. Alchemists. Even grey-coated lions. People who think they are better than others because kharma has given them something no one else has. Making them think they are *more* because of something they didn't earn. Judging others as inferior, weak, less. *That's* what I hate about people like you."

"And here, all along I thought you simply hated the beard."

"That too."

When the Seer smiled at her, she was confused so she rose to her feet, sheathing the dagger into the leather at her arm. She crossed the room, to take up her position in the corner once again.

Finally, there was the approaching sound of boots on hardwood and the door creaked open under the Captain's hand.

"Leave us."

"Sir."

She slipped out through the door, grabbing the heavy iron latch behind her. As the door closed, she heard the singing of steel and she risked a glance inward. The Captain was advancing on the Seer. He had drawn his short sword.

The door thudded shut.

Major Ursa Laenskaya stayed very still for a long moment, puzzling at this strange new sensation that was sinking her stomach like a stone. Finally, she shook her head and went down for breakfast.

***

"Good morning, Kerris your name was."

"And a very good morning to you, *sidalady* tigress. I hope you haven't eaten all the wontons."

"Nope. Saved the broken ones for you."

"How very considerate." Kerris lowered himself down to the table. "Is there any tea? I'm starving."

Fallon smiled at him, pushing her mug towards him with a slim, orange finger. "Hey, where's your tunic?'

He tugged at the blanket around his shoulders, wondering how in the Kingdom he could explain without really explaining, for in truth, he hadn't a clue. "Um, well, sort of, you know..."

"Look, I'm really sorry..."

"You are?"

"I didn't even think. I mean I just grabbed and well, you were just sort of *there* and well, you did say 'climb', so so I'm really sorry..."

"Right. Well, if I said 'climb' then..."

"Then..."

"Right."

He sipped at his tea or rather, *her* tea, perplexed.

"How do you feel, anyway?"

He glanced around for the innkeep, wondering if anyone was going to bring him some food.

"Well, not too bad really, all things considered."

"And your arms?"

"Funny thing about arms," he said, raising them in the air. "Can't live with 'em..."

"Can't cut 'em off!"

And the Great Room was filled with the sounds of sunny laughter.

Major Ursa Laenskaya stormed down the stairs.

"Inkeep!" she bellowed as she dropped herself on the bench beside them, "Bring me some tea!"

Within moments, several mugs of hot sweet tea were placed on the table as well as several platters of flatbreads, fruits and cheese. Pickled fish and strips of curried lamb were also presented, and soon both Kerris and Fallon were digging in, hungrily filling the gaps in their bellies as quickly as they could. The Major, on the other hand, seemed to have no appetite and merely stared at the mug in her hand.

"I don't think we'll be making the Palace today," said Kerris with a mouthful of fish. "So I'm thinking of going into the marketplace. Seems I am badly in need of a new tunic and cloak. Would either of you lovely ladies care to accompany me?"

Ursa slammed her mug down on the table. "No!"

"Well. Alrighty then."

"Mother," muttered the Scholar as she sunk low into her seat. "She needs something stronger than tea..."

With a snarl, the Major pushed herself up and away and began pacing in front of the Great Room's main hearth, arms wrapped tightly across her chest. Kerris shook his head.

"Really now Ursa, all this is a bit much, don't you think? You're tighter than the trigger on a crossbow."

"I don't have to tell you anything."

"True enough, I suppose. Sorry for caring. Forget I asked."

The Major whirled on him, her pale eyes flashing.

"*You* want to know why I'm so angry. *You?* You spoiled, insignificant excuse for a lion?"

"Well, not if you put it that way..."

"Do you really want to know?!"

Kerris swung around on the bench.

"Alright then, yes. Oh wise, unspoiled most significant excuse for a snow leopard, pray tell me. What is it that has made you so angry?"

"Your brother has just killed the Seer."

"What?" whispered the Scholar. "What did you say?"

"Oh, Life is not so funny now, is it, tigress? No smart comeback? No witty turn of phrase? Just *'What did you say?'* Surely you can do better than that."

Fallon glanced at Kerris, tears welling up in her eyes. She raised a trembling hand to cover her mouth.

"Would - would he do that?"

Kerris shrugged.

"Well, if Kirin does anything, you can be sure he has a good reason for it."

"But... but, I thought..."

"Maybe you didn't *think* at all," hissed Ursa. "This is not some game that you can play or a little while until you grow tired of it. When you swore your oath to the Captain, you placed your very life in his hands. Did you think that was a game too?"

"I –I..."

"Enough, Ursa. You don't need to make the girl feel worse than she already does. Besides, if Kirin had to kill anybody, it would be done swiftly. You can believe that. Kirin doesn't like killing. He never has."

"It's my fault. I thought I said the right thing."

"I'm sure you did."

"It *is* your fault," growled the Major. "You were the one who found him last night, Scholar. You gave him over. *You.*"

"...oh..." was all Fallon got out before crumbling like a tower of sand and she buried her face in her arms.

"Oh well done, Ursa. Why don't you go kick some old people while you're at it?"

The Major resumed her pacing and save for the occasional sob, there was silence in the Great Room for a long time.

Finally, Kerris pushed the tray away and sat back. He cast a worried look up the stairs, in the direction of the upper rooms.

"So," he said. "Where is he?"

"What?" Ursa scowled.

"Well, I've never actually had the pleasure of killing anybody myself, not intentionally and certainly not with a sword but I really can't imagine that it takes too long, now does it? Not if you have the sword and the other fellow doesn't. And Kirin is not the type to gloat over a dead body. He really doesn't like getting blood or bits of *stuff* on his uniform. A bit fussy that way, he is. So then, why hasn't he come down?"

Fallon raised her head from the table. "Why hasn't he come down?"

"That was the question, yes."

"Free my hands..."

"Come again?"

"He didn't kill him..." said Ursa, her voice unnaturally soft. "He cut the bonds."

They both glanced up at the Major. It was like looking into a stormy sky, one that was growing darker, more ominous by the moment. Suddenly, lightning flashed in her pale blue eyes.

"AhmniShakra!"

And like a thunderclap, she bolted across the room and up the stairs. Kerris and Fallon exchanged glances and followed.

***

two hearts pounding, ***madness****, the blood hot, too hot, racing, two lifetimes of memories mingling, merging,* ***utter madness****, sad old eyes smiling, weeping,* *three lifetimes now, your vision he is saying, the only key, rejoicing and* ***devastation****, your vision, old eyes,* ***Ancient eyes****, Ancestors, here and now, Captain*... ***no***... *See it*...***please, no***... *Know it*...***I don't want to know this***...

And suddenly, like a blow from a broadsword, Kirin's soul was rent in two, twisting him inside out as though his very heart were being torn from his chest. He heard a cry, a roar of pain that shattered his bones like a fall from a rooftop, until he realized it was his own voice he was hearing, his own and then somehow, his brother's and the room came spinning into focus.

He sat up, gasping for breath, fighting the pain and dizziness that threatened to send him back to the floor.

"Kerris, Kerris, what are you doing? Where is the Seer?"

"Are you alright, Kirin?"

"Where?"

Under the broken window the Seer huddled in a ball on the floor, groaning and clutching his head in his hands. Sprawled on top of him was the Major, pinning him as she had once before, this time with a fistful of mane and a dagger at his throat.

"Get away from him!" the Captain snarled as he lunged across the mahogany, throwing the woman's arms aside, sending her dagger clattering across the room.

"Sidi, can you hear me? Are you unharmed?"

"I think so," came the muffled reply. "Except..."

"Except?"

"Except I now have your headache."

With a deep puff of breath Kirin sat back and glared at the Major, teeth gritted, muscles in his jaw rippling with fury.

"What were you thinking?" he snarled, each word bitten in half.

"Sir." She drew herself up ramrod straight. "I thought he was attacking you, sir."

"What were your orders?"

"Sir—"

"Your *orders?*"

She steeled her jaw.

"To leave you alone. Sir."

"And earlier?"

"Not to touch him."

"Kirin, it did look rather odd," said Kerris. "It looked like he was cracking your skull like a coconut."

"Thank you, Kerris, but I don't recall asking your opinion."

"So sorry, dear brother, but—"

"Enough, Kerris. You have no business here, either."

"Please," Sireth moaned as he pushed himself to his knees. "No arguing. It's too loud."

"No business? No *business?* Kirin!"

"Later, Kerris."

"Kirin—"

"Too loud," the Seer moaned again, wincing as his own voice roared through his temples like a morning gong. Just as the sensation was beginning to fade, green-sleeved arms were flung around his neck and he was tackled by yet another woman. Thankfully, Fallon Waterford possessed neither the strength nor the fervor of the Major and she simply buried her tear-streaked face into his shoulder.

"I'm so glad you're alive."

"Thank you, my dear," he said, managing a thin smile. "I'm glad too."

She wrapped those arms around his waist and helped him to his feet.

The Captain stood, hands on hips and cast dark, scathing glances between the Major and his brother, as if deciding whom to behead first.

"Major," he said. "I relieve you of your charge of guarding this man. For the duration of the journey, you will be responsible for the care and maintenance of the horses."

"Sir."

There was the slightest tremor in her voice but she remained rigid, hands clasped tightly behind her back.

"Oh, giving away my job now, are you Kirin?" said Kerris. "Why don't you just go ahead and make her your guide. And make me a Major while you're at it. I need a new tunic and I think I would look smashing in all that white leather."

"Kerris, I said later."

"Captain, if I may," said the Seer, still panting as he slipped his gloves back over his hands. "The Major was simply 'doing *her* job', something you all take quite seriously it seems. You cannot punish her now because she is zealously concerned for your safety."

"You stand up for her now? After all she has done?"

"Not at all, Captain. I stand up for her for what she has yet to do."

The object of their debate stood still as stone, her eyes not wavering from the form of her Captain. For his part, her Captain ground his molars together, feeling the strain as he worked to control his rising temper. *This was not the way*, he reminded himself, not *his* way, but he feared *his* way was slipping farther and farther out of his grasp, and would very soon be torn from him, in favor of another, much older one.

It was madness.

"Very well. Major, you are reinstated as this man's guardian. You owe him your station. Do not forget that."

"No, sir."

"And Kerris..."

The Captain now turned to his brother. Kerris drew the blanket tightly across his shoulders, as if trying to retain some of the indignation that had fueled him earlier.

"Kerris, go put something on."

"I need a new tunic, Kirin. An expensive one."

"Fine. Fine. The Empress will pay."

Kerris brightened.

"Alright then. *Sidalady* tigress, shall we go to the markets?"

With a shrug, Fallon slipped from the Seer's side and accepted the arm that was offered her. The pair headed out the door and down the hall.

The Captain turned to regard the Major, as still and silent as her sword. Sireth benAramis stood at her side, towering over her as *Kathandu* towered over *Pol'Lhasa. Too bad he wasn't a snow leopard,* Kirin thought ruefully. The man actually might be a match for her.

"You may as well go too," said Kirin. "It will be a long tedious day while we wait on the Empress. See the sights. Buy what you will."

"Am I still under arrest?"

"No, but you are still under suspicion."

"So much better."

He was hard to ignore, this audacious mongrel but the Captain did admirably.

"Major, you are to accompany the Seer to the marketplace. You are to see that he returns safely, and enjoys himself while there. That does not include being threatened by your weapons nor by your tongue. I will not remind you of this again."

"No sir."

"Good. Now leave me alone. I much to think about."

"Sir."

He swung his back to them, crossing the floor to lean out the open window, signaling an end to the conversation. As Ursa and Sireth moved to leave, the Captain turned his face in their direction.

"I wish you had not shown me," he said softly.

"I wish I had not seen."

And they left him alone, for indeed, he had much to think about.

***

The morning was a bright and sunny one and by the time they reached the first of the stalls, the marketplace was full to brimming with bodies. Merchants, peddlers and beggars alike, calling for silver like so many children, eager-eyed and open-handed at a parent's return. Oxen lowed from narrow billets and headless geese swung against headless rabbits, as shop after shop beckoned for attention. From silken scarves to idols of jade, from sacks of rice to over ripe oysters, the sights, sounds and most of all, smells of the marketplace were a delight to the senses, tempting even the most sensible of souls with her bounty of goods.

The Scholar was drinking it in.

"Wow," she said as she picked up yet another item from yet another stall. "I've never seen anything like this."

"That's the fifth time you've said that this morning," said Kerris. "Really, *sidala,* I think you've led entirely too sheltered a life."

"Oh, well, yes. I suppose you would think that, wouldn't you? After all, you grew up in the Palace Courts and I grew up on a lowly pheasant farm in the jungle."

"That's not what I meant."

"Oh, really?" She picked up another item, the likes of which she truly never had seen. "So what's this, *sidi* world traveler?"

"What's what?"

"This. Tell me, Kerris your name was, what in the Kingdom is this?"

"It's from the time of the Ancestors, it is," came the gruff voice of the shop merchant, a jaguar with series of golden hoops running the lengths of both ears. Like the Inkeep, he spoke Hinyan, the Language of Commerce. "From the very first Dynasty, or thereabouts. Look, it's even got his Imperial monogram."

Kerris took the bangle from Fallon's hand, turning it over and over in his own.

"Hmm. *Saykoh.* Never heard of him. But I've seen this type of thing before."

She folded her arms across her chest, grinning a sly, lopsided kind of a grin.

"Oh really. You have."

"Really. I have. See."

He plucked at the pendants that hung round his neck. It was a confusing jumble, made all the more unmanageable by the blanket still draped across his shoulders, but finally, he held one out. It was made of silver as opposed to gold but the flattened disk bore a remarkable resemblance to the bangle in his palm. He turned the disk to face her.

"See, *Tymechs.* Some Old Fhae'roh, perhaps."

"Wow." Fallon received the bangle back from her companion. "But, but what is it for?"

"Purely ornamental. I've cracked a couple before and inside they're full of springs and wires and odd rusted chips of steel. Nothing much to them, really. Why don't you put it 'round your arm. Or maybe your ankle. Might look rather fetching down there."

"Why does it have twelve symbols?"

"Zodiac? You know, the monkey, the goat, the tigress..."

She didn't hear him, so intent was she on the face of the bangle, turning it one way, then the other to catch the light.

"Kinda looks like a sundial to me."

Kerris and the shopkeep exchanged looks.

"Right. Of course. That's it. A sundial that you wear on your ankle. Brilliant. Trust the Ancestors to come up with something like that..." He leaned in to the jaguar, waggled a grey finger between them. "We'll take it. Charge it to the big lion at the Inn. Right?"

"Just keep that little snow leopard out of my stall, is all I ask. I've already had my share of ears pierced!"

He roared with laughter. Obviously, news traveled fast around this little corner of the world. Or rather, on the very roof of it.

Kerris laughed as well, taking Fallon's elbow and ushering her away from the treasure trove of Old things. She was still pondering her new acquisition when suddenly she seemed to realize she was somewhere else.

"Hey! I didn't pay for this!"

"Not to worry. Kirin did. Or rather, his Empress."

Fallon slipped the bangle over her wrist, sliding it as far as it could go. On such a thin arm, it went up quite far.

"I think he likes her."

"Who?"

"Your brother. I think he's fond of the Empress."

"Mad about her. Absolutely starved for her love, I can assure you. Always has been, ever since we were children. But do you want to know something that's even stranger?" He leaned in to whisper in her ear, and suddenly, his very closeness caused her pelt to tingle. "She's mad about him too."

"No!"

"Oh yes. Why do you think there is no consort? No heir?"

"Wow..."

"Not a word, mind. Or it'll be my tail."

"I swear."

"On your father's father's father's grave?"

"And my mother's."

Kerris grinned again, hooking his arm through hers.

"That's what I love about tigers. They know how to keep secrets."

Fallon swallowed. She was getting rather good at keeping them.

***

Major Ursa Laenskaya scowled all around her.

"They are looking at us. Why are they looking at us?"

"This is a very isolated region, Major. These people see few visitors."

"I don't like it. It's bad for business."

"Perhaps your reputation precedes you."

"It should," she grunted.

They passed a large octagonal stall, each side spread with an elaborate variety of goods, from hot cooked fruit to leather slippers to weapons. It appeared to be a family operation for two men and one woman, ocelots all, moved from table to table under the rough yak-hide canopy, bartering and selling in many tongues. In the very centre, an elderly couple sat, observing all but saying nothing. They nodded as Sireth passed by.

From under a corner of a nearby stall, bright eyes darted in and out, hiding a small face behind a flap of curtain. A kitten, thin and dusty, having no more than seven summers to her credit was watching him with curiosity. Smiling, the Seer cupped fist to palm and bowed. The child disappeared.

"Nice work," he heard the Major say. "Where did you find it?"

"It has been brought by caravan," answered one of the brothers from within the stall. He was speaking Imperial quite admirably. "From the white plains above *Gobay.*"

"Hah. Stolen no doubt. From the corpse of some dead Dog."

The brother said nothing but merely watched as Ursa picked the weapon, testing its weight in the palm of her hand. It was a *jamviyah,* a short, sickle-shaped blade and her silver fingers curled about the hilt with relish. She held it oddly, Sireth thought, for the blade seemed backwards, curving beneath her wrist and into her body, as though she knew it intimately. But it was when she began to move, slowly, gracefully, swinging her arm out and away like a Chai'Chi mistress that he realized its lethal potential. It was an intimate weapon, a scimitar forged for close combat, a scythe as personal as one's very claws for it was common knowledge that Dogs had not the claws of Cats and envied them for it.

"You are from *Sha'Hadin,*" came a very frail voice in the ancient tongue of the Manda'Rhin. He turned to see the elderly couple, standing now at the table nearest him and for some reason, he was reminded of Petrus Mercouri. They were a small pair, ocelots with bright, glistening eyes, toothless smiles and fragile bones. *Almost Sacred,* he thought. It was a blessing how Age did that to people.

"Yes. I am," he responded in Manda'Rhin.

"The last of the Seven."

"Yes," he said softly.

They bowed deeply and the man held his spindly arms open wide.

"It is an honor to have you at our stall, *sahidi.* Anything you desire is yours."

"Thank you, but I have need of nothing."

"The monastery has been good to us, *sahidi.* It would please us to return some of that generosity. The *jamviyah*, perhaps?"

Sireth noticed the prick of Ursa's ears at the mention of the deadly weapon. It lay now amongst common daggers on another of the tables. He shook his head.

"*She* has need of nothing, either. But thank you again. You honor me with your offer."

Hungry young eyes peered at him again from under the dusty flap.

"Wait," he said as he turned to leave. "Perhaps there is one thing..."

"You need but name it, *sahidi.*"

He could see Ursa's gaze slide back to the blade. She seemed to be holding her breath.

Clasping his hands behind his back, he breathed deeply a sickly sweet scent.

"Is that the smell of honey-roasted bananas?"

"Our specialty, *sahidi.* Hanshan, bring the Seer a kz'laki!"

"Two?"

"Two kz'laki!" The old man bowed deeply once more. "You have honored us, *sahidi.* Enjoy them with our compliments."

Two bananas skewed on wooden sticks, crisp and crackling with candied honey, were passed across the table into Sireth's waiting hands. The Major gaped at him. He smiled and turned to walk away. She scrambled to his side.

"You are an idiot!"

"Sometimes."

"Did you see the goods in that stall? The silks? The leathers? The blades?"

"I saw them." As he walked, he clasped his hands once again behind his back, the kz'laki waggling like come-hither fingers. "I did not want them."

"Well," she snorted, "I will not eat those things. They are disgusting."

"Good. They are not for you."

"Candy for kittens."

"Precisely."

"And you are no kitten."

There was a flurry of movement behind them and Ursa whirled in time to see a tiny dirty figure snatch one of the kz'laki from the Seer's gloved hand and bolt off into the crowds. In a heartbeat, she had pulled one of her daggers, flipping the blade into her palm for throwing. Sireth caught her wrist.

"Major! No!"

"It has stolen your kz'laki!"

"Yes."

"It is a thief! It must be punished!"

"It was a hungry child."

The kitten had long since disappeared into the crush of bodies. Growling, Ursa sheathed her dagger.

"Children are not above the law. They must be taught order."

"And is that how you were taught, my wild Empress? Obedience at the point of a blade?"

She wheeled on him, eyes flashing and she stabbed a finger at his face.

"Stay out of my soul!" she hissed and with that, she spun on her heel and marched off through the stalls, fists clenched, hair swinging in straight, coarse lines across her back.

"Would that I could, Major," he sighed, shaking his head as he watched her go. "It is a very frightening place to be."

***

The shopkeep looked up from his whittling. There was someone entering his tent.

It was a woman.

"Go back to your husband, *sidala,*" he purred. "Women have no business here."

Long, speckled fingers reached up to remove the hood and the shopkeep almost hit the floor. Instead, he scrambled to his feet. "Of course, if you *have* no husband..."

"You are the tobacconist?"

"I am, *sidala.* Seller of fine pipes and finer tobaccos, imported from the furthest reaches of the Kingdom. Our incense is the finest. Even the Empress herself sees fit to call."

Heavy, golden eyes roamed the dark, smoky confines of the tent.

"I have need of a hookah pipe."

"Ah, don't we all, *sidala.* But of course, you know those are illegal."

"And a good measure of opium. Enough for one man, one night. I will take them now."

"*Sidala,* I would be more than happy to help you, truly I would, but the legalities are prohibitive. I'm sure you can appreciate my position."

She moved towards him, fixing him with her hypnotic stare.

"Of course. But I have my orders, *sidi.* I am directed to offer you whatever you need."

She was almost upon him now, so close he could taste the incense on his tongue. He breathed her in, deeply.

"*Sidala,* I'm sure you are aware of the visitors at the Inn. There is a lion who bears the Royal Standard. It would be madness to even consider—"

"It is in his name that I have come."

For some strange reason, his resolve was growing weaker by the moment and the tent spun around him as in a dream. He nodded and she pushed him away, turning her back to him as he began to gather the goods from deep and secret places. After several minutes, he handed her a package and she slipped from his tent without another word. Finally, he slumped to his seat and resumed whittling, as if nothing at all had happened.

***

"Well, what do you think?

Fallon looked up from the saris on the table as Kerris spun around for her, the cloak of midnight blue billowing like a banner around his body. The linen tunic was of the same color and spattered with starry embroidery – suns and moons of silver thread, with laces of grey and clasps of pewter. She sighed. He looked fantastic. She swallowed and looked back at the saris.

"Oh. Well. It'll do."

"Not good?"

"Oh! No, no it's good. Quite good, really. Good colors for you. Blues and greys and stars and all that. Yeah, good. Good."

"It's really expensive," he said, running his fingers along the sleeves. "Look at the needlework."

"Hm. Good."

"So I should get it, then?"

She moved away from him, keeping her eyes glued to the jewel-toned silks of teal and scarlet, orange and purple.

"Get what you want. I'm not your mother."

"Mummi would love it." He turned back to the seller of linens. "Despite what my friend here says I quite like the set. If you don't mind, I'll wear it out. Charge it to the lion at the Inn. Keep the blanket."

"And perhaps, a sari for your wife? The finest silks from *Bhen'ghal*—"

Fallon's head snapped up.

"I'm not his wife!"

"She's not my wife," echoed Kerris, grinning.

"Forgive me," sputtered the shopkeep with a modest bow. "I assume too much. Your mistress, then?"

"I'm no one's mistress! You take that back!"

The shopkeep turned from Kerris to Fallon, a bewildered frown on his face.

"But *sidi.* On your back, the scratches... Are they not made by... during...?"

"Her claws, that's true." The grey lion grinned. "Oh, yes. She's a wild thing, right and sure."

"I am not!" Fallon stamped her foot. "I am not wild. I – I - I am very *tame.* You tell him. You take that back!"

"See? Wild."

"More like a wife," said the shopkeep.

"Hm. Yes. Very. Well come along, love. Time to be getting back to the Inn."

"You can walk back yourself, Kerris your name was," she snapped. "I have no desire to be the object of your joking. And, and, and you can take this back, while you're at it. Add it to your little collection of trinkets, 'cause I won't be among them."

She pulled the bangle from her arm and tossed it at him before storming off through the stalls in the direction of the Inn at the Roof of the World. Kerris slipped it into a deep pocket, wondering how such an innocent affair could sour so quickly. And moreover, why in the Kingdom it should bother him so much.

He was comforted by the smell of incense.

"She is a sensitive soul," purred the Alchemist, as she slid up on him from behind and ran the back of her hand along his hip. "Accustomed to parents and sisters who love her and protect her and tend to her every whim. She has no experience with men like yourself."

Kerris turned to face her. Her mouth was only a kiss away. He grinned, breathing her in.

"And you do?"

"I do."

"Well then. I have no consuming desire to return to the Inn anytime soon and I could really use a drink. Care to join me?"

He waited a heartbeat, for he knew it was coming.

"Of course."

***

The road to the Inn was steep and winding, furrowed by ox-cart and carved by runoff. But the sun was now high in the afternoon sky and warm on his face. Sireth resisted the urge to close his eyes and enjoy it for if he slipped in one of the many ruts or gullies, he could not trust that the Major would catch him. And it was a long way down.

She was walking several paces ahead and had said nothing for a very long time.

"Major," he called after her. "I need to ask your forgiveness."

She said nothing.

"I spoke out of turn, earlier. I meant no offense."

Still nothing.

"I thought you were going to hurt the child. I assumed ill of your character and your family. For that I ask that you forgive me. Please."

She stopped dead in her tracks, and he almost walked into her.

"You assumed?"

"Yes."

"You *assumed?*"

"Yes, I assumed. I was wrong."

"You assumed. You did not *see?*"

"I was not 'in your soul,' as you put it. To do so without permission or purpose is dishonorable. But regardless, I was in the wrong. And I'm very, very sorry."

Her stare was cold, inscrutable, as if she were weighing him in the white, hot fire of her eyes. He allowed himself to be weighed in that scale for it seemed the only means by which she had to judge the world around her.

So beautiful a measure, he noted, *but the scales so dreadfully unbalanced.*

"You were not wrong."

And for several moments longer, her gaze did not waver until she turned, resuming the march down the steep road and leaving the Seer standing alone.

A golden-orange hand brought him back into the sunshine.

"Hey, can I join you?"

"Please do," he said. "Do you like these?"

And he held up the last kz'laki, the crispy honey coating only now beginning to melt and slide down onto the leather of his glove.

"A honey-roasted banana! I love honey-roasted bananas! My father used to make them for special occasions! Why? Don't you like them?"

"They're disgusting."

"Well, thanks! I love them."

He offered her his arm and naturally, she took it, leaning into him with such casual familiarity that he quickly forced the Major out of his thoughts.

"Did you have a good day, my dear?"

"Mmhmm," she said through a sticky mouthful, "Interesting places, markets. Real maelstrom of the feline condition. Great joy, great poverty. Everyone trying to claw out a meager little existence up here in the remotest of places, on the most barren of peaks. The past and the future meeting and mingling on one crazy, crowded, busy street. So, am I really going to have six kittens?"

Even though she was the one with the mouth full of banana, it was he who almost choked.

"What – what was that?"

"That's what you said last night. *'Kittens. Six kittens. Six grey striped kittens.'*"

"I said that?"

"Yep. I know 'cause I was there."

"Ah. Yes. Well..."

He began to wish that one of those deep muddy ruts might turn his ankle after all, for a fall might distract her long enough and prevent him from explaining. He cleared his throat.

"Now, that was not necessarily a vision, my dear. I was not in my own soul, now was I? You said so yourself. Perhaps, this, this tiger who speaks through me has, has a *family*. Yes, a family of kittens. And naturally, being tigers, they would be striped?"

She grinned at him. "You are a terrible liar."

"I know."

"Do you think I'm naive?"

"Did I say that too?"

"Oh no. No, just asking. Do you?"

"Well, perhaps. After a fashion."

She sighed and tossed the stick to the side of the road.

"Figures."

"But that's not necessarily a bad thing, my dear. It connotes a certain pureness of heart, one that is not encountered nearly enough in these days. It is something that we at *Sha'Hadin* seek for years on end to achieve."

"Naivety? You seek to achieve naivety?"

"No, but a form of it. Innocence. Guilelessness. Lack of prejudice. Those sorts of things."

"Oh. Wow. I should have been a monk."

He patted her hand, wisely choosing to hold his tongue, and together, they continued the last leg of the journey, down to the Inn on the Roof of the World.

And at a broken window, high atop the Inn on the Roof of the World, a lion stood, thinking and planning and wishing he had never seen the madness that was about to befall them, a madness which would so completely crack the foundations of the Matriarchy and send their Kingdom crumbling into utter chaos. As Kirin stood there, high above the Roof of the World, he cursed himself for ever thinking he could possibly be Enough.

Truth be told, he wasn't certain there was anyone who was.

INSIGHT AND FAR

The sun was sinking down behind strange, unfamiliar peaks, but in the distance, he could still count torches dotting into existence as shadows fell across home and farm alike. *Not so different,* Kirin thought, *and perhaps no different at all.* The thought afforded him some measure of comfort for he had found none these past hours as he sat by the broken window in the Inn at the Roof of the World. In fact, he was grateful for it, for tonight, comfort was a blanket he could not chance wearing.

Tonight, the falcon had returned.

There was a knock at his door.

"Come."

He recognized the footfall immediately and smiled as his brother dropped himself down at his side.

"Hello Kirin. You been here all day?"

"I have." He reached over, to run his thumb along the needlework of Kerris' new cuff. "Very nice."

"Glad you like it. You paid for it, after all."

That brilliant smile flashed for him, brighter even than the setting sun and for a brief instant, the Captain's burdens seemed to lift a little from his shoulders.

"The Scholar tells me you got a note from Lyn-ling tonight."

Kirin looked down. He was still clutching the parchment tightly in his grasp, crushed and well worn from reading. It smelled faintly of lotus.

"Yes."

"So we're heading out in the morning, are we?"

"Yes."

"But not to *DharamShallah.*"

"No."

"Can you tell me where?"

"I don't know."

"Ah. Well. That's always good news for a Guide, isn't it? Now how about why?"

Kirin weighed the question carefully.

"Kerris, there is a threat to the Kingdom. A threat which may overturn everything we know. Destroy our society. *Change* things."

"Dogs?"

"Worse."

"We haven't finished then, have we?"

He finally turned to regard his twin, as blue eyes met blue for several long moments.

"No, we have not finished."

"And you really don't know where we are going?"

"We should find that out tonight."

"Hence the opium?"

Kirin growled, his tail lashing once as it lay curled at his feet.

"How did you know about that?"

"I had a few drinks in the marketplace with the Alchemist. She said you're going to give it to the Seer in hopes of finding out where this 'tiger' is hiding."

"Something like that."

Kerris shifted position on the hard mahogany floor, chewing his bottom lip a moment before speaking.

"Well, now don't take my head off when I tell you this, Kirin, but I have sampled *minute* quantities of opium on rare occasions—" He held up a grey palm. "— when I was much younger, of course. Not much, though, or often, what with it being illegal, and all..."

The Captain glared at him.

"Yes. Right. Anyway, it's been my experience that opium tends to make things a little distorted and more than a little unreal. I would hesitate to trust anyone under its spell, let alone try to follow his directions. We could be riding in circles for days on end. In fact, we could ride straight off the edge of the earth."

"We have no choice, Kerris. Apparently, opium is an integral part in the Ritual of Farsight and that the monks of *Sha'Hadin* have been using it for generations. benAramis assures me it is quite effective."

"Oh, I'm sure it's effective, Kirin," Kerris grinned. "I just find it funny that you, of all people, would be so ready to bend Imperial law to accomplish this task. It's not like you."

"Yes, I know." Kirin smiled now. "Perhaps somewhere, underneath all this gold, there is a small streak of silver?"

His brother laughed easily, enjoying the compliment and the mutual good humor between them, for it did not come often enough. The Captain of the Guard was always busy with important matters, whereas nothing Kerris did was important. It was the way of things.

Kerris sighed and picked at a crust of mud on his yak-hide boots.

"So, do you need my help tonight?"

"Need it? No. Desire it? Always."

"I'm not sure what I can do."

"Neither am I."

Kerris turned to gaze out the window.

"Because I think I'm having problems again..."

The weight that had been so thankfully lifted began to slide back.

"Problems?"

"Forgetting problems."

"Oh. Those." He nodded slowly. *This was not good.* "You haven't had those for awhile."

"My arms. My back..." Kerris shook his head. "No recollection whatsoever."

"Do you remember the avalanche?"

"There *was* an avalanche, then? I told you."

"You did."

"So what happened?"

"You and the Scholar almost went over a mountain edge. She

climbed up your back."

"Ah. Right. *'Climb.'* I see. Is Quiz alright?"

"Quiz is fine. The Alchemist gave you something for the pain. Perhaps that has affected your memory."

"Well you see, that's not all."

Blast. This was very bad.

"Tell me."

"The other morning, when I was out with the Scholar, there was an incident. She remembers it all quite vividly, but me..." He shrugged, dropping his hands into his lap. "Maybe you should find yourself another Guide, Kirin. Someone who won't forget his way back home."

"Nonsense. You are the best Guide in the Kingdom, and there is no one I would rather have to lead our expedition, 'forgetting problems' or no. Do you understand this?"

Kerris said nothing, so his brother nudged him with the point of an elbow.

"Besides, First is luck and you are our lucky omen. You saved the Seer, remember? You told that little boy."

"Yes, I do seem to remember that."

"Good. Now, it is still early and we have many hours before the Second Watch. Have you eaten?"

Kerris grinned, shaking off the blanket of self-doubt with a toss of his head.

"No and it smells delicious. I say this Inn has quite the remarkable kitchen. Perhaps I shall retire here when I'm an old man."

"Then I will join you and we shall grow old together."

Like sunlight and shadow, or the interlocking wheel of Yin and Yang, the brothers rose to their feet and went down for supper.

***

Fallon stretched her slender arms over her head and breathed deeply the cold evening air. Despite being a jungle girl, she had to admit that the mountains in moonlight were breathtaking and she stepped out of the light of the Inn to afford herself a better view.

She could grow to like this.

Peaks of silver floated like ice floes over the wispy white water of cloud that rose up from the valleys. Torches burned from faraway homes and even farther still, she could imagine the Cave of a Thousand Eyes, pouring light in golden streams from its many eyes and mouths. That sight would stay in her memory forever. She could almost hear chanting.

No, she *could* hear chanting.

She drew her cloak tightly around her shoulders and followed.

This wasn't the deep, somber mantras that had underscored life in *Sha'Hadin*, but rather scales, throaty and sensual, sliding up and down in pitch like a tune on a zither. It was faint but growing as she tracked it back behind the Inn towards a large outcropping of rock. Silhouetted against the moon was a pile of boulders, precariously balanced as if by some playful giant, towering many times higher than a man out of the mountainside. And beyond that, she saw the singer.

Cross-legged on the very edge of the mountain, the Alchemist sat clutching the red satin pouch in her palms like an offering to the stars above. Silver smoke flowed from her lips into red satin folds and for a moment, the pouch seemed almost to pulse with life, throbbing like a heartbeat, swirling with smoke within. *Impossible,* Fallon blinked as she carefully braced her boots against ruts in the steep frozen ground. Slowly, al Shiva lowered the pouch to her side. There was no movement now as it floated and bobbed on its tether but the Scholar was certain the pouch was just a little fuller than before.

Go back to the Inn, whispered a voice inside her head. *This is no place for naive young tigresses with altogether too much curiosity and not nearly enough common sense. Go back and enjoy a cup of tea with that handsome grey lion, take another look at the Fhae'roh's bangle about his neck. Something, anything, other than be witness to such strange, otherworldly events.*

But with a scrunch of her nose, she silenced the voice and sneaked closer.

Next, the Alchemist produced a golden bowl, large and shallow, quite similar to her father's wok back on the farm. She held a clay cup up to the moonlight and it seemed as if that same silver smoke rose like mist from the depths of the glass. When she poured the contents into the bowl, there was a roar of rushing waters and the surface grew still.

"Sahidi," Sherah murmured.

"They live?" said the waters.

"Still, *sahidi.* But the way to *Pol'Lhasa* is barred. There was an avalanche."

"Your destination?"

"Tonight, *sahidi.* The Ritual of Farsight."

"Learn it."

Fallon craned her neck, for upon that strange, still surface, she could see a face reflected in the moon's pale glow. A striped face as white as the moon, as cold as the mountain peaks which surrounded them, stars sparkling deep within empty, soulless eyes.

She peered closer.

Those eyes flashed at her.

"Who?!"

Sherah whirled and Fallon jumped back, her boots slipping on the frozen ground. She yelped and grabbed for the rock, praying that her claws would hold and that she would be spared yet another edge-of-cliff adventure. She wasn't at all certain that the Alchemist would be such a ready climb.

Her claws clung fast, boots kicking at the shale beneath her feet, trying to regain some sort foothold. Sherah was beside her in an instant.

"You are safe," purred the throaty voice. "You shall not fall."

She offered Fallon a long, speckled hand, and the tigress accepted, picking her steps carefully to where the Alchemist had been seated. Together, they stood and gazed over the sheer cliff-face, where tiny bits of shale were already more than halfway to the valley floor below.

"Who was that?" asked the Scholar.

"Who was whom?"

"The face. The face in the water."

"There was no face in the water."

"But I saw—"

"Moonlight."

"And, and stripes. I saw a striped face in the water. I know I did."

Sherah smiled at her. "You saw your own face, reflected in the moonlight."

"But the voice—"

"There was no voice."

"But you were talking."

"I was praying."

"To whom?"

"Prayer is an intimate matter. But we should get you back to the Inn. You've had a bit of a fright."

"No. No, I'm fine, really."

Sherah turned slowly, and golden eyes held green.

"No. You've had a terrible fright. You almost fell from a cliff, yet again. We will go back now and I will tell no one. Perhaps then, they will allow you to remain with us for our work is not yet done. Otherwise, the Captain may have to send you home to the jungle, to your mother and father and all of your happy, married sisters..."

Fallon felt her thoughts floating away, just like those silver mountain peaks adrift on seas of cloud. The Alchemist reached up to smooth away the strands of orange mane that had fallen into her face. It was a soothing touch, reassuring, almost maternal and Fallon was surprised to find tears coursing down her own cheeks.

"Don't tell them, please? I don't want to go back."

"Shh. Of course I won't. It will be our little secret." al Shiva wrapped a protective arm around the thin shoulders. "Besides, the grey lion grows fond of you."

"Really? You think so?"

"I know so."

"Wait! Your things—"

Fallon tossed a backwards glance over her shoulder, to where the red satin pouch, golden bowl and cup had lain.

"Things?"

There was nothing there.

"Oh, never mind. My mistake. I've had a bit of a fright."

And like sunlight and shadow, or the interlocking wheel of Yin and Yang, the two women began the trek up the steep paths to the Inn.

***

"Major?"

There was no response.

"Major, are you quite alright?"

"I'm fine."

Sireth laid down his hookah pipe and rose to his feet. Major Ursa Laenskaya was already standing. She had been since he had retired to the room to meditate, smoke and prepare himself for tonight's journey. However, against his better judgment, she had insisted on remaining and as the night had worn on, the opium's heady vapors grew thicker, more noxious by the hour. Her usually sharp eyes had become dulled, her acid tongue less cutting until finally she had grown quite still. Somehow, she managed to keep her feet beneath her and he was in fact impressed that she was not swaying.

"It is time to go down now."

"Yes."

She did not move.

"Would you *like* to go down now?"

"Yes."

Still, she did not move.

"Perhaps you would like to *lie* down, instead?"

"Yes."

He took her carefully by the arms, turned her in a half-circle and walked her toward 'her side' of the torn cot. She did not even appear to notice she had moved. He turned her again and hands on shoulders, pushed her down onto the mattress. Her legs folded beneath her and she sat stiff and wooden, staring at nothing in particular.

"Lie down," he ordered.

"Yes," she said, but still, did not move.

With two fingers, he pushed her to the bed and she curled into a tight white ball around herself. He found the rough woolen blanket, draped it over her, tucking it into the folds of her body. One of the more notable effects of the opium was a sensation of cold and he did not want the Major to be chilled on his account. Her eyes were closed so he leaned in to her ear.

"How's that?" he asked softly. "Are you warm enough?"

"I will be when you join me."

He straightened up, suddenly feeling much too intimate for comfort. Perhaps the opium allowed more than Seers to peer into the hearts and souls of others, for in truth, he would have liked nothing better. But for every good thing there was always a bad, Petrus had taught him. Yang to each Yin. The toll was far too heavy for such folly, the cost far too steep. He had paid it once. Never again.

"You will be warm enough. Sleep well, my wild Empress. I'll check in on you later."

He debated on blowing out the room's only candle, but decided against it, and quietly closed the door behind him.

***

The Captain of the Guard was growing anxious.

It was the beginning of Second Watch, and the Seer had not yet come down.

The Alchemist and Scholar were sitting at a far table, braiding each other's hair and chatting like old friends, whispering and throwing the occasional sly look at Kerris who sat at another far table, grinning and drinking a bowl of sakeh and watching them both. All this flirtation made Kirin uncomfortable.

He sighed, opened his palm, and the parchment uncurled within.

He read it again.

My dearest Captain,

It was with great joy that I received your note. You have indeed proven that my faith in you is not, nor has ever been, misplaced. And for that, you have my eternal gratitude.

But it is with great sadness that I must ask one more thing of you and I fear it is a thing that shall pain you as much as it pains me. I must ask that you not return to Pol'Lhasa *until you have found this 'Soul', this murderer of my Seers. Whatever, or whomever, has caused these deaths must be found swiftly, and once found, executed without remorse. I can allow nothing less.*

The security of the Upper Kingdom depends on this one terrible act. And I must ask it of you alone. I trust you will understand.

My heart forever yours,

Thothloryn Parillaud Markova Wu

It was sealed with the Imperial seal and the scent of lotus.

He closed his fist, slipping the note into the sash at his waist and glancing around the room. No one had seen. This, no one must see.

He breathed deeply and steeled his resolve. They would find this 'Soul,' he was certain of it and once they did, with his very sword, the Captain of the Guard would kill him.

It was madness.

And what was worse, if the vision of Sireth benAramis was to believed, the man whom the Empress said was never wrong, then it would not only be madness, but blasphemy.

Kirin rubbed his temple. He had another headache.

High above, from a room down at the end of the corridor, he heard a door close and the footsteps of a long determined stride. Kirin looked up. Very much alone, the Seer was coming down the stairs. The Captain rose to meet him.

"Where is the Major?"

Sireth regarded him with eyes as sharp and shiny as a falcon's. Indeed, it seemed to Kirin that, at this very moment, both eyes could see.

"The opium," the Seer began. "It is a raw blend, strong and harsh, not at all like the sort we use at *Sha'Hadin.* Nonetheless, I am accustomed to its effects. The Major is not."

"Is there anything else you require?"

"Nothing."

He brushed past towards the main hearth, kneeling down beside the fire as if about to begin another set of meditations. Slowly, methodically, he removed his gloves.

From the far tables, Kerris, Fallon and Sherah watched with interest.

It was a ritual, that much was obvious, from the meticulous folding back of his wide sleeves seven times to the exaggerated depth of breathing. The Seer's lips moved with incantations or mantras or other such spells and the Alchemist sat forward, ears pricked, as if straining to catch and remember every word.

And without warning, the Seer turned and thrust both hands into the roaring fire.

"Mother!" Fallon jumped to her feet.

They were all standing now, watching in awe as the flames hissed and leapt about within the hearth, over and around the spotted arms. After several moments, the hands drew back unscathed and unsigned and holding six live coals, each as red as a new morning sun. They sizzled with heat and smoldering fire when the Seer crushed them between his palms, sending ash raining to the floor.

Kerris grinned.

"I think I'd need a pipe or two of opium before doing that..."

"Pain," muttered the Seer, "is simply a matter of perspective."

And reaching forward, he smeared the ash across the stone, creating a palette in soot. Eyes closed, he began to draw.

Fallon peered over his shoulder.

"Wow, it's the Kingdom. He's drawing the Upper Kingdom!"

Kirin narrowed his eyes. Sure enough, the Scholar was correct. He could make out the range of the Great Mountains slicing the palette in two, the southern horn that was *Hindaya*, the eastern provinces of *Nam*, *Shiam* and *Lan'Landesh* and all the way west to the deserts of *Hirak, Hiran* and *Sahood.* The coastlines were rough but recognizable. To the north, the Lower Kingdom was not drawn in at all for no cat had ever dared explore those barbaric lands where Pure Races meant nothing and Dogs bred at will.

After several minutes of drawing, Sireth straightened up, fixing his falcon-like stare on the Captain.

"Your scroll," he said evenly. With some measure of regret, Kirin removed the tiny parchment and handed it over.

"This is *Pol'Lhasa.*"

Carefully, Sireth placed the scroll over the exact location of the Palace in *DharamShallah*, deep in the heart of the Great Mountains.

"And this," he turned back to the hearth, retrieved a seventh coal and placed it just to the north of the scroll. "This is us."

"Wow," Fallon breathed. "This is so exciting."

"Hush," said Kerris.

Sherah circled them all like a shark, the tip of her tail twitching in anticipation as she feasted on the mysteries before her.

"In several moments, this last coal will split and as I begin my journey, so it will follow. No one must touch it, attempt to alter its course or interfere with its path in any way. Is that understood?"

They nodded.

"We are assuming that our 'friend tiger' will join us again tonight. As he does, it will be unlikely that I will be able to communicate in any way to any of you. Therefore, it is vitally important that no one touch me at any time during the evening for once the connection is severed, there is no way of getting it back."

"Yes," said Fallon. "Yes, that's what happened last night."

"Hush," said Kerris.

"And since none of you possesses the Gift of Farsight, then none of you can help me if that happens. If the connection is severed prematurely, *I* shall have no way of getting back and this ritual will have accomplished nothing."

"That will not happen," said Kirin. "You have my word."

"Is it Enough?"

"It will have to be."

"I believe you." He took a deep breath, held it for a brief second, released it with a rush. "Very well. I will begin. Oh and by the way, will someone please open the door?"

He let drop his hands to his lap and said nothing more.

Fallon looked to the Captain, eyes wide and questioning. He nodded and she scrambled for the door, swinging it wide and peering out into the darkness. There was nothing, save the wind.

She turned back to the room.

"Nothing."

She frowned and looked out one last time, ducking just as the falcon soared in over her head, bleating and catching several white-tipped hairs in its claws. It soared around the room, as if searching for a snow leopard upon which to perch, finally settling for the horn of a yak's head mounted upon the wall.

Fallon slammed the door.

"That was not funny, you... you scary little bird!"

"HUSH!" said the brothers in tandem, before a sound caused

them to look back to the palette of soot. It was a soft sound, a crackling, sizzling, popping sound, one that produced light and heat in its wake.

The seventh coal was beginning to split.

***

heartbeat growing quiet, faint and distant, heat and weight falling away, a cloak at sunrise, breath within lifting, peeling, carrying, up up up above them all, above the Great Room, between the blackened beams of ceiling, falcon-sharp eyes watching him, watching, chirrup and cry, a ripple as the roof passed through, cobwebs and rotting wood, and stars now, many jeweled stars and the moon, familiar friends, well-traveled roads of cloud and night-sky, one star not a star, a star prophesied, a prophesy of rejoicing and devastation, a star waking, hungry, dying - there was a tug and like lightning, he was gone

***

"It's really splitting. Wow..."

Four eager faces hovered above the coal, now completely split into two distinct halves. One of the halves began to rotate, eerily spinning on its axis. Kirin motioned them back, for fear that some hand or boot might inadvertently block the path if indeed the coal chose to move. Quickly, he risked glancing at those eager faces. The Scholar busily tugged at her laces, emerald eyes glued to the coal as if she was willing it to move. Likewise, the Alchemist was intently watching, her golden eyes darting between coal and Seer as if she could divine his methods and practice them herself. For the first time, Kirin sensed the curiosity that must surely drive her and for the first time, he found himself approving. Kerris sat a little further back, taking in the entire room with quick blue eyes, enjoying being caught up in something unusual, something mutually unexpected, likely as eager to see that little coal head into uncharted territory as Kirin was to see it stay closer to home.

There was a yelp as the coal shot like a firecracker between Fallon's knees, scuttling away from the map and across the floor.

***

fast, too fast, through clouds and valleys, violent ripples as mountain rock passed through, swifter than a falcon's dive, swifter still, the Great Wall below, snaking like a sidewinder through the peaks, beyond the Wall now, over deserts as turbulent as a sea, unfamiliar ranges, golden rock and white-wash, sand and scrub and patches of sage, faster now, blurring the Sight, pulling faster, farther than a cat should go, no stopping now, over a small sea, the land below bleeding with color like paint holding too much water, too fast, to loose, falling apart, falling still

***

"Where did it go?"

"Don't touch it!" Kirin leapt to his feet. "Whatever you do, don't touch it!"

"Oh ho, Kirin!" Kerris laughed. "I hope that thing's wrong or we'll be riding forever!"

"There!" shouted Fallon. "There, under the table!"

The coal still moved, rattling across the floor like a stone skipping across the surface of a pool. There was no constant direction however, for it would turn as sharply as a mountain pony and shoot off in another direction, under boots, under tables, forcing them to leap and spin to avoid being struck and impede its path. As if by magic, it managed to navigate table legs and benches like a river flowing through deep and craggy valleys.

Sherah narrowed her eyes and moved closer to the Seer.

"Captain?" she purred.

"Where is it now?"

"Here," barked Kerris, springing onto a bench as the coal shot under his boots. "No, no there!"

"Captain?"

The half coal skidded back towards the kneeling forms of Alchemist and Seer, crossing the palette of soot yet again, passing *DharamShallah* far to the north and west of the Great Mountains, slowing as it passed even the heart of the Lower Kingdom. Finally, the spinning ceased, its journey ended at the base of a far bench.

Breathless, Kirin, Fallon and Kerris approached the tiny projectile.

"Oh mother," gasped Fallon.

"Oh no," growled Kirin.

"Oh well," grinned Kerris. "Guess we can go home now."

Kirin glared at him.

"That's well past the edge of the earth, Kirin. Even our dear Kaidan hasn't traveled *that* far, believe me. There's nothing out there! Nothing. I'm afraid your Seer has had a little too much opium. I did warn you, didn't I?"

"No," growled the Captain once more, his tone almost desperate. "No, Kerris. This must work. We must find this 'Soul of a Tiger.' We *must.*"

"Captain?"

It was Sherah, still kneeling very close to Sireth, studying his face with gleaming golden eyes. Kirin straightened up, put hands to hips in frustration.

"What?"

She looked up at him, with a faint, crooked smile, made all the more exotic by the kohl-black streak along her cheek.

"Your Seer," she looked back now, the smile growing wider, almost dazzling in its brightness. "Your Seer is singing."

***

Kirin knelt forward.

It was true.

Eyes closed, hands still folded loosely in his lap, the seventh and last Seer of *Sha'Hadin* was indeed, singing.

But it was like no song he had ever heard before.

"He's really quite terrible, isn't he?" snickered Kerris. "Tell me, *sidalady* tigress, do all tigers sound that bad? I thought your people had the voices of angels."

"Oh we do. Tigers are the best singers in the Kingdom. Why, almost all the famous poems and ballads are written for tigers. I think it has something to do with the stripes on our throats - makes us warble and trill like little birds. Want me to show you?"

"Thanks love. I think I'd need another sakeh for that tonight."

Kirin cast a quick glance at the Alchemist. She caught it and threw it back, her smile more dazzling than ever before. It was clear she was fascinated.

Finally, the Seer sighed.

"I can't sing any more songs. If I have to sing one more song, I'll go crazy. Well, maybe given my particular situation, that wouldn't be such a bad idea. Okay, one more time, *'Just sittin' on the dock of the bay—"*

"Hello?" said Kirin.

Sireth benAramis nearly jumped off the floor, sending both the Captain and the Alchemist scrabbling out of the way to keep from touching him. After a brief moment, he pulled his hand from his face, searching the room with unseeing eyes.

"Hello? Hello, is someone there?"

"We are here."

"How long have you been there? Who are you? How do you do this?"

"Slowly, please," said Kirin. "We know as little as you but we will try to answer your questions if you will try to answer some of ours."

"I'm all ears."

"What is your name?"

"You first."

"My name is Kirin Wynegarde-Grey, Captain of the Imperial Guard."

"Imperial?"

"Her Most Honoured Excellency, Thothloryn Parillaud Markova Wu, Twelfth Empress of the Fangxieng Dynasty, Matriarch of *Pol'Lhasa,* and Most Blessed Ruler of the Upper Kingdom."

"Alrighty, then."

"Now *your* name, *sidi."*

"Dr. Jeffery Solomon," said Sireth. "The stuff after *my* name isn't nearly as impressive."

"Solomon?" Fallon smiled. "Are you a king?"

The Seer's head snapped up.

"Hey! Is that Fallon Waterford I hear? Scholar in the Court of the Empress?"

"Scholar in the Court of the Empress?" asked Kerris. "My, my, isn't that a fancy title."

She felt her cheeks grow hot.

Sireth shook his head but he was grinning. "Where are you people from, anyway?"

"From *Pol'Lhasa* in *DharamShallah.* And yourself?"

"*Pol'Lhasa?* Where in the world is *Pol'Lhasa?*"

"Please, *sidi.* It is important that you tell me where you are."

"Why?"

"Because we would like to help you but we need to know how to find you. We need to know where you are."

There was a pause.

"I'm in a bunker, 20 k outside of *Kandersteg, Switzerland.*"

The Captain looked first to his brother, then to the Scholar. Both shrugged, baffled.

"Swisser-land?"

"Switzerland. Please don't tell me you don't know where that is."

"I suppose then I won't tell you, *sidi.*"

"Great. Just great."

"This 'Swisserland', is it in the Upper Kingdom?"

"Upper Kingdom? You're from Egypt then?"

"I am from Aegyp, *sidi,"* purred Sherah.

"Enough," said Kirin. "Solomon, I must ask you more questions, but..."

His voice failed him as the realization struck like a cold wind. He was trying to find a man whose very finding would bring his death. It was dishonorable.

"How are you doing this?" said Solomon. "Are you using C links? Are you wired in to a Sat-com?"

"You are speaking through one of us, a man named Sireth benAramis. A Seer and Advisor to the Empress—"

"Seer? You mean like a telepath?"

"Your words are unfamiliar, *sidi.* These past two nights you have spoken and heard us speak through the soul of this man. Even now, his soul journeys to you to determine your exact location."

"Wow. My very own psychic hotline."

"In fact, he may be there, with you, at this very moment."

***

mountains rushing up towards at blinding speed, falling like a shooting star, faster, the earth closer, closer still, earth passing through, snow and earth, soil dark and rich and brown, passing through, falling still deeper, metal passing through, beams of steel, slicing at his soul, wires, cords, altars, ground, shock of ground, quietness, quietness and a voice, a single voice in darkness, absolute darkness, blacker than a panther's pelt, Shakuri? sleep, no -follow the voice, follow it now

***

"Now? Here? That's kind of eerie, if you ask me."

"Say his name. I wish to know if he is there. Say it. Sireth benAramis."

"Aramis? Like the Musketeer?"

"I don't understand you, Solomon."

"Never mind." His unseeing eyes searched the Great Hall. "Hello? Sireth benAramis. Your Captain wants to know if you are anywhere around. Hello?"

There was a long pause, and he shrugged.

"Sorry, I have the feeling it's just me and these creepy little animals down here - *Ow!"* He clasped a hand to his face. "Ow, dammit, something just poked me in the eye!"

A simultaneous cheer went up from Fallon and Kerris. Even Kirin could not help but smile.

"I believe it is you and the creepy animals and our Seer, *sidi.* Tell him to return at once but to map the area as he does so. We will be journeying into unknown territory and cannot rely on a steady quantity of opium to enable him to travel thus, very often."

"Opium. I *see..."*

Again, Kirin smiled. "Tell him simply to return. He knows what to do."

"Okay. Go home, Sireth benAramis and leave my eyes alone. I like seeing out of both them, thank you very much."

Fallon squirmed closer.

"Are you a tiger, Solomon?"

"A tiger?" he laughed. "Hell no, I'm a Kiwi. Born and raised in New Zealand before I moved to California. That was before the Pacific Shift, of course. Then I moved to Boston, then Brussels. But, if you don't know where Switzerland is, I'm betting you won't have a clue about California, Boston or Brussels."

"Sorry."

"It's alright. I guess things have changed since I went under. That was to be expected. I realize that, but this procedure has somehow gone wrong and I can't get the grid up. There's no light, no heat. At least there's food, even if it is just protein powder and vitamin squares. And the others... the others are all dead in their chambers. I think these rat-things have breached the outer bunker but inside, well I'm not sure. All six and I..."

Now it was the one called Solomon's turn to lose his voice, as a wave of despair crossed the Seer's face. He dropped his head and Kirin felt a rush of panic. They could not lose the connection now, not when they had come so close, gone so far. He gritted his teeth, took a deep breath and waited.

***

too slow, much too slow, he had come too far, would never get back, sleep now, try later, no -faster, concentrate, the Inn at the Roof of the World, the room full of people, Path - her quick fleeting thoughts, the Captain an able anchor, reliable and worthy, the others, were there others? he couldn't remember, fields of green and forests of dark trees streaking below, growing darker as he moved south and east, into the night, into the moon, too high, he was too high, clouds below, obscuring the Sight, a star pulling him higher, a star not a star, concentrate on the Inn, the Inn at the Roof of the World, soaring upwards soaring

***

"I'll kill him!"

There was the clacking of boot heels as Major Ursa Laenskaya stormed down the stairs.

Kirin glanced up. "Hold your tongue, Major."

She brushed past the single leopard guard and snatched a dagger from her thigh.

"I said Hold!"

Still she came.

The Captain nodded and the guard darted forward to catch her slim white arm but she swung her fist into his temple and he dropped like a stone.

"Major!"

"She's not hearing you, Kirin!" shouted Kerris, "It's the opium!"

Kirin was on his feet now, stepping forward to block the woman's path. It was obvious she was not seeing him either, her pale eyes wide and glassy, every muscle in her body as taut as a steel cord.

She plowed into him like a small avalanche, literally forcing him backwards in his effort to contain her. Her fists flashed again, claws extended. Expertly, Kirin avoided them, snagging her wrists and using his greater weight to push her off balance. His foot lashed out, knocking her ankles out from underneath her but she grabbed him and they both hit the floor with a crash.

With a strength and skill heightened by opium, she drew her feet to her chest and sent her heels thudding into his ribs. Pain exploded behind his eyes and before he could catch his breath, she was gone.

"Kerris!" He rolled onto his knees. "Kerris, see that she does not touch the Seer!"

The grey lion was already occupied in the task, pulling chairs and benches into her path but she kicked them out of the way like kindling. Dagger in hand, Ursa dove for the Seer.

Kerris grabbed her wrist before the dagger could find its mark, but her free hand slammed into his stomach like iron. The Captain tackled her from behind, and together, the three of them went down just as a bench teetered, threatening to shatter the coal that lay in it path. Without thinking, Fallon dove for it, just as it hit the stone floor with a crash.

The coal instantly turned to dust, scattering soot and ash in all directions. Helpless, the tigress glanced up and out of the corner of her eye, saw long speckled fingers reaching for the Seer's cheek.

"Solomon, are you a wizard?"

"Sherah, no!"

She touched him.

Sireth's head snapped up.

"An eye for an eye. A life for a life," was all he said before falling forward into the Alchemist's arms.

And suddenly, for a long, terrible moment, there was silence in the Inn at the Roof of the World.

***

like a boxkite with a snapped string, the spirit left him, and he began to drift, up up upwards, towards the star not a star, the Sight all but gone, clouds growing thin, dark, cold, the dying star not a star, he turned his soul to the star not a star but a dragon, a dragon of steel, a dying dragon with great fan wings and long segmented body and single eye, hovering just beneath the blanket of stars, watching the affairs of cats for years, more than years, years, he had been floating for years, too far, too long, dying

***

"No!"

With a roar, Kirin sent the heel of his palm into the Major's temple and she fell backwards onto his brother. He was at the Alchemist's side in an instant.

"What happened?"

"The connection severed," she lied. "I caught him as he fell."

The Captain's fingers found the spot on the throat where heart met soul and with a snarl, pulled the man out of her arms and onto the floor.

"Sireth, Sireth benAramis. Hear me."

It was not a plea and more than command.

"Come back. *Now.* You have a duty. You are needed. Here. Now."

There was no response.

"You must hear me. Now. You are almost home. You are almost here. You must finish what you started."

He glanced up at his brother, at the Scholar and the Alchemist, all looking to him for direction, for a way out of this bleak and desolate place. It was up to him. It was always up to him. He nodded to himself, swallowing back the rising panic. Indeed, it *was* always up to him for as always, he *did* know the way. It was inside of himself. *Bushido.*

With a deep breath, he slipped his hands around the Seer's head, thumbs to temples, and closed his eyes.

"Sireth benAramis, come back. Here. Now. To the Inn at the Roof of the World."

nothing

"Here you belong. Here with us. Here. Focus and find us. Find your way back to us."

two hearts beating, but only one soul, the other empty, cold

Another pair of hands on his, soft and slim and delicate, and without seeing, he knew it was the tigress. Her voice added to his.

"Come back here with us, Sireth. Find your way back. Please. We need you."

Three pair of hands, grey ones now cupping them all. Kirin felt a wash of gratitude. Felt them feel it, as they united in hearts and souls and wills to bring the Seer home.

***

annoying, how annoying, like a child tugging on an adult's tail, wanting attention, wanting to be heard, pulling him away from the dragon, annoying, ignore it, perhaps it will go away

***

"Come back. Here. Now. Here to the Inn at the Roof of the World. Now."

Kirin felt an odd sensation, a stir of emotion, irritation perhaps? He clenched his eyes tighter, and continued.

***

tugging, pulling, downwards, falling away from the dragon, tumbling through the clouds, many voices rushing past, many hands tugging, annoyance and irritation, go away, falling faster now, the mountains looming larger, larger still, plummeting like a falling star, the Sight growing sharp, hot, white hot, lights from the Inn, hotter, faster, too fast

***

"Too fast, *sidi.* Slow down."

***

too fast, slow down, faster, blurring, rushing, spinning

***

Kirin's head was spinning. Fallon's head was spinning. Kerris' head was spinning.

Quickly, Kirin tried to imagine hands, reaching upwards to slow the fall, stop it, felt the soul pass through like a shooting star, much too fast, they were all going to hit—

Four souls burst with the clap of thunder, throwing them in four separate directions across the room, knocking over benches, crashing into walls. Sherah threw her arms over her head to avoid the chaos and flailing debris. When finally all was still once again, she peered out again, three cats lying prone and barely conscious on the floor. The Seer, however sat up, eyes bright and glistening, breathing as if just coming in from some mad cross-Kingdom dash.

"Amazing," he panted, "Absolutely amazing. Now, please excuse me while I go outside. I think I'm going to be sick."

And with that, he clambered to his feet and staggered toward the door. He didn't quite make it to the threshold before his prophecy came true.

Fallon lay sprawled on her belly across an overturned bench. "Yep. Like trilling little birds, *layahlayahlai...*"

Kerris pushed himself up against a table and grinned.

"By the Kingdom, Kirin, we're going to need a great more than opium on this trip."

Major Ursa Laenskaya sat up, eyes glassy and unfocused.

"Opium," she growled. "I hate opium."

She pushed herself to unsteady feet and stomped up the stairs to her room.

And Kirin Wynegarde-Grey, Captain of the Imperial Guard, placed his hands over his face, for his own vision had proved faithful, his own prophecies true. Madness and blasphemy would rain down upon his head, for they were about to embark on a journey, a sojourn to the Ends of the Earth, to find this Soul, this Solomon, not tiger, not even cat, but the last of the Ancestors, revered and idolized by every living creature in all of the Nations.

A human.

And with his very sword, the Captain of the Queen's Guard would kill him.

SWISSERLAND

Somewhere, far to the north and far to the west, far beyond the boundary of even the Lower Kingdom, there is a range of Mountains splitting yet another part of the earth in two. There are peaks that rival *Charta*, spears that mock *Kathandu,* although none can come close to matching *Shagar'mathah*. She is ours alone. But there *are* mountains, up there on the Edge of the Earth and answers to mysteries from the beginning of time. Perhaps even before this.

This is a land of green grass and orchards, lush slopes and steep winding rivers, of wild goats and dahl sheep and otters, storks and cattle as sturdy as yaks. There are no cats. There are no dogs. There are no people of any sort, for one cannot in truth consider rats as people even if they do chatter and have the arms of monkeys. True monkeys, those called *Chi'Chen*, can hold a conversation. *Chi'Chen* have homes, raise families, barter and sell wares like people. *Chi'Chen* hate dogs, envy cats, enjoy laughter. Rats kill. There is considerable difference.

This land is full of rats.

The temples are old, more like the temples of *Gobay* made of paper and steel and stone. They are broken and ruined and supposedly carry on for days without end. There are rivers of stone, also broken and ruined and these run to and from the temples in confusing patterns, weaving and twisting like the most intricate *KallaShakra* wheel. For the most part, this land is dreadful.

And yet, there are mountains.

Magnificent, towering, powerful mountains, perhaps even a worthy consort for our Great Mother should she ever find the need. Mountains are a source of purity and strength, so perhaps once this land was likewise. But no more. It is the way of things.

High in these mountains, there is a village.

Rather, there *was* a village, so very long ago.

Kandersteg, Switzerland.

And buried deep beneath such an old village, beneath layers of snow and soil and rock, sat a man called Solomon, head in hands, waiting for the nausea to subside.

It was black, save for the dim emergency grid-lighting along the floor. It was also cold, which probably was a blessing since it seemed those horrible rat creatures seemed to have a preference for warmth. The air was stale, at least 500 years stale (but he couldn't shake the feeling that it might be older) and stank of rat urine, liquid nitrogen and blood. He had been able to chip ice from several of the cryo-tanks so he was in no danger of dehydration just yet but his stomach had long since given up rumbling for attention, having begun the process of metabolic enervation for what it assumed would be another long hibernation.

He wished it were so easy.

"Hello? Anybody there?" he called again into the darkness, knowing it would be futile. These stray contacts were fleeting at best, chaotic at worst, and this time had left him with a sensation of vertigo. But at least he was not alone. He was not alone and for that, he was infinitely grateful.

It had all started three nights ago. Actually, it had all started centuries ago, but he couldn't spare the brainspace to think of it now. MAX, the orbital satellite, had made a colossal miscalculation, somehow allowing him to waken before the revival process had been complete. Now, his first memories of this new time, of this new world, were those of extreme cold and panic. Even now, they continued to haunt him with their vivid sensations. It was a danger he and his colleagues had thought they had long overcome. In the beginning, prototypes had produced the same effect and the SANDMAN Project had almost been scuttled because of so many early fatalities. He shuddered to think of it. It would not be a pleasant way to go.

He paused in his thoughts.

They had saved him.

These strange, backwards people, people who used horses and shamen and terms like "sidi," had saved him.

For the first time since he could remember, he found a smile tugging at the corners of his mouth. The irony amused him. Actually, it kind of hurt, so he stopped smiling and ran his palm across his face, finding stubble in its wake.

Somehow, they had saved him.

The others had not been so lucky.

Six fellow supervisors had met grisly fates, frozen and contorted, their tanks little more than sophisticated Arctic tombs. And then the rat-things had done their work, smashing in the plexi and pulling what they could of the bodies onto the floor. Solomon remembered that first morning when he had crawled warm and dry from his unit and tumbled unceremoniously onto the cold metal floor onto part of someone's arm. Not the waking he had expected. Certainly not what they had planned. And the rat-things had been plaguing him ever since, likely the start of every evening but since he was underground, he wasn't entirely sure. He also wasn't sure how he had managed to stay alive for this long and avoid their many scrabbling hands, their sharp slicing teeth, their sheer savage numbers.

One thing he was sure of, however, was that unless he got the comm back online, they would surely kill him. And he had not survived this long just to become this century's version of frozen dinner.

Not when he had 2000 others depending on him.

"Okay, Captain," he announced to the empty room, "If you're coming to find us, we'd better be ready. Let's see if I can find the welcome mat..."

He pushed himself to his feet and staggered over to the main terminal in Ops.

It was black, like the past. Like the present. And very possibly like his own future.

He adjusted the wire at the base of his skull, pulled over a creaky, rattling chair, and got down to work.

THE GREAT MOUNTAINS

It is impossible to remember all the things that transpired that night as we worked into the very hours of morning. In fact, I'm not entirely convinced that any of us found more than an hour of sleep before we were forced to begin our preparations for the journey that awaited us. But truth be told, I believe none of us missed those hours for a challenge had gripped us in invisible claws, the knowledge that we were about to embark on a journey where no cat had journeyed before, a sojourn unlike any other. We would be riding beyond the very edges of the known world. Even I must admit it was exhilarating.

The Seer was repeatedly sick for most of the night, and cold too from the effects of the raw opium. But he aided us as best he could as my brother and the Scholar drew map after map, changing and refining them with Kerris' familiarity and the Seer's memory.

Soon it became apparent that where we would be traveling, no map existed, and I began to question the accuracy of the vision that was sending us so far from home. I also began to question whether the journey was necessary at all for if there was indeed only a single Ancestor so far from our Empire, it was doubtful that he alone could bring down devastation to cripple the Matriarchy. But I was under orders to kill him. Could I do this thing? Could I not? As the maps were being drawn, I sat and wrestled with these thoughts, all the while under the golden eyes of the Alchemist.

She disturbs me.

Not only that but my scroll is missing. I wish to believe that, in the madness of the night's events it was simply discarded, swept into the fire with the crushed remains of the coals. I pray this is the case for if one of these people were to discover that our quest is now one of murder then I am convinced that their assistance would be neither whole-hearted nor unsolicited. For the most part, they are not soldiers.

Finally, after several hours more, I called a halt to the process, for it was obvious that the maps were of limited value and my people were growing giddy with exhaustion. The Major had preceded us to the upper rooms after our unceremonious 'crash' from unnatural places, and I had assumed she was sleeping. I found out she was completely otherwise, and had thoroughly dismantled one of the beds. She had carved an intricate sign into the rough mahogany headboard and was carrying it down the stairs as we dragged ourselves up them. I noticed her eyes still manic with opium. The five of us stood on the steps and watched as she threw open the Inn's front door and pounded the headboard into the hard earth by the entrance. She then stormed up past us and disappeared once again into her room, slamming the door with such force that the black windows rattled in their frames. The Scholar trotted back down the stairs to take a look and returned promptly with the news that the Inn at the Roof of the World now had a name.

"The Mother's Arms."

I thought it fitting.

We retired for the rest of the night but were up at the first light of dawn. Every bone in my body ached but Kerris seemed bright and eager to set out. Perhaps it is simply the difference in our natures. I am Metal, a creature of habit, preferring the routines of my job and the stability of the Kingdom, whereas Kerris is Fire and thrives on adventure and change. We both serve the Empress well, however, for as I work to maintain that which we already have, he sees what might be, and works toward that end. I could not do what he does, living such a free, independent life, and I know for fact that he could not survive within the confines of my responsibility. It is the way of things.

At first light, I had sent the guards to the markets to load our packhorses with tents and supplies. I was beginning to believe that this journey would take weeks, if not longer. As the horses were made ready, I made certain to give the innkeep a promissory note for his lodgings, for so many meals and for the destruction of at least one window and two beds. The Major had no memory of the events of the night previous, and I found her, fresh and well-rested, admiring her own handiwork on the sign outside the Inn. The Seer still looked ill but as I bid him good-morning, he touched my arm and asked if I had indeed brought him back from the lost last night. I told him that, with the help of others, I had. Then he said to me a very strange thing.

He said perhaps I was *Enough.*

We set out immediately, for our aim was to follow the Shi'pal River *northwest through the Great Mountains. Although the* Shi'pal *flows west most of its course, and then east, and then south, ultimately it finds its source in the north. It does indeed meet up with the Great Wall along the way. I was hoping to head due north, and reach the Wall by sunset, for it is equipped with frequent battle towers, cisterns of fresh water, and level footing. However, Kerris disagreed, citing the unpredictable nature of our quest thus far, the treachery of the northern pass and the fact that we were a large party, traveling with heavy-laden horses. I was forced to concede. So, just after dawn, we left the Inn, 'The Mother's Arms', and the mountains of* Sha'Hadin. *I knew we would not be seeing them again soon.*

-an excerpt from the journal of Kirin Wynegarde-Grey

The morning mist had lifted, allowing them an unparalleled view of the Great Mountains. They were a study in contrasts, these mountains, laying down steep, U-shaped valleys of pink shale aside level plateaus of snow. Stone hedges ran at unnatural angles, as if some cat had devised to create Walls of his own in miniature. Rocks as large as yaks alternated with stunted cedars to speckle the land like the back of a leopard and in the distance, spires of white and purple ruled everything.

Kerris and Quiz had naturally taken the fore, leading the party down the narrow, winding road from the marketplace and into territory quite unfamiliar to any of the riders. There was little conversation en route for the horses were trekking single-file and the precious lack of sleep in the last few days was beginning to take its toll. Even the Scholar's usual banter was negated in favor of head-bobbing, bleary-eyed silence. It was then that Kirin first considered the notion that, of all the factors weighing against them on this impossible journey, exhaustion might well be the most dangerous of all.

So after several hours, the river of horses rode deep into a red sandstone valley, veering sharply away from the majestic views of the Mountains and into the coolness of her shadows. The shade was welcome relief from the sun and as they descended, the spring runoff that had been trickling across the paths remained frozen like slick entrails of dripping white. The walls of the valley echoed with the sound of rushing waters but the *Shi'pal* was still nowhere to be seen. It seemed as though Kerris were leading them straight into the very heart of the earth.

Above them, Path the falcon pivoted on a high wind and disappeared around the crest of a ridge that rose before them, apparently blocking their trail.

alMassay slid the last of the way into the ravine and suddenly, the ridge opened up before them into a great cavern that had been hidden by the angle of descent. It was wide, dark and low, a frowning mouth with jagged teeth, and quite naturally, Kerris and Quiz were riding straight into it. Both were swallowed in seconds.

The guard directly behind them swiveled in his saddle, throwing his Captain a glance. Kirin nodded and the guard was immediately covered in a cloak of darkness. From the Scholar to the Major, the party disappeared before his eyes and Kirin found himself holding his breath as alMassay stepped slowly into the breach.

Every inch of his body tingled as the blackness consumed him and every other sense scrambled to adjust. His pupils opened wide, seeing fragments of light bouncing from buckles and straps and swords. It was damp, smelled of old moss and bat droppings. He could hear those bats too, clicking at the unexpected visitors, imagined them snatching at the crest of his hair from their upside-down perches. *Unclean creatures,* he thought grimly, *almost as bad as rats.* He was glad he couldn't see them.

The cavern was colder than the trail into it and the further they went, the damper and colder it became. The rushing of waters was growing louder too, almost drowning out the clopping of hoofs. Through the darkness, Kirin could see slices of sunlight, stabbing down through the rock and he prayed something remarkable awaited them at the end of this black journey.

The exit was as sudden as its entrance, the sunlight almost blinding him and he pulled his stallion short as his eyes adjusted.

Several horse lengths below them, the *Shi'pal* roared through steep red cliffs, her cold spray pricking his pelt and chilling him to the bones. On both sides, the ravine's edges sheered straight up to the sun

"Wow, oh wow! Oh-oh-oh wow!"

The Scholar gasped in open-mouthed wonder, but in truth, the Captain felt the same. The Mountains never failed to inspire him. There were constantly new sights, new marvels within her ample bosom. She was a Good Mother.

Kerris waved at him and al Massay jogged up alongside.

"This road will take us a good way," Kerris shouted to be heard over the rushing waters. "The river is full of fish and the cliffs full of pigeons. We might even take a cliff buck or two. We won't have to touch our stores for days!"

It was a good plan.

"No swimming, though," the grey lion said with a grin. "The current will crush you against the rocks like a clove of ginger. Right? So, Kirin, we keep going?"

"No."

"What? No? What's that?"

"No."

"No?"

"It is just past noon," Kirin shook his head. "We'll stop for a rest and a light meal. Our people are tired."

Kerris sat back on his pony. "Well. Yes, they are. I didn't think you'd noticed."

"I noticed."

"Some hope for you yet, brother," he said. "Right, we'll stop here then. It's as good a place as any."

And with that, he sprang from Quiz's back like a hare, making his way down the line to the packhorses. Kirin swiveled in his saddle.

All eyes were upon him.

He cleared his throat and through gritted molars, forced a smile.

"Time for tea."

***

the darkness was swallowing the sun. Shafts of light pierced the clouds but, one by one, their beams snuffed out under the all-pervading blackness. Pol'Lhasa *was consumed by shadows, and like the torches of midnight, eyes flickered on all around her, thousands of eyes, an army of yellow, gleaming eyes advancing upon her, flowing up her many steps, surrounding her in a siege of blackness and incense...*

"Kirin?"

"Hm."

"Kirin, wake up."

The Captain sat up, blinking the sun and sand from his eyes. Kerris was crouching before him, his ashen grey hair wet and sticking up all over his head.

"You've been sleeping for almost 2 hours."

"That's not possible."

"'Fraid so. Ask Ursa if you don't believe me."

For a split second, he was sorely tempted and the Captain's gaze flicked to his Major. Her back was to him but he could see she was busy rolling several rows of fillets that had been drying in the sun. Her hair was wet too, twisted into a tight knot on top of her head, and her white doeskin was patched with dampness. Kirin straightened himself against the rock.

"You haven't been swimming, have you?"

"In that river?" Kerris laughed. "No, thanks. Fishing gets you wet enough. We caught four more. Big ones, too. Ursa's a good fisherman." He cocked his head in her direction. "Aren't you, Ursa my love? A regular fishwife."

"Watch it, stableboy," her long tail lashed behind her. "Or you will be tasting my hooks..."

"She adores me, really she does. Looks like you've found a friend, too."

Kirin followed his brother's gaze to the thick spotted tail resting across his thigh. Beside him, Sherah al Shiva lay curled in a patch of sun, her lean, black-clad body claiming it like a spotlight. He snorted.

"Alchemists."

"The horses are ready, Kirin. Just waiting for riders. Well, I'd better help Ursa with that fish. You know how she gets, living the life of domestic bliss and all."

And with that, he left his brother's side, his good-humor a distinct contrast to the Major's growling.

Kirin took a deep breath and looked around.

Two leopards were only now beginning to rouse themselves from their afternoon naps.

The other two were still standing sentry and he felt a pang of remorse. With only four guards left, their stamina would be pressed thin as the daily duty rotations took their toll. He would make a point of redistributing their hours some time soon.

Farther down the rock face, the Seer began to stir. The falcon was perched on his left shoulder but this time, she shared her host with the Scholar who had tucked herself, childlike, under his arm. Kirin found himself smiling, wondering if the lynx Tiberius would have approved such familiarity. Surely such innocence could damage no one's soul.

At his own side, however, the Alchemist was another story. Before sleeping, she had loosened the laces at her throat and the milky white pelt of her chest and belly stood out like beams of sunlight in a darkened cavern. The black and silver vestments at her hips splayed skirt-like across the rock beneath her, as did her mat of wavy hair. *All* too *familiar*, he thought darkly. He lifted her tail away with ginger fingers.

Claws, strong and black, slid from the tips of her fingers as she engaged in an elaborate stretch from tip of tail to top of head, forcing him to watch every arch and curve of her waking. With a long breath, she rolled to sit next to him, her shoulder brushing his. She turned her sleepy golden eyes on him and smiled.

"Time to go?" she purred.

She was hypnotic.

"Yes," he said.

More beautiful than the sun.

"Yes, it is."

Like the Empress...

"It's time to go."

The Empress.

He stood too quickly, feeling the blood rush from his temples and causing him to breathe deeply to re-orient himself to their new terrain. The *Shi'pal* roared beneath them and the Captain studied the path ahead. The spray of waters would be a tolerable nuisance, keeping them cool in the heat of the ravine and awake to any dangers it might possess. Ice still crusted her steep banks and he knew at some point they would have to cross. He hoped there would be a bridge for it would be impossible to forge such a river.

With a quick nod of his head, he strode away from the cheetah, not knowing whether the chill racing up his spine was caused by the cool waters or the golden eyes weighing heavily upon him.

Farther down the rock face, the Seer nudged the young tigress with his arm.

"Wake up, *Kallilah.* I believe the Captain wants to head out."

Fallon looked up at him with a wide, floppy grin, slowly blinking the sleep from her eyes.

"Hmm. *Kallilah.* That's an old name. My father used to call me that when I was a little girl."

"It suits you."

"Yeah. That's what he used to say."

He rose to his feet, waiting patiently as she had yawned so that her tongue curled inside her mouth and stretched so that every joint in her arms popped. Finally, she took the gloved hand offered her and allowed herself to be helped to her feet.

"Isn't this river beautiful? This is the *Shi'pal,* right? Did you know that the *Shi'pal* has many names? Some places, she's called *Shammah'puthra,* and some places she's called *Shang'bun.* Depends on your province, I guess. And wow, what fish! I can't remember eating better fish, although I probably have, 'cause we used to eat glacier-fish all the time, but I just can't remember. Maybe I was just really hungry. Yeah, that's probably it. Well, let's go then. I just can't wait to see what we see next."

And she strolled away towards her horse, arms swinging, feet bouncing, white-tipped tail tapping out some tune that likely played inside her head. Sighing, Sireth watched her go, cursing his lapse and fighting back the rush of sadness that threatened to claim him. The falcon on his shoulder chirruped, pushed his cheek with her hooked beak. He stroked her breast.

"Yes. Yes, I know," he said softly. "What's gone is gone. Thank you for your counsel."

With that, Path left his shoulder, rising on the updraft from the ravine. She was a silhouette in moments.

He sighed a second time and looked around at the people, all busy with the business of mounting horses. Suddenly, there was a cold breeze and he turned. The Major was scowling at him as she tucked several dried fillets into her saddlebag. He held it for a heartbeat, her icy stare, then made a point of turning his back and heading for his own horse.

"Right!" called Kerris from the back of his pony. "Everyone ready? Yes? Let's go then! Adventure awaits!"

And so, like a river beside a river, the trail of horses moved out, refreshed and renewed for the journey ahead.

***

They hadn't seen the sun for hours. It was growing dark in this deep mountain ravine, the only light reflecting from great sheets of glacial ice. The road had narrowed, the river grown swifter and it was clear that a waterfall must lie ahead, for here they found signs of Ancestors.

Signposts really, artifacts from ancient days, pipes of rusted metal and great grey boxes split open by the earth, containing nothing of value any longer. But these artifacts were dangerous, as dangerous as anything left behind by the Ancestors and cats had long since learned to be wary of such things. Sometimes, such things killed.

So it was with some measure of caution that Kerris slid from his pony's back and disappeared into a cleft in the side of the mountain. Unlike the cliffs of *Sha'Hadin,* this cave was symmetrical, chiseled with angular precision and reinforced with the smooth grey stone so common throughout the Older Civilizations. And like most examples of that grey stone, this too was cracked by vines and alive with the moss that worked to gradually consume it. A fence of twisted red wire lay by the entrance, ready to snag both pelt and cloth if one moved too close. It still kept things out.

"Right! Safe enough!" called Kerris from within. "This will do for tonight!"

One by one, the party dismounted and began to remove the tack from their horses. The animals would be left to forage on their own for the night for horses were fierce hunters, adept at finding a meal at the expense of the lesser creatures. It wasn't uncommon for them to go for days on only mice, rabbits and grass. Their riders, however, were more particular.

"Pigeons," muttered Ursa as she made her way into the Old cavern. "I smell pigeons."

She bent down to gather a few small stones from the floor. She bounced them in her palm, rolled them across her fingers and with a swift sharp motion, flung the stones toward the ceiling. The roof echoed with the sounds of impact and almost instantly she was showered in feathers.

Several bodies thumped to the ground.

Fallon's eyes were wide as she slipped under the threshold and into the Old cavern. She inhaled the musty scent, let her gaze linger over the stark architecture of the room. It seemed to be a series of rooms actually, slick with river spray and rich with moss. In the centre, Kerris had already begun placing the coals for the night's campfire and she moved to his side immediately.

"This is amazing, isn't it?" she breathed.

"Well, it's just a pile of coals."

"No, I mean, places like this. Old places. Places of history. It must have been a powerful place."

"Why do you say that?"

"Well." She wrapped her arms 'round her ribs. "We're near a waterfall."

He glanced up at her. "You don't really believe those old tales, do you?"

"Well..."

"It's just impossible, now isn't it? There is simply no way to take fire from water. Any other element, perhaps, but not fire."

He resumed pouring the oil over the coals. She knelt down beside him.

"But look at the oil."

"The oil?"

"Well, we use the oil to make the fire. And they were smarter than us. Why couldn't they have used water to make fire?"

"Because it would get it all wet, now wouldn't it?"

"But maybe they didn't use it to make *fire.*"

"But isn't that what we're talking about?"

"Yes." The tigress nodded.

"Right then."

He bent back down to his work, trying not to look at her. She, however, was still looking at him, as if expecting him to be thinking about something.

"Maybe you should go help Ursa pluck those pigeons," he suggested. "Feathers do terrible things to my digestion."

She stayed beside him, expecting for several moments longer. Finally, she said, "Okay" and left.

He shook his head.

It wasn't long before the scent of incense descended from above and he felt warm breath on his neck. He did not need to look up.

"'Rah?"

"Yes?"

"Do you think the Ancestors could take fire from water?"

"They were very powerful."

He turned his face toward her, knowing she would be but a kiss away.

"Can you?"

She smiled.

"Of course."

***

The stories began that night.

Kerris had always been a good storyteller, not only for his remarkable memory for legend and his wealth of personal experience but for the animated way he presented both. In the glow of this late-night fire under the low mossy ceiling that flickered with lamplight, he told his tales. He told them with his whole body, tail slapping, eyes dancing. Alternately on his feet then down to his knees. Kirin could not help but notice that, almost without exception, the entire party was spellbound, taking in the performance with obvious delight. Even the Major seemed to be enjoying herself for she sat cross-legged, picking her teeth with the sharp tine of a feather, her customary scowl replaced by something like a wicked grin.

Only the Seer seemed distracted and Kirin made a note to speak to him before the night was through.

"So there we were, hauling this beastly creature out of the poacher's pit when suddenly the weight increased a hundred-fold!" Kerris' eyes were as round as blue moons. "It was almost as if I was hauling the thing up by *myself!*"

Fallon let out a little squeal, hands clasped tightly under her chin.

"Does anyone have any idea how much a baby behemoth weighs? Any idea at all? No? Well, let me assure you that they are very heavy, more than ten men I should think. And it was struggling and bellowing the entire time. I finally got a hold of its long nose, then one of its great floppy ears, and pulled the horrid little thing onto the grass. When at last I caught breath enough to look around, what did I find? That it was true - I *had* been pulling it up by myself! The rest of my pack was gone, disappeared into the jungle like the dung-beetles that they were!"

Ursa's smile broadened. Kirin shook his head.

"So, there I was, me, by myself, saving this baby behemoth from the poacher's nets when I feel this puff of hot breath on my neck..."

Fallon squealed again and Kerris looked at all the faces, his pause dramatic and well timed.

"And sure enough, when I gather my wits and turn around, what do I see but baby's great big behemoth Mummi standing behind me!"

Sherah sat forward. "Tusks?"

"Huge tusks, my dear! Longer than your cheetah's tail. Pointed right at me, I might add."

"Tusks can be ground up to make many things."

"And so can lions, under those great flat feet! I was just sitting there on the grass and there she was, towering over me like the mountains. They have such long noses, you know that? And hers grabbed me, wrapped me right round the middle, and before I knew it, I was in the air, face to face with this baby's angry mother! I could practically see the red in her beady eyes!"

Kirin suppressed a smile. The story got better each time Kerris told it. But to his brother's credit, it was true, every word of it. He had no need of exaggeration.

"I've seen behemoths tear the heads from men's shoulders," Ursa snorted. "Split them wide open with one blow from those tusks."

"What happened?" yelped the Scholar. "What happened?!"

"She put me down. Just like that. She put me down and walked away, crunching through the trees with her baby holding on to her tail."

"Wow," breathed Fallon, "You're really lucky."

Kerris looked at his brother and grinned. "Yes I am, aren't I?"

"Have you ever seen an Ancestor?"

All eyes turned to the Seer, speaking for the first time all evening and Kirin cursed under his breath.

"Come again, *sidi?"* asked Kerris.

"I mean, images of Ancestors. Carvings. Reliefs. Books, that sort of thing."

"Oh yes. Many, many times."

"Tell me."

"No." Finally, Kirin rose to his feet. "Not tonight. It is time to rest. We have an early start in the morning."

Silenced, benAramis averted his eyes as though guilty of breaking some unspoken taboo. But the Scholar was eager.

"Please sir, I think we all would love to hear–"

"I *said*, not tonight."

She was crestfallen.

And the party rose to their feet, breaking the warmth of the fire circle and moving towards their respective bedrolls. Kirin grabbed the Seer by the arm, his voice low and threatening.

"Not you, *sidi.* A word outside."

It was not a question.

There was a spark of defiance, but only a spark and it died quickly under the Captain's glare. He nodded slightly and followed Kirin into the night. Only Ursa watched them go.

***

"What were you *thinking?!*"

Sireth said nothing.

"Please tell me, *sidalord* Seer, for I wish to understand what you hope to accomplish by this game."

Kirin paced a small, furious circle, fists clenching and unclenching as he sought to rein in his temper. Several lengths away, the cliffs of the *Shi'pal* dropped into her glacial waters, sweeping the mountain snows over the falls to far distant valleys. Even in the bright moonlight, she was as black as the night. The Seer stood staring at the ground, saying nothing.

"After all," Kirin continued, "It was you who said this was madness, wasn't it? That you could tell no one but the Empress the fact that we are seeking an Ancestor? That it would be - what was the word - *devastation,* if anyone knew?"

Still nothing.

"Do you think that they will be any more eager to find this, this 'Soul' if they know what we know? Do you wish to frighten them with all this talk? Or do you merely seek to satisfy your own curiosity? Please tell me, *sidi,* for I truly wish to know."

It seemed for a moment that the Seer was about to speak, but thought better of it and continued to stare at the ground. Growling, Kirin folded his arms across his chest.

"Very well then. You have nothing to say now to me, I expect you to have nothing to say later to *anyone.* I will have no more talk of Ancestors, is that clear? This journey is dangerous enough without—"

"I saw him."

"You what?"

Sireth looked up, eyes bright.

"Solomon. I saw him. Last night, I saw an Ancestor."

The Captain had no response for him. In truth, the very idea of seeing an Ancestor was enough to send chills up his own spine. They simply did not exist anymore, *had* not for Dynasties and their departure had been the cause of much speculation. In fact, differing beliefs regarding their demise had, on many occasions, nearly rent the Kingdom in two. It was a volatile subject, and cats are after all, a volatile people.

"I touched him, too. Well, almost." The Seer continued. "He was real, Captain, as real as you stand here before me now, he was real. And not at all like the images in stone and glyph that are scattered throughout the Kingdom. He was so much like us."

"Enough."

"He had brown eyes, just like me. It's *not* unnatural! I could have sworn—"

"I said enough!" Kirin turned away, mouth grim. "No more of this talk. The others—"

"But they should know. This affects them too. Their skills, their—"

"No. It doesn't."

"Of course it does!" Sireth threw his hands into the air. "How can the Scholar understand if she is not presented with all the facts? How can the Alchemist—"

"You trust the Alchemist, now do you?"

"No, but—"

"And now these 'facts'. You did not feel obliged to share such 'facts' with me back in *Sha'Hadin.*"

"I was afraid. Now—"

"Now *I* am afraid, *sidi.* This knowledge is dangerous."

"They have a right to know."

"They will know what I allow them to know."

"And how do you intend on keeping it from them, Captain? There will be many, many nights spent on this journey, and many, many of these strange late-night conversations. Do you intend on keeping them all to yourself?"

"If I must, yes."

"You will not be able to do it."

Kirin stepped in close.

"You would be surprised what I am able to do, *sidi.*"

High above them, the shrill cry of a falcon echoed over the roar of the river. The distant fire circle cast long, menacing shadows up the sides of the rock. The wind from the ravine whipped their clothes and hair but the two stood like stone, set against each other by the gods. *This knowledge is dangerous*, Kirin had said and he believed that. But there was something else, something less noble wrestling inside and try as he might, he simply could not push it from his thoughts.

He set his jaw.

"You will not speak of these things again. Do you understand?"

The Seer pulled himself to his full height, good eye glittering in the moonlight.

"You would be surprised at what I am able to *understand*, Captain."

And with that, he brushed past the lion, returning to the warmth of the fire, and the company of others.

Kirin remained outside for some time longer.

***

It had begun again.

"Okay, okay, tell me again where this *Pol'Lhasa* place is."

Kirin sighed and rubbed his temple. This time, Solomon was insistent, almost aggressive in his conversations, and the Seer's hands moved with quick, agitated motions.

"*Pol'Lhasa* is the palace in the Royal City of *DharamShallah,* which lies in the heart of the Great Mountains—"

"Mountains, mountains, which mountains?"

"The *Great* ones, Solomon. Those which separate the kingdoms."

The Seer was shaking his head.

Fallon sat forward.

"It's in the province of *Mepal,* if that's any help."

"Sorry, Fallon. I'm just not getting it."

Stretched out on the floor, chin in hands, Kerris was barely awake.

"You speak so strangely."

"So do you, my friends. So do you..." Solomon's voice trailed off and he seemed deep in thought.

"I'm going to sleep." The grey lion dropped his head into his arms. "Wake me if you need me."

"Wait a minute..."

"You *don't* need me. Really."

"What is the name of your palace again?"

"Pol'Lhasa," said Kirin.

"In the province of where?"

Mepal."

The Seer closed his eyes. "In the mountains."

"The Great Mountains, yes."

"Oh man..."

"Solomon?"

"Ohhhh mannn..." He placed a palm over his face. "You're in Tibet."

"Mepal," corrected the Captain.

"Acttally," corrected the Scholar. *"DharamShallah* used to be in the Province of *Hindaya,* until 200 years ago."

Kerris looked up. *"DharamShallah* was in Hindaya?"

"Yep," she nodded. "It became our capital when we lost the battle of *Lha'Lhasa* in *Shibeth.* Then the borders of all the provinces were redrawn and we conceded the new capital to *Mepal.* That's why we still squabble over *Shibeth."*

"We didn't lose the battle!" Ursa's eyes flashed. "It was a *Chi'Chen* concession."

"See? Squabbling. So Solomon could be right."

"Well done!" Kerris laughed from his bedroll. "Scholar in the Court of the Empress."

She felt the heat rise in her cheeks.

Kirin nodded.

"So, Solomon, you know the province of *Hindaya*, then?"

"Yeah. And the Great Mountains must be the Himalayas. Oh ho ho man. I am so screwed."

"He speaks so strangely," Kerris muttered from the floor but his brother sat forward.

"You understand, Solomon? Do these words mean something to you?"

"Yes, Captain. They mean that I'm screwed."

"Please, Solomon. Now *I* don't understand."

The Seer sighed. "Remember where I said I was?"

"Swisserland."

"Right. That's right. Well, Switzerland and the place you call

Mepal are half a world away."

"Beyond the edge of the earth."

"Something like that. And I have no idea what your roads are like anymore."

Kerris groaned. "Until we reach the Wall, the roads are no better than this one, really. Worse maybe."

Solomon continued. "Is it too much to hope that you still have cars?"

"Carts? We have carts but we are on horseback. It is the fastest—"

It was Solomon's turn to laugh. It was a strange laugh, big and hearty and lasting far too long, finally ending with a futile wiping away of tears from unseeing eyes. He shook his head.

"From Nepal to Switzerland. On horseback. Maybe I should call you Marco Polo."

There seemed to be a measure of despair in his voice, a measure Kirin was beginning to share.

"This is a long way?" he asked.

"Should take, oh, I dunno, a couple of *years*! But don't worry. I'll be fine. I'll just sit right here and wait..."

"Are you alone?"

"I have no idea."

"Then we shall hurry."

"Okay." A weary smile spread across the Seer's face, to be quickly replaced by a frown. "Okay, I'm losing you here. Can you still hear me, Captain?"

"Yes, Solomon."

"Captain? I can't hear you anymore, Captain. Or think you, or whatever we're doing. So goodnight all and Godspeed."

The Seer's eyes grew vague, then after a few moments, sharp. Only one focused on the Captain however, and this time, there was no hiding the contempt.

"Did you get what you needed?" Sireth growled.

"For tonight."

"May I go back to sleep now?"

"By all means."

He disappeared into the recesses of the cavern. Rising to her feet,

Ursa shot a glance at her Captain.

"You should not allow that," she warned.

She too disappeared into the shadows.

"Dream sweet, all," mumbled Kerris as he pulled the blanket over his head.

That left the Alchemist and the Scholar. They were both looking at him. For some reason, he could not meet their eyes.

***

"Kirin!"

The Captain jogged his stallion up past the river of horses until he was at Quiz's flank. Kerris looked grim.

"Bad news, I'm afraid..."

Kirin followed the pointing grey finger across the river. In the bright noonday sun, it was difficult to make out exactly what his brother was pointing at. The sides still sheered off into the *Shi'pal* below but the river had been progressively widening the further along they journeyed. Wider, slower and flatter she flowed, patches of ice clinging to her sides and sweeping her banks. And yet, as he scanned the high red ridges, he could see nothing to peak Kerris' interest.

"What is it, then?"

"The bridge."

"The bridge?" Pulse quickening, he scanned the slopes once again and once again, there was nothing. "I see no bridge."

"There you have it. The bad news."

His heart fell like a stone. "Are you certain this is the place?"

"Look down."

No more than a man's width from the road, there was a mound pushing out of the snow. It was a stump, a rotted post with a scrap of twine twisting in the breeze. Across the river, he could see a similar mound. The bridge was gone. Kirin sat back in the saddle, gritting his teeth in frustration.

"We cannot forge such a river. Is there no other way?"

Now Kerris sat back, brow furrowed, chewing absent-mindedly on a thumb claw.

"Well..."

Kirin waited for several moments. "Well?"

"Well, if we follow the river another day, the mountains fall away. It is still fast, but in winter the surface does freeze up some. A horse can get across. Well, at least a pony can."

"It is not winter," Kirin growled.

"Yes, well, that might be a problem."

"And we have ten horses, plus a pony."

"Many problems."

"Another day, you say?"

"Half-day, if we ride quickly."

"Then we shall ride quickly." He swiveled in his saddle. "The bridge is out! We must make good time to the next crossing. Is this understood?"

There were nods all around and al Massay forged ahead, his powerful legs carrying him easily past the pony. Quiz squealed and scrambled to catch up.

Behind them both, the Alchemist smiled at the Scholar, her golden eyes mere slits in the sunlight.

"Perhaps, you could build one of your 'cat-a-pults'."

Fallon blinked several times, glancing up at the sheer walls of the ravine, then back at her companion.

"No. No. Not really a good idea, not really. I mean, it would work, I could build it but it would take time and materials but one little mistake and *splat*, cat innards all over the rocks. And the horses. No, no, I don't think –"

"It was a joke."

"Oh."

The black mare loped forward, leaving the tigress craning her neck behind.

"That, that was funny! Really. That was a really funny… um, joke…"

The sound of Ursa's snarl was enough to spur her horse onward and the band picked up the pace toward the second crossing.

***

It was as Kerris had said. As they rode, the *Shi'pal* widened, her banks growing less steep with each passing hour, ice and snow clinging to her sides like hide on a brittle carcass. She had exchanged her previous roaring disposition for a more temperate one and many forks had left her like so many wandering children. Finally, a stretch of white from side to side with a promise of solid footing. Even so, Kirin found himself shaking his head. The sun had long since disappeared behind the edge of the earth, drawing the skies above them in her nightgown of purple. It would not be long before she hid her face completely, leaving them the impossibility of crossing this river in utter darkness.

"Well?" said Kerris, blowing warm breath into his palms.

"This joins the Great Wall?"

"Just beyond that ridge. It's actually closer here than at the rope bridge, but the river is far wider, as you can see. You can't bridge this."

The Captain dismounted, moving slowly to the edge of the river, sinking up to his boots into the drifts. There was still much snow in these parts, for while the mountains were less severe than in eastern *Mepal,* the west lived and breathed winter. It was the way of things.

He put his hands to his hips.

"It doesn't look safe."

Kerris grinned. "Neither did the rope bridge."

"You first."

The grin melted away.

"Yes. Right. No problem."

Slowly, he slid from his pony, his own yak-hide boots sinking up to the laces. Obediently, Quiz followed his rider, short sturdy legs completely swallowed by the drifts and together, the pair skirted down the steep bank and thudded onto the ice.

It held. With an audible sigh, Kerris began to cross, stepping carefully at first, but with increased confidence at each footfall. At the mid-point of the river, he paused and threw a wave back to the party watching his progress from the high bank.

"See! No problem! Strong as the mountains!"

And for emphasis, he thumped his boot several times before resuming his trek. Kirin was not cheered by his brother's claims however, for the mountain pony was wire-tight, nostrils flared, ears as straight as a plumbline. Nevertheless, within minutes, they had reached the far bank and up safely on the other side.

Kerris waved again.

"Come on!"

A leopard next, and then the Scholar. It was slow going as the Captain made each rider dismount and lead his horse across. The sun was all but gone and eyes were straining in the twilight sky. Kirin had sent the last guard on ahead, leading both his own mount and the last packhorse. The man's voice carried across the ice, speaking in alternately calm and stern tones. One of the horses was snorting nervously, its hoofs slipping and scraping the surface and Kirin cursed the shadows, for he could see little of what was taking place. Then, a sudden squeal and the sound of a great weight hitting the ice and more curses. Finally, Kerris' voice echoed across the river.

"Get on, man! Ride him across!"

"But the Captain said —"

"Do as he says!" Kirin boomed and within moments, the last leopard guard had reached the shore.

That left the Captain. He reached up and stroked the long, proud nose of his stallion, patted the thick arched neck.

"Are you ready, my friend? Of course, you are. Let's go." *More dependable than soldiers, more faithful than men.*

With a leading hand on the reins, the pair slid down the snow and onto the ice.

He could barely make them out on the other side until from out of nowhere, a candle flickered into the darkness and then another. The Alchemist. He could make out her kohl-rimmed eyes, the curling stripe along her nose and cheek, her haunting smile. She was a beacon, calling him to shore and he could not help but come. Step after step in near darkness, great hoofs pounding the ice behind him, he had reached the mid-point of the river when alMassay stopped.

"No. Come, 'Massay. We are almost—"

There was a sound, a low grating sound, the sound of grinding wheels and massive weight, and the ice shifted beneath his boots.

"Kirin!" shouted Kerris from the far bank. "Run!"

The sound was angry now, snapping away from him like

fireworks, squealing like many ponies. alMassay bellowed, rearing back and yanking the Captain off his feet. Hands and knees took the impact as he came down on the hard surface of the ice, and Kirin felt freezing water splash his face. alMassay backed up, swinging his great head, reins whipping about his neck. Kirin scrambled to his feet and leapt for the reins, ignoring his brother's cries from so far away. There was water everywhere, seeping through the cracks and flooding the surface of the ice. Sharp stinging water that bit his tail and hands and face. Finally he caught the leather and at the contact the horse lunged forward and forward again, splashing and slipping when suddenly, the great sheet gave way. alMassay plunged downward and Kirin went with him.

Kerris was on the move. He had not needed to see the struggle to know how it would end. He raced to one of the packhorses and pulled a coil of rope from the supplies. When the *Shi'pal* opened her great mouth, Kerris was already scrambling down the bank.

"Ursa! Hold!" He tossed one end of the rope to the Major and continued with the rest onto the river. She did not follow his order, however, and pushed the rope into the Seer's gloved palm.

"You. Hold."

She didn't wait for a response before following the grey lion out onto the ice.

Open water is blacker than night under a starry sky but the pair could make out the silhouette of the Imperial stallion, haunches submerged, chest and forelegs heaving forward, scrabbling for any hold. Kerris had great difficulty, however, picking out his brother from the mass of buckles and wet leather but Kirin was holding fast to the saddle, his own claws failing to make any headway against the slick, sharp ice. The current was strong, his cloak heavy with water, pulling his face under every time he made progress. The horse's legs churned the river like iron.

"Kirin! Here!"

Crouched low to the ice, his own legs stretched wide, Kerris reached for his brother. The Captain shook his head.

"N-n-no," he said, teeth chattering in the cold. "G-get Massay f-first."

"No, you first. Take the rope."

"And if-f it was Q-quiz?"

"Right. I'm coming around. Pass it under his haunch."

Immediately behind him, Ursa was stunned. "What are you doing? Get the Captain!"

"We get the horse!" he snapped. "Listen and obey!"

And before she could argue, he'd scrambled behind the stallion, laying the rope across the sinking back. Weighted by the heavy cloak, Kirin struggled to pull himself through the water along the saddle and girth. His hands were numb, fingers fumbling across the stiff leather and frozen buckles and finally under the dark water to slide the cord beneath his stallion's haunch. The water bit like many teeth.

"Kirin? Got it?"

"Y-yes…"

"Wing! Per!" Calling two of the leopards by name, Kerris motioned them onto the river, tossing them the last of the rope and waving them back before they got too close.

And then, back to the horse, sliding across the ice and crouching low under alMassay's straining neck. Kerris grabbed the bridle.

"Kirin, you ready? Kirin?"

In the killing cold of the water, he found himself growing strangely quiet. Kerris threw the Major a quick look before scrambling out of the horse's path and straightening up several lengths away.

"Now! Pull!"

The cord snapped under the stallion's haunch, providing him impetus and support and with powerful force, he lunged forward. Like a massive pendulum, the stallion threw all his weight onto the fore, hoofs churning up a path through the ice and dragging his rider along with him. On the bank, all hands were on the rope, backs heaving, boots deep in snow. The stallion stumbled up and onto the ice like a newborn foal but Ursa was at his head in an instant, grabbing the bridle and guiding him toward shore. Kerris grabbed his brother and worked to pry the stiff fingers from the saddle. He slipped a shoulder under the heavy arm just as Kirin's legs buckled beneath him.

"Blankets!" shouted Kerris. "We need blankets!"

There was a flurry of activity on the shore and many hands

reaching to haul them onto the *Shi'pal*'s snowy banks.

Kirin glanced around. His eyes popped in the darkness as faces moved in and out of his vision. His chattering teeth threatened to crack his skull.

"M-Massay... where's alMassay?"

Suddenly, there was a blanket around his shoulders and Kerris was leading him away from the others.

"Will someone start up a fire and Sherah, tea if you please?"

"Kerris, please… Massay?"

"Ursa has him. She'll take good care of him."

"No. Kerris, you do it. You know him. He trusts you."

"I will. I will, but first," Kerris turned him and began to tug at the frozen buckles. "You've got to get out of this. Leather freezes stiff. So will you."

Kirin tried to push his hand away, but his own were thick and useless.

"No, no, I'll be fine."

"No, you'll be frozen." The heavy cloak hit the snow with a thud, the brigandine a close second. "We have plenty of blankets to keep you warm."

"But Kerris—"

"But nothing."

He caught his brother's wrist.

"Kerris. I can't."

Kerris cocked his head and waited, patience wearing thin.

"Kerris, there are women..."

"Oh, by the Kingdom, what vanity!" Kerris laughed. "Here I thought you were just being modest. Beautiful as you may be, Kirin, do you really think they will abandon their wills at the sight of your disrobed body?"

He shook his head, still grinning. "Our female companions are discreet and self-controlled, Captain Wynegarde-Grey. Shame on you for thinking otherwise."

Kirin lowered his eyes.

"Yes, yes, you are right. And I am very, very cold..."

"There you are, then. Let's get you warmed up by the fire." He began to pull at the laces of the uniform. "Trust me, dear brother, no one will be looking at you."

***

"Wow. Will you look at him?"

"I am looking, Scholar."

Fallon bit her lip but could not tear her eyes from the sight of Kirin Wynegarde-Grey, sitting by the fire, a blanket around his hips, another over his shoulders, and drying his waist length hair between his hands. Beside her, Sherah al Shiva was doing the same, watching and running her tongue along a sharp feline tooth. Ursa crouched beside them, sharpening her blades. She glanced up at them.

"See his chest?" she said.

"Oh, oh yes. I - I see it."

"It is a good chest," said Sherah.

"Rather hard to miss," said Fallon again. "All big and golden and, and *big* like that."

"See that white scar in the center?"

They narrowed their eyes, trying to pick out the one she was meaning. He was a soldier. He had many scars.

"The one by his heart?" asked Fallon. "That one?"

"I gave that to him." Ursa grinned at the memory. "I almost killed him."

Next to him, Kerris sat, exchanging wicked glances with their female audience. The Captain however seemed oblivious, frowning at the ripple of a wave in his normally poker-straight hair.

"Wow, what a mane," sighed Fallon. "Why doesn't Kerris have a mane like that?"

"Can't." Ursa snorted. "Won't grow."

"Why not?"

Her pale eyes flicked up, darting between the other women before she shrugged, picked at the hard earth with a dagger.

"It's just a story."

Fallon knelt beside her. "Tell me."

"There is a story among the ranks. They say he called down lightning when he was a kitten. That is how their father died – he was carrying Kerris on his shoulders and Kerris called the lightning and killed his father. That he killed a cousin the same way. That he can still call the lightning to this very day, which is why he spends so much time alone."

Fallon sent a long look to the brothers – so different, sunshine and moonlight, and suddenly she felt very sad.

"That's why it sticks up all over his head like that." Ursa bent back to her blades. "He's not like a real lion at all."

"My, my, my," purred a rich voice and Sireth slipped up from behind. "What is going on here? Is this our Captain you are leering at, our proud and noble leader? I wonder if he would appreciate knowing about your rather base attentions?"

Ursa snorted again. "You're jealous."

"Absolutely."

He smiled at her and left their company, lowering himself down next to the lions with quiet grace.

"This will not do," the Captain growled. "There should be no ripples. Kerris, why haven't you found my comb?"

"Sorry."

"I will not be pleased if this continues."

"At least you're alive."

"No point in being alive when your mane has ripples."

Kerris grinned at Sireth, who, being part lion, had a long dark mane that fell past his shoulders. But, being only part lion, it rippled like a river. Sireth shrugged. Kerris rose to his feet.

"Right then, Kirin. It looks like you're in good hands. Rest. I'll go tend alMassay."

"Yes please. And Kerris, I think he may have sliced his forelegs. If he needs stitches—"

"I'll take care of him, Kirin. Rest."

He left the fire and disappeared in the shadows. Silence followed in his wake.

Sireth sat staring into the flames and out of the corner of his eye, Kirin watched him. The man seemed to want to say something, but was unsure how to begin. This time, the Captain felt no inclination to help him. He drew his blanket across his shoulders and fell into his own thoughts. His comment earlier had not been the truth. He *was* lucky to be alive, he knew. The water had been bitterly cold and if he'd stayed under much longer, it would have killed him easily. He shuddered at the thought of being swept beneath the ice, water filling his mouth, his nose, his chest, the breath splitting his body like a brittle wineskin. It was bad enough simply to have gotten wet.

He looked up to see the Alchemist watching him from across the clearing. Her candles burned all around them, flickering warmly against the snow and rock, as she quietly brewed fresh tea. The art of *chado* was apparently hers along with that of alchemy and Kirin found himself grateful for it.

"I, for one, am glad you're alive, ripples or no," said the Seer.

"Are you?"

"Of course. Why shouldn't I be?"

Kirin turned back to the fire. "If I were dead, you could go home."

"And if *I* were dead, *you* could go home." His smile faded. "You *are* joking, aren't you?"

Kirin said nothing. Sireth stared at him.

"You're serious."

"I am always serious."

"Why would I wish you dead?"

"We argued last night. The last time we argued, three of my men died."

"You think I did this? Like the avalanche. You *still* think I'm doing all of this?"

"I think you are a man accustomed to keeping secrets."

"Of course I keep secrets! " Sireth snarled. "I am one of the Council of Seven. It's is simply my *job.*"

The outburst caused not only the women to stare but the leopards as well, a definite breach of discipline. Kirin gritted his teeth.

"Perhaps, *sidi,*" he growled. "But not now. Not with me. Did you cause this?"

"Perhaps *she* is the firestarter. Have you ever considered that?"

"Answer the question."

"No. I did not cause this. I did not cause the avalanche. I did not kill my friends."

"Did you kill a lion serving in the National Guard?"

The man's head snapped up.

"Who told you that?"

"Did you?"

The Seer stared into the fire for a long moment and Kirin could see tiny muscles twitching in his bearded jaw. He turned back to the Captain, leaning into him like an old friend.

"Another secret," he purred. "But perhaps, I shall tell you sometime..."

He rose to his feet, brushed the snow from his robes and smiled.

"Besides, we all have our secrets, don't we, Captain? Some knowledge is simply too *dangerous* for the ears of others. You might do well to remember that. Goodnight."

He snatched his bedroll and, like Kerris earlier, left the warmth of the fire. The flames leapt a little higher, roared a little louder, at his passing.

***

"That should not happen," growled Ursa. "The Captain should not allow that."

Sherah inclined her head. "And what should the Captain do?"

"He should fight him. He should beat him."

Golden eyes scanned the rocky clearing. The guards were checking perimeters. Kerris was with the horses. Fallon had gone to find him. The Seer had disappeared and the Captain continued to dry his hair by the fire.

Sherah smiled and poured two cups of tea.

"He shouldn't kill him?"

"No. We need him."

She stirred in the honey. "You grow fond of him."

"What?! I *despise* him! I hate him so much I could kill him!"

"Then, do it. Do your Captain a favor. Fight him. Beat him. Kill him if you wish. I will say nothing."

"I cannot."

"He has killed lions before. It is only a matter of time."

"What? Blasphemy! Where did you hear this?"

She passed Ursa a mug before raising one to her own lips.

The steaming liquid bit her tongue, her throat.

"Only a story," she smiled. "Among the ranks..."

***

Fallon watched as he muttered and fussed and rubbed the great animal with an affection that men seldom spent on their wives. She had often wondered why men did such things and had come to two conclusions. One, that men believed their lives depended more on their horses than their houses and Two, that horses were lovely to look at, yet easily controlled. Of the two, she did not know which was closer to the truth.

In the cold night air, a squeal echoed down from the mountains and she realized that Quiz had made a kill. A rabbit perhaps or a grouse. Something more substantial than a mouse, at any rate. She shuddered. It was so easy for animals to kill animals. It was natural. It was the way of things. But for people to kill people, that was something she had never understood. Even for a cat to kill a dog was beyond her reason. Dogs had longer noses. Dogs couldn't retract their claws. Dogs married freely, without thought to race or caste. Perhaps this was why they were considered animals. Still, she could never kill one.

The great horse, alMassay, nickered and stretched out his neck, nostrils blowing softly in her direction. It was only then that Kerris noticed her.

"Oh, hello *sidala.* Can you grab that green pouch over there? The one on the rock?"

She found it and brought it to him.

"Open it up will you?"

She did, and immediately her nose was assaulted by the most hideous of smells.

"Wow. What is it?" she asked, trying not to look too intrigued when he stuck his hand in the bag and pulled out a glob of black slime.

"Salve for his scrapes. See here," Grey hand took orange, guiding her down the powerful leg to a series of cuts across the bone. "From the ice. Took off a big slice of his pelt here."

"Is it serious?"

"Could have been if it had been boggy water and we hadn't had the salve."

"Boggy water?" Her eyes lit up. "Do you have any idea the creatures that live in boggy water?"

"Not edible ones, that's for certain. Anyway, what are you doing out here? Shouldn't we all be bedding down for the night?"

"Oh, yes, well we are. That's mainly the reason I came to find you. To tell you. We're bedding down. For the night."

"We are?"

"Yes."

"You and me?"

"No!" She laughed nervously, snatching her hand from his and taking several steps back. "Nononono, ha haaah…Uh, no."

"Same as usual?"

"Yep. Same as usual."

"Too bad. I think Kirin snores. Or maybe that's me."

She watched him rub the salve into the wounds and wipe the residue on his trousers. *So different from a normal lion,* she thought to herself. The Captain would never do that.

"Ursa says you call down lightning."

"Ahhh…"

He frowned but did not look up.

"I – I'm sorry. I shouldn't have said anything."

"No, no. It's alright." He straightened, wincing as the stitches pulled in his back. "It's hard to describe. I don't call the lightning. The lightning, she calls me."

"The lightning calls you?"

"Yes. Lots of things do, really. They all have voices."

"What do?"

"You know, the air, the earth, water. Most especially water."

"Oh."

"But the lightning is the loudest. And the angriest."

"Oh."

"But I don't remember much when it happens."

"Like the cobra."

"What cobra?" But he grinned at her, and she was amazed at

how, even in the dark moonlight, his smile still shone like the sun. "Alright then. We'll walk him back. I don't want him far from the group tonight."

"Just in case."

"Exactly."

The snow was soft under their boots, the night silent and still, but Fallon's heart was pounding like a herd of wild yaks. She cleared her throat.

"You were pretty amazing tonight. With your brother, I mean. And, and, and the river."

"Yes well, just my job, you know. Saving people and all."

"I was really proud of you."

"You what?"

"I, I, I was just, you know, really proud of you."

"You were?"

"I was."

"Well." He smiled again. "Thanks."

"You're welcome."

"Happy to save *you* again sometime."

"Looking forward to it."

They walked back to the camp with a great Imperial horse between them.

***

"Lion-killer."

Sireth groaned and rolled over, wrapping his arms over his head and pressing his face into the snow.

"Lion-killers are executed. How come you were never executed?"

"Because it was my kharma to face a slow, miserable death with you."

And he pulled his bedroll over his ears.

Ursa crept even closer, pausing only when she heard the chirrup of the falcon perched on a rock above.

"You should not talk to the Captain like that."

"Why not?"

"It is dangerous. It shows no respect."

He lifted his face to look at her, rested his chin on his arms. She was also on her belly no more that a breath away, eyes intense, mouth a tight line, hair spilling all over the snow. It was difficult to distinguish snow from leopard.

"And this bothers you?"

"It should bother you. He is within his authority to kill you."

"Why do you care?"

"The mission would fail. That would not reflect well on him."

"Come closer."

The same look, a flash of fear and resistance, crossed her silver face. But he had issued a challenge and she was no coward.

She inched forward.

"You love him," he said.

"I respect him. He is a good leader."

"But you don't love him."

"I love no one. No thing."

"Closer."

They were so close now that he could feel her breath on his forehead, see the pulse of her throat. Her pupils were wide, black.

"Who has done this to you?"

"Done what?"

"Turned you to stone."

She snorted. "Life has turned me to stone."

He did not touch her.

"I *have* killed a lion," he said. "And Life has killed me a thousand times over. But you... I fear you are more dead than I."

After several long moments, she drew back and opened her bedroll. She flapped it out onto the warm snow and sat, pulling her cloak about her shoulders and wrapping her arms around her knees.

"Go to sleep," she ordered. "I will watch over you."

"I know you will," he said softly. "I know."

***

His muscles ached as he bent down to pull on his boots. He had not realized how easily the water could cripple and while the fire had rendered his uniform warm and soft, inside he was still bitterly cold.

He badly needed to sleep as well but soon, Solomon would come. Kirin would not leave that to the others. Sighing, he looked about the snowy ground for his sash.

"I can help," said a voice, and the Captain turned to see Sherah standing immediately behind him, black cloak and hood hiding all but her face. He didn't want to think how long she had been standing there.

"I can fix this."

And she held up the sash of gold, the symbol of his rank in the Queen's Court, embroidered threads catching the moonlight like falling stars. It was torn at one end.

He took it from her, turning it over in his hands.

"No," he said as he began to wrap it round and round his waist. "No, I wish to show the Empress the extent of our travails when we return."

"We will return?"

"Of course. Why wouldn't we?"

"I thought..."

When she did not finish, he turned to study her.

"What kind of mission did you think this was, *sidala?"*

"The kind from which one does not return."

"You will return."

"We have lost four already."

"Too many." He shook out his cloak, patted the snow from its dark golden folds and pulled it over his shoulders. "No more."

"A promise?"

"A wish." He began to walk back to the campfire, Sherah a silent shadow at his side. *"Sidala?"*

"You may call me Sherah."

"Sidala, the Seer has accused you of being a firestarter."

"Of course he would."

"You deny it, then?"

The hems of their cloaks swept across the snow and rocks as they walked. Black and Imperial gold. It was like a heartbeat.

"The military has always been wary of the Gifts and the Arts, *sidi.* These cannot be seen nor touched, nor therefore, killed. And what cannot be killed must be feared."

He couldn't stop a smile.

"Do they train you to speak like this?"

"Of course." She smiled back. "But you see, I know you are concerned with the pragmatic. If either one of us was a firestarter, how would that change *you?*"

He paused. It was a good question.

"Kirin! *Sidalady* cheetah!" It was Kerris and the Scholar, the stallion's shiny body a solid block between them. "There you are. Heading back to camp?"

"Kerris, how is he?"

Kerris slapped the great beast's chest.

"Sound as a yak. Those scratches shall heal up nicely. Sherah, any chance we could get a last cup of tea before bed?"

She was already moving, a ghost of black slipping through the night. But she did turn her face as she left, golden eyes gleaming through her hair.

"Of course."

***

It was well past second watch. The falcon swooped down over the camp, the floppy body of a rabbit in her talons. She soared over the figures in bedrolls, scattered around the fire, the Captain and the brother, the Alchemist and Scholar. Two leopards slept nearby, and she circled them, before arching her wing and rising higher. She spied the other two, standing sentry on the surrounding rocks and chirruped to them. One raised a hand to her, a greeting from a fellow watcher.

She had seen the Wall tonight, had taken the rabbit at its very base. It was not far, a day's travel at most. There were plenty of rabbits. It had been a good night.

She angled downward toward her master, calling him with his falcon's name. He did not respond, for his sleep was deep, deeper than any of the past nights. At his side, the silver soldier lay. *A kindred spirit,* thought Path, *lover of pigeons and blood.* She lit on a rock high above them and began to tear at the soft rabbit fur to the still-warm flesh beneath.

Tonight had been a rare night, for tonight, Solomon did not come.

THE GREAT WALL

The Great Wall is unlike anything in the Upper Kingdom. It finds its source high in the Land of the *Chi'Chen,* protecting monkeys from the marauding of dogs. It is not known how long ago it was begun, for truth be told, cats did not begin it. It is said to have originated in the time of the Ancestors. I believe it, for it is very well made and architecture is always a true test of culture. This is a fact well understood by cats and when we undertook to continue the task two Dynasties ago, we were hard pressed to maintain its integrity. By the time it guards our borders, the Wall reaches heights of ten men and an army can travel several horses across. Battle towers are frequent, at least one every hour and more frequently along disputed borders like *Shibeth* and the *Phun'jah.* Few have ever seen it or trodden its stone. I have. It is marvelous.

For the most part, the work is done by tigers. Tigers who labor day and night, stoking kilns and making bricks and carting stone from quarries as far away as *Gizah.* Tigers who lay brick upon brick, filling gaps with mortar and shaping clay by the ton. Some leopards work as fine masons, some jaguars as engineers and of course, the project is overseen by lions. Only lions can keep the sort of order required for such a task. A few of Sacred blood have positions in the financing and purchasing of stone, kilns and equipment, but for the most part, the work is done by tigers.

No one is entirely sure why.

Starting high beyond the easternmost canton of *Xhiangxing*, it winds its way southward through the Arms of our Mother, the Great Mountains, skirting her peaks like a leaf on a river. It hems the provinces of *Bhushan, Shibeth* and *Mepal*, only to rise upwards once again, meeting the *Zashkar Pass* in the beautiful, terrible province of *Phun'jah.* There, it is a magical place of glaciers and waterfalls and deep jungle valleys, a broken place of salt flats and ruins and dry, dead plains. Where *DharamShallah* is the roof the known world, the *Phun'jah* is its breast. Beyond that, the tigers still work.

So, it was with some measure of satisfaction that Kerris saw it stretched out before him, the gold serpent that was the Great Wall, a flash of order traversing the unbridled Mountains. He couldn't help but grin for he knew Kirin would be pleased. It seemed little this morning had pleased him.

Kerris had been rudely awakened by the sound of his brother cursing and scrambling out of the bedroll next to him. It had also been terribly early, Kerris remembered this distinctly, for the sky was not yet pink and a thin layer of snow coated the sleepers. He could hear the cursing for some distance beyond the fire and, not really caring to know the reason, he had started the tea for breakfast.

They had slept through the night.

For the first time in many nights, the little party had slept through the night.

"How could you have heard nothing?" Kirin had growled at the Major after ushering the pair back to the fire. "You sleep like a hare. You hear everything."

"I don't know, sir. I, I —"

"Perhaps there was nothing to hear," said the Seer in her defense. "Perhaps Solomon was preoccupied."

"No." Kirin began to pace, his jaw working on some invisible piece of flesh between his teeth. "No, this is too regular, too predictable now. I don't believe Solomon has any more control over these episodes than we do."

"And I think he looks forward to them," offered the Scholar, sitting by the fire and munching on a slice of orange. "He sounds so lonely. I think he needs to talk to us."

Kirin whirled on the Seer. "And you remember nothing?"

"I never do."

"These oranges are great," said Fallon.

She peeled off a slice and tossed it to Ursa. It struck the snow leopard on the chin and she scowled, wiped the juice with the back of her hand.

"What does it matter, Kirin?" Kerris asked. "Whether Solomon has taken a little break or whether he forgot, what does it matter? We will reach the Wall by sunset and if he comes tonight, good. Fine. We can continue to *Lhahore*. If he doesn't, then we have a direct route back to *Pol'Lhasa*. This time, *time* won't be a factor."

With a heavy sigh, Kirin placed his hands on his hips. As usual, Kerris met his gaze, as undaunted by his brother's temper as the others were mindful. Finally, Kirin nodded.

"Yes, Kerris. We carry on to the Wall. We will decide our course tonight."

"Right then, let's get cracking."

And the grey lion sprang to his feet, leaving the group and its dark *shar chi* for the company of horses. The others followed suit.

Fallon sidled up to the Captain.

"These are really great oranges," she said as she offered him a slice.

"No but thank you, *sidala.*"

"Really, you should try one. You need your breakfast, after all."

"No. Thank you."

"She's been drugged."

Slowly, he turned to face her.

"Ursa." She popped the slice in her mouth. "She's been drugged."

"How do you know this?"

"Pupils are still wide. Not sharp little slivers of black like usual. She's moving slower too. She would have normally caught the orange I tossed at her. Didn't even see it coming."

"Who would have done this?"

She shrugged, still chewing.

"Anybody, I guess. Sherah or Sireth, most likely. But any one of us could have. Even you."

His blue eyes narrowed. "Why?"

"Oh, I don't know. Maybe she owes you money or something."

"No. Why would someone drug the Major? What would that accomplish?"

"Well, we wouldn't talk to Solomon, then would we? That would be my first guess. I can't think of any other reason. Ursa has always been the first one to wake when he starts talking, if she even sleeps at all. But that's only one possibility. I could be wrong. Maybe she's just really tired. Now *that* would be scary. Dangerous, really. Well, better get to my horse. I like this one much better than my old one. My old one was so slow."

And she ambled off, completely oblivious to the state of alarm in which she had left her Captain. His eyes roved the backs of his party, from the four surviving leopards to the civilians, from his brother to the Major. And now he was certain of it too, Ursa Laenskaya was not moving with her customary swift, bird-like motions. Or was she?

First expedience, then paranoia. *How many masters would he serve on this journey?*

He shook his head and headed for his horse.

***

It was late afternoon before the Wall came into full view. It had been, for the most part hidden by the mountains, allowing a glimpse of its snake-like body only now and again, a thread of gold woven through a basket of bamboo. It seemed small from far away, but the nearer they rode, the greater, the more impressive it grew. Towers could be seen all along its length, battle forts offering the promise of food and shelter and fresh, clean water. It is common knowledge that tea tastes all the better when made with fresh water. This is an important consideration.

Kirin held up a tawny hand, and the trail of horses wound to a stop. He had taken the fore this day, being short on patience. Now, he jogged alMassay back to the Seer, pulling up alongside.

"Where is the falcon?"

"Hunting. Why?"

"Call her back. I wish to send a message to the Tower guards at

Sri'Varna."

"Is that necessary?" Sireth asked sharply. "Soldiers have been known to shoot falcons."

"Not *my* soldiers."

"Not *my* falcon."

"Call her back."

The man sighed and cast his gaze skyward. In moments, a shrill cry echoed through the valley and a shadow crossed the sun. The falcon swept over the heads of the riders, bleating and crying her displeasure, finally chirruping softly as she settled on her master's arm. The Seer pulled a set of talon leathers and bells from a goatskin pouch.

"Your message?"

A thin scrap of parchment, bound in thread and sealed with Imperial gold, was passed over and tied securely to the wiry leg. Sireth placed two fingers over the dark, shiny eyes, and closed his own. Kirin watched this, marveling at not only how a man could speak to animals, but how he did so without words. With a chirrup and a jingle of bells, the bird lit from his arm, wings capturing the wind the way a kite breaches the clouds. She was a speck in moments.

"Thank you," said the Captain after she disappeared entirely from his sight. "The guards will have a hot supper awaiting us, a change of clothing, and maps."

"Maps?" Kerris brightened as they started on the way again. "Say, do you think Solomon knows about the Wall? He seems to know about a great many things."

"Perhaps."

"Because if he does, then maybe he could tell us how far along we should travel before heading north into the Lower Kingdom. If we could make it all the way to *TheRhan,* we'd be well along indeed."

"Yes."

"Why do you think he has a different word for everything, then?"

Kirin sighed, not wanting to be discussing anything at the moment, least of all Solomon.

"I don't know, Kerris."

"Did *he* kill the Seers?"

"I don't know, Kerris."

"I think he's a dog."

"What?"

"I mean, we don't know for certain that he's a tiger, now do we? He just speaks poorly, like so many tigers do. Dogs speak pitiful Imperial, you know that, if they speak it at all. And for a tiger to be so far beyond our borders—"

"He's not a dog."

"But how do you know?"

"Kerris—"

"Was there an expedition I wasn't told about?"

This time, the Captain's sigh was one of relief.

"No, Kerris. There would never be an expedition that you wouldn't be a part of."

"Because if there was—"

"There wasn't." He saw his chance to diffuse the conversation, seized it without hesitation. "You are by far the Empress' preferred guide. You know that as well as I."

Kerris grunted affably, nodded as his blue eyes scanned the terrain.

"Besides, who else brings back the little trinkets you do? You have the best nose for treasure in the Kingdom."

Another grunt, another nod, and Kerris shot out his hand, grey palm curling open under Kirin's nose. A single shimmering pearl, nestled amongst a sea of shark teeth.

"You see?" Kirin smiled. "This tiger is lucky indeed, to be rescued by the likes of you."

"Hah! Thicker than honey, dear brother. Save it for Lyn-ling!" He spurred Quiz into a gallop. "Perhaps she'll shower you with kisses when we get back!"

"Kerris!"

But he could not resist laughing and spurred his own horse to catch up, and the party of horses burst forth like a whirlwind, kicking up a cloud of dust as they went.

***

They came upon the garrison town of *Sri'Varna* at sundown. It was a small community of tigers, leopards, jaguars and smaller cats, people whose very livelihood was dependent on the Wall. They were the families of the builders and potters who specialized in maintaining the great kilns needed for such work. They were the farmers and tradesmen who supplied the Wall with food and linens and oil for alarm fires. Of these provisions, the oil was by far the most important. Without oil, they were defenseless.

It was quiet by the time they rode down the only road in town and Kirin found himself approving. It was sunset, time for quiet reflection and evening tea. Time for all people of good breeding to be settling in for the night, trusting the safety of their homes to the Wall and the soldiers who guarded their borders. *It was a good sign,* he thought to himself, *reflecting the prosperity and stability of the Kingdom.* And of course, the quality of the soldiers.

A door opened from a far garden gate and light poured onto the street. A figure could be seen silhouetted under the lintel, a lantern swinging the familiar patterns of welcome. Kirin rode alMassay toward it.

It was an elderly lion, his mane silver and twisted into a high knot on the back of his head. His robes marked him as a judge, the highest authority in these small towns but it was he who greeted Kirin with a deep and formal bow, cupping fist in one palm.

"Captain Wynegarde-Grey," the man said in the Imperial tongue. His accent was classic, rich like Kirin's and Kerris' and for that matter, Sireth's. "I am Shah Kim taeKanawae. It is an honor to have you at our garrison."

"It is we who are honored," said Kirin with equal formality but being a lion in the Court of the Empress, he did not bow. Indeed, he did not even dismount his horse. "Our party has traveled for many days. We look forward to the amenities which the Wall can afford us."

"And you shall receive them, *sidi,*" he said, bowing again.

"Thank you then, and good evening."

With that, Kirin pulled his stallion back onto the road.

Fallon leaned over to the black-cloaked figure riding at her side.

"Wow," she whispered. "That was easy. Much easier than, oh,

say, back at the Inn. Now that was *not* easy."

"Such is the way of lions," purred Sherah.

It was nearly dark now but the great shape of the Wall rose high above them, its geniculated cornice black against the purple sky. Torchlight beamed from small windows and the scent of curry and lamb wafted down on the breeze.

Three guards awaited them at the gate. They were leopards, naturally, but educated ones, for the parchment had been opened, read and tucked deep inside a bronze sash for safekeeping. Out on the Kingdom's front lines, reading was not a luxury. The three bowed with perfect precision.

Kirin dismounted. "You have carried out my instructions?"

"As best we could, *sidi,*" said one. "I have summoned others from nearby towers to assist with the horses."

Kerris was at his brother's side in an instant.

"Linaments and wraps for each leg, straw bedding, and once they've rested, strong mash, ground organ meat and fresh water." He rubbed Quiz's crescent of white. "They've worked hard for you, today Kirin. They deserve as much."

The Captain turned to his party, just now beginning to slide from their saddles and onto solid ground. They were weary, it was obvious, but Kerris was right. They *had* made good time that day and he would see to it that cats, as well as horses, would be rewarded.

"These men will see to the horses. We have other things awaiting us."

"Ooh, yes, 'amenities'," grinned Fallon as she dismounted. "Oh wouldn't a good scrub be nice? A good scrub, fresh clothes and warm slippers. I feel scratchy all over."

Sherah smiled at her.

"Then a nice soft bed, full of feathers and tea. Not – not tea *in* the bed, mind you. Just *with* it. Beside it, you know. Beside the bed."

"You are very amusing, Scholar."

The tigress passed over the reins and staggered on wobbly legs into the tower.

"And a book, a big fat book, and supper. Wow, look at that Wall..."

Kerris fell in between them, catching both women by the elbows.

"Did you say supper?"

The screech of a falcon drifted down the stairwell and Sireth paused before entering. He glared the leopard.

"You shouldn't tie her like that. She's hungry."

"She bit several of my men. *Sidi.*"

"Good."

Ursa shoved him and together they disappeared through the doorway. Kirin shook his head and followed.

***

A high-heeled white boot hit the stone floor.

"Ursa, how um, how exactly do you walk in those things?"

"Very well."

"Heh. That was funny."

Fallon Waterford wrinkled her nose and looked around the room. It was not large but it was cozy. A wood stove burned in one corner, casting golden shadows across the bricks and toasting the linens at its hearth. The 'amenities' had been most satisfactory, in her estimation. Fresh, hot tea had been provided and a guard stood outside their door for their clothing, which would be taken to the garrison town and cleaned and fire-dried by morning. Curried lamb and dumplings, noodles and cabbage awaited them up the winding stone stairs that led to the very top of the tower. The very roof of the Wall.

She pulled off her own suede boot and stretched her toes, enjoying the feel as her claws stretched as well. In the jungle, back at her father's farm near *Parnum'bah Falls,* she was barefoot most of the time and she preferred it that way. In fact, back home she would most often be found in one of her father's old tunics and little else, for because of her penchant for tree-climbing, experiments and dissections, it was impossible to keep her own clothes in good repair. Life at the University had changed many things.

She watched as the Major peeled her uniform of white doeskin and threw it to the floor. Fallon shook her head in amazement. Even such simple motions caused the muscles to ripple across the snow leopard's back. The marbled pelt was striking to behold, *much more elaborate than tigers,* she thought. Bars and bands and rosettes of silver in glorious patterns, like snow-ripe clouds on a moonlit lake. *Yes, much better than tigers.*

Sherah had also stripped from her catsuit of black and the vestments made tinkling sounds as they struck the stone. Fallon studied her markings as well, the cheetah pelt of butter-cream, the spots tiny and regular, accentuating her narrow waist and the swell of her hips and the long, thick curve of her tail. Her throat and belly were milk-white, her chest full. A woman's chest. Fallon frowned as she looked down at her own.

"Good thing I don't have kittens. They would die of starvation."

Turning, Sherah smiled.

"They grow bigger."

"Oh, no I don't think they will."

"Pah. Who wants kittens," growled Ursa as she grabbed a brush of hog bristles and began to scrub the fur of her arms. "Better to be dead than to have kittens."

"Well, *I* would love to have kittens, but I wouldn't want them to die of starvation."

"They would not starve," said Sherah as she too began to brush her long spotted legs.

"So? How do you know?"

"I have had kittens. They grow bigger."

"What?" Fallon's head shot up. "You're married?"

"No."

"Pah." Ursa rolled her eyes. "Bastard kittens. Better to be dead."

"How many kittens?"

"Four."

The cheetah did not bother to look up but she smiled as the bristles ruffled the smooth hair of her feet. *Elegant feet,* thought Fallon. *Not like my flat skinny stripy ones.*

"Wow. What are their names?"

"I do not know."

"Pah! Bastards."

"Sherah, don't you know your own children?"

"They were taken as newborn, to monasteries other than *Agara'tha.*" She paused as golden eyes slid up to meet emerald.

"Alchemy begets alchemy," she purred. "My skills are strong.

They breed true. It is a great honor."

"And the sires - all cheetahs?" asked Ursa.

"Two."

"Bastard mongrel alchemist kittens. That should not be allowed."

"Wow." Fallon sat back on her stool, arms draped across her knees. She let out a deep breath. "Wow."

"Bad enough to be a Pure-born child, let alone a mongrel. This very thing is the cause of all the problems in the Kingdom." Ursa pulled a rough linen tunic over her head. "It is a weakness."

"Children?" Fallon frowned again, thinking of her own family, happy parents who had welcomed as many daughters as the jungle would give them. "Children are a weakness?"

"Stupid girl! What did I say? *Bastard. Mongrel. Alchemist. Kittens.* What don't you understand?"

Fallon shrugged. "You."

"Pah." Ursa snorted and tossed her head, her hair whipping across her back. The conversation was ended.

"Pay her no heed, Scholar," Sherah said, her eyes gleaming. "Perhaps she needs another cup of tea."

***

In the Upper Kingdom, there are a great many rituals and ceremonies. Ceremonies for taking tea, ceremonies for taking a wife, ceremonies for writing letters to people in faraway lands. So, then, for a people graced with such glorious pelts, pelts that are the envy of all other Nations, it is not unusual for there to be a ceremony involved with the art of brushing. All is taken into consideration - the correct brush with the correct bristles, the correct pattern for brushing first against the hairs, then with, and most of all, the consideration to help a friend when brushing the back. The back is difficult, most difficult to reach with claw or comb, and it is a great gift to offer one's service in this very deed. Brushing is a fastidious business and cats are, after all, a fastidious people.

"Lower, lower, now in the middle, there! That's it, Kirin, aaahhhh..."

"Kerris, your foot."

"Sorry."

The Captain could not help but smile. His brother so loved to have his pelt brushed. As a child, he had spent hours letting their mother brush and brush and brush. When other kittens were anxious to get about their studies, or dash outside for a game of sham'Rai or Chicken-poke, Kerris was just as happy to let himself be brushed. Feed him and brush him and Kerris would purr well into the night.

"Your wounds are healing well, brother."

"They itch like mad warthogs."

"The stitches will have to come out soon." Kirin tapped the bristle brush into his palm and laid it on the stool beside him. "There. You are done."

"Oh please, just a few minutes more."

"No. I wish to go over the maps before supper."

Kerris straightened and stretched, rolling his grey head 'til his neck popped.

"Ah, maps and supper. Can't say which I'm looking forward to most. What about him?"

He inclined his chin towards a corner of the small chamber where the Seer was sitting, slowly folding a long orange sash seven times.

"Make the offer if you wish. I have no time."

"Right. Go then. We'll be up soon."

He gathered his uniform, snatched the rough wool cloak that completed the tunic, wide trousers and warm hide slippers he now wore, and strode swiftly from the room, closing the door behind.

Kerris glanced back to the Seer. For the most part, he was still clothed in loose dark linens, remnants of life in the Cliffs of Thousand Eyes. He had taken great pains to remove the leather robe and the wide sash that had wrapped him at shoulder and hip, and folded them both as if they were the Queen's very bedclothes. Likewise, gloves and boots had been placed at right angles to each other, symbols of higher, loftier things. Such concentration on trivial matters seemed a waste of time to Kerris, especially when a pot of curried lamb lay waiting upstairs but he knew that most people relished their rituals, *needed* them almost, to keep the shoots of their lives contained. It was the way of things.

So, with a puff of breath, he pulled his new tunic overhead, grabbed the bristle brush and crossed the room.

He bowed deeply, enjoying the form, if not the formality.

"Might I have the honor?"

"No."

"No?"

"No."

"Ah." He frowned, looked around the chamber, rocked back and forth on the pads of his feet. Finally, he sat down on a wooden bench. "You see, there you have me. What am I supposed to say to that?"

"I don't know." Sireth shrugged. "But I do not wish you to brush my back."

"Why not?"

"Why should I?"

"Didn't you brush each other's backs in *Sha'Hadin?*"

"Yes."

"So? What's the difference?"

"You are not from *Sha'Hadin.*"

Kerris leaned back against the cool brick wall, laced his hands behind his neck. He grinned.

"Shame on you."

Now, the man did look up, tilting his head like a falcon hearing a faraway sound. "I beg your pardon?"

"Can you see out of that other eye? The good one?"

"Of course."

"And can you see color with it?"

"Yes, of course."

"And what color am I?"

benAramis sighed. "Grey."

"And how many grey lions are there in the Kingdom?"

"I have no idea."

"Two. Exactly two, although I do believe Robin neeCornWallace's mother may have dabbled once or twice with a certain white tiger. No stripes mind you. He's as grey as quarried stone. But even still that makes only two grey lions in all of the Upper Kingdom. Far less than the number of mongrels, I'd wager."

He sat forward, still grinning.

"So then, what makes you think I care whether you have spots or stripes or for that matter, purple monkeys tattooed on your back? Am I such a typical lion that I should care?"

"You are far from a typical lion," said Sireth quietly.

"And you are the highest ranking mongrel in the history of the Upper Kingdom. So let's call it even, shall we?"

The Seer smiled. "You are very different from your brother, Kerris Wynegarde-Grey."

"I am indeed." Kerris smiled back. "But don't think to poorly of Kirin, *sidi.* He has a hard job and he prides himself on doing it well. Offence is a small price to pay for peace."

"Yes. Thank you for your counsel."

"But you still don't want me brushing your back."

"No."

"Fair enough then. Do you still want to know about Ancestors?"

Sireth almost fell off his stool. *This man was sharp, sharper than he let on.*

"Yes," he said, forcing himself to breathe evenly. "Yes I do."

"Well, what do you want to know? It is a rather broad subject."

His hands, gloveless and spotted, were shaking.

"What did they look like?"

"Well, that depends. The glyphs in *Aegyp* are far different than the glyphs in the Land of the *Chi'Chen.* The statues in the jungles of *Hindaya* not at all like the ones in *Shiam.* Can't tell about the ones in *Hiran* or *Hirak.* They have most of their heads smashed off."

He leaned back again, began chewing on a thumb claw.

"For the most part, I think they looked rather like us. Two legs, two arms - for the most part I say again, for some of the statues, seemed to have many arms, like Khali." He shuddered at the thought. "Now where was I? Oh yes, two arms, short noses, like us, not like dogs. Um, no tails, two eyes—"

"Brown eyes?"

"No offence, *sidi,* but brown eyes are unnatural."

"Yes, of course. Please continue."

"Dogs have brown eyes. Are you certain there isn't any dog in your particular mix?"

"Not to my knowledge."

"No matter. I found an odd book once. The pages were stiff and clear, save for paintings of red and blue, and they looked to me like paintings of like paintings of innards."

"Innards?"

"Yes. Blood paths and hearts and lungs and stomachs and the like. It was gruesome. I think they were a gruesome people."

"Why do you say that?"

Kerris leaned forward. "Have you ever been to *Calcah'thah?"*

Sireth leaned forward. "I grew up in *Calcah'thah."*

"There are still parts of the city that none of us can reclaim. It is devastated."

"I know."

"There are areas in *Hiran* and *Shyria* that even still nothing grows. Cats who pass through become sick within a fortnight. I think they were a powerful, gruesome, warrior people who killed themselves off in a great war. Or many great wars." He shrugged, as if catching himself in a blasphemy. "I think."

Sireth sat very still. These were not things he wanted to know.

"But they were marvelous, as well. Here. Look at this."

He pulled the sleeve from his wrist. Something flashed in the firelight.

"What is it?"

"Not sure, entirely. The Scholar thinks it's a sundial. But you know her. Actually, I bought it for her, but she didn't want it. Threw it back right in my face. She's a puzzle, that one is..."

He slipped it off and passed the bangle over into Sireth's eager *hand melting flesh melting heat blasting blinding light fire consuming death death lungs burning burning blood bursting eyes mouths ears bursting death dying earthshake shake and collapse wailing kittens six kittens cool water spray oceans lion tiger man*

Sireth gasped for air as Kerris finally managed to wrench the bangle from his iron grip.

"Are you alright? *Sidi?"*

He couldn't speak for his head was still pounding, the power of the Vision strong in his soul.

"What happened? You weren't breathing."

He nodded.

"Did you see something?"

"Devastation," he whispered.

"Right." Kerris slipped the bangle back on his wrist and rose to his feet. "Well, I um, I should go up. Kirin has maps, and all. And supper. Are you coming for supper? I'm quite hungry, aren't you?"

"Hunger is simply a matter of perspective."

"Yes, well from where I'm standing, the perspective smells quite good. Are you sure you're alright?"

The Seer nodded again.

Kerris took several steps toward the door, paused before leaving.

"Be sure not to mention this to Kirin, will you? He has enough to think about."

"I won't."

"Right then, I'm off."

And with a snatch of his wool cloak, he disappeared out the chamber. Sireth sat for some time longer before he slipped off his own tunic, revealing not only spots and stripes but a tapestry of black, white and blistered scars that would have paled even the greyest of lions.

***

Fallon filled her chest with cold air as if this action might bypass the necessity for kitten bearing. Her belly was similarly inclined, filled full with lamb and dumplings. The curry had been too mild for her tastes. Her father's had always made her tongue tingle for days afterward and again, she found herself smiling at the memory of family.

She sighed. She had always assumed everyone felt the same about family.

She had left the brothers in the battle tower, poring over map after map and speaking together in quiet voices. In this rough linen clothing, it was almost difficult to tell them apart from behind, save for the occasional swat of a tufted grey tail, and yet, they were so different. Hard to believe they were twins. Ursa and Sherah had disappeared shortly after the evening meal, and Sireth had not taken supper at all. She worried about him and his sullen ways. Such solitude could not possibly be good for the soul.

She leaned out over the parapet, between the rectangular rises and dips in the cornice. The north wind plucked at her hair and she leaned out even further, imagining what it might be like to be the first to see an approaching army, to dash to the great oil lamp in the tower and light it ablaze so that all of the Kingdom would know by daybreak. She imagined hundreds of troops marching in unison down the length of the Wall, the Imperial Standard waving over their head. Harder to imagine, however, was the ensuing battle, the hooks and cables flying upwards, spears raining down, blood seeping between the stones like mortar. No, this she could not imagine at all.

It did not look so different, she thought as her eyes scanned the borders of the Lower Kingdom. These were still the Great Mountains, Mother to cats of all Races and yet it seemed she belonged to dogs as well, her peaks as rugged and bountiful as those in *DharamShallah*. Perhaps dogs had jungles as well and fertile valleys and dry plains, and perhaps not all was desert and desolate wasteland. Perhaps dogs were as proud of their Mother as cats and just perhaps, she was Good Mother to both.

"Ah, there you are. Hot cocoa?"

She turned to see Kerris standing directly behind her, holding up two steaming mugs of foam. Her eyes grew round.

"I love hot cocoa. My father used to make it all the time." She took a big gulp, wincing as the bitter brown milk scorched her tongue. "Yep, forgot the honey. Just like father."

Kerris grinned and leaned out next to her, cupping the mug in both hands for warmth. She tried not to watch him out of the corner of her eye, cursed the maddening pace of her heart, the sudden unwelcome loss of thought.

"This preoccupation is childish and foolish. I'm acting like a little girl."

"What's that?"

"What's what?"

"You said something about a little girl?"

The heat rushed to her cheeks as she realized she had been thinking out loud.

"I – I – I…" She waved a hand out over the edge of the Wall. "I never dreamed I would see this, all this, when I was a little girl."

"The Lower Kingdom?"

"Uh-huh. The Lower Kingdom."

"Quite far from the pheasant farm, eh?"

"Yes." She looked away quickly, a new heat rising on her cheeks. She took another gulp of cocoa.

"It's not so bad, really. Some of it's quite lovely."

"Kerris your-name-was, have you ever seen a dog?"

"Many times."

"Have you ever killed one?"

"No." He smiled. "Not a dog."

"I don't think I could."

"No, I don't think you could, either." His smile broadened when he looked at her and suddenly, he was reaching for her. "Hold still."

She froze, heart pounding. His fingers touched her chin, his thumb brushed her mouth, and with one smooth motion, he wiped the foam from her lip.

"There. Now you don't look like our friend Seer." Still smiling, he made no move to take his hand away. Instead, he stroked her chin with the lightest of touches. "Say, you're soft, aren't you? I never knew a tiger to be so soft. Did you have a good scrub?"

She swallowed, not hearing a word he was saying. In fact, she could have sworn she heard music.

"Hmm?" she squeaked.

"Actually, you have quite lovely markings. I never noticed before." He stopped, glanced around. "Do you hear something?"

She almost melted into his arms. "You mean the music?"

"Yes. Music."

"Oh that. It's only in my head. I hear it all the time. Not like this though. Usually just funny little kitten songs. I never knew anyone else could hear it. But really, nothing to worry about."

"You do hear it, then." He stepped away from her, moving to the tower's easterly edge and peering out over its side. She could see him smile in the moonlight.

The music in her head was louder now, a wailing, rhythmic pulse like wind on blood, calling her by name, calling. She followed, leaning out between the cornice high above the eastern rim. On the

Wall down below, among a circle of candles and incense, Sherah was dancing.

***

"Curse that woman," growled Sireth as he stormed along the westerly Wall, away from the tower. "She is destroying my concentration."

Ursa was doing her best to keep up. "What are you talking about?"

"That infernal music."

"Music? What music? You have gone mad."

"The music!" He whirled on her. "Can't you hear it?"

"I hear nothing but your grumblings, Seer."

"Bah!" He threw his hands into the air and continued, his long strides carrying him fast and furious, muttering as he went. "This is not Alchemy. This is Vision-sharing. She should not be able to do this."

"So, stop her."

The words stopped him.

"What? What did you say?"

In the rough linen tunic and baggy trousers she wore, she looked very small, but she challenged him with one flash of her eyes.

"You are one of the Council of Seven. You advise the Empress. You speak to falcons and dead people. It should be nothing to stop the songs of a witch."

"Yes," he said slowly. "Yes, you're right."

He was very still for a moment, before he nodded.

"It is done."

"What? That's it?"

"That's it. Thank you for reminding me, once again, of what I am. You are very good at that."

She did not seem to know how to respond, so he held out a gloved hand, careful not to touch her.

"Come."

"Where?"

"Walk with me."

She refused his hand but fell in at his side, taut as a strung bow. They walked a little further in complete silence, until he found a spot, a particular place on the Wall where the energies converged, the *feng shui* pleased and the moon shone brightly across the stones. He turned several small circles before folding his legs and lowering himself to the road so high above the ground. He motioned her to sit as well, and to his surprise, she did.

"What do you know of meditation?"

"Nothing I care to."

"Ah. But you have studied *Chai'Chi?*"

"Yes."

"It is the same."

She snorted. "Far from it."

"You are familiar with the Warrior Pose?"

"Of course."

"And how long can you hold it?"

"Forever."

"Major Ursa Laenskaya, you are a soldier. Your body is a weapon. You must care for it, keep it constantly sharp for battle. Your tools are a sword, crossbow, dagger and claw. But I think your best tool is your body, for you know it so well. It obeys your simplest thought. If it were wounded, you would know. You would feel wrong and you would not fight well."

She was nodding so he continued.

"I, on the other hand, am a Seer. My soul is my weapon, if you will. Vision and Farsight, these are my tools, *my* sword and crossbow. I know my soul so well and it obeys my simplest thought.

"Since that night in the kitchens of *Sha'Hadin,* my soul has been wounded. It is not my own and for me, this is wrong - *I* am wrong. And if I am to heal it, I must meditate, focus my thoughts and emotions into a single, pure weapon, a steel that can pierce any darkness, destroy any guile. What the Warrior Pose does for your body, meditation does for my soul. It is not a luxury, it is not a ruse, it is my life. And without it, I cannot fight well."

She looked away so he studied her profile, her deep set eyes and high cheekbones, her short straight nose and small mouth. Now and then, the wind lifted her hair, swirled into her face and she made no move to push it aside. It was as if the hiding were part of her mystery. *Nothing at all like Shakuri,* he thought. Perhaps, much more like himself.

She turned back to him. "Meditation is discipline for the soul."

"Exactly."

"Teach me."

His smile froze. "Ah."

"It is not even close to the Second Watch. We have time."

"Yes, bu—"

"If my soul becomes disciplined, my entire being becomes a weapon and I am pure as steel. I become a much better fighter. Teach me. To refuse would bring dishonor."

"Very well."

He removed the thick leather gloves, turned his palms upwards and reached the tips of his fingers to her. She took a deep breath and gave him her hands.

***

She was cloaked in stars, her hair the wind, her eyes candles, as she danced on the Wall in the moonlight. Neither Kerris nor Fallon could pull themselves away, so hypnotic her movements and the music, exotic and rhythmic, pulsed their very blood. Dimly, Fallon became aware of the Captain as he moved in beside his brother, drawn in the same way. The leopards now, all watching, each one joining the cheetah in her movements as if they danced with her, their feet hers, long arms and sinewy body simply they themselves captured in a dream. She was a whisper, a spirit, a ghost cat moving through shadow. It was marvelous.

Abruptly, the music ended and the spell with it. In fact, as they stood high above her, there was nothing below save a woman in rough linens, lighting candles. She sat cross-legged, humming.

Kerris scratched his head. "Oh hello, Kirin. Is anybody hungry?"

"I wonder if they have any cocoa," said Fallon, and the pair ambled back to the tower. The leopards, loathe at finding themselves so far from their posts, slipped away as silently as they had come. Only the Captain lingered a little longer.

***

breathe in, heartbeat beat beat, breathe out, heartbeat beat beat, breathe in, heartbeat beat beat deep, breathe out, heartbeat beat beat, deep dark, beat beat beat, deep dark places, beat beat beat, shame, beat beat, deep dark shame, peace, *shame, beat beat,* peace, calm*anger, shame anger beat beat,* calm and strength, peace, *beatbeat beat,* peace and strength, strength like steel, *beat beat beat,* like steel, ***eyes one thousand eyes black robes fire and blood and alchemy***

It was like a fist, the way he pushed her out and Ursa snarled, about to give him a fist of a different sort when the falcon sliced the air between them. It circled frantically but could not, would not, land. The Major looked back to the Seer.

His head was bowed deep into his chest, back rounded, fingers reaching to the stars.

"It is not time, not yet time," she growled. "Solomon, is this you? Solomon?"

There was no response. The falcon was still circling and she raised a hand to it.

"The Captain! Go find the Captain!"

And knowing nothing of falcon-speak, she formed a picture of the golden lion in her mind. Path arched her wing and soared toward the tower.

He was moaning now, shaking his head and gasping for air. It reminded her of the first night in *Sha'Hadin,* when Solomon had seized him, so she grabbed his shoulders, determined to break whatever grip he was caught in. It worked and she felt the tension drain from his muscles.

"Sha'Hadin..."

"What?" His voice was a whisper, so she bent in. "What of *Sha'Hadin?"*

"Sha'Hadin..." He looked up at her, his face streaked with tears. "Has fallen."

***

"It is done."

Empress Thothloryn Parillaud Markova Wu could have been carved stone, a statue, silent and straight and barely breathing. Her elaborate robes fell in razor-edges to the floor, her golden headdress caught the lamplight, reflected it along the scarlet walls. The stained glass high above was dark, for it was night, and a heavy cloak of clouds hid the moon. Across her shoulders, a mongoose raised its tiny head, its small eyes glittering like black pearls. She stroked its throat with a thin finger.

"Tell me again this was necessary, Jet."

"It was necessary, Excellency."

"The transition has been smooth?"

"As polished glass, Excellency. The brothers are relieved at having order restored. Some have even petitioned for leave to visit family and friends now that the monastery is in such good care."

"Good. I cannot tell you how much this matter disturbs me."

"I am aware, Excellency. However, this is only a temporary solution until the Council, or some semblance of it, returns."

She would not let him see her heart. "They will return, Jet."

And she waited, for she knew it would come.

"Of course."

With a long breath, the Empress turned to study the man standing directly behind her. He was an impressive figure, his black and silver robes a startling contrast to his white striped pelt. Jet barraDunne, First Mage of *Agara'tha,* alchemist and priest and noble council, a white tiger from a line of white tigers that had served the Royal House for more years than she could recount. His hair was white-streaked steel, the top roached like a horse's mane, the length of it gathered in a long braid down his back. It was impossible to determine his age, though she knew him to have had more than forty summers and, as was whispered among the Courts, almost as many wives. His eyes were as white as the moon.

"Take heart, Excellency," he said, his voice round with the accents of the Middle Courts. "I have managed to locate Yahn Nevye from his sabbatical in *Sahood.* He has only been away from *Sha'Hadin* two years and has agreed to assume responsibility for the monastery for as long as needed. Naturally, he will stay on to rebuild the Council if benAramis so wishes."

"We should tell them."

"benAramis will know."

"Even so, I wish to tell them."

"Of course."

The Empress turned away, folding her hands within her wide sleeves and moving slowly back towards the throne. He fell in behind.

"Is there word on their party?" she asked.

"They have made the Wall at *Sri'Varna.*"

"Intact?"

"They have lost four leopards."

"So soon? That is not good." She lowered herself into the ages-old seat, the only thing simple and unadorned in the room. "I will dispatch one of my falcons at daybreak. They must know that *Sha'Hadin* is in good care. Then, they can continue their journey unmindful."

"Naturally."

"You disapprove?"

"Not at all, Excellency. I understand your concern for..." He stared at the floor, a gesture of respect but it made her study him all the harder. He had no need to finish the thought. He knew her, knew of the secret places within her, her reticence in choosing a suitor and the reasons for it. She had held an incomparable standard since kittenhood in the Imperial Nursery, a kittenhood shared with the brothers Wynegarde-Grey. He had never spoken of it however, never would, and she trusted him with this knowledge. It could destroy her.

"Thank you, Jet."

"Is there anything else, Excellency?"

"No."

"Then I shall be leaving for the monastery in the morning." He bowed. "Good night, Excellency."

"Good night, Jet."

Thothloryn Parrilaud Markova Wu let her golden eyes roam the Throne Room, now empty save for the Leopard Guard lining the walls. Lamps and lanterns burned well into the night, for in truth, they were never allowed to go out and were refreshed daily with oil and cloth. Three peacocks slept at her feet, their tiny crowned heads buried in the blue of their backs, their great tails folded and still. She could feel the rapid, even breaths of the mongoose on her shoulder and knew it too was asleep. All was quiet in the Throne Room of the Empress. All was in order.

She missed him.

The wealth of the Kingdom was hers for the asking, temples of gold, incense and idols, all hers to hoard or give away. Soldiers and armies and horses, mountains and deserts and jungles, people by the thousand, hers to command. During her short reign, she (with the help of Kaidan) had brokered peace with the *Chi'Chen,* forced the *bab'Hundi* back tenfold in their quest for land along the Aegypshan border and furthered the Wall like no other before her. It was a noble lineage of Sacred blood, a mantle of power which she wore so very well.

And yet, she missed him.

"When you return," she promised the emptiness. "When you return."

The emptiness did not answer.

***

The Captain of the Guard shook his head.

"You are certain of this?"

Sireth threw up his hands and continued pacing. The disrespect set Kirin's teeth on edge. He ground them tightly to rein in his temper.

"Of course you're certain. Forgive me. Tell me again what you saw."

"I saw *Sha'Hadin* overcome by Alchemy!"

"Are you speaking from a clear glass, *sidi?*"

The Seer glared at him and steeled his own jaw, apparently as angry with himself as with the Captain. He took a cleansing breath.

"I saw eyes, and the Cliff of One Thousand Eyes. The seven gates of *Sha'Hadin,* with cats in black robes flowing through, 5 of 5 per gate. I saw soldiers in black leather filling the Valley of the Seers, carrying swords and spears and the Standard of *Agara'tha.* I saw the snuffing of torches, the drawing of chalk circles and the spilling of blood in the Hall of the Seers." He turned his face to the Captain. "I saw Tiberius, beaten and weeping in the snow."

The mention of Tiberius was like a blow to the stomach and Kirin battled to keep it from crowding his thoughts. "This could not have been a future event?"

"No. They have a different sense."

He turned to the Alchemist. She was leaning against a wall, braiding feathers into her hair.

"Why would *Agara'tha* do such a thing?"

"We do not know they have."

"*I* know!" snapped Sireth, tail lashing.

"So you say."

"You knew about this, didn't you?"

"Did I?"

"You may beguile the others, Sherah al Shiva or whatever your birthname was, but you will not catch me in your games."

"I do not play games."

Fallon Waterford sat forward, another mug of hot cocoa in her hands.

"I hate to say this, Sireth, but it's really just your word against hers. We have no proof that anything at all has happened to the monastery."

"I saw it too," said a quiet voice and all eyes swung toward the Major.

The Captain put his hands on his hips.

"You? How?"

She cast a furtive glance at the Seer before responding.

"He was teaching me to meditate. It is discipline for the soul."

"And you saw this...this 'taking' of *Sha'Hadin?*"

"Part of it, yes sir, I did."

As if vindicated, Sireth folded his arms and cocked his head, brows raised. Kirin turned to the Alchemist.

"And you know nothing of this plan to take the monastery? The First Mage never mentioned anything of the sort?"

"How could I? I am here. They are there." She held his gaze, undaunted. "Unlike the Seer, I do not engage in Soul-Travel."

There seemed to be something about her, however, something in her tone or rather, *not* in it. It puzzled him.

"Well, let's look at it this way," said Fallon. "What would *Agara'tha* have to gain by taking the monastery? What could Alchemists possibly want with Seers? Or what would Alchemy need of Farsight and Vision?"

"Unification," said the Captain and Sherah's eyes flashed. "You said so yourself, *sidala.* Unification of the Gifts and the Arts. An Alliance, as you put it for the good of the Kingdom."

"What?! That is ridiculous!" Sireth threw his arms up again. *"Sha'Hadin* would never accept such a joining!"

"They may have no choice now," said Fallon. "And it's the perfect opportunity. The Council is abolished, and if I'm right, and I usually am, there are no Elders left. At least, none that command the Gifts the way the Council did. Right?"

She looked at Sireth. He nodded, but numbly.

"Sha'Hadin is vulnerable, for the first time in generations. Yep, it's the perfect opportunity."

The Captain growled under his breath. *"Sidala?* What are your thoughts?"

Sherah pulled at the feathers in her hair. Gone were the baiting airs, the sensual self-confidence that characterized her occupation. In fact, to the Captain, she almost seemed worried.

"Sherah al Shiva, answer me. Is it possible that, during our absence—"

"Or *because* of it," chimed the Scholar.

"Yes, or because of it, that the First Mage has seen fit to make a move toward Unification?"

Slowly, very slowly, she inclined her chin. "It is possible."

"I knew it!" Sireth snapped, a kite in a strong wind. "We must leave at once!"

"No."

"What?!"

"I said no. At first light, we will dispatch the falcon. She should make *Pol'Lhasa* in two days time. We shall see what the Empress herself decides."

"That is completely unacceptable, Captain."

"That is not your decision, *sidi.*"

"Tiberius trusted you, respected you. He believed that you had saved *Sha'Hadin.* And now you have handed them, and him, over to the darkness. How could you betray us like this? Have you no honor?"

Kirin's palm slammed the table with such force that everyone jumped and he loomed over it like the great lion statues in the palace courts. But when he spoke, his voice was low, quiet and completely controlled.

"We wait... on the Empress."

Sireth straightened to his full height, stone-faced and seething and when he turned, Fallon noted that even without the swirling dark robes, he was still impressive. He strode toward the tower door. And stopped.

Suddenly, he swung back to the room, grinning from ear to ear.

"Hello, my friends!" said Solomon. "I've got great news!"

***

"I don't know that I'd call it a Gift exactly," said Kerris as he watched from a distance. "More like a bloody nuisance, wouldn't you say? I mean, first it's you, then it's not you, then it's you again. A person could get lost in all those souls, traveling about, bumping into each other. And what if you did get lost? Could you just pop into someone else's body, take him out for a spin, then give him back when it was convenient? No thank you, I'll just take the grey pelt myself and get on with it."

No one answered, because of course, he was talking to himself. He had slipped out of the room as soon as Kirin and the others had appeared and had nabbed the last bit of cold curried lamb and dumplings. Two of the dumplings he had pocketed for Quiz, being as they were the pony's favorite snack. He made a point to check on the horses, to see that they were bedded down for the night in a high tower stable. It was ironic, he thought, to see horses sleeping deep in straw on a stone wall so high above the ground. It was typical of feline culture to go to such great lengths to demonstrate their mastery over the natural world. It was in its own way, peculiar. But cats are, after all, a peculiar people.

He waved at the leopards, Wing and Per, Luke and Oded as they too bedded down for the night. With the extra sentries already available from the Wall, the Captain had given them the night off and Kerris knew they sorely needed it. His brother could be thoughtless when it came to subordinates, believing that everyone could function as he did, on strength of will alone. Kirin had remarkable will.

"Not me," he said to the stars. "In fact, I don't have remarkable anything. Just as well, I suppose."

He leaned out over the cornice, feeling the wind upon his face. It was cold and grumbling, and more than a bit angry. There was a storm coming, he knew it. It would hit before morning. They would have a hard day of it tomorrow. He pulled two sticks from his pocket.

Dharma and *Red.*

Odd.

With a deep sigh, he blew the moon a kiss and started back to the tower.

***

"Power? What do you mean 'Power?' Power over people?"

"I mean, just the *power.* I think I can get the power on. What, don't tell me you people don't have electricity?"

Kirin frowned. "We have cities."

"Okay, fire? You have fire, right?"

"Of course we have fire. It is one thing of many that separates us from animals."

"Dogs have fire," Fallon whispered and the Captain cut her off with a glance.

"Yeah, okay, whatever," said Solomon. "Well, electricity is kind of like fire under harness."

"Ah, a lantern. Yes, we have these."

Solomon laughed again. He was in a good mood tonight. This 'finding of power' was obviously a good thing. But it was also very likely an Ancient thing and Kirin had no wish to be discussing Ancestors tonight, or any night.

"Solomon, where were you last night?"

"Oh, that. Well, I've had to go deep into the bunker to get the auxiliary generators up and it took me all night to break into the vaults. This place is crawling with those rat things. I had to be very careful but I don't think they are very smart."

"They are not," said the Major. "But they do have a keen sense of smell, and excellent hearing."

"I thought so. That's why I was so quiet. When I felt - I don't even know what to call it - this connection-thing with you people, I tried to talk to you a few times but I could only talk in whispers. I heard nothing back, so I gave up and got on with my work. '

Kirin nodded. So Solomon *had* come but had been very quiet about it. Whether or not the Major had been drugged, she might not have awakened at all. This did nothing to prove one thing or the other, nor did it help to alleviate his concerns.

Solomon went on.

"So, anyway, I think I can get the power back on, possibly by tomorrow. Then I can get the comms up and running, maybe get some supper, and find out what it's like up there." He grinned again. "And hey, we've got some pretty nifty ATV's and a Humlander in storage. Even a couple of choppers, if I'm not mistaken. I'll be able to meet up with you folks in style."

For some reason, Kirin found himself looking at the Scholar, hoping that she of all people would understand anything of what this strange soul was talking about. But she was as lost as he, delighted in the conversation, but lost nonetheless.

"Solomon, we have to talk to you about maps—"

"Shh!" The Seer's eyes darted around the room. "I hear them."

"Who? The rats?"

"Yeah! Gotta go!" Sireth bolted to his feet, scrambling backwards toward the door. "I'll talk to you tomorrow night, okay? Tomorrow night!"

"Solomon! Wait!"

Kirin was on his feet too, as the Seer spun on his heel and dove for the doorway that led out to the Wall, the black night and the precarious drop to the ground below.

"Major, stop him!"

She lunged.

Perhaps it was the last of the drug, working its way through her body. Perhaps it was the change of clothing, making her more bulky, the Seer less so. Perhaps it was simply the unexpected nature of the motion, the unforeseen, unforeseeable action of this foreign soul. What ever it was, something caused Major Ursa Laenskaya to do something the Captain could never, in all his years' association with her, remember her having done before.

Major Ursa Laenskaya missed.

To her credit, she did manage to snag a leg but he swung free, striking her jaw with his heel and sending her back into the Captain. By the time they were steady, he was out the door. Both she and the Captain were behind him in a heartbeat.

Blacker than black against the bright sky, they could hear more than see him and they were like two arrows bearing down on the fleeing figure. There was another figure on the Wall before him, there was no mistaking who—

"Kerris! Stop him!"

The Seer whirled, hesitated but a moment, then sprang onto the cornice of the Wall, baggy clothing billowing in the night air. Kirin skidded to a halt, terrified.

"Kerris," he called. "Carefully now."

The grey lion was within touching distance.

"Solomon," he asked, looking up with a mouth full of dumpling. "Is that you?"

"Sh! The rats! God damn these rats!"

Kerris threw a glance at his brother and the Major as they moved slowly, tautly, like coiled springs, towards them. He looked back up at the Seer.

"They gone?"

"I think, maybe, *shh...*" He flung his head wildly around, dark hair whipping in the wind, eyes seeing nothing, not the Wall, nor moonlight, not the steep deathly drop to the cliffs below.

"You know, that's not really a good place for you, or for our Seer. How about you come down here where we can help?"

He reached up, grabbed the man's spotted, un-gloved wrist.

ocean water earth and lightning forking, breaking the road, breaking it into a thousand pieces

A gasp, a sag, a sharp release of breath. Sireth blinked, swayed, took a step backwards to steady himself—

"Kerris!" shouted the Captain.

The grey lion braced himself as the Seer toppled backward. The stone of the cornice caught him mid-thigh, scraping his trousers and grey pelt down to the knees. He yelped but held fast when the Seer struck the stone as he fell. In fact, the momentum almost pulled the grey lion over the edge with him, but Kerris held with a strength he should not have had.

Within a heartbeat, however, Kirin then the Major were there with him, pulling the Seer over the cornice and onto the parapet. Kerris flopped down beside him.

"I hate this," the Seer grumbled, rubbing the scrapes along his bearded chin. "I really, truly hate every aspect of this entire affair."

"You hate this," muttered Kerris, and he too rubbed at the scrapes along his thighs. *"I'm* going to end up a black-and-blue panther by the time this journey is finished."

"You should have let me fall," Sireth said to Kerris but he was staring at Kirin. "Then you could have gone home and spared yourself the bruising."

"Yes, but that would have been dishonorable, and my brother would have made me clean up the mess as punishment." He glanced up. "Kirin?"

The Captain shook his head, letting his eyes follow the line of torches dotting the Great Wall. They seemed to go on forever.

"Kirin, are you alright?"

Four leopards dead. Bandits, avalanches, icy rivers and now the Wall. He had so hoped that by reaching the Wall, they would end their trials and ride smoothly, effortlessly, to the end of this sojourn. He had hoped to kill the Ancestor with a clean, honorable sword, and return home to his Great House, to his office, to his Empress.

But he knew now that *Bushido* would not allow this, and *Bushido* was his master.

He knew it now, in his heart of hearts, the only way to serve both

Empress and master.

He would kill the Ancestor, then kill himself. Honor would be restored with his own death.

He would not be returning home.

THE BROKEN ROAD

Most Honoured Excellency,

Our party has experienced a difficult few days, as you have no doubt been informed. I regret to report the loss of four of your Leopard Guard and I alone bear the responsibility for this. I cannot shake the fear that they will not be the last casualties on this remarkable journey.

Your Seer, Sireth benAramis, claims to have seen a Vision of Sha'Hadin, *overcome by the brothers of* Agara'tha. *Since we cannot confirm the truth of this, I humbly request your direction in this matter. We shall return or continue as you wish. We are yours to command.*

For the moment, we continue to Lahore. *We await word from you there.*

In Your Service,

Kirin Wynegarde-Grey

The morning had started out angry, a fact that did not surprise anyone. The sky was so thick with clouds that one need only reach out over the Wall's edge, it seemed, to catch one. The sun was hiding, having conceded the dawn to her rival the moon and their mutual suitor, the wind, howled madly for them both. Today, he was a strong suitor.

The pace of the horses was dismal. Along the Wall, smooth straight stretches alternated with steep steps as it rose and fell with the Mountains. Usually, horses could maintain a steady trot for the most part but today, a trot was impossible for in that bouncing two-beat gait, a horse was suspended for a heartbeat above the ground. Today, the wind was such that, in that heartbeat, a hoof could easily be snatched from the stone and both horse and rider sent tumbling over the edge. Today, like their souls, they crawled.

Kirin tucked his head deep into his hood, once again Imperial gold, fresh and clean from the garrison town. *At least it wasn't raining,* he thought darkly. That would be the ultimate insult, but then again, clouds so often were insulting. Dog-like they were, constantly reaching for the Kingdom's skies, muffling her warm sun and pelting cats with water.

Briefly, he allowed his eyes to scan the party of horses in front of him. Kerris and Quiz took the lead, the mountain pony looking very sorry with its head low to the ground and its wild mane and tail a victim of the gales. A more satisfying view was that of the Imperial horses, manes shaven, tails bound, plowing through the gusts like water buffalo through a river. Two leopards in the fore, followed by Alchemist and Scholar, each clutching cloaks over their heads, one black, one green. Next, the Major and the Seer, faces forward and uncloaked, as if daring the wind to beat them. Kirin shook his head. *Ursa Laenskaya - meditating.* Never would he have thought such a thing. And never would she have let a man touch her, as surely he must have. A shame he wasn't Pure. He would put a stop to it at once.

Finally, the last two leopards brought up the rear, leading the packhorses behind them. This way they traveled for hours, passing battle tower after battle tower before the Captain called a halt at noon.

They huddled chilled and weary inside a tower keep, sipping hot tea and soup provided by the keep's guards. Messages were sent between towers daily via kestrel. Despite the wind, the kestrels had managed to alert other towers to the approach of the Imperial party, and preparations had been hastily but efficiently made to accommodate them, should the need arise.

Kirin did not find it odd, then, that not a single word passed between them during the short break for lunch. He hadn't even needed speak to the tower guards to be presented with several skins of hot soup for the journey that he accepted with gratitude and a good measure of pride. He never failed to be impressed with the consistency of their training. Then again, consistency was the very heart of *Bushido.* He could not imagine otherwise.

So again, they set out into the driving wind. It wasn't long before the Captain found himself losing track of time. Hours blended and the afternoon crept forward, a constant struggle against the gale. Once, he saw motion from under his hood, knew instinctively that a horse had stumbled, and a sharp wave of alarm swept through him. Even alMassay was blowing hard, the sounds rumbling around his great chest like thunder. *This was madness,* the Captain thought to himself. They would stop at the next battle tower for the night.

The wind picked up again, drowning all sound but its wailing, as they neared a great, unfamiliar mountainside. The Wall rose to meet it, steps mirroring the steep angle as she prepared herself to climb again. 20 steps then plateau, 20 steps then plateau. With increasing fury, the wind blew, snatching snow from the rock face and throwing it in bitter circles across the stone corridor. Even this had become a weapon against them. Kirin could see Quiz begin the treacherous climb, skittering as his small hoofs fought for traction. 20 steps, then plateau. The leopards next, a struggle even with greater horses. 20 steps, then plateau.

Stumbling and skidding, the party of horses ascended the mountain on the back of the Great Wall, 20 steps then plateau. In fine weather, this would have been difficult enough but in this gale, it was misery. Kirin could see nothing of the others as alMassay struggled with the climb, his view restricted to the steps directly in front of him. And finally, when he was certain the stallion would drop from exhaustion, the steps ended and they stood on the rampart of a large battle tower, Imperial Standard whipping defiant and proud.

Tower guards met him, taking alMassay and ushering the Captain inside, where he was greeted with warm blankets and hot tea. His ears were still ringing from the wind as he surveyed his people, sprawled against the walls of the keep, too numb to move. He slid down next to his brother.

"Will tomorrow be the same?"

"Worse," muttered Kerris. His eyes were closed, chin to chest, and his night-blue hood pulled over his head. "Tomorrow, the skies will fall."

The Captain had barely placed his empty teacup on the stone floor before he surrendered to the blackness.

***

blackness, blackness and candles, books burning, journals, 100 summers of journals burning in circle of chalk, old eyes weeping, painted walls, painted panthers, scrubbed free with sulphur and acid, paint burning, searing, golden eyes curling into wet ash, Tiberius beaten and weeping in the snow

"Captain."

Noble Tiberius, Wise Petrus, Sha'Hadin *broken and weeping in the snow*

"Captain?"

He awoke with a start.

"Yes?"

A leopard was kneeling before him.

"Sir. The second watch has begun."

"Thank you."

With a deep breath, he roused himself. The coal brazier in the centre of the room cast long flickering shadows up the tower's brick walls. His people lay scattered around it like living mats. Even his own leopards slept with them this night, as deserving of rest as the others, perhaps more so. The wind howled outside the tiny windows, but unlike those in *Sha'Hadin,* these had been wisely fitted with the thickest of glass.

Quietly, he padded over to the Major. She was awake, her sinewy arms wrapped around her knees, her hair all but covering her face.

"Major, have you slept?"

"No."

"That's unwise. I told these men to wake us at second watch. They can be trusted."

"Yes sir."

"After this, you will sleep. I have no desire to be catching you when you fall off your horse in the morning."

His attempt at humor fell on deaf ears. He knew her well, knew her shame of the other night and her fierce desire to prove her honor in the face of it. Her own *Bushido,* a warrior-way of a different nature. Still, he understood her well.

"Yes sir."

He looked at the near-by form of the Seer, slumped against a warm brick wall, head in his arms, sleeping. He deeply wished that the falcon would bring them orders to come home, to return to *Pol'Lhasa,* or *Sha'Hadin,* and make things right. Armies and alchemists, these he could handle, but this journey into an angry man's soul, this impossible search for a being that could not exist and finally, this murder of Ancestors, all this was indecorous to him. Dishonorable. But if it was demanded, it would be done. And he knew the way *Bushido* would demand he handle it. He would take the dishonor upon himself by killing the Ancestor, then restore it by killing himself. The Empress would be blameless. It was the only way.

He did not look at the Major.

"You will not meditate again."

"Sir."

She had hesitated before responding. This disturbed him, perhaps more than all. He was about to say more when there was motion beside him.

The Seer was shaking his head. Kirin leaned forward.

"Solomon?"

No response, just shaking.

"Solomon? It is the Captain. Are you there?"

"Go away."

"Solomon, are you quite alright?"

"I said go away."

"What is wrong?"

The Seer raised his head, tears streaking the sandy pelt of his cheeks.

"They're all dead."

"Major, leave us."

He could feel her glance, the frosty chill of her eyes, but she obeyed, rising and moving out of earshot. Satisfied, he leaned in closer.

"Who, Solomon? Who is dead?"

"The stench. I couldn't - it's those god-awful rat-things. They smashed all the units, tore out bits and pieces, I couldn't..."

Kirin gritted his teeth.

"There are others?"

"I got the power on. They scattered like rice, but it's too late. Too late..."

The utter despair in that voice gripped him. He was grieving for a man he was bound by duty to kill. *What could he possibly say to that?*

"I'm sorry, Solomon."

"Have you ever thought about killing yourself, Captain?"

"No," he lied.

"Me neither. Until now."

"Solomon..."

"I can't talk, Cap, okay? Just go away this time. Just this once. I - I'll talk tomorrow, okay?"

"Tomorrow. Promise me."

"Yeah."

The Seer dropped his head back into his arms but Kirin knew the connection had not yet severed for he was still shaking his head in mourning. He motioned the Major to return, and rose to his feet. With a deep breath, he moved to one of the windows, leaned his forehead on the cold pane. Outside, it was as Kerris had said. The sky was falling.

***

When snow breeds with rain, it becomes miserable. This is yet another proof for the integrity of the Pure Races. Even at its worst, snow is cat-like, having a certain nobility of form and even at its best, the dog-like rain is simply that. Rain. But breed the two and you have a recipe for anarchy neither Kingdom should ever suffer. So it was this mongrel sleet than rained down on them the next morning but even still, under Captain's orders, they set out.

The Wall provided more of the same, rising with the mountain peaks, falling into the valleys. The altitudes were so varied that the architect of this section had chosen to build high, rather than broad, to level the way as much as possible. Therefore, across this section, a party could ride only two abreast and there were dangerous low dips in the geniculated cornice. In fact, it seemed that the mountain wind had ground many of the bricks smooth over the years since its construction and parts of the parapet were missing entirely. Soon, Kerris had assured them, they would be leaving the mountains for more hilly terrain but for the next few days, it would be like riding a great dancing dragon, never knowing when one might get slapped off and trampled or caught between its teeth. It would be, Kerris had assured them, a miserable few days.

The tower guards had provided them with wet-coats – thick leather cloaks soaked in oil and hand-rubbed with bee's wax. They were heavy and smelly but with the hood laced tight, very effective in keeping pelts warm and dry. They did also stop the bite of the wind though not its force and the horses slipped and plodded and fought every step of the way.

This day, they did not stop for lunch but ate as they willed on the soup and dried fish they each carried. At one point, they were forced to concede however and stood their horses in a circle on one of the few plateaus, taking shelter from the wind. Kirin promised them they would finish early for the night, although that did little to cheer their cold, wet, buffeted spirits. It seemed they had grown numb to the world. They set out again.

So, it was with sluggish reflexes that Kirin noticed far ahead of him, at the base of yet another set of ascending steps, a strange unusual movement. Movement not coinciding with the steady plodding of horses or flapping of cloaks. Rather, a flash of red, a flare of black. It was something that should not have been seen on this narrow, climbing section of Wall.

Above the saddle of the Alchemist's horse, the scarlet pouch, a symbol of unnatural, otherworldly things, was unraveling, and the Alchemist was reaching for it.

Not just reaching, but standing, twisting in her saddle even as her horse began lunging up the steps. Bending her long body, cloak flaring like a cobra's hood, she stood in the stirrups to reach behind and over the horse, her inexperience deadly for she kept one hand on the rein.

"No!" the Captain shouted but his words were torn from his

mouth. Directly behind her, the Major and Seer were doing likewise, trying to warn her but they too were deafened by the wind. He tried to urge alMassay faster but the stallion was putting every effort into simply moving forward. In horror he watched the mare's head pull back, nose high in the air, mouth wide. He could see the white panic in her eye as completely unaware her rider was destroying her balance. To keep from toppling head-over-tail, the mare swung her haunches across the steep steps and into the Scholar's mount, forcing it backwards toward the edge of the Wall. The Scholar's horse took several steps back down the steps, reared and fell.

Fallon Waterford had been unprepared. Truth be told, she was completely elsewhere, awrap in thoughts of warm, sunny jungles and loving smiles and long walks through deep dark quiet green.

So when the saddle suddenly jerked and rose beneath her, she was thrown first sideways, then back and finally out of it altogether. Her knee wrenched, her ankle twisted and she smacked the stone of the step with her cheek. But only for a heartbeat, for she was caught by a foot in the stirrup and the horse was tumbling down the steps of the Wall, pulling her along with it.

Immediately behind was the Major's horse. Battle-trained and sure-footed, it reacted swiftly, executing a perfect capriole, gathering up on its hind legs and leaping over the thrashing form that was sliding downwards. But elevation and the bitter sleet were ruthless enemies, and it did not land cleanly. Hooves skidded and slipped, and it too went down. The Major sprang from the saddle before she hit, striking the step with palm and shoulder, pain shooting through her like arrows.

In many a cat's life, there comes a point of decision, a junction or crossroad as it were, in which a choice is made and a path followed. It is called the 'Broken Road' by the more poetically inclined, as though life were a journey, unknown and unscribed, which of course, cats know it is not. It more often than not involves a measuring of self, of what is right against what is want. Often, these points of decision carry him(or her) down roads that, later, are regretted and even cursed. So was it with Sherah al Shiva that day. In less than a heartbeat, she saw the chaos, the danger to people she had come to know, a danger she herself had caused. She saw the Scholar pulled under her horse, the Major thrown off hers and the Captain bracing his for impact. But in that same heartbeat, the demon wind grabbed the pouch out of her grasp, its spider-threads unraveling like wool. She saw the people. She chose the pouch. She leapt out of the saddle onto the narrow parapet to catch it.

At the base of the stairs, the Captain had maneuvered alMassay into the falling horse's path, swinging him sideways – a wall of muscle and iron-will. It hit like a boulder, that horse, legs flailing, head thrashing and Kirin fought against the wave of pain that swept up from his thigh. Instead, he swung from his horse and onto the other, throwing his wet-coat over the animal's head. Its fall halted and unable to see, the horse grew quiet.

Eye for an eye. Life for a life.

As if hearing a voice very far long ago and very far away, Sireth turned his head slowly toward the wall, even as he was sliding from his saddle to help the Major. He could not believe his eyes and he watched in horror as the Alchemist clung to the worn parapet like a great black spider, cloak and wet-coat billowing behind her, longs arms reaching for the pouch, reaching...

She snagged it but the wind barked and pushed her over the side.

"Captain! Major!" he cried.

The others could not hear him, nor had they seen. In fact, he could barely see *them* through the sleet as they struggled with frantic horses on the steps below. He glanced back to the edge, caught sight of a flutter of black and abandoned his own horse to rush towards it.

She was dangling by the hem of her wet-coat, one clawed hand scrabbling at the bricks, the other clutching the pouch to her chest like an infant. He thrust his hand over the side.

"Here!"

She looked up, eyes wide in terror and sent her free arm shooting upwards toward his.

"Reach!" he shouted and she stretched like a serpent, legs swinging, tail lashing. Their fingertips brushed *Let her go said Petrus Mercouri Let her go and save yourself the bruising*

He froze.

Never before had he heard voices of the dead. It was not part of his, or any other Seer's Gift. That was the realm of the Black Arts.

He shook his head, reached for her again.

Let her go said Petrus You know what she is

"No! Woman, release that thing!"

But she would not, and tucked the pouch deeper to her chest, even as the hem of her coat began to tear.

"Release it!"

She has chosen a violent path One of death and fire and blood Will you do likewise

He felt the strain in his legs as he bent further over the edge. The Wall plummeted so steeply that he could not make out its base. Snow and sleet threw themselves all around, vainly trying to claim another soul for their Good Mother.

Let her go or you will not be able to stop what is coming Listen to me Let her go

There was a moment. He could pull back, do nothing, allow the mountains and the sinister nature of her craft to swallow her whole and no one would be the wiser. She had fed him blood. She deserved to die. For a moment, he was tempted.

In fact, there were two cats that day on the Broken Road. Two.

She lunged again and he grabbed her wrist.

The jolt almost pulled his arm from its socket but he held fast. She cried out furiously and with a kick of her long legs, propelled herself high enough for him to catch her with the other hand as well. Her boots scraped the bricks, searching for a toehold but finding none. Her weight was wild and swinging and he had no balance. She was pulling him down with her.

Very well It is yours to give Now find peace

He closed his eyes and was elsewhere, *in a jungle far to the east and deep in the south, a jungle without bugs. Shakuri's night-black hand in his, weightless as a leaf or a flower, yes a flower, he was reaching into the grass to snip a flower from its stem, lifting it, lifting a weightless little flower up up and onto the grass beside him, up and over and onto the* Wall beside him. The Alchemist collapsed into a black-cloaked ball on the stones, clutching the pouch to her chest, weeping.

You are stubborn my friend But such is the dharma of choice It has begun You cannot stop what is to come

"Forgive me," the Seer said wearily as he sank to the stones beside her.

The Scholar was not moving. The Captain had managed to free her foot from the iron stirrup and pull her out from under her horse. The Major was at its head, wrapping the wet-coat securely over its eyes and she threw him a grim look. The animal stood now but one hoof dangled like a pendant, bearing no weight. Ursa looked at the tigress.

"Is she dead?" she asked.

"No," he answered, noticing for the first time the Major's arm, cradled up into her ribs. It was the same one that had suffered the arrow, so many days ago. "You are injured."

"No."

"The Alchemist will tend you both."

He gathered the tigress into his arms, paused when she slid open her emerald eyes, just a crack.

"I'm sorry, daddy," she whimpered. "About the pheasants..."

He smoothed the white-tipped hair from her forehead.

"Hush, child. Sleep."

And he lifted her from the steps. Kerris was bounding down them, ashen hair and night-blue cloak whipping madly. He was flanked by unfamiliar leopards.

"Battle-fort just up ahead," he panted. "What happened, Kirin? I didn't see—"

"I know. See to the horses."

And he turned back to alMassay, laying the tigress across his saddle and beginning the long trek up the mountain.

***

Someone was stroking her hair.

It felt warm and familiar and she breathed in the scent of leather. Fallon opened her eyes to see the bearded face smiling down at her.

"Welcome back, *Kallilah.* You had us worried."

She scrunched her nose and frowned, tasting the sharp tang of blood in her mouth. She tried to stretch for she felt knotted and cramped all over, but that only brought pain rushing up and around her body.

"Owww..."

"Lay still. You've had a bad fall."

"It hurts..."

Another voice, and now a face, this one a beautiful butter-cream.

"Is there pain in your belly?"

"Um..." She tried to sit up, wincing as her muscles cried against the movement. "No, not pain really, just, just oww. You know? Just awful and owwy all over. But my foot—"

"Twisted, not broken. I have applied liniment and bound it with strips of tanned hide. It will heal quickly." The woman glanced up at Sireth. "It will heal."

His expression was unreadable, but if anything, Fallon thought, a little sad.

"Yes," he said. "She will heal."

With ginger fingers, Fallon touched her face. Her cheek ached, and the soft tissue around her eye was puffy and tender. Likewise, her jaw hurt when she pressed against it, and she frowned again.

"I think my horse fell... Oh, my *horse!*"

Suddenly, the room came into focus and she saw they were in a battle tower, the brick walls, small windows and charcoal brazier exactly as they had been in every tower along their route. At one far end, the Captain stood, hands on hips, staring out at the gale, his stillness heavy as iron. There was no one else in the room.

She opened her mouth to say something, but Sireth put a finger to his lips. He shook his head. Quickly, Sherah lifted a tea cup, the green-gold brew steaming and fragrant.

"Oolong," she murmured, "With ginseng for strength, and tao-root for healing."

Quiet descended on the little room for some time.

Steps echoed on the floor above them, then a pair of high white boots began to descend the pole-ladder. First the Major, then Kerris jumped the last few rungs to the floor. The grey lion flashed Fallon an appraising look before approaching his brother. The Captain did not turn.

"Sorry Kirin," said Kerris. "The pastern is shattered."

She could see him nod, take a deep breath and lay one hand on the hilt of his long sword. Kerris looked at the floor.

"I can do it if you wish."

"No. We must redistribute the supplies and refit the last packhorse. That is your arena."

He turned and started up the pole-ladder, leaving the heavy stillness behind with them.

"Do what?" asked the Scholar.

Ursa snorted, jabbing a finger at the Alchemist.

"It's your fault. *Kunoichi!*" And she spat on the ground.

"Enough of that, Ursa," growled Kerris. "It's bad enough we have to fight the weather. We don't need to fight each other."

"Do what? What does the Captain have to do?"

"You don't need to think about that now, my dear," said Sireth, but Kerris shook his head.

"Your horse has a broken leg. Shattered the bones in his pastern, in fact. That's the sunken spot right above the hoof."

"But Sherah can fix it?"

The Alchemist continued to stare into her tea.

"Kunoichi," Ursa hissed again. *"Nin'jaah.* You sabotage our journey at every turn."

"I said enough!" snapped Kerris and for a fleeting moment, he resembled his brother in more than just face. When he turned back to the Scholar, he was Kerris once again.

"Nothing can heal this kind of break, *sidala.* And since it's an Imperial horse, Kirin has to take care of it. But not to worry, his sword is sharp, his aim sure. The creature will be dead before it even knows it has been struck."

"Oh...oh no..." Emerald eyes brimmed.

"Yes, well." Kerris huffed and looked round at the faces. "I guess I'd better get to those provisions. We have only one packhorse now. We may have to leave some books—"

"Not my books—"

"And some Alchemy stores." He glanced at the pouch, bobbing and full at the end of its tether. "You might want to consider leaving that."

"No."

"Believe me, *sidalady* cheetah, Kirin is not too well-disposed toward it at the moment. Or for that matter, you."

She looked up at him. The paint around her eyes had streaked with her tears and she looked almost vulnerable.

"I cannot leave it. It is my life."

"No." said Sireth. "It is your death.

"I cannot leave it."

"I can leave my books," said Fallon, biting back her own tears and wincing anew. "If I can get them when we come back."

"You shall have them, then," said Kerris and he started up the pole-ladder. The silence he left behind roared louder than the wind.

***

He *was* handsome, she had to give him that.

In fact, Andreas Wolchenko Verona Chiraq was perfect.

He was young and courtly, as well mannered as any in her Imperial company. He held his tongue when it was wise to do so, and offered opinions that made her think. His family was Sacred and very old, dating back to the Second Dynasty and well spoken of by the people of the region. They had governed *Abyssinia* throughout the ages and *DharamShallah* had grown used to their tithes and tributes.

And, as all of his people, he was gold. Like a lion.

The Empress had to smile to herself. The man had been chosen by the First Mage himself, his pick for suitor for the Empress' hand, and she knew in her heart of hearts the very reason. Not the only reason, however, so as not to offend with the error of simplicity. Still, she found herself reminded in many ways of her Captain. His eyes, while not blue, were as green as jade and reflected a depth of thoughtfulness and humor that she found most appealing. His laugh was effortless and natural, but not overdone, his discretion commendable. He was well read, well taught, well groomed. All in all, the perfect match. The First Mage was not valued counsel for nothing.

As they reclined on silk cushions of crimson and blue, she studied Chiraq over her plum wine. It had been a lovely evening. They had dined on roasted pheasant, set out on platters to look in death as they do in life. They had tasted the chocolate from *Hindaya* and the marzipans from *Hirak*. They had been entertained with the koto and sitar and bamboo flute. He was altogether pleasant, in form, in manner, in conversations, and she found herself counting the reasons why she should be grateful for such an agreeable match.

There was, however, a problem. With his eyes.

She could tell when someone was impressed with her. She could tell when someone was overwhelmed with her position, her opulence, her power. She could tell when someone was fearful, proud, cloying, false or deceitful. She could also tell, from close inspection of one set of blue eyes in particular, when someone was absolutely and unconditionally in love with her, enthralled with her every nuance, would lay down his life in a heartbeat. She was skilled at discerning all these things, so it was not difficult at all to tell when someone was hiding something behind the deep spheres of color that were his eyes.

"What is her name?" she asked over her cup and smiled when his gaze lowered. Again, to his credit, his composure remained secure.

"You are every bit as wise as I was told, Excellency. It is inexplicable."

She did not lower her own gaze, however, this alone informing him that his comments would not suffice. He took a deep breath.

"Bellethsa di Montagne, Excellency."

He smiled shyly. She wondered if her Captain might look the same when confessing the name of the one he loved.

"That is not a Sacred name, Andreas."

"No, Excellency. She is a scribe from our courts. An ocelot of good breeding."

"You know this cannot be, Andreas."

"I know, Excellency. As does she. But I would not presume to lie to my Empress."

"But you would *marry* your Empress."

"It would be an honor, Excellency."

Marvelous, she thought to herself, *how kharma works in us all.* She brought her cup to her lips.

"The First Mage has chosen well. Perhaps too well. You are everything I would want in a suitor. Yes, you are a perfect choice." She nodded, sipped her plum wine. "Perhaps he knows me too well."

The night went on like lemonade, sweet and bitter, and by the end, she dismissed him with riches to bless his family and the family of Bellethsa di Montagne, the ocelot scribe in the courts of *Abyssinia.*

***

Kirin watched her with sharp, sifting eyes, wishing for once that he might see as a Seer sees, deep into the hearts and souls of the unwary. She confounded him, this woman of blackness and incense, even now as she sat cross-legged on the stormy parapet, her candles wavering but not going out, her tangle of hair lifting and falling like the wings of a raven. She was drawing chalk circles on the stone, dropping pebbles in between the interwoven lines. She shook her head and repeated the process many times. All the while, she hummed but it was not a sweet singing.

He stepped out of the shadow of the tower.

"Sidala."

"Sidi."

"Your actions today were unforgivable."

She had still not looked up at him, and he thought this was a large part of her power. She forced one to act, forced one to move, when out of courtesy and propriety, it should have been her obligation. He would not tolerate it.

"Sidala, look at me."

It was almost his undoing. Her eyes were wide and wondrous, no longer blackened by the thick paint she wore and they shone like lanterns in a gale. He steeled himself against them.

"I have killed an Imperial horse, tonight, *sidala.* Perhaps in *Agara'tha,* they have little value, but here and now, they are all we have. Do you understand this?"

"Of course."

"Do you?"

"I do." She nodded, no hint of duplicity now in either voice or expression. She was somber and serious but preoccupied and she turned back, waving a hand over her circles. "This cannot be."

He stepped towards her now, towering over her, a dark shadow against the darker sky. "What cannot be?"

"The numbers. The numbers do not lie. They can tell nothing but the truth."

"And what is the truth they are telling?"

She shook her head again.

"Sidala." It was not a question.

"Six," she whispered. "The numbers keep saying six."

Something told him he should know this, should know the significance of what she was saying, and somewhere, it rattled him to the very core.

"What of it?"

"Seven is the number of perfection, *sidi.* But six..."

"Yes?"

"Six is the number of man."

Blast, he thought. She was a diviner as well. He should have known. He should have been told.

"The numbers are wrong."

"The numbers are never wrong."

He crouched down low to her, meeting her gaze directly. Then with a slow, deliberate motion, he wiped away her circles and gathered her pebbles. He pressed them into her palm.

"The numbers are *wrong.*"

Golden eyes dropped to the floor. "Of course."

"And we will not speak to the others of their error."

"No, *sidi.*"

"Two nights past, after we crossed the *Shi'pal*—"

"Yes, I did."

Cocking his head, he sat back on his haunches. "You drugged the Major?"

"In her tea. Two tablets of hawk's thorn."

He was surprised at his own mild response. He should be furious.

"Why?"

Again, she looked at him and the force of her almost pushed him over.

"You required sleep. When Solomon comes, you do not sleep."

"Thank you, *sidala,* but my needs are not your concern."

"Of course."

Rather quickly, he rose to his feet.

"You will not do this again."

She bowed, almost touching her forehead to the stone. With a deep breath, he left her to her chalk and candles.

***

Solomon did not come again that night but this time, somehow Kirin was not surprised. He and the Major had sat up for the entirety of the second watch but the Seer had slept like a kitten, without even a flicker of an eyelid to disturb him. The Captain himself was so exhausted that he welcomed the respite and found sleep came quickly once he laid his head. He had no dreams that night.

The next days were like the previous, wet and cold and stormy. They were entering the *Zashkar Pass*, the Wall cleaving the Great Mountains like a magician's trick. The Upper Kingdom claimed the south-eastern range, for it was these that boasted the most spectacular peaks. *Kathandu,* and *Charta,* and her greatest daughter, virgin *Shagar'mathah*, Empress of the Earth. There were others, to be sure, such as her sister *Mathah'kalu* or consort *Khanshen'kalu* but none could rival *Shagar'mathah* for size. Cats of all races had tried to scale her but all attempts had failed miserably and their bones fed her avaricious slopes. She alone was virgin. She alone was pure.

Unless, of course, one believed the recent exploits of Kaidan. Legend Kaidan, onetime hostage then first ambassador to the *Chi'Chen.* Myth Kaidan, cat of unknown Race, in one story lion, in another tiger, in yet another ghost. Clever, wily and untouchable Kaidan, hero of the people, heralded by bards everywhere. Now, the most current of these tales being that Kaidan had indeed conquered *Shagar'mathah,* that he had wooed her and won her and left his cloak like a flag on her very summit. On that matter, Kirin did not know what to think. He usually tried not to think about it. Thoughts of Kaidan invariably gave him a headache.

Now, the Lower Kingdom had been ceded the northwestern ranges, for reasons inexplicable to cats. It was not that they had not been defendable. The Great Mountains offered cats great protection and the Wall had only proved that fact, simply reinforcing this natural barrier. Rather, it seemed that somehow, at some time, a cruel bargain had been struck, and someone had delivered over to dogs a portion of their Good Mother. Perhaps it had been Her own plan for with her strong arms, she could at once embrace her chosen people and keep their enemies at bay.

So having begun at *Sri'Varna* all the way to the garrison town of *Panther* in the *Zashkar Pass,* the Mountains were angry and steep, howling and raging because of this unworthy bargain. But west, beyond *Panther*, the anger subsided and the mountains grew bored, the wind lost interest and the Wall leveled to more manageable straights. Even still, it took five days before they could see the domes and spires of *Lhahore.* Solomon had not come at all, on any night during their trek and Kirin found his spirits buoyed at the chance of returning home. On the eve of the sixth day, they arrived at a battle tower high above the city to find a falcon, not Path, awaiting them.

It bore a parchment, sealed with the Imperial seal and the scent of lotus.

My dearest and most noble Captain,

I trust this falcon finds you at the tradestown of Lhahore, *well and strong on your journey, and that your people are likewise. Our Mother, the Great Mountains, is sure to bless you with safety and good speed as you make the difficult pass through her breast.*

I am pleased to inform you that the First Mage of Agara'tha, *Jet barraDunne, has graciously agreed to assist in the supervision of the monastery of* Sha'Hadin. *His priests have already begun the delicate procedure of assuming the daily operations, and he has succeeded in locating former Council candidate, Yahn Nevye, to oversee that the transition is smooth. Jet has assured me that none of their unique traditions or practices will be lost during his stewardship. Rather, he insists that my Seers might be strengthened and supported by the presence of their brothers in the Arts, during this time of bereavement and change.*

Although I wish in my heart of hearts to see you and your party return to the safety of Pol'Lhasa, *your mission has not changed. Imperial justice must be sure and swift, and I know you to be both.*

With highest and most honorable regards,

Thothloryn Parillaud Markova Wu

He folded the tiny slip of parchment and slid it into his sash, frowning. There should have been two but perhaps it was all for the best. The first held his loathe secret. It was better to be ashes on the scarlet Inn's floor.

With a sigh, he turned back to his party, now in the process of removing the tack from their horses' backs. He watched them all in turn, the Major with her quick, sharp movements, the Alchemist with her slow, languid ones. Naturally, Quiz required no untacking so Kerris was being useful as he aided the still limping Scholar with her new mount. He pulled the saddle from the high back and slipped the bridle over the long, rather Roman nose. She was chatting constantly, even as his back was turned, and hobbled around behind him like a kitten, leaning on the Seer's twisted bamboo staff for support. The Seer, himself, shouldered his saddle as the Captain approached.

"Who is Yahn Nevye?"

"Yahn Nevye?" The Seer paused before lowering the saddle to the ground. "What of Yahn Nevye?"

"Who is he?"

"He is a Seer from *Sha'Hadin.* Or at least, he was. He's on sabbatical. Why?"

"He has charge of the monastery."

"Really?" The man raised his brows. "Now that is interesting."

"He was a Council candidate?"

"Yes. He was expected to take Chen Bundi's seat two years ago."

"But he didn't."

"No."

The Captain waited, knowing there was more but benAramis turned back to his horse and reached for its bridle.

"How did they find him?"

"The First Mage located him."

The reins swung as the man spun round.

"The First Mage? I was right, then!"

"Sireth benAramis is never wrong."

He had not seen her move, but she was there, a smoke-wraith at his side.

"You have news of the First Mage, *sidi?"* breathed Sherah.

He ignored her and folded his hands behind his back. "So then,

Sha'Hadin is in good hands."

The Seer shook his head. "I have seen nothing from them these past days. Nothing. For me, this is unsettling. My attempts are met with walls, my thoughts deflected like light on mirrors. That is not natural."

"Perhaps there is nothing to see," suggested the Alchemist.

"And perhaps that is what the First Mage wishes us to believe."

Kirin had no patience for squabbles. "Is Yahn Nevye a powerful Seer?"

"Yes."

"More powerful than you?"

"No."

"Is that why you were chosen to the Council Seat instead of him?"

"No. Yahn Nevye cannot speak to falcons."

"What of it?"

"It is the falcons who choose."

Kirin shook his head, finding it ironic that seven of the most powerful, influential cats in the Kingdom were chosen by birds.

"We are not going back."

"As you wish."

The man tried to smile, but the Captain thought it was a thin smile, the smile of a man struggling to resign himself to something. Something far deeper than the loss of *Sha'Hadin.* He could not consider it now.

Kerris looked up from checking one of the horse's feet.

"Well, if we're not going back, then where *are* we going? I mean, Solomon hasn't put in an appearance for many nights now. And we can't navigate on the maps we made back at the Inn. They are nowhere near accurate."

Kirin folded his hands behind his back. "I have an idea."

All eyes were on him now. He shouldered their scrutiny well. "Tonight, the Seer and I shall hold *AhmniShakra.*"

The Seer stared at him. "You're serious."

"I am always serious, *sidi.*"

"But you are not gifted. We will only reach the second level. It won't be enough."

"It will have to be."

"Very well. Since *I* shall be doing the bulk of the work, you *will* allow me to prepare? Have 'the stableboy' see to my things."

And without awaiting permission, Sireth turned, robes swirling, and strode into the massive tower keep.

"You should not allow that," growled Ursa, before trudging after her charge.

"I know," said the Captain. He too turned and left the rampart for the company of soldiers.

***

They had dined well that night, as the Guard did most nights in the battle tower over the tradestown of *Lhahore,* on wild boar and brown rice and quail-egg soup. The atmosphere in this tower seemed almost animated as if the proximity of the town cast her own busy reflections up to the Wall itself. As the sun lay her head down, her warm, golden mane spilt over her clouds and bathed the skies in beauty. From high above, torches began to spring to life within the town's dark centre and temple bells and gongs summoned her people inside for the night.

Fallon yawned and stretched, reaching her arms high above her head and enjoying every tweak and twinge of muscle that it brought. She was almost healed, the bruises from her fall paler and less painful with each passing day and her ankle could hold her weight for a rather good length of time. She was certain that, between the Seer's bamboo staff and the Alchemist's wraps and remedies, she would be walking on it in no time.

Quite casually, she approached the Captain as he stood conferring with the tower guards.

"Hello."

He turned, face stern. *"Sidala?"*

"Um…" It was only then that she realized her breach of protocol. "Um…"

"Yes, *sidala?"*

"Um, well um, nothing really, I mean, nothing important, it's just, um..."

His face grew even more stern.

"Um, do, do, do you know where Kerris is?"

"He has gone into town with the Alchemist. She needs supplies."

"Oh. Oh okay. Okay thanks. Sorry if I bothered you. Sorry."

She back-pedaled out of the chamber and lay flat against the wall beside the door.

"Oh, mother. What was I thinking? He's the Captain of the Guard! And I'm just a skinny little tigress. *'Scholar in the Court of the Empress.'* Hah. Who am I fooling? Not me. And certainly not him. I am utterly, completely hopeless."

With a deep sigh, she pushed off and began to wander, knowing that with the approach of darkness, she should sleep and sleep well for the journey had been long and relentless and showed no promise of ending. She wasn't tired however and to her surprise, she had been holding up rather well. Her stamina had grown each day, and she was delighted at finding new muscles in her slight, slip of a body. Sometimes, she would even pretend that she was the Major, a mistress of swords and discipline. Even now as she walked, she spun on her heel, thrusting and parrying her bamboo staff and swinging it in a wide arc that would be sure to slice an enemy clean in two.

She lost her grip and the staff sailed out of her hand, through an open doorway.

"Ai!"

It was a dark chamber, lit by only a single earthen oil-lamp in the centre. Before the lamp, Sireth benAramis sat cross-legged, holding the staff and rubbing his head.

"Oh! Oh, sorry, I'm really sorry!"

He smiled at her.

"Now you have one on me, my dear. I didn't see *that* coming."

She bustled into the room and flopped down beside him.

"I'm hopeless."

"Well, that was a rather good throw, if you ask me."

"That's not what I meant."

"Ah. What did you mean, then?"

Her gaze was despondent, her eyes downcast. "I'm a girl."

"Ah."

He nodded and nodded again, not entirely certain what to say in response.

"Yes," he said finally. "A girl is what you are."

"Yep. A girl."

"Yes."

"Not a woman."

"Ah! Yes."

He paused, remembering how Petrus Mercouri would handle difficult questions with questions. How he had maintained that people always knew their own answers. They only needed help finding them.

"And why would you say that?"

She rolled her eyes.

"Well, I will have eighteen summers this year, and here I am, so far from home, but I have no home, no husband, no kittens, certainly no kitten-inspired chest. I draw little pictures in my books. I hear little songs in my head. I entertain little passions on the Captain's brother."

He opened his mouth to speak, but she wasn't finished.

"I can't use a sword. I can't make magical potions. I've had two horses literally killed out from under me. I pretend that I'm all smart and knowledgeable and fine with all this, but deep down, I just want to go home."

He smiled.

"And with the notable exception of the Captain's brother, exactly how does that make you any different from me?"

"Well, *you* haven't lost any horses."

"Good point. And the passions *I* am entertaining would likely see me drawn and quartered if they were ever found out."

She laughed now and he secretly thanked Petrus for his wise, wise ways.

"Give me your hands."

"My hands?" Even as she asked, she was giving. "Why?"

The touch of her fingers made him smile. It sent warm sparkles all through him, sparkles and sunshine and shooting stars.

"I wish to hear your songs."

***

The Captain sighed and leaned out over the Wall. *Lhahore* nestled in shadow now, her torches flickering eyes in the darkness. The Great Mountains were no longer her protector, rather her lover for they enfolded her with wide arms. Small hills and grassy plains stretched out as if forever, and lights from battle towers could be seen all along their length. Far to the northwest lay the old ruins of *Roar'pundih,* a former dog-city that had been the site of a fierce battle during construction of this section of Wall. It had also very likely been the site of a fierce battle in Ancient times as well. Bits of architecture still remained, temple peaks and gray roads and metal, red and brittle with age. Few cats lived there. It seemed impossible to overcome the devastation. The rats, however, were plentiful and *Lhahore* was in constant danger from their invasions.

The Major appeared at his side. "They will be closing the city soon."

He growled softly. "Fetch him, please."

"Shall I bring a guard?"

"You can handle it."

"Sir."

With a swift nod, she spun on her heel and was gone, her boots echoing down the vast stairwell of the tower keep. He watched from above for some time longer.

***

"Well, that was easy," said Kerris, tucking a package under his cloak. "I believe that if you could steal an Imperial seal, you could write orders on a blade of swamp grass and they would be obeyed."

Sherah al Shiva smiled and took the arm he offered her. The streets were growing dark, lanterns lighting the path to and from the apothecary's where they had just been. Soon, town watchmen would come along to inspect the streets, send good people home, and at the hour of the boar, the town's gates would be shut up, closing all cats, good and not so, in for the night.

"Not to mention the things you could buy. Think about it – I'll take those boots over there, see this Imperial seal here? And those puzzle rings and that sash and oh yes, a pint of your best ale, thanks. Just send your bill to my dear friend, Lyn-ling, at the Palace.' Yes, I think it would be quite easy."

"Of course."

"Say, we have some time before they close up the gates. Care for a drink? I'm sure we can find a tavern or two."

"I have no money."

"That's alright." He grinned at her, raising the small, leather ring stamp his brother had given him. He waggled it in the lamplight. "I think the Empress has enough for us both."

"That was for supplies."

"If I recall correctly, which is never a thing of certainty when it comes to me, the exact words were 'Get what you need' and I distinctly need a bowl or two of sakeh."

She let one long speckled hand slide down the length of his thigh. "Is that all that you need, sidi?"

"Well," he grinned some more as they headed toward a brightly lit window. "It's a start."

***

Little Blossom made a sash, Made a sash for her love
Little fingers worked the sash, Worked the sash with silken thread
Made the sash for her love who worked upon the Wall
Upon the Wall, Upon the Wall,
For her love upon the Wall, Little Blossom made a sash.

Little Blossom traveled day and night, night and day to see her love
Little feet traveled night and day, On little slippers small and fine
Day and night, night and day, she traveled to the Wall
To the Wall, To the Wall,
To the Wall, Little slippers traveled far to see her love

Little Blossom found the Wall, long and gold, a serpent's tail
Little hands caught their eye, Called the soldiers guarding there
Soldiers saw that little hand, from high above the Wall

Above the Wall, Above the Wall
Above the Wall, the soldiers saw her calling for her love

Ten strong tigers lifted her, in a basket of bamboo
Ten strong arms, in a basket of bamboo Little Blossom went
Like the bread or fish or rice, in a basket of bamboo
Up the Wall, Up the Wall
Up the Wall in a basket of bamboo, Little Blossom went

Little Blossom wept and moaned, at the news of her love's death
Little heart broke for love was dead, fallen from the tower high
Her love was dead for many days, fallen from the Wall
From the Wall, From the Wall
From the Wall, her love had died, fallen from on high

Little Blossom took the step, with the sash clutched to her breast
Little step across the side, into the air, over the edge
To death's dark heart, she followed her love over the Wall
Over the Wall, Over the Wall
Over the Wall Little Blossom stepped, with the sash clutched to her breast'

"That was beautiful," said Sireth, after several moments.

Fallon sighed. "It always makes me cry."

"You see? You needn't keep those songs in your head. Others might enjoy them as I did."

"I never had the courage to sing in front of anyone but my family. My father was a great singer. When he opened his mouth, the whole jungle shook."

He could not stop himself from smiling. Neither did he chase it from his face when he noticed the Captain standing in the doorway. Suddenly, the tigress noticed him too. She covered her mouth with her hand.

"Oh, mother..."

"He was right. You sing beautifully."

The Captain crossed the room, folded his legs and lowered himself next to them.

"It is time."

"Already?" chirped the Scholar, glancing toward a high, small window as if she could tell the very hour from the blackness. "Wow, where is everyone?"

"We will start without them." He turned to study the Seer. "Are you sufficiently prepared?"

"For second level?" Sireth snorted. "I should hope so."

"You can do better?"

"Well, from what we'd been able to determine at *Sha'Hadin,* the seven Levels of *AhmniShakra* do not apply in my case. There is no measure as to how far, or how deep my gifts run. According to Petrus, there isn't a man living today who can match me. Not even *he* could fathom their depths. Why, Captain," he leaned forward, his good eye gleaming in the lamplight. "Can you do that which Petrus Mercouri could not?"

It was barbed and acerbic, this banter of theirs, and it made Fallon nervous inside. Whenever two lions argued, she had heard tell, it frequently ended badly for one. These two had been sparring since the beginning, and she kept waiting for the flash of claw or show of steel that would inevitably signal the challenge. She wasn't sure why it hadn't happened yet.

"Now third level would be a possibility," the Seer continued, "If you were prepared to be completely open to my Sight. I would know everything about you, every thought, every memory, every secret, every right and every wrong. Likewise, you would know the same about me. Are you prepared for such revelation?"

The Captain ground his molars.

"Level Two should suffice. I simply wish to determine if Solomon is still alive."

"Fair enough. Give me your hands. We shall begin."

***

She was magnificent.

In fact, Kerris was not alone in his observations, for the entire tavern was spellbound. She danced in the middle of the room, its beaded curtains and satin pillows and smoky incense-pots a fitting stage for such an exotic show. Somehow, the laces at her throat and chest had loosened, and her belly flashed against the blackness of leather. She used her cloak as a veil, hiding and teasing with glimpses of gold and her hips swayed with the oboe, tambour and hurdy-gurdy rhythms. The patrons were from all Races, some jaguar, some tiger, some not-quite-certain, and from all walks and stations as well. But even with such a large, appreciative audience, she danced for Kerris, and Kerris alone. He lay across a cushion, entranced.

The music ended and she fell to the floor, folded backwards on her knees, her face only inches from his, her lips parted, breath rushing, mixing with his. Upside down, he kissed her and the tavern cheered.

The spell was over and the music started up once more, this time a new dancer taking the floor. The Alchemist rolled over and propped herself up on the cushion next to the grey lion. She declined an offer of wine from a passing leopard, opened her palm to show Kerris the gold coins held within.

"Well," he grinned as he took another gulp of his ale. "We could go into business, you and I. You are an alchemist, a magnificent dancer and apparently, a thrifty little businesswoman as well."

"And you?"

"Inspiration?"

"Of course."

She smiled and, slipping her hands into his unruly hair, she kissed him again. He felt his head spinning, his thoughts leaving in a swirl of incense and passion and truth be told, he didn't care overmuch. She tasted good on his tongue, and he was tired of this journey, tired of his brother, so very tired.

The tavern door slammed open, chill night winds gusting over the floor and snuffing many of the candles. Grumbles and snarls could be heard from the tavern's patrons, and sharp angry clacking filled the room. A white fist grabbed handfuls of grey mane, yanking the lion's head back so that his teeth cracked against the cheetah's. He yelped.

"OW! Ow! Let go! Ursa, by the Chancellor's beard, let go!"

She flung her hand away, as if it had been touching a scorpion.

"They have shut the gate, fool. Your brother wants you back."

Kerris shook his head, tried to shake away the vertigo that had threatened to overcome him. The Alchemist was already on her feet, cloak draped over her figure, eyes gleaming at him from under the hood. He wasn't entirely certain what had just happened, but he didn't like the way Ursa was lookng at him.

"Right. Right, let's go."

He rose to unsteady feet, began to sink back down. The Major grabbed his arm with remarkable force.

"You are drunk! Pathetic."

"I don't believe I am drunk. Am I?"

He looked to Sherah, but she was already gone, a whisper of black in the crowd. A shadow crossed his line of vision.

"Our friend don't want to leave, Little Sparrow."

It was a common accent, spoken from a common tiger, but he was definitely uncommon in his bulk. In fact, Kerris had only seen two or three men of that size in his lifetime and now that man had squared off against the Major, looming over her like a behemoth over a ladybird. "

He's paid for our drinks, he has, and we likes his company."

"And we likes his dancer," jeered another voice.

"Get out of my way," the Major hissed, her pale eyes slivers of glass.

Kerris held up his hands. "One more round, then and we're off. Right? Now, where's my package?" He glanced around the cushions. "Anyone seen my package?"

"See? He don'ts wants to leave. He wants to stay. Little Sparrow should goes home to their own man, push their own around for a time. Leave our friend be."

"I said get out of my way."

"Ah, there it is. Right, let's go—"

"Maybe Little Sparrow can dance too, eh, like the raven?" The tiger moved in closer, reached his thick fingers to touch her silver hair. "Maybe Little Sparrow dance for me."

Kerris winced and looked away, for he knew what was coming. It was like a child winding a spring too tight and waiting with terrified glee for the thing to suddenly snap. Only with Ursa Laenskaya, the snapping was a matter of fact and there was nothing evenly remotely gleeful about it. She was savage. Her boot heel was a blur as she hop-kicked in place, sending his huge chin snapping back and his great bulk reeled on top of several patrons beneath him. His companion lunged for her arm, grabbing her and swinging her towards him. It was a foolish move, for she let him swing her, harnessing his strength and adding it to her own. Her knee caught him mid-chest, her palm into the bridge of his wide nose and she landed lightly. He, however, added his body to the pile of tiger on the floor and did not move to get up.

"Little Sparrow says no dancing today," said Kerris as he bundled his package under his arm and grabbed for one last gulp of ale. Ursa whirled on him and he scrambled to the door before she could do him any harm.

***

two breaths, merging, two heartbeats mingling, beating together, united as one, one heartbeat, one breath, one blood coursing through two bodies, one

Kirin fought the rush of panic as his every movement, every inner working, became the Seer's. He had never enjoyed the loss of control in any area of his life, and this was no different. It was suffocating, this *AhmniShakra,* but at the same time, strangely exhilarating, as though he was allowing himself to fall and be caught by another. Even at this second level, he was out of his depth.

Hush, said a voice, *focus your thoughts, Breath and Heartbeat, these are your masters*

He obeyed, quieting his misgivings and surrendering to the single breath, in and out, and the single heartbeat beat beat that controlled them both. He sank deep into himself, into the very heart of *Bushido* and deeper still. With a wonder he had rarely experienced, he felt his soul open like a flower.

Good, said the voice, but no thoughts now, just be

???

Be

It required all of his discipline to *just be* like this. Under normal circumstances, his controlled exterior masked a sharp, active thought-life, the planning and oversight of so many trivial events that made up his days. His career was founded on this very ability, to be mindful of everything, to do what needed to be done when needed and to delegate the rest. But this place, quiet and peaceful as a candle-lit cavern, was also known to him. It was perhaps, the very source of his strength. It was, at once, heart and soul and will, the centre of his being.

Be-ing.

He felt a wash of good humour. From himself or the Seer, he could not tell, but he surrendered all the more, tempted for the briefest of moments to ask for level 3. He felt himself pull back from it, however, knew the Seer felt it too. Instead, he focused all the more on the shared heartbeat, the shared breathing and found himself pushing against the Seer's soul to keep him out.

Suddenly, that soul disappeared.

It was like the ice on the *Shi'pal,* one moment strong and solid, the next simply gone. He found himself falling, falling into a space of nothing, and even the panic could not pull him out. For the briefest of moments, he could not breathe, was certain his heart had stopped too until, as with the *Shi'pal,* he resurfaced, chest aching, head spinning and he knew in an instant he was not in the tower at *Lhahore.*

Far from it. He was in Swisserland.

***

"Open the gate."

The sentry guard in the gatehouse of *Lhahore* peered out through his tiny window.

"Impossible. Go home."

Major Ursa Laenskaya curled her hands into fists at her side.

"We are with the Imperial party traveling the Wall. We must join our Captain."

"In the morning."

"No. Now."

"Sorry, *sidala.* I would be my head if I open the gate."

"It will be another part if you don't."

Behind her, Kerris leaned on the arm of the Alchemist and laughed.

"You are truly terrifying, Ursa my love. Scare him some more. Just for me."

Her hand fell to the short sword, the kodai'chi at her side and with only the light of the moon to guide her steps, she charged the wooden gate that walled the city. Kerris closed his eyes to avoid the sight of her crashing but before she hit, she coiled and sprang, swinging her short blade in a fierce arc, the momentum carrying her high. The sword stabbed the rough wood and she held fast, drawing her boots underneath her. Again, she sprang and again she swung, sprang and swung until she perched atop the gate, hawk-like, under the arched lintel.

She tossed her sword down at their feet.

"Next."

Sherah al Shiva picked it up, turning it in her long, strong hands as if to scry its magic. Then, she too sprang upwards, her lithe body scaling the gate like a serpent, long tail whipping beneath her for balance. Soon she too was straddling the gate, smiling her inviting smile and willing him up beside her. She tossed him the sword.

Kerris picked it up, touched the tip with the point of a finger and winced.

"Well now," he mused. "This looks far too tough for such a spoiled, insignificant excuse for a lion as myself."

"Hah. I thought as much."

"'*Two lovely ladies sitting on a gate, One filled with passion, the other filled with'* – well, you know..."

He grinned and slipped the sword into his boot. He began to back away.

"*'One lonely lion, what's he going to do?"*

Ursa glared down at him.

"Get back here, you idiot."

"Find himself a bar and drink himself a brew!'"

"Get back here!"

"What? Can't hear you, my love. You're too far up." And he continued backwards. "Tell Kirin I'll see you all in the morning. Night night!"

He bumped into something and turned around.

He looked up and up into the glowering face of a very big tiger. A very large fist came rushing into view and Kerris remembered little else for the rest of the night.

***

Bright light, garish and white, flashed across walls of dark moving pictures, walls of moving, flashing greens and yellows and alarm-reds. He could see fingers - not his fingers - *pale and pelt-less, drumming on a steel grey table before moving with many little, sharp motions over surfaces he could not fathom. He felt himself take a deep breath* - not his breath - *and push that pelt-less hand into his hair* - not his hair. *He cocked his head* - not his head - *and looked out into the garish light.*

"Hello?"

Solomon.

"Whoa, this is different. Cap, is that you?"

Yes Solomon.

"Uh, okay. This is weirder than before, you know. This time it feels like you're in my head."

I may be. It is strange for me too. But we have not heard from you-

"I know. Sorry. I wasn't sure if I was worth having you people trek all the way from Nepal to find a corpse."

Ah. You are well, then?

"Sort of. Alone, though. Most definitely alone. All my people are dead."

I am sorry. How many were there?

"2000 subs - sleepers, that is. And 7 of us supers."

Supers?

"Supervisors. We were supposed to run the place. We were supposed to be in charge."

What happened?

"I don't know. I think we've been down here a lot longer than we were supposed to be."

How long were you...supposed to...be down there?

"Don't worry about that. You wouldn't believe me anyway. But I think there's been a malfunction in the satellite. It's not responding."

Saddle-light?

"Never mind. It's too complicated to give you a tech lesson right now, especially if you're at the level I think you're at."

I am at level two for the moment. It seems good enough.

"Huh. Right. So where are you guys now?"

We are in a battle tower above the trade town of Lhahore *in the province of* Phunh'jah.

"Not in *Nepal* anymore?"

Phunh'jah. *We should make* KhahBull *in five more days.*

"KhahBull? You mean Kabul? Afganistan?"

Khanisthan. *Is Swisserland close?*

"No. Still far north and farther west. How far does your Kingdom extend?"

Far. All the way to Aegyp.

"Well, I guess the human race hasn't done too badly after all."

Hmmm. What do you look like?

"Oh. Um, hang on. I'll show you a clik. I think I can pull one up..."

Pale fingers of skin and dirt and short flat claws moved across the strange surface, another surface coming to light, a painting-that-looks-like-life flashed in front of his eyes - *not his eyes* – brown eyes, intelligent but unnatural in their brown-ness, pale skin, crinkles, tiny folds, as if carved by tiny tiny claws, straight nose, the nose different, not as broad as cats and without a pad, a wide smiling mouth, similar mouth, similar lips, small ears, bushy brows, high cheekbones, no pelt, no pelt.

No pelt.

The face of an Ancestor.

"There you go, that's me. At least, a clean me, without this scruff of a beard. So how about you? What do you look like, my friend?"

He had to tread softly here.

Gold, he said finally. *Gold hair, blue eyes. I am a soldier.*

"Is Kerris your brother? He sounds like you."

Yes. He is. He is our Geomancer and Guide in these regions.

"So," the body seemed to shift, settle, get comfortable, as one might when conversing with an old friend. "How many are traveling with you, then? And what's your society like, anywayyyy. iisss ittttttttt vvvverrrymmillitaaaaaaaaaaaarrr....."

His painting was blurring, the dark, bright room was blurring, fading. His fingers - *not his fingers* - split and peeled away, growing fainter, fainter, and suddenly, his fingers *were* his fingers once again.

He let his hands fall away from the Seer and glanced around the room. He needed to catch his breath. He needed to find his balance. Fallon Waterford knelt beside them, her emerald eyes wide with wonder.

"Wow," she breathed. "Did it work?"

"Captain."

He turned in the direction of the voice. Ursa stood in the doorway, the Alchemist a black shadow behind. The Major did not look pleased.

"Major," panted the Captain. "Where is my brother?"

"Kerris..." She spat the name out, scowling and lashing her tail. *"Kerris* is in jail."

THE PHUN'JAH

Kerris awoke to the jangling of keys.

It was not altogether an uncommon sensation, for it was not altogether an uncommon occurrence. He had often found himself waking in various locations, from *Chi'Chen* palaces to watery ocean caverns. And yes, on the odd occasion, jail cells. It always involved tigers, these penitentiary occasions, and this time he could distinctly remember stripes. Ah well, at least he was waking. The how's and why's of it were never particularly important to him. With a deep breath, he pushed himself up to his elbows to see his brother silhouetted in the doorway.

"Oh, hello Kirin."

He could tell by the unnatural stillness that his brother was angry. Furious, in fact. Kerris couldn't help himself. It was too rich, really it was.

"Shall I pretend to be dead? Would you be happier to see me this way?" He lay back down, folded his hands across his chest. "Cold? Stiff? Dead? Deceased? Tripping merrily down that Last Road?"

"Kerris."

"I could say hello to Father for you, if you wish. He won't be wanting to be talk to *me* anytime soon, now will he, given the circumstances of his passing."

"Kerris..."

"Say," he said, pushing back onto his elbows. "I could ask those Seers what really happened, couldn't I? They would be fairly new here. Shouldn't be too hard to find."

"Stop!"

The command was a whip, and a terrible silence descended. A line had been crossed, both ways. Slowly, ever so slowly, the grey lion rolled onto his feet, dusting bits of straw and ages-old jail grease from his tunic. He stared at his brother, silver against gold. It was Kirin who looked away first, letting his eyes roam the features of the tiny cell. The cobwebs, the black walls, the unwashed chamber pot, tipped and reeking from weeks of overuse. There was no window, no candle, nothing to commend it to its royal occupant. Nor the one who had come to free him.

"Why do you do this, Kerris?" he whispered.

"Same as ever, dear brother," Kerris answered. "Same as ever."

Kirin turned, not wanting to see it, the flash of that which he knew lived, deep and darkly, behind those eyes. He began to walk away.

"I wasn't drunk, Kirin," his brother called after him. "For once, I wasn't drunk."

He ignored him and left the cell alone. But the door was open.

***

He led alMassay up the winding stone stairs of the battle fort. The corridor echoed with the sound of hoofs and snorts, creaking leather and tinkling buckles. The stallion was getting quite good at navigating such unlikely stretches, and his attitude was, as always, willing and ready. He reached up to pat the great neck. *More dependable than soldiers, more faithful than men.*

And much more predictable, too.

Kerris had gone on ahead, not stopping to dismount, but rather leaning forward and burying his face in wild tangles of mane. Quiz had sailed up the steps like a mountain goat, not remotely winded by the lion on his back. The sound of his hoofbeats had disappeared within moments.

Morning sunlight streamed in from above, and with a grim set of his jaw, he led his horse out onto the rampart of the Great Wall.

Blue eyes quickly scanned the party assembled before him. Four leopards and their mounts, one remaining pack horse, very heavily laden now. The tigress, the cheetah, the snow leopard and one Imperial horse, notable for its empty saddle.

Kirin felt his claws curl into his palms.

"Where is he?"

The Major swung down from her grey. "Sir, Kerris has started out ahead of us. I tried—"

"Not Kerris. The Seer."

"Oh." She glanced up, high up the tower, squinting in the sunlight. "He won't come down, sir. He says he's waiting."

"For what?"

She shook her head, but did not snort or spit. She frowned.

"I can not kill him. I cannot carry him. I am at a loss."

"Major, you and the others head out. The Seer and I shall follow presently."

"Sir?"

"Head out."

But his back was already turned to her, hands on the hilts of both swords, disappearing into the doorway of the battle tower of *Lhahore.*

***

Sireth benAramis leaned out over the Wall, breathing in the colors laid out before him. Perhaps he could see it more clearly from within, the gold of the hills, the purple of the mountains, the blue of the skies. He could never paint this, never could have, not even before the blinding. There were simply not enough colors in the palette to capture every nuance, every expression in the face of their Good Mother. She was unmatched, magnificent.

He closed his eyes.

Petrus? Petrus, can you hear me? Petrus, are you there?

"Long or short?"

He turned to see the Captain striding towards him from the tower keep.

"What did you say?"

"Long or short? Which is your preference?" In a swift flash of steel, both katanah and kodai'chi were held out to him. "I would suggest the long. It would afford you more reach."

"Swords? Captain, I won't fight you."

"All I asked was that people be ready to leave upon my return. All you needed do was get on your damned horse. Was that so very difficult, *sidi?"*

His blue eyes were blazing, the tips of the outstretched swords quivering in the morning stillness.

"Insolence and defiance at every turn," the Captain went on. "I will not have this mission compromised by your presumptions. I simply will not. Now choose. Long or short."

"I will not fight you, Captain. Not now."

"It was you who issued the challenge, so long ago, *sidi.* Or have you forgotten?"

"I have not forgotten."

"Then take it up now. And perhaps tomorrow you will be more amenable."

"It wouldn't be fair."

"You should have thought of that before issuing the challenge, *sidi."*

"I meant it wouldn't be fair," Sireth smiled. "To *you."*

That took him completely unawares. The arrogance of it, the sheer absurdity. Looking back on it, Kirin wondered if his mouth had been hanging open, for the Seer seemed compelled to explain.

"I have been meditating all morning. I am fresh and well rested and at peace with our situation. You, on the other hand, are far from it. You are angry with your brother, yet you seek to set your claws on me. Your blows would be misdirected from the start. It would be child's play."

"You would beat me?" He was stunned, incredulous, unable even to form a response. "At a duel of swords, you propose to think that you would, that you could *beat* me?"

"Like a rug, Captain."

The audacity, the sheer nonsense. He had run out of words. The *absurdity.* It made him laugh. And it came out of him, even as he tried to contain it. First it shook his chest, rattling about like a cobra in a basket. Then his shoulders, heaving them like many wild horses. Finally from his mouth, bursting forth like a river breaking a dam. He laughed a long time, even as he sheathed the swords and walked over to stand beside the Seer, to lean out over the high geniculated cornice. And even then, as he wiped the tears from his eyes, shook his head in futility, he was still laughing.

"Ah yes." He shook his head again, laughter all but spent. The smile that remained, however, was sad. "Yes, you are right. Sireth benAramis is always right."

He could make out the party of horses, fading into dark shapes on the grey-gold Wall.

"I am angry at my brother. He confounds me sometimes."

"It would seem a great many people do."

"That is true, *sidi.* A weakness?"

"The way of lions. Do you want to know the first thing I learned when I came to *Sha'Hadin?"*

"Yes, I would."

"Well, actually, the first thing is that they have no window panes and it's insufferably cold. But the second thing," and he paused, seeing if the Captain was with him, "The second thing is that the only glass we can polish is our own."

Kirin thought on this, long and hard, leaning out that morning over the plains of *Lhahore.*

"I don't know if I can," he said softly. "His actions are inexcusable. It is a matter of honor."

"There is no such thing as honor, Captain. There is only desire, and the sorrow that it brings."

"Spoken like a true Brahman, *sidi."*

"Brahman *and* Untouchable." The Seer turned to him, raising two fingers theatrically. "Tell me then, where is the *Bushido* in that? In the accepting of one's caste, or the rising above it?"

And he turned his fingers, held his hand high. Path the falcon, unseen for days, settled onto them, talon bells jingling, a slip of parchment bound securely in place.

"You see, she asked me to wait. How could I refuse?"

Kirin cursed himself, his lack of patience, his dark, dark glass. He had so much to learn.

Sireth unwrapped the message, passed it to the lion, slipped the hood over her eyes. The bird hopped to his left shoulder, home.

"There is no honor, Captain. Nor is there *Bushido*. But there are a great many other things. You must simply look for them and accept what you find."

They turned and crossed the parapet, towards the cedar door to the stone stairwell. As they headed down the steps, Kirin threw the man a sideways glance.

"You truly believe you can beat me?"

"At a duel of swords?" The Seer grinned. "Like a rug."

***

The trek from *Lhahore* to *Gujar'Rath* was a long one, but manageable due to the evenness of the Wall and surrounding terrain. For some reason, from *Lhahore* to the *Pass KhyaBar,* the Wall had been built on the plain, not the mountains, and it had long been a subject of debate and speculation. In fact, if Kirin remembered correctly, it was Chancellor Ho's pet project, to rebuild this section of Wall and push the northern border even further north, to the *Khash'koran*. A feline claw into the belly of the dog, he had said. Kirin suspected there was more to it than that.

He had had no part in these discussions, naturally. It was not his arena. He had no national say. His was solely the defense of the Empress, the maintenance and training of her personal Guard. But he was familiar enough with Court politics to know there was more involved than a simple policy of national security. The *Phun'Jah* could easily be protected by increasing the allotment of guards and improving their supplies. An expansion of the Wall along such sweeping lines would be met with war. Dogs were fiercely territorial, even more so than cats. Cats were, in fact, innately generous - one only had to understand the terms of the *Chi'Chen* concessions to know this. Before you could take the Wall into the mountains, you would have to take the mountains. This, against a massive army of dogs and the innumerable swarms of rats that infested these foothills, would be no easy task.

He let his gaze drift over the peaks now distant in the east. The land sloped and rolled and stepped and he had no doubt it had once been quite beautiful. There was the bed of what may have been a powerful river, now dry. It was a desolate land, abandoned save garrison towns, mining villages, gypsy caravans and bandits prowling the salt flats. Chancellor Ho cared for none of this. No, this was not about the *Phun'Jah.* This was about the Mountains. The Great Mountains. This was about strength and unity of a Kingdom known for these very things, about a people who identified themselves by the majesty of her peaks and the depths of her valleys. It was pride and it was purity and she was their Good Mother. Theirs and theirs alone.

It was a vein of nationalism that Kirin shared, but to a degree, feared, for it led down roads he would rather not travel. It spoke of pragmatism over people, a trait he was seeing far too much in himself of late. The Scholar and the Seer had been swift to point it out. The Seer, riding two horses ahead, had lived on such roads. It had scarred him, made him barbed and defensive and hated by those in the Imperial Courts. He was seen as a compromise to order and stability and to the accepted way of things.

Kirin, on the other hand, embodied this ideal.

He had been proud of it too, before embarking on that fateful road to *Sha'Hadin.* Now he was not so confident. He had become aware of the glass.

The Seer had been right. He could forgive Kerris, he knew he could. Dharma had been hard on him. A grey lion born into a world of gold. It was remarkable and therefore marked him different in a world where difference was shunned. He had been entertained as a curiosity, no more. Tamre Ford-d'Elsbeth would never have considered a match with Kerris Wynegarde-Grey. No family with highborn daughters would. Even his own mother had pushed the marriage on Kirin as the only eligible heir, when she knew, she *knew* his heart belonged elsewhere.

He grinned to himself. Another road best not traveled. Chancellor Ho probably hated him too.

It was late in the evening he pondered these things, as torches from the towers of *Sri'Gujar'Rath* came into sight. A troop of guards awaited them there, led by a handsome, dark maned lion. The Captain called his own troop to a halt.

"Sir," said the lion. "I am Major Lucas Roth-Dhaliwar, commander of *Sri'Gujar'Rath*. We have been expecting you."

And he executed a most formal bow, fist to cupped palm.

Naturally, Kirin did not. "Good," he said, swinging down from his horse. "And the parchments?"

"All we could muster, sir. As you might imagine, there is not much call for paper here."

"We will take only our need. Please, have someone see to the horses. Has my brother arrived?"

Roth-Dhaliwar exchanged glances with the leopards at his side.

"The grey one, *sidi?*"

Kirin steeled his jaw, finding the comment suddenly grating.

"Yes, that would be him."

"He's, ah, he's in the stables, sir."

"In the stables. Of course."

"Yes sir. Actually, he's cleaning them..."

***

The legs, Fallon thought. Definitely the legs.

Or perhaps, the pelt, buttercream and white with fine black spots, begging a lingering stroke of the fingers. Or the hair, black as night and down to the fullness of her chest, drawing the eye as it went. Or the way her body curved and arched when she moved, a hint of possibility and stealth or or just the *way* she moved or or or her eyes, all painted and golden and knowing, or her voice, deep and dark and breathy...

Fallon sighed. Who knew what it was that made men look at Sherah al Shiva the way they did? She had seen it happen time and time again and could tell the immediate disjunction of self from soul when it did. It was if they were transfixed, lost in the sheer art of her. She couldn't dismiss it, however, their base, primal, powerful reactions, for at that exact moment, she was looking at Kerris Wynegarde-Grey in precisely the same fashion.

He was cleaning the stables.

He was forking the last of fresh straw onto the newly scrubbed floor. Both cloak and tunic were discarded, tossed over a cedar beam and the pelt of his chest was a glistening dark grey. She thought – with an odd, detached sort of thought – that he wasn't nearly as broad as his brother, his musculature not nearly so defined, and his pelt not nearly so littered with battle scars. The ones she had given him, however, stood out like stripes, white tiger stripes down the length of his back. His pendants swung and snapped as he worked.

With a deep puff of breath, the lion paused to wipe his brow with a forearm. He surveyed the stalls, and nodded swiftly.

"Well, I think that's it. Looks much better. Smells better too. Horses deserve so much better. Why don't people understand?"

And then he noticed her, standing at the foot of the stair.

"Oh, hello *sidala.* You're all here now, are you? It's about time."

She separated from the protective cover of the stairwell.

"Yep. We're all here."

"I suppose Kirin wants me up for supper, or something. Well, tell him I've already eaten, thanks. I was starving."

He stepped over to a far wall, leaned the fork with others along the brickwork.

"I think we'll have to rethink our portable lunches. Soup may be tasty, but it's nowhere near filling enough for this kind of journey."

Her mind was racing, thinking of all sorts of interesting and appropriate responses, but she had suddenly gone mute. It seemed important to listen now, taking in what he said, and more importantly, how.

He snatched a straw broom from the same wall and began sweeping small loose flakes into the stalls.

"So I was thinking milk-paste. We'll need to arrange for goats somewhere along the line, or cattle, or now - wait a moment, a nursing mare. Yes, that might do it. She could come with us, wouldn't slow us down..."

His voice trailed off as he swept, swept, swept.

"Milk-paste?" she asked hesitantly.

"Yes. You dry milk into a paste, put it in a canteen with some rice or millet, add water first thing in the morning, and by mid-day, you have porridge. Not very tasty but it fills your belly for the rest of the day."

She brushed a stray lock of hair out of her face and stepped forward again. Her heart was in her throat.

"Are you alright?"

"What? Me? Oh yes, I always talk to myself. Not to worry."

"I mean, after last night, and and and this morning, I just wondered..."

She shrugged, feeling very inadequate and young.

"Ah, yes, well." He looked down for a moment, shrugged too. "Too many vices, I suppose. They catch up with me from time to time."

"I, I just thought..."

"Thanks." He smiled at her, a different one this time, sadder, a glimpse of starshine usually hidden by sun. "Say, how's your leg?"

"Oh, that..." She glanced down, raised her ankle, gave it a shake. "Funny thing about legs..."

He laughed and she flushed with pride that she had caused it.

"Kerris!"

They hadn't heard the jingle and clop of horses and suddenly the Captain was there, leading the great Imperial stallion down the stair and into the stable. Kerris was at his side in a flash.

"Here, let me take him. I've cleaned this place up, top to bottom. It wasn't fit for a yak."

He caught the reins, led the horse to a large corner, pointing and shouting directions as the others filed down the stair.

"Over there, over there, and you, ah, over there! Kirin, I've been thinking, we really should consider milk-paste for our mid-day rations, once we reach *KhahBull*. We will, of course, have to arrange for a mare..."

And Fallon stepped back to watch it all, the shift sudden like a closing door, and she understood a great deal more than she had expected, but still nowhere near what was there.

***

The meal had been bland, tasteless but filling. Root vegetables and salt pork, unsweetened green tea. It was the way of things here in *Sri'Gujar'Rath* and Kirin had assured Major Roth-Dhaliwar that improvements would be made in their station. So now, like so many nights before, they huddled round the charcoal brazier, embers creating warm edges on everything, waiting for Solomon to arrive.

Fallon hugged her knees to her chest and looked around. The Seer was sleeping, the Major curled at his side. It seemed that she too slept but she saw a sliver of ice-blue behind black lashes and realized otherwise. She shook her head. The woman was relentless.

The Alchemist slept as well and Fallon studied her face for a long time. There were no baiting airs in sleep, no place for suggestion or lure. Her lips were parted slightly, like a child's and the tigress felt a wave of guilt wash over her. It was so easy to presume with this one, to assume and infer and to judge this mother of kittens, regardless of the circumstances of their births. She was what she was, or more likely, what life had made her. Who knew what truly lay beneath?

Then the brothers. She shook her head again. What puzzles they were, trading strength for strength as day trades with night. Sun for moon, clouds for stars, gold for silver. It couldn't have been easy, being who and what they were, born to privilege and duty, weights to bear whether or not they were wanted. She couldn't fathom such a life, for either one. Double-edged swords, they were, brilliant and sharp and grave and quick. Perhaps that was it. They were, after all, twins. Two edges of the same sword. They both cut deep.

And so they sat, the Captain, the Scholar and Kerris, around the brazier, spokes of a waiting wheel. The Captain was running an ivory comb through his long golden mane, ensuring no ripple or snag in its satin finish. With his hair down like this, he looked very young.

"We need maps," sighed Kerris, sitting in a ball, chin in hands. He always looked young.

"I know. But Kerris," Kirin looked up. "I honestly have no idea how we can get them. After *KhahBull*, I honestly don't."

For a moment, he was not the Captain but a man, a brother, a fellow traveler on a dark road.

Kerris chewed his bottom lip, frowning.

"I mean, if we still go west, we have the many roads and the Wall *is* under construction for a very long way past *KhahBull.* North all the way to through *Khanisthan* to the *Khash'phian.* And from there, there is still work through *Shiryia,* and the Dead Lands. They are laying foundations in *Aegyp,* you know."

"But that's south."

"Oh. Yes, you're right." He sighed again. "Well, we must know something by *KhahBull.*"

The ivory comb caught in a very small tangle. The Captain glowered at it and continued to comb all the more.

"What about Solomon?"

"What *about* Solomon?"

"Well, he seems to know something of the land. Remember how he sounded when he realized where we were?"

"And his strange words. But Kirin," he straightened his back as they moved well into his territory. "You can't draw maps from hearsay. Not accurate ones."

"We may have no choice."

"And if he says, 'Go north to the big mountains', and meanwhile, on the way to the big mountains, there are more mountains? And you think 'Are *these* the big mountains' or are these just medium mountains and the 'big' mountains are even farther beyond? If so, where's the pass? Or perhaps there's a canyon in between? Or a lake?" He sat forward now, "Oh yes, a lake, right between us and the big mountains. Do we take the left bank or the right? Because invariably, one leads to the big mountains, and the other to the very heart of *Gowrain* country and we are all shish'khebabs for supper."

Kirin laughed softly and Fallon would have too, had she not been in deep, wheel-spinning thought.

Kerris grew serious.

"Why is he there, Kirin? I would very much like to know how a tiger comes to a place where even Kaidan hasn't been."

Fabled Kaidan. Legend Kaidan. Kirin shrugged, grinning.

"Perhaps Kaidan *has* been there. Perhaps he's simply… forgotten?"

At that, Kerris laughed so loudly that everyone roused from their slumbers, even the leopards.

"Shush," shushed Kirin, but even he was still grinning as his brother fought for control. Fallon was grinning too, but she didn't really know why. Something to do with Kaidan.

"Oh my, oh my," Kerris panted, wiping the tears from his eyes. "Now that was terribly funny, Kirin. Really, it was. Some hope for you yet."

The Captain nodded and the others, not particularly awake but not anymore sleepy, rolled to sit, bleary eyed and patient. She waited until it had gone very quiet again, very still, before

Fallon cleared her throat.

"I, I think I have an idea."

The Captain eyed her from under his curtain of hair. "That *is* why you're here, *sidala.*"

"Yes," purred Kerris. "A Scholar in the Court of the Empress, you know."

She felt the heat rush into her cheeks and thankfully, the Captain seemed to notice.

"Go on," he said softly.

She squeezed her knees. "Well, do you remember the night at *Sri'Varna?* When Sireth almost went over the Wall?"

"Rather memorable one, that. My legs are still sore," grinned Kerris, but the Captain had furrows on his forehead, eyes steely as he scrambled to follow.

"It, it's an observation I've made since the start, since the very first night back in the monastery."

At the mention of the monastery, Sireth rose and like another spoke in the wheel, took a place by the brazier. The Major did likewise. Only the leopards and the Alchemist did not.

"When Solomon comes," Fallon went on. "He not only exists in Sireth's soul, but in a way, in his body as well. When the cold came, Sireth froze. When the rats came, he ran. I think, for that very brief span of time, for however long they are connected, they *are* connected, body and soul."

It was there, just beyond his grasp. What the tigress was saying made sense. He knew where she was going, but she had made a leap in reasoning that he simply could not make. He was soldier, not scholar, after all. But it was there, right there, just at the edge of his reason...

"If he does really and truly know our lands, then Solomon could draw our maps in Swisserland. There and therefore," she inclined her head to the Seer. "Here."

She glanced around, prepared for the laughter that was undoubtedly coming, or the ridicule and scorn or other such things as she had experienced in her short, sheltered lifetime. It was always like that at home. Her father and her sisters had smiled and patted her head, shaken their heads or laughed in outright dismissal.

Funny though, she thought in retrospect, *her mother never had.*

"Brilliant," said the Captain. "That is brilliant, *sidala.* Once again, you have rescued this mission. I thank you."

He stood and twisted his long mane into a queue down his back.

"Kerris, get the parchments and chalks. The good ones, the ones that last, inks and brushes. Tonight we find *Swisserland.*"

As the lions set about their work, Fallon sat by the brazier, hugging her knees and smiling, thinking she was the happiest she had ever been in her life.

***

When Solomon came that night, he was very optimistic, jovial even, and had actually asked if this had been the idea of Fallon Waterford, 'Scholar in the Court of the Empress.' But then, as he began muttering about databases, flash screens and C-spikes, political maps versus geographic ones, and a myriad of unlikely word combinations such as 'continental drift', his mood changed. He would need a day to access it all, for something called the 'TemPower Sell' was low. He would be ready for them tomorrow night, he promised, and had mentioned his excitement at finding a 'Hum-lan-der' intact and operational. By the time the connection had faded, Fallon was convinced that this man was no ordinary tiger. *If,* she suspected deep down inside, if he was tiger at all.

She suspected he was dog.

That, she also suspected, would be a definite problem.

So, on this night of little victories, she bedded down restless, trying in vain to stop her mind from wandering and spinning in darker directions. That night, in her dreams, the pheasant farm by *Parnum'bah Falls* was gone.

***

The sky was red. Clouds stretched across it, long purple fingers covering the last glimpse of the sun as she laid her sleepy golden head on to her pillow, the Great Mountains. On a normal evening, the sight would cause the Captain to marvel and wonder and even wax philosophic if he had the time. He was such a lion. But this hour, any of these hours of late in fact, he was in no mood for marvels or wonders or philosophies. These past hours, there had been no room for sun.

Today, they had made *Roar'pundih.*

Roar'pundih. Once a jewel among dogs, now a thorn in the paw of the Upper Kingdom. This thorn had not been pulled. Rather, it had been patched, bandaged over and left to fester and rot. The land in the last few hours had told them as much. Fields of parched grass, rubble and twisted metal and stone. The Mountains seemed angry, snappish and small. Indeed, it seemed as if she were a different Mother, one with brittle claws and yellowed teeth. Or perhaps, all the years of canine infestation had simply made her that way.

Or the rats.

They had started the Wall in quiet good humor since morning, determined to maintain the course of the night before and, indeed, they had made good time. But the deeper they journeyed into the *Phun'Jah,* the deeper their spirits had fallen like kites with no wind. Towers had become more frequent along the way and they were manned almost every 100 paces. Leopards, for the most part, but there had been some tigers, some jaguars, and some of the smaller Races, ocelots and servals and sandcats. More than a few snow leopards too. They had not spoken but he knew they watched. It was their job to watch.

So it was in the middle of this red evening that the huge battle tower came into sight, tall and gleaming, her stone and brickwork worn smooth from years of wind and sand. *Roar'pundih.* As they drew near, Kirin could see the stories, the scorch marks and oil slicks and broken carapaces along its length, stone scars from too many battles. Not so different from the land and surrounding mountains, he thought, but high above, the Imperial banner still waved, and he had taken some measure of comfort in that.

They had been ushered into that great red tower by the commander, a greying lion named Nehru Tripp-Jonesthon. They were fed the same meal as the previous night and so they sat, mugs of hot tea in hand, parchments and inks and chalks scattered around the brazier, waiting for Solomon to come.

"They rushed to their hut once they heard what had happened, but it was too late. Pure Gold had tasted the poisoned plum, and lay, still as stone, on the cold, hard floor. And this is how the young Rajah found her... "

Once again, Kerris had managed to enthrall his audience, for this time, even the Seer seemed caught up in the ages-old tale, *Pure Gold and the Seven Chi'Chen.* It was a sad tale, poignant when well told, and more than once, he had seen his brother bring veteran soldiers to tears. Despite his many flaws, Kerris was a brilliant storyteller.

"They built for her a glass sarcophagus, embellished it with gold and rubies and sea shells, and laid it out in the depths of the jungle, to be guarded day and night by all seven monkeys. The young Rajah stepped down from his palanquin the moment he saw her, placed his fingers to the glass that covered her. He wept, for she was as beautiful in death as she had been in life, and it was with a lilting *Chi'Chen* blessing that he knelt down to kiss her lips. The Old Rani's magic was too powerful, however, her secrets too dark, and with a terrible breaking heart, the young Rajah took the poisoned plum into his own golden hands and bit deeply of it. They laid him next to his love and sealed the sarcophagus with anhonda paste and tree gum and left it to the vines of the green, green jungle. And so there they have laid for a thousand years, less a day, covered in gold and rubies and sea shells..."

His quick blue eyes scanned his audience, searching for those most caught. They fell upon the tigress.

"Perhaps one day, the spell will break and the lovers will rise. Perhaps one day, someone will find the sarcophagus, but it is said to be guarded by the spirits of seven dragons now. Until then, however, and even today and perhaps forever more, they lie together in a sleep as still as stone, deep in the green, green jungle, covered in gold and rubies and sea shells..."

The silence was praise enough, for true storytellers prefer a hush over a cheer. Kerris lifted the tea to his lips, waiting to see who would be first to break the spell he had woven. It would not be the tigress, he was sure of this. She was staring into her mug, shaking her head, fighting back tears.

"Admirable, Kerris, as always," said Kirin. "The kabuki is also effective."

"I beg to differ, dear brother,' he said. "Kabuki are rarely effective."

"Mmm," purred Sherah. "A man can never play a convincing woman."

Kirin turned to her. "You think not? With the face made white, and the lips red? And the wigs and kimonohs? I think it rather amazing."

"A woman is more than white face and red lips, *sidi.* No man can plumb her depths."

"But a Kabuki is not meant to capture depth, *sidala.* It is a treat for the eyes. Nothing more."

"And you have just lost your point, Kirin. Kabuki is a treat for the eyes," Kerris sighed. "But a well-told story is a treat for the soul."

"Hm," said Kirin.

"It is a stupid story," said Ursa. She slid a glance at the Seer. "I'm sure *you* like it."

"I do," said Sireth. "I think it's lovely."

"*You* like k'zlaki."

"In fact, I don't like k'zlaki. But I do like kittens. And this is a lovely story for kittens."

"Pah. Kittens, stories and k'zlaki. I don't know which is worse."

Sherah rolled onto her belly, crossed her ankles in the air, cupped her chin in her hands. Her golden eyes were glued to the Captain, her gaze stickier than anhonda paste and tree gum.

"You like kabuki, *sidi?*"

Kirin cleared his throat. He felt suddenly uncomfortable, as if needing to choose his words as he would swords.

"In truth, I have not seen many. This one, yes, when I was a child. A few others..."

"Perhaps you shall take your children some day."

It was an innocent comment, he told himself over and over, an innocent topic. *So why did it boil his blood so?*

"Perhaps."

"If *I* have kittens," said Fallon in a quiet voice, "I will tell them this story, but, differently."

Kerris cocked his head. "How so?"

She looked up at him, her eyes serious and round.

"I think I would make Pure Gold a tiger."

Everyone stared at her, just like they used to at home. Except Sireth benAramis. He was smiling.

"Well? Why not?" Fallon sputtered, "It's not fair! The stories are always about lions and lionesses! Why can't I tell stories about *my* people? Why does everything have to be about lions?!"

No one had a response for her, and she glanced from face to face, begging to be told if and how she was wrong. The Captain avoided her gaze. Kerris seemed amused, intrigued even, that she would have the nerve to ask. She could see the wheels behind his eyes turning. The Seer reached over and squeezed her hand.

"You will have many stories to tell your kittens, my dear," he said. "But a great many of them *will* have to do with lions."

And then it came.

whoompf

Kirin's head snapped up.

whoompf whoompf whoompf

He was on his feet in a heartbeat, pressing a hand onto the dark window glass, the Major at his side.

One by one, cauldrons of blue flame leapt to life all along the Great Wall.

"Rats," he growled. He swung around to the people behind him. "No one is to leave this room. Kerris, bolt the door and open neither it nor the window unless either myself or the Major commands you do so. Is that understood?"

It wasn't a question.

And with that, he, the Major and the remainder of the leopard Guard strode out the door and Kerris slid the bolts home.

***

Rats are a terrible thing. It is said they are born in the depths of the earth, formed from clay and worms and decayed monkey flesh for indeed, they have some marked similarity to monkeys. Mostly in the arms and fingers and face, but with the jagged teeth, the iron claws and the whipping, scaly tails, they are the worst of all creatures. They sometimes move on all fours and sometimes on two and the big ones come almost to the knees. They do not speak, but rather chitter and squeal and the scraping of their limbs over rock lives in nightmares all throughout the Kingdom.

They move by the hundreds.

It is also not sure why they move as they do, what causes the swarms to destroy villages and farms alike. But the only thing that is sure to stop them is oil, brute force and fire.

Like a single living thing they swarmed up the Wall, a mass of shiny blackness and Ursa could see the leopards of *Roar'pundih* fighting to stop their advance. They poured great vats of boiling oil, they loosed flaming arrows into the slick, and even as the creatures burned, others came, crawling atop their dead like stepping stones. Everyone with a sword was into the fray, and she could see her Captain, swift and methodical, swinging as a farmer harvests wheat, severing heads and limbs and torsos with lethal grace. As always, she admired his technique.

She thought, with a frown, that he seemed to have more than his share to battle.

With both swords drawn, she waded in toward him.

***

"Wow," breathed Fallon, hands and nose pressed up against the glass. "They can't stop all those rats not like that. There's, there's too many."

"There's always too many," said Kerris, beside her. "You stop them any way you can."

She bit her lip. From up here, even with the blackness of the night sky, she could see it all silhouetted in the flames. The great cauldrons burned blue, blue being the color for rats, orange for dogs, yellow, *Gowrain.* She was sure in the far Southwest, in the lands of *Aegyp* and *Sahood*, the cauldrons burned a different color for *bab'Hundi.* It seemed every creature wanted its share of the Upper Kingdom. From what she had seen on this remarkable journey thus far, she could understand why.

A rat slammed into the window glass at her face and she screamed.

***

This was wrong, he thought to himself. *Pivot, swing, swing, strike. All wrong. There were too many, too many and this time, they moved with precision. Dodge, step back, strike.* It was as though they had a goal, an aim to their usually aimless invasions. Teeth dug into his leg, just behind the knee. He sent the short sword back, heard the squeal, swung the body into the face of another, impaled them both before stepping back again. Far too many and their goal, it seemed, was him.

Another now, the same knee. Pain threatened to blind him but he pushed it from his thoughts. There was room for nothing save the fight, save the analysis of their offenses, which was separate but the same. The knowledge that their bites brought with them poison and disease, even this he pushed from his thoughts. He brought the hilt of the long sword down, splitting a skull the size of a baby's, slicing so many more as he followed through, the motion mirrored by an opposing sweep of the short. *Step, pivot, swing, swing.* He could hear the army of *Roar'pundih,* shouting commands and pouring oil by the vat. Smoke and fumes were heavy in the air, and the stench of burnt flesh, and blood. His own blood. He could taste it in his mouth. Yes, it seemed they were after him. But why?

Stepped back, felt a scaly tail under his boot, crushed the spine with the other. *Swing, swing, pivot, strike.* Harvest them like wheat, he kept telling himself, like ripe, bloody wheat.

***

The glass cracked with the veins of a spider's web as the hairless, monkey-like fingers scrabbled at it. They were hanging from their scaly tails, smashing at it with things they held in their hands.

"This is wrong," said Kerris as he pulled the tigress from the window. "This is all wrong."

They could see the grotesque faces, the black glittering eyes and lipless rasp-toothed mouths, raking the panes as if they could chew it like meat. But what was worse, was the fact that within their scaly hands, were stones.

"Tools?" Fallon dug her claws into Kerris' arm. "I didn't think they used tools."

"They don't."

The grey lion wrested free her grip and sprang to the packs, rummaging through in desperation. The window split with a groan, and many scrabbling hands pried at the shards. They still hung upside down but now there were more, using their fellows as ladders, smashing the panes with their skulls.

"Knives, forks, did they leave us nothing?"

"My staff?" It was the Seer.

"Good."

"Fire powder?" It was Sherah and Kerris' head snapped up.

"Better! Where? *Where?!*"

She, like the Seer and Scholar, was standing in the middle of the room, and she seemed as terrified as the others. She pointed a trembling finger.

"The sealed bag, with the scarlet clasp."

There was a thump overhead and sprinkles of wood rained lightly down onto their heads.

Fallon looked up. In the middle of the high ceiling was a wooden hatch with a long rope serving as a latch keep. The hatch was bumping.

"Oh mother," Fallon swallowed. "Hurry..."

***

Pain had turned his eyesight red. Time had slowed too, and the battle, to Kirin, was a dance. He could not miss a step, every movement vital, one slip would be his death. He felt too heavy for this dance, the poisons he knew, and his knee twisted whenever it bore weight. *Pivot, pain, swing.* Even his swords, normally an extension of his very hands, were heavy and slow. They slipped in his grip from the blood on the hilts. It was only a matter of time.

Something struck his shoulder between the blades, and he staggered forward. *Wrong,* he thought, *bad move.* His balance was compromised. Even through the leather brigandine, and the leather underneath, he could feel the claws. Teeth sank into his neck and he sent the short sword back to pierce the skull.

He heard the squeal but a second set of teeth closed across his wrist.

It was only a matter of time.

***

"Hurry!" shouted Fallon. "The hatch!"

It began to lift away from the ceiling. Black, scaly fingers pried into the gap. With barely a thought, she leapt for the latchkeep, caught it. Still they pulled her up, fingers scraping at her hands, her legs swinging wildly as her feet left the floor. Mercifully, arms wrapped round her waist, and she did not need to look down to know it was the Seer, adding his weight to hers.

The cord burned in her palm but together, they pulled it back down, closing off the terrible squeals. Severed fingers dropped to the floor like twigs.

Kerris was at the window, flinging handfuls of fire powder around the panes. There was a sharp shattering sound as the window spat its glass across the floor. The creatures followed, squeezing over their fellows, impaling each other on the slivers and shards, but oozing through nonetheless. With a deep breath, he tossed a torch into the powder and ducked away as the entire frame burst outwards, sending flame far out into the night sky.

The hatch thumped and thumped again. Splinters of wood rained down into Fallon's face. Blinking them away, she could see gaps now in the wood above her. Her heart leapt to her throat. They were using their stones now to dig and chip. The wood was strong, but she wasn't at all convinced that it would hold against this.

"Kerris!" she shouted, but he couldn't hear, leaning out through the pane as he was, staring up to the very top of the tower. His ashen hair whipped in the winds.

"There's more of them," he called out. "By the Kingdom, how did they get all the way up there?"

"Kerris!" she shouted again, and almost lost her hold on the rope latch. Her hands were aching and raw, and the hatch jerked and bumped as rats tugged the other end. "Kerris-your-name-was!! Up here! Look here *now!!*"

He turned – "Damn." and took a step toward them when chittering caused him look back. "Double damn."

They were at the window again.

***

He didn't remember stumbling. He didn't remember the wave of creatures crash over him as he went down to his knees. He did however, distinctly remember a woman's voice, carrying over the howl of the winds, and the flashes of steel as throwing stars and *shir'khins* whipped past him and beside him and above. He did remember the slice and tang of swords and death squeals of rats, and it all blurred into one last roar until the quieting of the night and the welcome clacking of high boot heels on stone.

When he had finally caught his breath and wiped the blood from his eyes, her face was there, brows drawn, mouth in a tight line. He was able to smile at her, for everything had worked out right after all. He had known it would.

It had only been a matter of time.

***

"The staff!" shouted Kerris. "Where's the staff? Never mind! Found it!"

The light in the tower hold became eerie and dark as the grey lion snatched the remaining torch from its perch on the wall. He flashed it at the creatures climbing through the window, pushing them back, but only so far, as their numbers forced them, uncaring, into the breech. The ones that made it through, he smacked hard with the staff. Flash and smack. Flash and smack. It was not a particularly effective strategy.

The noise above her grew louder. Not just chitters and squeals now, but a growl, a low, gutteral drone like the buzz of angry bees. Fallon yelped and was almost torn out of the Seer's grasp. A chunk of meal wood struck her in the forehead and she could see faces through holes in the hatch. They were trying to squeeze themselves through.

One from the window launched itself onto Kerris' shoulder and he staggered, the tip of the staff touching the window. Rats began to climb it instantly.

Like a wraith, Sherah was suddenly at Kerris' side, snatching the creature from his shoulder and hurling it toward the others. She spun and snagged the powder bag next and began to circle the room, spilling a trail of black behind her. For a brief moment, Fallon could see her, understood immediately what it was she was doing, had an idea of her own.

"What is she doing?" growled the Seer from below. "Alchemists and their infernal circles."

Once Sherah had completely surrounded the room, Fallon twisted an aching hand free. A rat was climbing down the rope latch toward her.

"Quickly!" shouted the tigress. "Sherah, throw me the bag! Get Kerris!"

The cheetah did as she was bid, tossing the powder and pulling the grey lion away from the window. She wrested the torch from his hand and threw it onto the circle.

The room was engulfed in flames. Fallon felt the Seer shudder and press his face into her back. With a deep breath, she shoved the bag into the rat's scrabbling, scaly hand and let go of the rope.

The hatch swung upward, taking the rat and the bag of fire powder, with it.

"Get down!" she shouted, dropping to the ground, the Seer falling with her. "Don't breathe! Close your—"

The boom drowned her words as the flames were sucked upward, up over their heads, threatening to take them all with it, up and into the night sky above. Then a second boom, pushing them down now, forcing the air from their lungs, scalding their rounded backs with heat. The flames thundered and roared all around them, until, finally, after what seemed like ages, there was silence.

Fallon coughed and coughed again. She lifted her head. The tower hold was in blackness, lit only by moonlight from the shattered window. Even the flame circle had burnt itself out. But, she noted with some satisfaction, there were no rats.

Kerris rolled onto his knees. A slice of moonlight illuminated his face. It was scratched and sooty, but for some reason, he was grinning at her.

"Well, *sidalady* tigress," he said, "That's one story you can tell to your kittens. And see? Not a golden lion in the lot."

There was a pounding at the door. Kerris disengaged himself from the others on the charred stone floor. He threw open the bolts and swung open the door.

"Ursa, my love. Welcome to the *Roar'pundih* Rat and Grill."

"Idiot," Ursa snarled. "Your brother is wounded. Come if you care."

With that, she spun and disappeared down the stair, Kerris a reeling grey shadow at her heel.

***

It is an odd place, that place between waking and dreamless sleep. Some things can be recalled with razor sharpness, like voices or snatches of conversations. Other things, like passing time and pain, can be recalled only in vague and twisted ways. At one point, he found himself wondering if this was the Vision plain, the road of Farsight where Seers journey and falcons soar through the souls of men. It was certainly not the *Nihr'Vannah*, for it was neither empty nor enlightened. In fact it was a terrifying place, he decided, not a place he would tarry, and he fought its grip whenever he was aware. Somehow, long, strong hands kept pushing him there, to this very place. It had given him a headache that had rent his skull for days.

Or perhaps, that was the incense.

So he knew how it would be when finally he left that place and found himself staring into the golden eyes of the Alchemist.

"There you are," she purred. "Lie still. I will fetch some tea."

It seemed prudent, so he obeyed, letting his own eyes adjust to the darkness, to the soft light flickering across the stone ceiling. Candles, he noted, no torch. Alchemists were strict believers in *feng shui,* the Art of *Chi.* And, he also noted gratefully, as she knelt with a steaming cup in hand, of *Chado,* the Art of Tea.

She helped him sit, propped several stiff cushions behind his back, and knelt back, a curious smile playing with her lips. It was only then that he noticed two things. First, his uniform was gone, and second, Kerris, all grey and night-blue, face down on a bedroll beside him.

"Where?" His voice scratched in his throat. He cleared it. "Where is my uniform?"

"Being repaired," she said. "Rats are not respecters of good leather."

He frowned. A wrapped tunic and sarong were not his choice of attire, no matter what his situation.

"It will be repaired soon?" Not quite a question.

"Soon. But hush. You will disturb your brother. I believe this is the first time he has slept since you were stricken."

"How long?"

"Three nights, two days..."

"Not—"

"Not plague. Just poison."

He sighed this time, shoulders sagging. So much time lost. Too much. He sipped his tea.

Kerris mumbled in his sleep and lifted his head from the pillows. He seemed about to roll over and go back to sleep, but for some reason, he paused, blinking as if not comprehending the change in scenery. Kirin allowed himself a small smile now. His brother looked terrible.

With a startled yelp, Kerris bolted to his knees.

"Kirin! Oh, how do you feel? Are you fine now? Are you? Really?"

"I will be fine when I am in uniform."

"Oh that. Yes, well, that's out for—"

"Repairs. Yes, the Alchemist told me."

With bright, brimming eyes, Kerris turned to the cheetah. He was wringing his hands.

"Is he alright, really? The poisons are gone?"

"The poisons are gone. It does not usually take so long, but…" She turned her face to the Captain. "There were many bites."

"I seem to recall," Kirin said, moving his knee at the memory. "It was unnatural the way they attacked."

"Yes, that's what Ursa said. Like they had marked you, singled you out somehow." Kerris sat forward. "Kirin, they were using stones to crack the window glass. I've never seen them use tools before."

"I will need to speak to Commander Tripp-Jonesthon about this. He may have an explanation."

He shifted on the blankets, just now realizing that he was on the floor. Somehow, it had seemed much more comfortable only moments before.

"Was anyone else hurt?"

"Several of the soldiers, but our Alchemist soon put them to right with her ointments and her tea." He beamed at her, high praise from the prince of such. "Dear Sherhanna. She's been a godsend these past few days, haven't you?"

Kirin looked at her.

"Sherhanna?"

The woman smiled again, cast her eyes downward. "An old name. One I have never gone by."

"But it is your true name," said Kerris. "You told me so. The one your parents gave you before your consecration."

He looked back to his brother.

"Sherhanna al Sha'er. Beautiful, isn't it?"

"Yes," Kirin said softly. "It is."

He was oblivious then, as Kerris glanced from his brother to the woman and back again, noting the strange thing that had suddenly come into being, and just as suddenly, shut him out. He touched Kirin's arm.

"So, so how's your knee? It was pretty buggered up."

"Kerris, mind your tongue."

"Well, it was. How does it feel?"

Kirin flexed his foot, stretched his calf muscle, and finally, bent his leg into the thigh, aware now for the necessity of the sarong. The flesh of the joint itself was exposed, a portion of the pelt cut away cleanly, and drawn in with only a few stitches, leaving most of the wounds open to drain. It felt remarkably strong, however. He said so.

"Yes, well that's our dear Sherhanna," said Kerris. "She did the same with my back and arms, remember?"

"I didn't think you did remember," said Kirin.

"I have you for that, now don't I? Remembering everything I don't."

"You're exhausted," said Kirin. "Go get some sleep. I am in good hands."

"Yes. I can well imagine," said Kerris. He dragged himself to his feet. "Anyway, I am glad you're feeling better. Really, you have no idea. So, ah..."

"Goodnight, Kerris."

The grey lion stared at him a moment.

And he padded from the room, not looking back as he closed the door behind. It had taken all his will not to look back, not to sneak a glimpse of his brother and the cheetah and the warm candlelight and he stood quite still for several long moments. He glanced around the stairwell of the battle tower of *Roar'pundih.* It was dark and imposing and bleak and he felt a rush of sadness. He had tried to fight it, really he had. For weeks now, it had dogged him. In fact, as he stood there, alone and dismissed, he feared it never really left him, no matter how much he ran or how far. Even now, it lapped at him, beckoning like the waves he loved so much.

No, it never really left.

He sank to the stairs and covered his face with his hands.

***

Sireth could see *Khanisthan* from up here, from the top of the tower of *Pesh'thawar,* the very border of the *Phun'Jah.* And the distant twinkling lights that lead to the city of *KhahBull.* They had ridden two days hard since the Captain's recovery, through mountains red and gold and squared, through the famed *Pass KhyaBar,* through ruins and battle towers aplenty, all to make up for lost time. Or so the Captain said. Still, the Imperial banner waved above them all, unifying this diverse land with its one elegant symbol. He found himself shrugging. These were very strange days.

He had never been to *KhahBull* but as he sat, cross-legged under the purple sunset atop the battle tower, he thought that it looked like every other large city he had ever seen from so far away. *Cal'Cathah, Old Delhih, Phankoth.* Like them, it spread out as if limitless, as if cats knew nothing of restraint. As if the very land owed them their homes, farms and inns, and they should spread like mushrooms over a dead tree, to consume it and beat it down and turn it to earth.

The pattern was the same, even. Lights burned bright in the heart of the city, scattering rings like ripples on a pond, growing fainter as they neared the horizon. Torches and lanterns and hearths, glowing with peace and contentment and the promise of life. Like jewels of the people, they were evidence of their mastery over the natural world. They glittered like stars, those jewels, like the carpet of bright twinkling stars over his head. He looked up now, at the one star, the new one, the *dragon,* and at all the others, constellations still familiar despite the distance from home.

Home. How he missed it. He knew that even if he did return, which was unlikely, it would not be home. For him, home was a fleeting thing, lasting only a few years at best, before his mistress, Dharma, chased him out. Oh yes, she would forget about him for a while, and he would have peace and respite, even the pretense of happiness, until she remembered him and chased him out again.

He must have been very bad in his previous life. She chased him without mercy.

Petrus? Petrus, are you there?

He shook his head. He couldn't speak to the dead. It was not part of the Gifts. He was a fool for thinking so much of it these last days, since he had stood at the Broken Road and touched the Alchemist and heard his friend speaking inside his head. It had to be a ploy, a ruse to distract him, to darken the glass and keep him from quieting his soul and receiving the visions as he should, with single-mindedness and focus.

He closed his eyes and filled his chest with cool night air.

He did not strive, did not reach, he just was. The visions would come. They always did.

***

"Hey, Kerris your name was! Come and join us!"

The figure in the doorway waved but turned his back and trotted down into the stairwell of the tower towards the stables.

"He's gone down to check on the horses, *sidala.*" Kirin shook his head. "He has no use for *Chai'Chi.*"

Fallon Waterford shook her head now, even as she swung her arm in a graceful controlled arc over her head. She pivoted on her right foot.

"There's more to life than horses," she muttered.

"I have told him that very thing."

Kirin, likewise, swung his arm in a graceful controlled arc over his head. He pivoted on his right foot.

"No talking!"

Pale eyes blazed, but Ursa Laenskaya's arm swung of its own accord, supremely graceful, marvelously controlled, the arc a silver and white rainbow over her head. Her pivot was music.

"Chai'Chi does not respect conversations. Without focus, the discipline is lost."

"Yes, Major," said Fallon.

"Yes, Major," said Kirin, but he fought back a smile. For the past several evenings since they had left *Roar'pundih,* she had led them in the exercises of *Chai'Chi.* She was very good and surprisingly patient with the tigress who was often as graceful as a yak. Sometimes, the Alchemist joined them, sometimes, the leopards, and sometimes, soldiers from the towers themselves. Never the Seer. And most certainly, never his brother.

Tonight, it was just the three of them, Captain, Major and Scholar, and she had taken them through their stances efficiently, no energy wasted on instruction. Next, she would begin the Sun Salute of *Chai'Yogath* but here and everytime, it had proven to be too much for Kirin's knee. Here and everytime, he had opted out to sit and watch and appreciate the poetry of the gentler Martial Arts.

Tonight was no exception.

He sat with his back against the stone, breathing deep and enjoying the sensation as his muscles relented. The air smelled dry, of sand and wind and would now for weeks as they began their journey through this very large desert province. At *KhahBull,* they would leave the Wall, which turned and traveled northwest to the wide expanse of water known as the *Kashphian.* They had chosen the roads, which led them more west than north, for it seemed Solomon was taking them deep into the unknown, through *Hiran*, then beyond. Roads afforded a greater flexibility with possibly straighter stretches and therefore better time. Kerris had been pleased. Naturally, Kirin had not.

So he sat, filling his chest with cool night air, wishing once again that he was standing at the top of the One Hundred Steps under the black beams of the Palace, counting the torches as they flickered to life in the Imperial City. It occurred to him that he would never count them again.

His heart was heavy. It was the way of things.

In the morning, they would send out the falcon. She would carry their goodbyes.

***

alchemy, alchemy had reached Lhahore, *5 of 5, black robes and candles and red satin pouches filled with souls, killers of falcons had reached* Lhahore, *5 of 5 on angry black horses, following the Wall, following in a trail of blackness and incense and candles*

His eyes flew open. The Captain. He had to tell the Captain.

Sireth bolted to his feet and swung around, when he saw the impossible, standing directly behind him.

He staggered at the sight, her night-black pelt, her smiling golden eyes, the sweep of silk that was her hair.

"Shakuri," he gasped.

She took a step toward him. She was wearing his favorite sari of blue sateen, embroidered gold at shoulder and hem. Her many earrings caught the moonlight, as did the delicate hoop that pierced one nostril.

"Shakuri, how? *How?*"

He was trapped on the vision plain, he had to be. He glanced around to orient himself.

"Hush." She took another step. "I've missed you."

The words were gone from lips, the thoughts from his mind. This was impossible. First, Petrus, now... this...

Her mouth twisted at the corner, her particular grin.

"Soladad is well."

At the mention of his daughter, he almost fell to his knees. His heart was beating too fast.

He was dizzy from the sight of her, his legs weak. He could barely stand.

"Shakuri..."

She was so close now, passing an ebony hand across his brow and eye, almost but not quite, touching the scar.

"I am so very sorry for this."

"No," and he pressed her hand to his cheek. It was cool where his face was hot, dry where it was streaked with tears. There was a sudden memory of flames, but it was gone before it brought its companion horror, and he found himself sinking into her, hands trembling as he pulled her to him. Her hair was scented with orange and ginger and something else he could not place, didn't care to try. She lifted her chin and smiled, her eyes as gold as sunrise. He had found himself, once so long ago, in those eyes, and lost himself every time thereafter. She was his home.

He kissed her.

She tasted of orange and ginger, and the salt of his tears, and he breathed her in, felt his own breath leave his mouth. She would empty him completely and leave him with nothing, no anger, no fury, no fear. She was his home, his peace, his respite. He surrendered willingly, he always had. He had no secrets from her.

Strange. She was taller than he remembered.

Like the pull of a sinking stone, he opened his eyes.

***

Odd, Kirin thought to himself. He had just been thinking of the falcon, and there she was, streaking to the top of the tower in a jingle of bells. He followed her with his eyes, trying to make her out against the purple sky, could see her only when she blocked stars as she passed. She was flying in tight circles, crying and bleating in that sharp, shrill voice of hers.

A woman's scream tore the night in two, and in a heartbeat, he was on his feet and racing into the stairwell.

***

He met benAramis on the way down. The Seer obviously had no intention of stopping, so he grabbed the wide-sleeved arm, swung him around on the step and was met with a gloved finger thrust into his very face.

"If she *ever* touches me again," the Seer snarled, "I *will* kill her!"

He yanked his arm free and stormed passed the lion and the tigress, and finally the Major, who needed only one look from her Captain to turn and follow her charge down the winding stair. Kirin quickened his pace as he headed up.

It was very dark up on the tower with only moon and starlight for guidance. But he saw movement and rushed toward it, black and silver against purple. She was pushing herself up from the stone floor, and at the sound of his boot, looked up through her tangle of hair. Their eyes met. It was his undoing, for there was blood at her mouth, and a sob tore from her throat when she saw him. He knelt beside her and gathered her into his arms.

"I'm sorry," she pleaded. "I am so very sorry."

And she buried her face into his chest.

Several long moments he held her, until finally her weeping began to subside. He brushed the hair from her forehead, wiped the tears from her kohl-rimmed eyes.

Standing directly behind them, Fallon Waterford watched, her arms wrapped around her ribs.

"You are safe, now," said the Captain. "No one will hurt you."

She nodded and took a deep breath, touched the corner of her mouth with tender fingers. The Captain did likewise.

"What happened?"

Fallon couldn't help but wonder at the tone in his voice. She could also hear footsteps, faint at first, but frantic, growing louder as they raced up the tower steps. Kerris leapt up through the hatch behind her, pausing only to orient his eyes to the darkness of the sky. And he too bolted to the cheetah's side.

"What happened?"

Sherah looked from brother to brother, chin trembling, tears threatening to spill once again over her lashes. Instead, Kirin helped her to her feet. She leaned against his arm, and Kerris stepped back.

"What happened?" he asked again.

"Not out here,' said the Captain. "Let's get her inside."

His brother nodded and together they led the woman to the hatch, Kerris sliding down first to take one hand, his brother going through last, keeping the other.

Leaving the Scholar alone on the roof under the last of the purple sunset.

***

"Where are you going?" Ursa shouted down the dark stair.

He didn't answer, but he was headed to the lower level, she knew. Where they kept the horses.

So, she stopped when she came there, watched as he moved with swift, angry motions. He found his saddle, snatched it up. Then the bridle, then the horse he had ridden since that third morning so long ago at *Sha'Hadin*. He threw the reins over the great wide neck of the beast and led it out of its stall.

"Where are you going?" she asked again.

"Away."

"That's not your horse."

And noticed with some satisfaction that she had given him pause.

"It does not belong to you. It belongs to the Empress."

She knew him well enough now to know he considered. He did not look at her, rarely did when his temper had the better of him. She could tell by the stiffness of his spine. Could see his shoulders relax, then reset. *Discomposure, amendment, decision.* He released the rein and pushed the horse back into its stall. Methodically, he put the tack back where he had found it and finally swung to face her.

"I shall walk."

"All the way home?"

He threw up his hands, let them fall to his sides with a slap.

"Why not?"

And brushed past her towards the door, towards the last level of the stair.

"You can not leave," she called.

"You can not stop me," he called back.

He was at ground level now, striding toward a uniformed leopard guard. The guard would stop him, she told herself. At night, it was against orders to open the outermost door to anyone, save a lion.

The guard opened the door.

He was outside now and she had to move quickly to catch him. With a singing sound, her sword left its scabbard and she ran in front of him, turned it into his chest.

"I can not let you leave."

"Stop me as a soldier, then, or join me as a friend. Either way."

His good eye flashed at her. And with remarkable constraint, he grasped the blade in one gloved hand and pushed it out of his way. He pushed past and she stared at the steel, stunned now to see it glistening with a slick of red blood.

She slid it back where it belonged, and scrambled to catch up.

***

She should be doing something, Fallon told herself. Making tea, fetching water, something. Something other than standing here, watching the three of them navigate these muddy waters on their own. She tightened her grip on her ribcage and puffed. Not that she would be much help in this area. *She* didn't even have the courage to step off the shore.

Kerris sat beside the Alchemist, holding her hand in both of his. Kirin was standing behind them, hands on hips, staring out the window. The city of *KhahBull* glittered in the distance. His tail, normally held poised and still, rapped the stone floor of the tower keep in agitation.

"Tell me again," he growled softly.

Sherah nodded. She was composed now. She had lit an incense stick and placed it in the brazier. Water was boiling for tea. A candle was burning in front of her, and she kept her gaze locked on it.

"I went to the roof. I wished to do my divinations there. It is better to be private, away from curious eyes." She did not look up. "The Seer was there. Meditating I presume. It was the posture.'

She paused, ran a tongue across the crust at her lip.

"I was leaving, not daring intrude, but he began to speak to me, and I thought…" Now, she did look up, but at Kerris. "We have not got on well, the Seer and I. He has not hidden his contempt of me or my Order, so when he approached, I was, I was hoping..."

"Hoping?" prodded Kirin.

"For better."

Fallon Waterford frowned then realized with a rather quick, quirky thought, that she had been frowning a lot lately. She remembered how her father had insisted her face would stick that way if she frowned too much. But there was cause for frowning, for mixed in with the baiting airs and calculated phrases, there was something else, something not quite as tangible. Perhaps, though, more disturbing.

"What did he say?" asked the Captain. He had still not turned round.

"He began to call me *Shakuri,* the name of his late wife. He said how he had missed me, how he was sorry for causing my death, and then…"

"Then?"

"He kissed me."

Now, the Captain turned.

"He kissed you?"

"Yes."

"And you did nothing?"

"He saved my life, that day in the storm. I owe him." She pouted. "It was a good kiss."

Oddly enough, the Captain's tail lashed at this.

"And then?" he growled.

Fallon thought he was doing a lot of growling lately. She wondered if his voice might stick that way.

"Then he hit me."

"Once? Twice? What?"

"Once, and he left the rooftop. And then... you came."

Waiting, waiting, *there!* Fallon shook her head, for in an execution of flawless timing, the Alchemist finally turned those golden eyes upwards. Had they been swords, they would have delivered the killing stroke.

Fallon sat forward. "So when did you scream?"

All eyes turned now, for the first time tonight, to her.

"What does that matter?" asked Kerris. "A woman screams when the scream wills, not the woman."

Again, Fallon shook her head. "But when? I mean, before he hit you? After?"

The Captain looked down at the cheetah, inclined his chin like a hawk.

"Well?"

"After, *sidi.* I believed he was going to strike again but the falcon flew in between. He stopped and left the rooftop."

Kerris stood up, releasing the long speckled hand, and placing his own on his hips. His brother's gesture. Fallon had never seen him do this.

"Well, that makes two for three, doesn't it? I mean, first he hits Ursa, now Sherah. Perhaps, *sidalady* tigress should be very careful."

"I'm not afraid of him."

"Perhaps you should be."

She tugged at a well-tugged lace, but said nothing.

In fact, no one said anything for some time. The water began hissing in its pot, and Sherah moved to tend it. Kerris stopped her, however, catching her hands, and moving them aside.

"No, no, *sidala.* Let me tonight."

"Actually, Kerris," said the Captain. "I will do this."

Fallon's heart thudded. *There! There! Oh no, please don't!*

"Oh, it's quite alright, Kirin. I'll do—"

"No, Kerris. I want you to find the Seer."

Why couldn't he see?

For within that heartbeat, everything changed.

Kerris' head snapped up.

"Why?"

"Because I need to speak to him."

Something glittered in Kerris' blue eyes.

"Isn't that what we have Ursa for?"

The golden lion felt it, Fallon knew he did, but he gritted his teeth and continued, nonetheless.

"And, I need to speak with the lady, alone."

"Alone? Really?" Kerris rose very slowly to his feet. "Why alone?"

"Kerris, please."

Reinforced with a rap of the golden tail on the floor.

Oh, it was terrible, those next few moments. Fallon very carefully had begun edging herself towards the door. Despite her natural and boundless curiosity, this was not something she wanted to see. Finally, Kerris looked down at the Alchemist, eyes still strangely glittering.

"Be gentle with him, *sidala*. He is a sensitive soul. Accustomed to mothers and courtiers who love him and protect him and tend to his every whim. He has no experience with women like yourself."

"*Kerris!* Enough!"

But the grey lion executed a very formal bow, and spun on his heel, out the door and down the stairwell before his brother could thrash him for it.

Fallon slipped from the room, unnoticed. A fact that did not surprise her.

***

The night was perfect and cool, if a little strange. There were no torches lining this road, no guards or sentries, and she thought it odd. The road itself was cut between small red mountains, squared by nature and rounded by wind. It was in reality, not a road, but a simple dirt path. All the way from the Wall to *KhahBull*. Unlit. Unguarded. Ursa shook her head. It was nice enough however, she thought, to walk on something other than stone.

She had no idea where he was going, nor for that reason, how she was going to get him back to the Wall. She did know, however, that wherever he went, she would follow. She was his protectress, his very own Imperial guard, and she would die before she let him slip away. And at the pace he was walking, she would be earning her salary tonight.

"What did she do that you should hit her?" she asked as she strode very swiftly at his side.

"It is none of your concern."

"I didn't say I was concerned." He did not respond, so she pressed him. "I will ask and ask and ask all night until you tell me. I am good at that."

His tail lashed and she could hear him growl under his breath. She lifted her chin, stared defiantly into the night as she walked even more briskly.

"I will ask and ask and ask and ask..."

"She kissed me."

She stopped, dead in her track. He did not pause, but kept on walking, right through those red mountains. The way he was feeling, he could have walked forever. Until he heard it, and it stopped *him,* dead in his track.

Major Ursa Laenskaya was laughing.

Laughing so hard, she was holding her sides. Laughing so hard, she was bent over double, her thick tail lashing from side to side. Laughing so hard, she was actually wiping tears from her cheeks. It infuriated him.

With a swirl of his robes, he marched back to her.

"It is *not* funny, Major!"

"No," she gasped. "No. Not at all."

"Then why are you laughing?"

"You hit her for kissing you!"

"Yes!"

"That is something *I* would do."

Try as he may, he could not keep it, not in the face of this irony. In her skewed, pragmatic view of the world, it had to be more than amusing. And so after several moments, he too smiled.

"It is *not* funny," he protested weakly. "And I am still leaving."

And so he did, turn his back and walk away, but this time, much more slowly. She fell in at his side, grinning in the moonlight.

"So, then. Do you always hit women who kiss you?"

"Try me."

"Pah! No wonder there are no women at *Sha'Hadin.*"

But he noticed with some satisfaction, that she was still grinning.

***

Kirin had never been good at this. His hands were too big, his grip too tight. He was accustomed to holding sword, not teapot, and the steaming brew splashed over the rims of both cups. He would have failed *Chado.* Good thing it was not a requisite in the training camps.

"I may have let it steep too long," he said, passing her the cup. "But it is a good blend."

She accepted it with lowered eyes. "No one has ever made me tea before. I am honored."

"Try it first," he said. "It may not be such an honor."

They struck him now, her eyes did, with the force of the sun. She could kill with one look.

"Your kindness is the honor, *sidi.*"

He sat beside her, around the charcoal brazier in the center of the room. He held the tiny cup with both hands, but did not drink. There were matters. He cleared his throat.

"One more question, please."

"Of course."

"He called you a name?"

"Shakuri." She smiled into her tea. "It is a lovely name."

"Yes."

"From *Lan'Lahdesh.*"

"The name of his late wife?"

"Yes."

"How did you know?"

There was a sudden sharpness glinting within those golden orbs. He could see her thinking and rethinking and thinking again. She had slipped and he had caught. It had only been a matter of time.

"*I* did not know,' Kirin continued, the ropes of his net tightening around her. "Even, that he had been married, let alone the name of the woman. It disturbs me that you know so much more."

"The First Mage is not valued counsel for nothing."

"You have said so before."

Not the first time on this journey had Jet barraDunne, the First Mage of *Agara'tha*, made a veiled appearance. Their Seventh rider, perhaps? He shook his head. Yet another road best not traveled.

"What else has the First Mage seen fit to tell you?"

"The histories of the men sitting—"

"Sitting on the Council, yes you have said. *Sidala,* I will not ask you to betray your lord. Nor will I ask you to betray his confidences. But this I must know. Is there anything that can affect the course of this journey?"

She was frightened, it was obvious, but so well trained as to mask it beautifully. Or with beauty. Her skill a weapon, as much as his very swords. She plucked at her bruised bottom lip. Drawing attention to it and away from the issue.

"He has killed before..."

"As have I. As, I might presume, have you."

"I have never killed a lion."

"Would you?"

She did not answer. He narrowed his eyes.

"Would you?"

"Not any more."

"What is your mission, *sidala?"*

"To assist you in ensuring the survival of the last Seer of *Sha'Hadin."*

"We have accomplished this. So now? What is your mission now?"

"It has not changed."

"Is it also your mission to kill the last Seer of *Sha'Hadin?"*

"No." *Emphatically.*

"That is not something the First Mage asked of you?"

"No. He has not asked me this."

"Not even to ensure Unification?"

"It would be sacrilege."

"Answer the question."

"Not even to ensure Unification."

He believed her.

"You swore an oath in *Pol'Lhasa.*"

"Of course."

Part of him wanted to grab her, to shake until the pretense flew from her like chaff. But even though it would be allowed, honorable even and in keeping with the code of *Bushido,* he found himself wading in different waters. She was a koi. Beautiful and cunning and she swam deep. She had not survived so long by being easy prey.

He sipped his tea. *The only glass you can polish is your own.*

She sipped her tea. She shifted by his side. She glanced from the brazier to her candle to her cup.

Still, he sipped his tea.

"Have you ever," she began. "Been given orders...orders you were loathe to obey?"

"Of course," he said, imitating her, and he smiled. It was met and returned, gratefully. He could have sworn he saw a glimmer of tears, but she fought them back.

"And what did you do?"

"Obeyed them. But that...is *me.* If there is anything, *anything,* that may in any way compromise this journey, you must tell me. Now."

She looked back into her tea.

Beautiful, yes, he thought, *but not a koi.* Rather, a hawk, wild and untamed, used to coursing on its own, now forced to accept morsels from a master's hand. She could be tamed, he was sure of it. It was a much better life for the hawk, receiving safety, shelter and purpose in exchange for freedom. Yes, it had to be much better.

"My heart, my soul and my will..." Yes, there were tears again gathering behind her lashes. "Are yours."

He finished his tea. That was all he needed to hear.

***

They stood on a knoll, overlooking the city of *KhahBull.* It's lights spread out as far as they could see. It was a huge city.

"You want to go...there?" Her lip curled even as she asked. She had no desire to go to *KhahBull.*

He cast his eyes up to the sky. The falcon swooped and arched a wing, heading left.

"Left," he said with finality. "We are going left."

He turned and took a step, then swayed as if pushed by a strong wind. Ursa, fully expecting this, caught him before he fell.

"Hello? Hey, Captain, are you there? I have maps..."

"Not tonight, Solomon," she said. With a silver hand, she touched the Seer's cheek.

moonlight and silver, he will die in her arms

And with that touch, Solomon disappeared. Sireth staggered to regain his footing.

"Major?" he asked, blinking and obviously disoriented. "Was that Solomon?"

"He left."

"Left?"

"Left," she said with finality. "We are going left."

***

"Are you following me again, *sidala?* By the Kingdom, if you keep this up, someone might think you were a-courting me."

Kerris didn't pause in brushing the pony's shaggy mottled coat. In fact, he didn't even look up. The heat, all-to-familiar of late, rushed to her cheeks.

"Sorry," Fallon said, "It's just, well..."

"It's past your bedtime, is what it is."

She would not give him this and stayed, pressed into the shadows of the stair.

"I can't sleep."

"Ah, well. On a night like this, who can?" Then after a moment, "Pity."

"Pity what?"

"It might have been nice to think someone was a-courting me."

She said nothing. Truth be told, she couldn't think of a single thing to say. *Couldn't even step off the shore.*

"There you are, Quiz my boy. As clean as you're going to get."

With this, he slapped the pony's rump and straightened up, tossing the bristle brush into a saddlebag in a corner of the stall. Quiz snorted and began to turn tight circles before dropping himself down into the straw.

Fallon suppressed a yawn.

"Really, *sidala,* you should go to bed. Excitement or no, you'll pay the price for it in the morning."

"No, really. I really can 'not' sleep. The bedrolls are in the keep," she yanked a thumb toward the ceiling. "Upstairs."

"Aaah." He nodded, a shadow of something crossed his face. "Ah, yes, well. I could make you a bed down here, a little nest, as it were, of your very own. Quiet, peaceful, undisturbed by lions or other lesser animals."

"I'm sure it's not what you think."

"I'm sure it's exactly what I think, *sidala.* I should be happy for him. Really, I should."

"It can't. It isn't. He won't." She shook her head, thoughts spinning, tumbling, colliding. "I mean, I don't know him very well, but he's so, he's so, well..."

"He's a lion."

"Exactly. And she's a cheetah. I can't see him even considering it."

"And that's the problem," he said, "He's not considering it at all. He's in love with someone else he can never have."

"The Empress?"

"The very one."

"Oh," she said. After that, there seemed little else to say.

He studied her face in the darkness, light from a single torch casting long shadows across her face. She was too young for this, not even a woman, a kitten with potential, no more. And yet, she had taken the first step the other night. Pure Gold *could* have been a tiger. And that said in the presence of lions. Perhaps, then, just perhaps...

"If he were considering it," he began, strolling over and folding his arms as he leaned against the stair beside her. "What would you think?"

"Who, me? What would *I* think?"

"That was the question, yes."

"Why would it matter what I would think?"

"You don't think the opinions of others matter to our people? You, the proponent of changing all fairy stories in favor of tigers?"

"But that was a fairy story."

"Not real life."

"No, not real life."

"In real life, lions court lions, tigers court tigers."

"Well, that's the way of things, isn't it?"

"And mongrels be damned."

"No! That's not what I meant!"

"What did you mean, then?"

"It, it, I," she huffed, frowned, and suddenly, her emerald eyes flashed at him.

There, he thought with some satisfaction, *that's what I want to see.*

"I think that if someone loves someone else, it shouldn't matter what anyone else thinks."

"Really? That's a very dangerous idea."

"I know. But, but I, I believe it."

Still leaning against the stairwell, he turned so that he was facing her and very close. He caught her with his stare, entangled her in the depths of blue that were his eyes. She fought him, though, made her own stare defiant and proud, did not pull away at the brush of his hip. Still, she was a koi, a small, skinny, minnow of a koi, and he so loved to fish.

"Well, then," he purred, "If say, there was ever a time when a lion came a-courting *you,* it would be fine?"

"It, it, it," she swallowed this time, regrouped, tried to parry. "It would depend on his intentions."

"Not yours?"

"Well—"

"Then say, for the sake of argument, that his intentions were noble. That he wanted to marry you and be the father of your kittens, what would you say?"

Kittens Six kittens Six grey striped kittens

Oh mother

She thrust out her chin.

"Then I would say fine."

His eyes began roving now, following the stretch of milky white from her throat on down through the laces between her breasts. Up now, around her face, tracing the tiger stripes with his gaze, up, up even as they ran into her hair. Over her shoulders again and back down again. Her heart was beating hard in her chest, and this, he seemed to study with even more interest, and suddenly her ideas about size seemed irrelevant under his scrutiny.

"Still fine?"

"Yes," she breathed. "Yes, fine."

His hand moved up, caught a white-tipped curl, twirled it with a finger.

"But what about the university?"

"What about the university?"

"You couldn't stay there, you know. Not with a marriage like that. They would force you out. All your books and thoughts and philosophies, abandoned. Just like that."

"There's, there's more to life than books."

"True enough. What about your family? Have all your sisters married tigers?"

This was becoming too much for her. She could feel the sting of impending tears. She would not let them spill.

"Yes," her voice small and struggling.

"And they have kittens?"

"Yes."

"You're an auntie."

"...yes..."

"That's lovely. Really, it is. I'm sure your parents are very proud."

"Why are you doing this? What have I done to you?"

"Well, you see, I don't think your parents would be very proud at all of mongrel kittens. If they don't ostracize you and your family, then they themselves will be ostracized. No one will buy your father's pheasants. No one will buy his eggs. It will be his ruin. He may lose the family farm. All because of you and your dangerous ideas."

The tears came.

He almost stopped, he should have. She was right. She did not deserve this. She was but a kitten herself, and he a cruel, cruel man for torturing her so. But he was angry now, and tired, and determined to break this young heart early on. It would spare her, anyway, in the end.

He wiped her tears with his hand.

"So it seems, there is yet one more thing you haven't stopped to think about. But it does make sense now, doesn't it? Lions court lions. Tigers court tigers. Mongrels be damned. It is the only way to be safe and secure in our pure, pure Kingdom. It is the way of things. Kirin knows this. And now, *sidalady* tigress, so do you."

He stepped back, gathered her hands in his, raised them to his lips. Then, he spun on his heel and headed up the steps, forgetting her in a heartbeat.

"And *you?!*"

The stairwell rang with her anger. It shocked him, her tone. Intrigued him too. He turned and looked down at her, the torch now casting long shadows across the other side of her face. He could barely distinguish stripes from tears, as they ran down her cheeks and into her mouth. But her eyes were blazing and it set his blood racing.

"What about *you?*" she snarled. "Do *you* know this, *sidalord* grey lion?"

He had never seen her angry, let alone furious. *She was,* he thought to himself, *rather pretty.* Perhaps, he had not been so cruel after all.

"No one courts grey lions, *sidala.*"

And turned one last time, leaving her to the horses and the pony and her tears.

***

It was the sound of the pipes, at first, the soft sad trill of hill pipes that drew them. Then laughter and singing, and the roar and crackle of a late night fire. By the time they approached the caravans, tucked into the mouth of one of the many caverns that rabbited these mountains, they had been sighted, and all sound, save the fire, had died away. There were many faces turned to stare at them.

"Good evening, my friends," said Sireth, stopping a distance from the group and bowing, most formally. His hood was drawn over his head, and with only moonlight and the long shadows cast by the fire, it was impossible to see his face. His lion-like tail, however, swayed visibly behind him. Ursa was at his side, hands on the hilts of her swords, hair blowing in the breeze. Several men, and some women, rose to their feet.

"Good evening, *sidi, sidala,"* said one, a barrel-chested man of indeterminate race, and when he bowed, it was as stiff as it was wrong. He spread wide his hands.

"We are a peaceful band, *sidalord* lion. Your weapons will not be needed here."

"Coincidence, I'm afraid. To protect us from bandits, not become them."

The man nodded, and glanced at his companions.

"How may we help?"

Sireth held out his hand. The sliced glove shone bloody in the moonlight.

"Water?" he asked, "And a wrap, if possible? We will not make *KhahBull* tonight and my palm is aching badly."

The man turned and called out in a strange tongue. Ursa narrowed her eyes. *Shaharabic,* she wondered? People scurried to fetch the required items. They wanted her gone as soon as possible, she knew. Were afraid of her, or more likely, what she represented. It was the way of things. She tightened her grip on her swords.

The man smiled nervously, bowed again, as if the very act could appease this wraith of a lion and the armed ghost at his side.

"You need only ask, *sidi.* We are also servants of the Empress."

"Indeed? Then, perhaps, a place at your fire? As I said, we will not make *KhahBull* tonight. I would sleep much sounder to the songs of your pipes."

Ursa threw a scowl at him. That was not the plan. To her credit, she kept her tongue.

Likewise, the man seemed just as uncomfortable with the idea. In fact, activity slowed to a stop and now all people exchanged nervous glances. The man clasped his hands.

"Yes, of course, *sidalord* lion, you would be welcome, of course, but..."

"But?"

"*Sidi,* we are a gypsy band. Our means are simple, our accommodations more so. We are not accustomed to entertaining those such as yourselves."

"There was a day," Sireth began, "When gypsy hospitality was not as exclusive as the company of lions. All were welcome in the name of Dharma."

There was a moment of silence, then the man threw wide his arms.

"Come and be welcome. What little we have is yours."

"The water and wrap would be fine," Sireth stepped forward into the firelight and pulled back the hood. "Of course, if you have any famous *KhahBull* khava..."

A cheer went up from the company, along with a good number of relieved sighs, as one mongrel joined his own. Ursa, suddenly feeling very alone, kept her hands on her hilts, and followed him into the fire.

***

She learned more about the Seer that night, than in all the days they had shared company. She learned he had been born to a caravan of gypsies, much like this one, on the outskirts of *Calcah'thah.* That he had been the younger of two sons, that his grandfather had been a Pure-blood lion who also traveled with the company, his mother a dancer and fortune teller, and that he had never known his father. In fact, he was so open with these people, complete strangers as they were, that she more than once found herself wondering what it was that made him so different in the presence of the Captain and the others.

It was, of course, the issue of Race.

As she scanned the faces of the men and women and children up at this late hour, drinking the bitter strong mixture called khava and listening with sleepy ears to the stories, it was obvious that none of them could lay claim to a particular Race of people. Tiger stripes were mixed with leopard spots, jaguar rosettes with tufted tails. Even the smaller cats seemed indeterminate, as caracals and sandcats and ocelots merged and blended, with ear tufts and bobbed tails alternating with alarming ease. She could have sworn there was a woman with Sacred blood running through her veins, masked however by lynx-like ribbons of grey.

There was, it appeared to her, no discrimination whatsoever when it came to breeding, their caste uniformly Untouchable, but to the last one they seemed happy and tried very hard to make her feel welcome.

She shook her head. The Scourge of the Kingdom. She knew that every last one of them should be killed, but tonight, she would draw sword against none.

So, as the last watch of the night crept to a close, the barrel-chested man, whose name was Thomas Adonalli, brought them two bedrolls and bid them goodnight.

Sireth flapped his open and stretched out, lacing his fingers (he had removed the gloves at some point during the night. She was surprised. She hadn't seen him do so) across his belly and closing his eyes. Ursa stared at him for a moment, then frowned.

"What are you doing?"

"Going to sleep."

"We have to go now."

"We're not going anywhere."

"We're not staying here. We have to go back. The Captain will be furious."

With a deep sigh, the Seer pushed himself up on his elbows.

"I told you I was going away. Did I not break it down into words small enough for your Pure ears?"

She stared at him.

"A-way. *A* way. Not *your* way. Gone. Leaving. No more to be present in your company."

"The Captain—"

"The Captain is under the spell of a witch. I will not ride with such as she."

"You ride with me. And I will not stay here."

"And that is your choice." He shook his head. "I gave you the option of stopping me as soldier, or joining as friend. Do you intend to kill me now?"

"I have to bring you back."

"How?"

She sat back on her heels, cast her eyes to the pink horizon. She was thinking. He could tell by the furrows on her brow, the particular way she pursed her lips. *moonlight and silver* She looked at him.

"I will beat you senseless, commandeer one of these oxen and take you back like a sack of millet."

He stroked his beard.

"That would work, yes..." A thought struck him. "Or...or you could tell the Captain you tried to bring me back, I resisted, and you were forced to kill me. You still, I believe, have my blood on your sword."

"You, a priest, council to the Empress, would have me lie?"

"To keep my freedom, I would do anything."

"You are running away."

"Yes. Absolutely," he said. "It is the only thing that has kept me alive all these years. Major, look at these people. There is not a one of them older than I. What does that tell you?"

"They are not good at it."

"Don't make me go back."

Again, she paused, studied this time the stars, the faint glow of sun at the first murmurings of day. Longer this time, for when she looked back at him, her stare was level and calm.

"I will not lie. But I will not tell him where you are."

In fact, he could not believe her. It was something bigger than he'd thought her able, and an unexpected wave of guilt carried over him.

moonlight and silver

"Thank you," he whispered.

he will die in her arms

She rose to her feet, silver hair blowing again in the breeze.

"He will barricade off the city, so I suggest you do not go there. He will also have many, many guards at his disposal, so I suggest also you go quickly. Do not travel with this caravan. It is too conspicuous."

And with that, she turned on her heel, and walked away, feeling his one-eyed gaze on her back and wondering exactly what method the Captain would choose to kill her.

***

There was something about the dawn that always drew him outside. Even as a child, he would be found practicing *Chai'Chi*, back in the cobbled courtyard of the House Wynegarde-Grey, or on one of the many fields or hillsides surrounding the manor. It was as if the air was newer, the sunlight purer, than anytime later in the day. Indeed, he believed it was. Each day started off like a mewling babe, fresh and innocent. It was the aging that made every thing dark and complicated.

So it was this morning, the morning after the chaotic night-before, that Kirin found himself performing the Sun Salute on grass for the first time in a long time, just outside the Wall and the first leg of their journey in *Khanisthan.* He had not slept at all, but was not weary, as the Major came into view. She was alone.

Her silver hands were curled into fists at her sides. Her lips pursed and tight, her posture stiff, she walked straight up to him and bowed most formally, something he had rarely seen her do before. He held up a tawny hand, released the last cleansing breath, and turned to face her.

"Major?"

"Sir. Captain, the Seer..." She seemed lost for words. In fact, for a fleeting moment, she seemed quite simply lost. But it passed, and she looked up at him, shoulders square, chin raised. "The Seer..."

"Is obviously not as fast as you are, Major."

And he looked over her shoulder.

She turned to see the Seer trudging over the rise in the path behind them.

"That was not wise, Major," Kirin said. "He could have slipped away had he the will. And then, I assure you, I would have had to kill you. I would not have liked that. Really, I would not."

She said nothing, her ice-blue eyes fixed on the man now approaching them. He stopped before them.

"Captain."

"*Sidi,* we need to speak."

"I thought as much. I simply needed to get... Away...for a time. The Major was good enough to accompany me."

"Indeed." Kirin raised a brow, but inclined his chin. "Now, it's my turn."

And the two men turned their backs to the woman, and walked away, into the bright pink dawn of a new morning.

***

And so, it was that day, they passed out of the *Phun'jah* and into the province of *Khanisthan.* They made good time during those next days, made good maps during the nights.

There were no more rats. There were no battles, no bandits, no brushes with death. In fact, there were no other remarkable incidents to mar the journey at all, and it seemed they had fallen into an ease with each other that was, Kirin felt, extremely commendable.

Something had happened, however, and some *things* were happening that, while not openly evidenced, were running swift and strong, dark undercurrents in a still lake. Alliances were being forged, others burned, and a tapestry was taking shape, threads shuttling and weaving in intricate patterns to make a banner of bright color and terrible darkness. There is a saying, 'All roads lead to *Pol'Lhasa.'* Here, the roads had broken, shattered, and were taking vastly different, dizzying directions, but leading slowly, inexorably, to the same terrible place.

They were passing through the glass.

End of Part 1

To be continued in

To Walk in the Way of Lions

(Book 2 from Tails of the Upper Kingdom)

An Excerpt from Book 2

To Walk in the Way of Lions

By H. Leighton Dickson

KHANISTHAN AND DESERT HORSES

Most Beloved Excellency,

We are leaving the Phun'jah and the Great Wall, for the roads and byways of Khanisthan. It is now difficult, if not impossible, for us to contact you by falcon. Therefore, accept this message as a farewell, until and unless our fates lead us otherwise. There are messages bound herein from those of us who wished and I know that you will see to it that each is delivered to the appropriate hand. My own is also enclosed for yours alone.

Captain Wynegarde-Grey

It has often been said that, as *DharamShallah* sits high on the Great Mountains as the jeweled crown of the Upper Kingdom, then *KhahBull*, in the eastern flank of Khanisthan, beats its bloody heart. She is a wild city, a proud city, an angry city. She has a history, to be sure, but one so shrouded in myth and folklore that it is impossible to determine which tales are true, and which merely wish. It is easy to believe that this one city fought off for ten generations a siege of dogs. There is no rat problem in such a city, as her legends would tell of a lone piper, leading all vermin from within its walls to scorching death in the salt flats beyond, and that even today, bodies of the vile creatures still can be found, etched in red stone. It is easy even to believe the boasts of unearthing relics from Ancient days beneath her very foundations, statues of *Asherbupal* and *ThanThanagoth*, and the restoration of their feline faces smashed in from ages long past. These cats are such people.

No matter its history, glory or riches, the one thing that cannot be ascribed to *KhahBull* is Kaidan. Kaidan belongs to *DharamShallah*, to *Mepal* and to the Royal Houses. The Great Mountains are his mother, *Shagarmathah* his bride, the courts of *Pol'Lhasa* his home. (I know this is true, for I know Kaidan himself. He is everything people say of him, and more.

They had been entertained that night in the governor's mansion, a fine house overlooking the minarets of the city and the ribs of the Mountains. The governor, a small, grey-striped man of Sacred blood, had been most intrigued by their journey, for it was not often that he had guests from *Pol'Lhasa.* Of course they said little, but accepted his hospitality nonetheless, and slept well in beds stuffed with feathers for the first time in weeks. That morning, they left the horses with the governor's stable commander, a fine lion by the name of Harrison Omar-valDelane, and made their way into the fabled heart of the city, the *Waterless Gardens.*

Now this is an odd name, to be sure, for it is neither garden, nor waterless. It is paradoxical and poetic, but cats are, after all, a paradoxical, poetic people. It was a marketplace, as huge as most cities, with shops under tent flaps and shops in three-story buildings. There were shops that sold pearls, and shops that sold elephants. There were shops that sold meats and shops that sold animals to make the meats sold in other shops. In fact, next to the canton-city of *LanLadesh* and the sprawling bustling wreckage that is *Cal'Cathah,* it is said that *KhahBull* is the busiest, most profitable marketplace in all the Upper Kingdom. This too, is easy to believe. Many taxes are gathered there.

The Captain hated it on sight.

As he stood at the entrance to the markets, hands on hips, blue eyes sifting the crowds that moved all about him, he was a most impressive, imposing sight. His long mane, held off his face in its simple queue, fanned in the dry breeze, along with the tattered golden sash. His tail, normally so still and reserved, whapped the dusty ground in frustration. Like a rock in a river, he just stood there, tides of people flowing around him, buyers and sellers alike, coming and going, ebbing and flowing, everyone giving him a wide berth. He was a lion. He wore Imperial gold. It was, and still is, the way of things.

He set his jaw and turned to face his people.

"This is to be an enjoyable day," he said, forcing a smile. "You are all free to do whatever you wish. Go wherever the desire takes you. The governor has given us unlimited credit. All you need do it present your rings—" He indicated the ring he wore on his right thumb. It bore a stamp pressed in gold. "And the merchants will indulge your purchase. One of the few benefits of our stations, I should think."

"It hardly seems fair," muttered the Seer. "To work hard for a living, only to be left with only a promise of remittance at the end of the day..."

"They will be reimbursed," he said.

"Will they?"

"Of course. The governor is an honorable man."

The Seer gazed at him for several moments, then looked away. "Of course he is."

Kirin ground his molars. *This was to be an enjoyable day,* he reminded himself. It would not do well to start it off with a futile debate. "We must meet here tonight, at or just before the curfew gong. Is that understood?"

Everyone nodded, but no one moved. They were still looking at him.

"Very well. Go. Enjoy yourselves. Go." And he spread his hands, feeling for all the world like a mother ushering her children to a forbidden playground. *"Go."*

Without a second look, the Seer whirled and strode off into the crowds, the Major his silver shadow. They were gone in moments. The tigress too, and the cheetah, and finally the leopards, still in uniform, but off duty, all disappearing into the crush of bodies that was the *Waterless Gardens.* All but one.

He turned to see Kerris, leaning against a stone wall, arms folded, the end of a smoking cigarash in his teeth.

Trust Kerris to know there was something else afoot. Things had been strained between the brothers these last days. An unnamed but familiar wall had sprung up between them and neither had possessed the will to bring it down. It had always been there, it just ebbed and flowed like the tides, never really cresting, never reaching the shore. Dark eddies under the surface, swift currents running deep. It was the way of things.

"I pulled the sticks this morning," said Kerris as the Captain moved to lean against the wall at his brother's side. "They said 'Lightning' and 'Red'…"

Kirin's heart sank. He glanced up at the sky, vast and blue with only wisps of clouds.

"…But I hear no storm. The air is quiet."

Kirin frowned. "Maybe the sticks are wrong?"

"Maybe."

They said nothing for some time, and neither of them looked at the other. The smoke from the cigarash was giving him a headache. He sighed.

"Are you up to a little shopping?"

"Depends," Kerris said. "On the governor's coin?"

"Mine. I believe our party is ill-prepared for the next leg of our journey. I would like to improve this situation."

"Hmm," the cigarash waggled up and down as he thought. "Leather uniforms have no place in the desert. You and Ursa and Sherah will be dead of sun sickness before the week's up."

"So...?"

"So. We need new clothing and…"

"And…"

Kerris' eyes dropped to the ground for a heartbeat, deciding the best approach to his next request. He looked up now and set his jaw. "And horses."

"Horses?" Kirin blinked. *That was most unexpected.* "But we can avail ourselves of the Governor's Stables—"

"Not *Imperial* horses, Kirin. Desert horses."

He studied his brother's face for a long time. He honestly didn't know what to think. Kerris was such a puzzle. He continued.

"Desert horses are smaller, tougher than Imperial horses. They are bred for desert living, can go for days without water, like khamels. In fact, I was considering whether or not we might need khamels, and if our journey was to remain in these dry places, I would seriously recommend them. But if this 'Swisserland' is so much farther beyond, then horses are still preferable. Khamels are a bugger to ride in mountains and jungles both, and they can't be trusted to forage during the night and return back for duty the next morning. Horses can."

Kirin let his own eyes wander the crowded streets of the *Waterless Gardens* as he thought it through. It was a sensible request.

"I will not give up alMassay," he said finally, turning to look back at his brother. "I would rather die with him in the heat than leave him in some Governor's stall."

"And I Quiz," said Kerris, smiling for the first time in days. "I don't think he'd let me go anyway. He'd tear the damned place apart and catch up with me even if I was on the other side of the world."

Kirin grinned at the thought. "The Major might need some convincing…"

Kerris pushed himself off the wall, puffed a few good smokey puffs on the cigarash before tossing it to the ground and crushing it under his boot.

"Oh, her grey can come, that's not a problem. As long as we have desert horses as the majority of the caravan, we should be ahead of the game. Besides, I've found a local breeder who happens to have a few nursing mares. Remember that milk paste I was talking about…"

And side by side, the brothers left the gate and disappeared into the currents of the *Waterless Gardens,* and for a time, the light and dark halves of the interlocking Tao wheel fit.

To be continued

Books by H. Leighton Dickson

TO JOURNEY IN THE YEAR OF THE TIGER

TO WALK IN THE WAY OF LIONS

SONGS IN THE YEAR OF THE CAT

SWALLOWTAIL & SWORD

COLD STONE & IVY: The Ghost Club

DRAGON OF ASH & STARS

Coming Soon:

SNOW IN THE YEAR OF THE DRAGON

COLD STONE & IVY 2: The Crown Prince

ABOUT THE AUTHOR

H. Leighton Dickson is a zoologist who has been writing stories of some sort since she was a kitten. She currently lives with three dogs, three cats, three kids, one horse, and one husband, in the rugged beauty of the Canadian Shield.

Join the Conversation at
www.hleightondickson.com
or on Facebook at
https://www.facebook.com/HLeightonDickson

Made in the USA
Middletown, DE
30 December 2016